Moonlight on Butternut Lake

Moonlight on Butternut Lake

Mary McNear

HARPER LUXE

An Imprint of HarperCollins*Publishers*

MOONLIGHT ON BUTTERNUT LAKE. Copyright © 2015 by Mary McNear. All rights reserved. Printed in the United States of America. No part of this book may be used or reproduced in any manner whatsoever without written permission except in the case of brief quotations embodied in critical articles and reviews. For information address HarperCollins Publishers, 195 Broadway, New York, NY 10007.

HarperCollins books may be purchased for educational, business, or sales promotional use. For information please e-mail the Special Markets Department at SPsales@harpercollins.com.

FIRST HARPERLUXE EDITION

HarperLuxe™ is a trademark of HarperCollins Publishers

Library of Congress Cataloging-in-Publication Data is available upon request.

ISBN: 978-0-06-239279-4

15 ID/RRD 10 9 8 7 6 5 4 3 2 1

For Suzanne McNear

Chapter 1

"**M**iss? *Miss?*"

Mila jerked awake and stared, uncomprehendingly, around her. "Where are we?" she asked, and her voice sounded strange to her.

"Butternut," the bus driver said. "This is the last stop."

The last stop. That sounded ominous, she thought, as her hand moved to massage her stiff neck.

"I saw you'd fallen asleep," the driver continued, almost apologetically. "But I remembered your ticket said Butternut. And I thought if you could sleep through that baby's screaming, you must really need the rest."

Mila nodded, annoyed at herself for falling asleep. That was stupid. She was going to have to learn to keep her guard up. And not just some of the time, but *all* the time. She started to stand up, but her cramped legs rebelled. She sat back down.

"Take your time," the driver said genially, looking every bit the grandfather Mila imagined he must be with his thick shock of white hair and pleasantly crinkled blue eyes. "You've been the only passenger since Two Harbors. Not many people travel this far north, I guess. Why don't you take a minute to stretch and I'll get your baggage out for you."

Mila nodded, then stood up again, slowly this time, and tested her legs. They were stiff, but otherwise functional. She gathered up her handbag, which she'd been careful to wedge between herself and the side of the bus, and made her way down the aisle.

When she climbed down the bus's steps, she saw that the driver was holding her suitcase and looking around doubtfully.

"Is someone meeting you here?" he asked.

"They're supposed to be," Mila said, a little uncertainly.

"Good," he said, handing her a slightly battered suitcase. "Because they don't get much traffic out this way. I don't know why they have the bus stop out at this junction, instead of right in the town."

But Mila had no opinion about this. A week ago, she'd never even heard of Butternut, Minnesota. Still, she had to admit, what she'd seen of it so far didn't look very promising. There was no bus station here, for instance, only a rest area, whose cracked asphalt was overrun with weeds, and whose sole amenities were an old bus shelter and a lopsided bench.

"I hope your ride comes soon," the driver said. "I hate to leave you here alone, but I've got to be getting back to the Twin Cities. My grandson's got a Little League game tonight," he added.

"Well, good luck to him," Mila said. "And thank you."

He started to get back onto the bus then, but Mila had a sudden thought. "Excuse me, sir," she said. "Can I ask you a favor?"

He stopped, halfway up the bus's steps, and turned around. "Name is Bob," he said, indicating his name tag. "And you can ask me a favor. I'll be happy to do it for you, too, if it doesn't take too long."

"It won't," she said. "I was wondering if . . ." Her voice trailed off. She had no idea how to phrase this. She thought about it and started over. "I was wondering, Bob . . . if someone was looking for me, and they tracked me down as far as, say, the bus station in Minneapolis, and they asked you if you'd seen me . . . if they, you know, described me to you, or showed you a photograph of me, could you . . ." She hesitated again. "Could you tell them you haven't seen me?"

Bob frowned. "Are you asking me to lie, miss?"

"Not lie, exactly." Mila hedged. "More like forget."

"Forget I ever saw you?"

She nodded.

Bob shifted uncomfortably. "Are the police looking for you?" he asked. "Because if they are—"

"No," Mila said, relieved to be telling the truth. "No, I promise, it's nothing like that. I'm not a criminal. I'm just . . ." She paused again here. "I'm just someone who's trying to start over, that's all."

Bob gave her a long, speculative look. "So you want a fresh start?

"Exactly."

"And you don't want to bring any old baggage with you?" he asked, with a smile.

"None," she said, smiling back. "Except maybe this," she amended, swinging her suitcase.

"Okay, that's fair," Bob said. "If anyone asks— anyone not in a uniform, that is—I'll say that I've never laid eyes on you before."

"Thank you, Bob," Mila said gratefully, swallowing past something hard in her throat. But she caught herself. *Don't you dare cry, Mila. Because then he really will remember you. Besides, he can't start comforting you now. The man's got a Little league game to get to.*

"Well, good luck," Bob said. He climbed up the rest of the steps, slid into the driver's seat, and pulled the lever that closed the bus's door.

"Thanks again," Mila called, relieved that the danger of her crying had subsided. Bob held up his hand to her in a good-bye gesture, started the engine, and eased the bus back onto the road. Mila watched him drive away, then dragged her suitcase over to the bench. She sat down on it, but no sooner had she done this than it began to rain. Not a hard rain. Just a dull, gray rain. Although it had been an unusually warm spring in Minnesota, today, the third day of June, was shaping up to be cool and wet.

So she stood up and carried her suitcase over to the bus shelter's narrow overhang, hoping to get a little protection from the rain. It was better there, but not by much. She shivered in her thin cotton blouse and skirt and wished she'd worn something warmer. But she'd tried to dress as innocuously, and as forgettably, as possible, and this was the outfit she'd settled on.

She saw something then out of the corner of her eye, and she flinched. But when she turned to see what it was, she realized with relief that it was nothing more than a crow alighting on a nearby telephone line.

Would this ever end? she wondered. This constant looking over her shoulder? This fear, always, of being followed? Of being discovered? She had a sinking feeling that it would not. Unless the unthinkable happened. And he found her.

"**Reid?** *Reid?* Are you listening to me?"

"Of course," he lied, though, in fairness to him, he had *tried* to listen to what his sister-in-law, Allie, was saying to him. But the painkillers—the painkillers that didn't seem to kill the pain—were making him a little foggy.

He watched now as Allie lifted her six-month-old daughter, Brooke, out of her stroller and settled her onto her lap. *Cute baby,* he thought, and, almost as if she knew what he was thinking about her, Brooke wriggled in her mother's arms and smiled at him, a toothless, charming smile. And then, for an encore, she balled up her tiny fist and shoved the entire thing into her mouth. *Very impressive,* Reid thought. Funny how he'd never known before how entertaining babies could be. Much more entertaining than adults, he decided, as he watched Brooke suck mightily on her little fist.

But apparently, while he was doing this, Allie was trying to talk to him, because now her voice intruded on him again. "Reid? Please try to stay with me, all right?" she asked. "Just for a few minutes." She sounded exasperated. Exasperated and something else. Concerned. Reid tensed, warily. Because if there was anything he hated, it was being on the receiving end of concern.

"Do I sense a lecture coming on?" he asked now, finally tearing his eyes away from the baby. And his voice, even to him, sounded odd. Thick, and cottony. As if he didn't use it that much anymore. Which, of course, he didn't.

"A lecture?" Allie asked now, raising her eyebrows. "No. Not a lecture. Not exactly."

"Because that sounded to me like the beginning of a lecture," he said, reaching for the glass of ice water on the table in front of him. It was hard to reach from his wheelchair, though, especially since when he leaned too far forward, the full cast on his left leg dug into his thigh, and his still mending ribs ached from the effort. Still, he reached for it, and, misjudging the glass's distance, his fingers only brushed against it, knocking it off the table.

"Damn it," he said, as the glass shattered on the floor. And, as if on cue, Brooke started to cry.

"Shhh," Allie said, trying to soothe her. "Caroline," she called out, to the woman who owned the coffee shop. "We're going to need a broom and dustpan over here."

Reid reached down to pick up a piece of broken glass, but the side of his wheelchair limited his range of movement.

"Damn it," he said again, giving up.

"It doesn't matter, Reid," Allie said, reaching over to pat his hand, which was resting on the arm of his wheelchair. "It's just a glass. I'm sure it happens all the time here."

"But I scared the baby," Reid said, wondering what kind of a jerk you needed to be to scare a baby.

"Reid, she's fine," Allie said, putting the baby up on her shoulder and patting her on her back. "She's just tired, that's all. She's overdue for her nap."

Caroline appeared then with a broom and a dustpan.

"I wish I could tell you this was our first broken glass of the day," she said to Reid, sweeping up the fragments of glass. "But it's our third. And today was a slow day, too." Reid looked away and mumbled an apology.

Caroline left with the dustpan and broom and came back with another glass of water, this one with a bendy straw in it. She handed the glass to Reid and waited until he had a firm grip on it before she let go of it.

"Thanks," Reid said, sipping from the straw.

"There you go," Caroline said, sounding pleased. But Reid felt himself sink a little farther into his wheelchair. *Is this what it's come to?* he wondered. *Holding my own glass and drinking from a bendy straw now constitutes a major accomplishment?*

"Allie," Caroline said. "Why don't I take Brooke for a little while? You and Reid are obviously trying to talk."

"*Trying* being the operative word," Allie murmured. But she smiled as she handed Brooke over to Caroline. "We just need a few minutes," she said, shifting her gaze back to Reid. *A few minutes,* Reid thought hopefully, as the sound of the baby's fussing receded into the background. Even he could handle a few minutes of being lectured to.

"Look, Reid," Allie started again, "I can only imagine how difficult it's been for you since the accident. And Walker and I have tried to be patient, and we've tried to give you time to adjust to all the changes in your life. But, Reid, sometimes we feel like we're the only ones who *are* trying."

Reid sighed wearily. So this was about his attitude. Which, admittedly, was pretty poor. But he was in a wheelchair, for Christ's sake, dependent on other people for all but his most basic of needs, and there were days, still, when the pain was so bad he was convinced the pills he took were nothing more than placebos.

"Look, I'm sorry," he muttered now. "I'll do better, okay?"

"Reid, you said that the last time we had this conversation."

"Well, I mean it this time."

Allie didn't look optimistic. "Reid, as of last week," she reminded him, "you've been through two home health aides."

"I know that," he said, still sipping from his straw. "But I can't help the fact that they were both completely incompetent."

"That's a matter of opinion," she said. "Walker and I, for instance, are of the opinion that they were both perfectly competent."

"Right. Well, maybe that's because you didn't have to live with either of them."

"Maybe," Allie conceded. "But the fact remains that both of them quit, Reid. And they both gave the same reasons for quitting, too. They said that you were condescending, rude, and uncooperative."

Reid, knowing this was a fairly accurate representation of his behavior, chose not to defend himself.

"The agency we've been using, Reid," Allie continued, "has refused to place another aide with you."

He shrugged. "No great loss there. They were clearly scraping the bottom of the barrel already."

Allie frowned, and a line appeared between her pretty hazel eyes. Reid immediately felt bad. He *liked* Allie. Most of the time, in fact, he liked her even more than he liked his brother, Walker, who, though younger than Reid, had lately developed the annoying habit of behaving like an older brother. But still, Allie didn't understand what it was like to have these people—these home health aides—living in his house. These people whom he had nothing in common with, but who were nonetheless privy to every detail of his life. He shuddered now, just thinking about the enforced intimacy he'd had to endure with the last two aides.

"Look," Allie said, pressing on, "I know how much you value your privacy. And I know having someone you don't know well living with you hasn't been easy, Reid, but it has been necessary. Because as much as we'd like to take care of you ourselves, we can't. We have Brooke and Wyatt." Wyatt was their nine-year-old son. "And Walker's running the business by himself until you're ready to come back to work, and I'm heading into the busy season for the Pine Cone Gallery," she added, of the gallery where she'd worked for several years before buying it from the owner the previous summer.

"Allie, look, I know how busy you both are," he said. "But I don't expect either of you to babysit me. In fact, I don't *want* either of you to babysit me. Especially since I'm capable of taking care of myself. As in a*ll of the time,*" he stressed. "Really, Allie. I'm ready to live alone again."

At this, Allie crossed her arms across her chest and leveled Reid with a *you have got to be kidding me* look.

"I'm not kidding," Reid said, to her unspoken comment. "I'm completely serious. I'll be fine on my own. And, if I need help, you and Walker are only a phone call away."

"No, absolutely not," Allie said, shaking her head. "You're not living in that cabin by yourself."

"Why not? You two had it completely retrofitted while I was in the rehabilitation center. I can use the bathroom by myself, get in and out of bed by myself—"

But here Allie interrupted him. "Look, it's great you're able to have some independence. But someone needs to be with you at all times. I'm sorry if that's hard for you to accept. But you were in a serious accident, Reid. You almost *died.* The doctor said it's going to be months—*many months*—before you fully recover."

"*If* I fully recover," Reid offered. After all, it was what they were both thinking.

"I didn't say that, Reid. And I didn't mean it either. You *will* recover. But it's going to take time. And during that time, you're going to need help. However galling it may be to your pride."

What pride, Reid wondered, looking down at his damaged leg. It had been a long time since he'd felt anything even remotely resembling pride.

But if he was wallowing in self-pity now, Allie chose not to see it. She had something else on her mind, Reid realized. Something else she needed, but didn't want, to say to him. He watched while she bit her lower lip, something he knew she only did when she was nervous.

"Allie, what is it?" he asked quietly. "What'd you bring me here for? I mean, other than to tell me I need to improve my attitude?"

Allie sighed. "Reid, that *is* why I brought you here. That, and to tell you that we've found another home health care aide. This one from Minneapolis."

"Minneapolis?"

She nodded. "We had to find a new agency, remember? Anyway," she said, glancing at her watch, "Walker's picking her up at the bus stop right now, and then he's bringing her here to meet us."

"Like a blind date?" Reid asked, cringing at the thought. "Is that really necessary?"

"Yes, it is, Reid. Because this time, you're going to make an effort. This time, you're going to be civil, right from the start, in the hopes that your civility will be habit forming. Because Walker and I have both agreed that if this placement doesn't work out . . ." She hesitated here. "If it doesn't work out, you're going to have to go back to the rehabilitation center."

"What?" Reid said, aghast. "Allie, you can't send me back there."

She wavered, and Reid knew how difficult this was for her. She liked him. Even when his and Walker's relationship was at its most acrimonious, Reid and Allie had always gotten along.

"We don't *want* to send you back there," she qualified. "But we will. If you can't make in-home care work, we won't have any choice, Reid."

He shook his head, disgusted. When he'd first arrived at the rehabilitation center, after three weeks in the hospital, he'd been in too much pain to really know where he was, let alone to care. But as he'd started to improve, and to take stock of the situation, he'd come to appreciate how truly depressing the place was. Even thinking about it, he could smell the disheartening odor of disinfectant overlaid by furniture polish, and he could hear the constant drone of a roommate's television set, always tuned, somehow, to the same inane game show.

"I won't go back there," he said now.

"Then make this work," Allie said, almost pleadingly. "It's only for three months, okay? After that, hopefully, you'll be ready to live on your own again. In the meantime, just . . . just be nice to this woman. Her name is Mila. Mila Jones. And, for some reason, she wants to spend the summer two hundred and forty miles from her home in the Twin Cities. And, not only that, but she comes highly recommended from the woman who owns the agency in Minneapolis. So please, Reid. Please try."

He looked at Allie. She looked hopeful. Hopeful and trusting. But more than that, he thought, she looked tired. And it made him feel guilty. Paired with the arrival of a new baby, his accident, he knew, had been a lot for Allie and Walker to handle. Not that they ever complained about it. They didn't. They left the complaining to him.

"All right, I'll try," he said finally, forcing himself to smile one of his increasingly rare smiles. "This time, I'll really try."

Chapter 2

Mila had been waiting in the bus shelter for five minutes when a pickup truck finally rumbled into view. She assumed it was there for her. She hadn't seen any other traffic on the road since she'd gotten off the bus. Still, she waited, warily, under the shelter roof until the driver, a man, pulled up, got out, and came around to her side of the truck.

"Ms. Jones?" he asked.

"That's right," she said, taking an instinctive step back.

"Mila Jones," he clarified. "From Caring Home Care?"

She nodded anxiously. "Is there . . . is there something wrong?"

He shook his head. "No, there's nothing wrong. I'm just surprised. You seem . . . younger, somehow, than I expected you to be."

"I'm twenty-five," Mila said, hoping her youthfulness wasn't a problem. If it was, there was nothing she could do about it.

But in the next moment, the man shrugged and smiled. "I'm sorry. I don't mean to be rude. And I already knew you were twenty-five. It was in the fax the agency sent. By the way, I'm Walker Ford," he added, holding out his hand. "And it goes without saying that you can call me Walker."

"Okay," Mila said, tentatively, looking at his outstretched hand. *He wants you to shake it,* she told herself. And she did shake it, but because she'd hesitated a moment too long in doing so, he looked at her a little more closely, something she didn't especially want him to do.

In the next moment, though, the handshake was over, and Walker was picking up her suitcase and opening the pickup truck's back door. "Is this it?" he asked, setting the suitcase on the floor of the backseat.

"That's it," Mila said. "I'm a light packer, I guess."

And if Walker Ford thought there was anything strange about her bringing a single suitcase for an entire summer, he didn't say so. He only shut the back door and opened the front passenger door, looking expectantly at Mila.

But again, she hesitated. *Does he want me to ride up front with him?* she wondered anxiously. But of course he did. Where else would he want her to ride? In the backseat? No. This wasn't a taxi, or a limousine service.

So Mila stifled her inhibitions, smiled at Walker, and climbed up, a little awkwardly, into the truck. And as he closed the door, and went around to the other side, she reminded herself that she'd have to be careful about how she responded to social cues. Like shaking someone's hand. Or letting someone open a car door for you. Until she started to feel like a normal person again, she was just going to have to act like one. Or try to, anyway.

Walker got into the truck then and slammed the driver's-side door. "I'm sorry you had to wait out here," he apologized, simultaneously fastening his seat belt and turning on the ignition. "I don't know why the bus stop can't just be in town."

"The bus driver said the same thing," Mila murmured, trying hard to appear relaxed. Walker pulled out onto the county road, and she looked out the truck's window. There wasn't much to see yet, though. Only pale green fields, giving way to darker green stands of pine trees. As she watched the countryside slide by, she reviewed what she'd learned about Butternut at the public library in Minneapolis a couple of days earlier. According to its website, it was a town of about twelve hundred people situated in the northernmost part of the state, a part of the state that Mila associated almost exclusively with frigid winters. But it had summers, too, apparently, because most of the photographs were of nearby Butternut Lake, looking resplendently blue in the sunshine and featuring people fishing, canoeing, and waterskiing. Still, if the town's website made Butternut Lake look both accessible and populated, the view of the lake from Google Earth told a different story. It was a big lake—almost twelve miles long and, in places, over a hundred and twenty feet deep—and part of it, one whole end of it, in fact, was managed by the National Forest Service and appeared, to Mila's eyes anyway, to be virtually unpopulated. Even the more "developed" end of the lake, she decided, with its town beach and its dozens of cabins and lodges, seemed barely to puncture the dense wilderness pressing in all around it.

But as she was considering this, Walker said abruptly, "What, exactly, did the agency tell you about my brother?"

"Oh," she said, turning away from the window and trying to compose her thoughts. "Well, they gave me a copy of his medical file. So I know about his injuries, if that's what you mean."

"Do you know anything else about him?"

She shrugged her shoulders, not entirely understanding the question. "I know his name and his age."

But Walker shook his head. "No, what I mean is . . . has anyone told you that my brother isn't exactly the easiest person in the world to get along with?"

Mila paused. Ms. Thompson, the woman who owned the agency, had said something about that, only she'd said it a little less politely than Walker had said it. But Mila ignored that question and said, tactfully, "Well, if he's not easy to get along with right now, that's not that surprising, is it? I mean, his injuries would be enough to put anyone in a bad mood."

"So the agency told you about the accident?"

"It was in the file. A car accident, right?"

"That's all it said in the file? That he was in a car accident?"

She nodded. "Why? Is there more?" she asked, glancing sideways at Walker Ford. He didn't say anything right away, though; he just sighed and ran his fingers through his hair. And Mila realized that when he was concentrating on the road, and not on her, she felt more comfortable. She felt comfortable enough, in fact, to steal another look at him. He was about thirty-five or forty, and he was tall and athletically built with short, dark hair and vivid blue eyes. Right now, he was dressed in clothes that gave him the neat, buttoned-down look of someone who was coming from an office, but the way he drove his pickup truck, and the tan he was already sporting so early in the season told her that whatever he did for a living, he didn't do it sitting at a desk all day.

"Yeah, there was more," he said now. "He *was* in a car accident. But he wasn't found right away."

Mila frowned. "What do you mean?"

"He was driving on the Arcola Trail, a pretty remote road that runs along a nature preserve outside Minneapolis, and he lost control of his car. I don't know what happened. And neither does he. He said he wasn't drinking, or texting or anything like that, and I believe him. He said he just . . . went off the road. But nobody saw him do it, and his car went into a ravine, so the crash site wasn't visible from the road. As it was, it was almost three days before some man walking his dog stumbled across him. Then it was several more hours before they could get rescue equipment to the scene and cut him out of his car."

"Oh my God," Mila said softly.

"You didn't hear about it at the time? It got a lot of play in the media. At least in the Twin Cities area. It's pretty rare that someone survives three days alone in a car after a crash like that," he added.

Mila shook her head. "No. I must . . . I must have missed it," she said. The truth, of course, was that her life before now, such as it was, hadn't lent itself to lingering over a cup of coffee and the newspaper every morning.

Walker nodded, but kept his eyes on the road. "My wife and I were at my brother's apartment in Minneapolis when the state police called us and told us he'd been found. We'd driven down from Butternut the day before because we were worried about him. He wasn't answering his cell phone, or his e-mails, which, if you knew my brother, was cause for concern. He is— *he was*, I should say—a complete workaholic. Anyway, the authorities caught up with us there, and we met my brother at the trauma center they'd airlifted him to. He was in bad shape, *really* bad shape," he said, and when she looked sideways at him again, she saw his face was aggrieved. Reliving this, she saw, was literally painful for him.

"Anyway," he continued. "You saw the file. Hypothermia. Dehydration. A concussion. Facial lacerations. A collapsed lung. Broken ribs. A fractured left tibia . . ." His voice trailed off.

"Those first days, after the accident, must have been very difficult for you and your wife," Mila said, and for a moment, she forgot her own apprehension.

"You have no idea," Walker said. "Reid, of course, was pretty out of it. But my wife and I . . . the first night we spent at the trauma center felt like an eternity for us. And it was touch and go there with Reid for a while. Luckily, though, he was in pretty great shape before the accident, and that's probably what pulled him through. And when he started to turn around, after the first couple of days, my wife and I wanted to celebrate. But one of the doctors warned us. He said, 'The hard part's not over yet. Because now is when it really starts to get difficult.' And I thought 'now'? As if what we'd already been through hadn't been hard enough? But you know what I've realized since then? He was right. Because then reality set in. And we realized, all three of us, my wife and I and Reid, that it *was* just the beginning."

"It's a long road back," Mila said quietly.

"Well, if it's a road, then it's a highway, and we haven't even gotten on the entrance ramp yet," Walker said, a little wearily. And then, looking over at her, he asked, "Can I be honest with you, Ms. Jones?"

She nodded.

"It isn't just Reid's injuries I'm worried about. The injuries, at least, you can see. And treat. It's . . . it's the other things I find more troubling."

"You mean, your brother's been different since the accident?"

"Very different. I mean, he was never the easiest guy to get along with. He was always . . . intense, I'd guess you'd say. Driven. He could be hard to be around. He didn't really know how to relax. My wife used to say he didn't have an off switch. But now . . . now he doesn't seem interested in anything. Or anyone."

"Well, depression is not uncommon after a serious accident. Has he had a psychological evaluation?"

"No. He's refused to have one. He doesn't deny that he's depressed. But his attitude is 'why shouldn't I be depressed?' It's depressing, he says, being stuck in a wheelchair, and being dependent on other people for almost all your needs." Walker sighed. "We've urged him to see a psychologist. We've even gotten a referral for one. But he won't go. Even before the accident, he wasn't a big believer in talk therapy."

"All right," Mila said. "But what about taking medication for depression? I'm sure his doctor would consider prescribing it. Would he consider taking it?"

"No. We suggested that, too. But he says he takes enough medication as it is. And I can't argue with him there. He takes *a lot* of medication. A lot of pain medication. Too much pain medication, probably."

"What do you mean by 'probably'?"

Even in profile, Walker looked sheepish. "I mean, I'm not sure how many medications he takes, and how much he takes of any of them."

"Well, who's giving him his medication?"

"He's giving it to himself."

"And you don't know if he's taking the correct dosage or not?"

"No," Walker said, obviously embarrassed. "But I do know that a couple of the medications he's taking can be habit forming."

Mila sighed inwardly. This was one complication she hadn't foreseen. But if she was going to do her job right—and she was going to do it right—then she'd obviously have to take charge of the situation.

"I'll speak to your brother," she said calmly. "And I'll tell him that from now on, I'll be the one dispensing the medications. He'll take the correct dosage, at the correct time. No exceptions."

Walker looked relieved. "Thank you," he said. "I appreciate that." They lapsed into silence then, and Walker drove, staring straight ahead, for several hundred more feet before he suddenly pulled onto the gravel shoulder of the road, put on the brakes, and shifted the truck into neutral.

"Look," he said, turning to a startled Mila. "There's something else I need to talk to you about before we take the turnoff for Butternut. And it's important that I talk to you about it before you spend your first night at the cabin with my brother."

"All right," Mila said, a little uncertainly. She'd wondered about this, about being alone with a man again, especially in close quarters, as she was with Walker Ford, and she'd wondered if she'd be afraid. But she wasn't afraid, she realized. She wasn't for the simple reason that she knew, intuitively, she had nothing to fear from this man. He was tired, and stressed out, but he wasn't dangerous.

"Look," he said now, "my brother, Reid, has these dreams." Then he corrected himself. "No, not dreams. They're nightmares. And you'll know when he's having them, too. Because you'll hear him. He . . . he screams, I guess, is the best way of putting it. Though sometimes, honestly, it sounds almost . . . not human. Sometimes he screams things you can actually understand. You know, like 'help,' stuff like that. But sometimes, he just screams. And it's worse, somehow," he said, with a visible shudder. "It's worse when you can't understand him. But if you wake him up, which I've done a couple of times, he says he doesn't remember what he was dreaming about. But I think it's pretty obvious, don't you? I mean, what must that have been like for him? Being trapped in his car for three days? Drifting in and out of consciousness? And in horrible pain?"

Mila didn't answer. How could she? Nobody but Reid Ford would ever know what that had been like.

Walker looked at Mila now and then looked out the window and onto the empty road. The rain, which had been a light drizzle, had started to come down a little harder, and Walker turned on the windshield wipers, which squeaked rhythmically, almost comfortingly, against the windshield. He started to say something, then stopped, then started again. "The nights with my brother are going to be tough," he said. "No doubt about it. But the days, the days might be worse."

Mila looked at him questioningly. He blew out a long breath, and she knew whatever he was going to tell her next was something he didn't really want to tell her. "I know I said before that my brother isn't the easiest person in the world to get along with, but I think I might have understated the problem. It's why we've had trouble keeping home health care workers. Two of them, in fact, have quit already."

"I know that," Mila said. "The agency told me."

"Did they?" Walker said, surprised. "And you still agreed to come all the way up here?"

"A job is a job," she said simply. *And a job two hundred and forty miles from my old life was just too good a job for me to pass up.*

"Well, some jobs are worse than others," Walker said, with a wry smile. "But I'm glad you feel that way. And I'm glad we had this talk, too. It was my wife, Allie's, idea. She suggested we try to prepare you for the worst. You know, 'forewarned is forearmed'? That kind of thing. It was also her idea to give Reid an ultimatum this time. She's telling him—right now, in fact—that if this falls through, we'll have to send him back to the rehabilitation center he was in after the accident. Obviously, though, we're hoping things turn out differently this time. Because between my wife and me, we have two children—one who is an infant—and two businesses. And to say that we're holding our own right now would be to give both of us too much credit. Most of the time, we're barely keeping it together. And that's on a good day."

As he said this, Mila felt a wave of sympathy for him. She knew what he was talking about. "Barely keeping it together" had become her stock-in-trade recently. But Walker Ford didn't need to know about that. What he needed to know was that she could help him. *Help them.* Because if she couldn't help people, she'd need to find a new career.

"Look," she said now. "Don't worry about your brother. Let *me* worry about him. I'm good at getting along with people." *Or I used to be, anyway.* "I'll find a way to make this work," she continued, smiling her encouragement. "And that way, you and your wife can concentrate on the rest of your lives, all right?"

He looked surprised and relieved. "Thank you" he said simply.

"Now, is there anything else I need to know?" Mila asked, feeling, for a moment, like the competent person she had once considered herself to be.

"You mean, is there anything else you need to know about my brother?"

"Or about the job. About my responsibilities."

"Well," he paused. "We've already discussed his medication. You'll give that to him, right?"

"Right."

"And, let's see, what else . . . Well, there are a few things my brother can do on his own now. Fortunately, the cabin he's staying at right now—it's where my wife and children and I lived before his accident—already had doorways wide enough for a wheelchair. But we've also installed an entrance ramp, and a hospital bed, and ret-rofitted his bathroom, so he can handle his basic needs."

"What about bathing?" Mila asked.

"Oh, I help him with that."

"Well, I can take over now."

But Walker shook his head. "I don't think so. He won't let anyone but me help him."

"But are you trained to help him?"

"Trained?" Walker repeated, looking sheepish again. "Not really. I just kind of, you know, wash him up." He made a washing gesture with his hands.

"All right, well, I'll wait to broach the subject with your brother. But ultimately, I think I should be the one doing that. Now, what about the cooking? What will that involve?"

"Nothing on your part. We've hired someone to do the cooking and the housekeeping. Her name is Lonnie Hagan. She comes every day, from 8:00 A.M. to 4:00 P.M. She brings Reid his breakfast and lunch—he prefers to have them in his room—and she also prepares his dinner before she leaves. All you'll have to do with it is heat it up and take it to him on a tray, then collect the tray when he's done."

Mila almost asked, *Why are you taking him his meals on a tray, instead of having him wheel himself in to wherever his housekeeper or his home health aides are having their meals, too?* But she didn't. Still, it was her opinion that if Reid wasn't a complete invalid, he shouldn't be treated like one.

"Okay," she said. "No cooking or cleaning. But there must be other things you need me to do?"

"Well, Allie and I have been taking him to his doctor's appointments, but I'm hoping that Reid will eventually let you take him, too. Same with his physical therapy appointments. Those should start as soon as he gets his long leg cast off, which, unfortunately, is still several weeks away. In the meantime, though, we'll need you to pick up his prescriptions and run an occasional errand. Oh, and check his vital signs and monitor his general health. But that's about it, I guess."

"I can do all those things," Mila said, "and I'll still have plenty of time left over to provide companionship for your brother."

"Companionship?" Walker echoed skeptically.

"Uh-huh. Taking him for walks in his wheelchair. Playing board games. Or even just having conversations."

"Conversations?"

"Yes, you know, talking," Mila prompted.

"Yeah, about that," Walker said, looking worried. "Maybe I didn't really make myself clear before. But Reid doesn't do the whole . . . companionship thing. He doesn't do the conversation thing, either."

"You mean he doesn't talk?"

"I mean he doesn't *like* to talk. Not since the accident. He likes to be alone. In his room."

"What does he do in there?" Mila asked.

"Nothing," Walker said. "We've offered to put a television in there. Or a computer. But he said no. I even bought him an iPad, which I couldn't get him interested in. Honestly, I don't know what he does all day. Stares out the window, I guess. Except he doesn't do that, either, because he likes to keep the shades down. It bothers me, actually," he added, "that it's so dark in there all the time."

"Well, then I'll add raising his shades to my to-do list," Mila said determinedly. "It will come right after confiscating his medications." But something else was bothering her now. "Mr. Ford—"

"Walker," he corrected her.

"Walker," she amended. "If I'm not providing companionship for your brother, I'm not . . . I'm not going to be very busy. I mean, the responsibilities we've discussed will take, at most, a couple of hours a day."

"That's probably true."

"But you're paying me to work full-time."

"That's definitely true," he smiled. "Is there a problem with that?"

"No problem, except that what you've described, it's not a full-time job. I'm not even sure it's a *part-time* job." Even as she was saying this, though, Mila was regretting saying it. Because what would she do if he decided not to hire her to live in, full-time? And where, exactly, would she go? There was no backup plan. Not for her, anyway.

"Look," Walker said, shifting in his seat. "It doesn't matter how many hours a day you'll actually be working, especially when what little time you spend with Reid will probably seem like much more time than it actually is. What matters is that you'll be there if he needs you, especially if he needs you at night. If you can be that person for him, Mila, you'll be giving my wife and me our peace of mind back, and right now, honestly, I couldn't even begin to put a price on that."

Mila hesitated, still uncomfortable with the idea of working only a couple of hours a day. She had a formidable work ethic, and so far, this job description was not jibing with it.

Walker sensed her ambivalence but misunderstood the cause of it. "Look, don't worry about being bored this summer," he said. "Especially if you like the outdoors. The cabin is right on Butternut Lake, and it's beautiful, really. And when Lonnie's there, during the day, you're welcome to explore the area, on foot or in one of the boats we own. Then, on your days off, you can borrow one of our cars and go into town. There's not much to see there, of course, but it should provide a few distractions. It's got a good coffee shop, for one thing, and a handful of other stores, some of which even sell things you might need. It's not exactly the Twin Cities," he added, with a smile. "But we like it."

"I'm sure it will be fine," Mila said quickly. "I don't need a lot of entertainment." And besides, she was planning on spending as little time as possible in public.

The cabin's secluded location suited her just fine. It was the perfect place to get lost. Or at least to not be found.

"All right, then," Walker said, with obvious relief. "I think we've covered everything." He glanced at his watch. "We're late," he said, shifting the pickup into drive and pulling back onto the road. "I kept you too long. We were supposed to be at Pearl's, the coffee shop I mentioned, fifteen minutes ago. Are you ready to meet Reid?" he asked, stepping on the gas.

"As ready as I'll ever be," Mila joked. But she found herself wishing that Walker had been a little less forthcoming with her. The more she heard about his brother, frankly, the less confident she felt that she could do the job.

"Here they are now," Allie said, watching the front door at Pearl's. She shot Reid a warning look and, in the next moment, composed her face into a welcoming smile. Reid followed her eyes to his brother, Walker, and the young woman with him, as they threaded their way through the coffee shop's tables.

"Hey," Walker said. "I'm sorry we're late. My meeting ran over at the boatyard, and I found Ms. Jones waiting in the rain."

"Walker," Allie said reprovingly. And then, to the young woman with Walker, "You must be Mila."

The young woman—Mila—nodded her assent, but there was something about hearing her name said out loud that seemed to unnerve her. She cringed, almost imperceptibly, and glanced furtively around. Reid frowned. That was odd. He watched her thoughtfully as Walker made the introductions. She wasn't unattractive, he thought. Far from it. She was petite and slender, with straight shoulder-length brown hair, watchful brown eyes, delicate features, and fair skin. But there was something about her that Reid found slightly unsettling. Maybe it was because, when she and Walker joined them at the table, she chose a chair that faced the front door and then looked up every time it opened and the little string of bells above it rang. Or maybe it was because of the way she sank down, ever so slightly, in her chair, drawing her slender shoulders together, as if she were trying to make herself smaller. As if she were trying, he realized, to hide in plain sight.

All this was interesting to him. For about two minutes. And then it was just annoying. Because this was the trouble with bringing virtual strangers into your home. They didn't just bring their actual baggage with them, they brought their personal baggage with them too. All their problems, big and small, not to mention all their annoying personality quirks and irritating habits.

Mrs. Everson, for instance, who'd been his first home health aide, had brought with her a fondness for cheap red wine, though she'd been careful to drink it only at night, and only in her own room. Reid hadn't mentioned it to Walker or Allie. He'd figured her habit of drinking herself into a stupor every night gave him a modicum of privacy he wouldn't have if she were sober. But he'd wondered, idly, what would happen to him if there were a nighttime emergency, as Allie and Walker worried there might be. A fire, or a tornado. In either of these unlikely events, Reid knew, Mrs. Everson—lying facedown on her bed, snoring lustily into her pillow—would be useless to both of them. Still, as much as Reid had enjoyed speculating about how Mrs. Everson smuggled all those empty wine bottles out of the cabin without attracting the notice of Lonnie or his brother, he still hated having her there. Because the truth was that for someone who liked to drink so much, she was surprisingly little fun, and once Reid made it his mission in life to make her quit, she was really no fun at all.

Mrs. Bolger, the home health care aide who replaced Mrs. Everson, didn't have a drinking problem. But she did have a grating tendency to have long, one-sided conversations with Reid, most of which were about her relationship with her daughter-in-law—which was lousy—or about her beloved collection of china dolls, which she referred to as if they were actual people. Add to that her constant, tuneless humming, and the cloying, too sweet odor of her perfume, and, within three days of her arrival, Reid found himself longing for the return of Mrs. Everson.

And now, he thought, watching Mila Jones as she tentatively sipped the iced tea she'd ordered, now someone else would be living with him. Someone who was acting as if she'd robbed a bank and was waiting for federal marshals to catch up with her.

"Isn't that right, Reid?" Allie said, interrupting his thoughts.

"Isn't what right?" he asked, entering into what he imagined would be an interminable conversation.

"Mila's welcome to use any of the recreational equipment in the boathouse. The kayak, for instance, or the Jet Ski."

But Reid barely grunted.

"Oh, that's not necessary," Mila said quickly. "I'm sure I'll find plenty to keep me busy."

"Don't count on it," Reid mumbled, under his breath.

Allie shot him a warning look and then turned her attention back to Mila. "Mila, what do you like doing in your free time?"

Reid watched her hesitate for a moment and then shrug. "I'm not used to having a lot of free time," she said, her eyes cutting to the coffee shop's front door again. Reid felt another wave of annoyance. His promise to Allie, he knew, was about to go right out that door.

"Can we stop this?" he asked now, addressing the table at large. "Can we stop pretending that Ms. Jones and I are going to become good friends? Because we all know that's not going to happen. If we're lucky—very lucky—we'll be able to stand each other just enough to tolerate the very short amount of time we'll need to spend together every day."

Allie's face flushed then from some combination of anger and embarrassment, and Mila, Reid saw, was startled. But only for a moment. Because in the next moment she slid down a little more in her chair and drew her shoulders even closer together, as if she was hoping to simply disappear altogether.

"Oh, come on," Reid said. "I'm only saying what everyone here already knows. I don't want Ms. Jones to be here any more than she wants to be here. I'd like to live alone now. Something, by the way, I'm perfectly capable of doing. And Ms. Jones—well, I don't know Ms. Jones well enough to know what she'd rather be doing—but I imagine it's almost anything but this."

"But this *is* what I want to be doing," Mila said, sitting up a little straighter. "Taking care of people, I mean."

Her apparent sincerity threw Reid, but only for a moment. "Well, you may want to do it, but you can't be very good at doing it," Reid pointed out. "Because if you were, your agency wouldn't have to send you two hundred and forty miles away to do it, would they? What'd you do, Ms. Jones, at your last job? Steal a patient's fur coat? Or was it their family silver?"

"Reid, that's outrageous, even for you," Allie objected, and she looked, Reid thought, like it was taking all her willpower not to strangle him. "Mila was referred to us by a reputable agency. And her record, I'm sure, is spotless."

"Actually," Mila said, looking not at Allie, but at Reid, "I don't have a record yet. This is my first placement."

Reid rolled his eyes, ignoring the warning hand Allie had placed on his arm. "Great," he said. "So you basically have no idea what you're doing. Which means you're going to be even *less* competent than your predecessors. Who, trust me, already set the bar pretty low."

He'd expected this to silence her, but she continued to look steadily at him before she said. "I can't speak for whoever came before me, obviously. But I can promise you that I've received excellent training, and that I'm fully qualified for this position. So I'll do my best to make you comfortable, Mr. Ford. And, if you're concerned about your valuables, I suggest you keep them locked up. But since you don't strike me as the kind of man who would own either a silver tea service or a mink coat, I don't think my stealing them is a real possibility, do you?"

Reid, surprised, sat back in his wheelchair, but Mila was still staring at him, a challenge in her brown eyes. And then she seemed to remember herself, and she glanced around, nervously, as though she'd said too much.

"Okay, fine," Reid said, still not quite willing to concede the point. "I won't worry about my valuables. Especially since I don't have very many of them to worry about. But I still think it's strange that you'd want to spend your summer so far from home, with someone you've never even met before. I mean, seriously, if that doesn't smack of desperation, what does?"

"Reid, stop," Allie said, but Mila interrupted.

"Actually, the reason I chose to come here was because I was ready for a change of pace," she said. "I've lived in the city all my life, and I thought this might be a nice change, living here for the summer."

"Change of pace?" he repeated, not bothering to hide his skepticism. "I think we both know that's not why you're here. I think it's much more likely you're running away from something. Or someone. A bad breakup, maybe? Or some guy in Minneapolis who—"

But he stopped when Mila stood up from the table so suddenly that she knocked over her iced tea, and then he watched, silently, as she rushed out of the coffee shop, bumping into a few more tables and chairs on her way out.

"Uh, Caroline," Reid called out to the coffee shop's owner, who was still hovering nearby, holding the baby. "I think we're going to need your help over here again."

He glanced over at his brother and sister-in-law, who both looked appalled.

"What?" he said, with mock innocence. "I thought that went very well."

Mila was standing down the block from the coffee shop, under the dripping awning of the hardware store, when Allie caught up to her. She'd brought her baby with her—a girl, judging from the pale yellow sweater she was wearing—and the baby, as if sensing somehow how miserable Mila was, smiled at her.

And Mila, trying not to cry, smiled back at her. Even in her present misery, it was impossible not to. Most babies were cute, she supposed, but this one seemed especially so, with her downy brown hair and wide blue eyes.

"She likes you," Allie said encouragingly.

"She's adorable," Mila said, watching as the baby now sucked contentedly on her chubby little hand.

"She missed her nap today, in all the excitement," Allie said, resetting the baby on her hip. "So far, so good, though. But I'm . . . I'm sorry about that." She gestured in the direction of the coffee shop. "I'm not going to ask you to excuse Reid's behavior, since, obviously, there is no excuse for it."

Mila shrugged, but she didn't say anything. She was afraid if she did, the tears would start. She could feel them gathering behind her eyes and burning in her throat. They were tears of anger, and humiliation.

"Look," Allie said now. "He's not like that *all* the time. *Most* of the time, yes. But sometimes, every once in a great while, he can be *almost* pleasant to be around." She smiled at Mila, and Mila saw that she was joking. *A little.* Mila tried to smile back. She didn't blame Allie for her brother-in-law's behavior. She and her husband both seemed like nice people. A little overwhelmed, maybe. But nice.

"No, seriously," Allie said. "He was different before the accident. I mean, don't get me wrong. Even then, he didn't expend a lot of energy on, um . . . personal relationships. But that was mainly because he was a complete workaholic. It was *all* about the business with him."

"The business?"

"He and my husband own a couple of dozen boatyards, all over the Midwest," Allie explained. "Walker did some of the work, of course, building their company. But Reid was the driving force behind it. He worked all the time. We're talking sixteen hours a day, seven days a week. And he'd be on the road two hundred and fifty days a year. It was crazy." She shook her head. "Walker and I visited him once at his apartment in Minneapolis, and I swear, he had nothing in the refrigerator. Nothing. Not even, like, a jar of mustard or something. The only sign that someone even lived in that apartment, as I recall, was some dry cleaning hanging in the hall closet." She shuddered at the memory.

"Anyway," she continued, "that was the way he lived then. If he had any friends who weren't his brother and I, or his business associates, I wasn't aware of them. There were some women, of course. Quite a few of them, actually. But I never met any of them. I don't think he was interested in a real relationship. I think he was the kind of guy who didn't like to stick around in the morning, if you know what I mean."

Mila knew what she meant, but she was having trouble believing it. Reid, the man in the wheelchair, didn't look like he could have been a womanizer for the simple reason that no woman in her right mind would have been interested in him. It wasn't that he was unattractive. He wasn't. Even his long hair—long enough to be falling in his eyes—and his scruffy beard couldn't hide the fact that he was a good-looking man. But his *personality* was so unattractive. *Yuck,* she thought. Who would have wanted to spend time with someone as boorish and as rude as he was?

But Allie, seeing the skepticism on Mila's face, only laughed. "No, it's true," she said. "Women liked him. He was good-looking. He *still* is good-looking, somewhere under all that facial hair. And as for the rest of him, well, he could be very charming when he wanted to be."

Mila considered this. It seemed unlikely. In fact, the man in the coffee shop was so *un*charming that she was having difficulty imagining how she was going to spend the next three months with him. And Allie, watching her, sighed and shifted the baby to her other hip.

"Mila, I understand how you must be feeling about Reid right now. I really do. But you have to trust me when I say that there's a nice guy in there somewhere. In fact, I'll tell you something about Reid that'll prove it to you."

Mila raised her eyebrows, curious in spite of herself.

"When my husband was growing up, Reid was the closest thing to a parent—a *good* parent—that he had. His actual parents had a terrible marriage—you know, one of those relationships that makes kids feel like they were living in a war zone—and then, when they finally got divorced, things got *worse*. They still fought all the time, only now they used the kids as weapons against each other. Finally, though, their dad just kind of washed his hands of all three of them, and their mom just kind of checked out. I mean, she was there, but she wasn't really *there*."

Mila nodded. Her own mother had belonged to the same school of parenting, the there-but-not-there school. Except, of course, that in her case she really *hadn't* been there a lot of the time. When she had been there, though, it hadn't been much different.

"Anyway," Allie continued, "that left Reid to be both parents to Walker, even though he was only a few years older than him. And you know what? He did it. He really did. He went to all his Little League games, and he helped him with his homework, and once, when Walker was having trouble with a class, he even went to a parent-teacher conference for him. Honestly, if it hadn't been for Reid, I don't know where Walker would have been. On his own, I guess."

Mila knew something about that, too.

"So there you have it," Allie said, shifting the baby back to the other hip. "That's how I know Reid can be a good guy. When he chooses to be one, of course. Which, admittedly, doesn't happen very often anymore. But, Mila?"

"Yes," Mila said, relieved that the urge to cry had finally passed.

"Walker and I really need this to work out," Allie said. "And I'm guessing you need it to work out, too."

Mila looked at her sharply, wondering what Allie knew about her. But then she realized that Allie knew only what the agency had told her, which wasn't much. Only her professional qualifications. What she'd meant, probably, was that if Mila had had any other offers, she probably would have taken one closer to home.

Mila studied Allie then and decided that she liked her. She was pretty, with long, shiny, golden brown hair and bright hazel eyes. But more than that, she seemed nice. Genuine, open, and warm. Mila couldn't let her guard down around her, of course. She couldn't let her guard down around *anyone*. But when it came to working with Reid, she figured she could use an ally, and the sooner, the better.

"So what do you think?" Allie asked hopefully. "Are you willing to give it a try? Walker and I are only three miles and one phone call away. And I promise, both of us stop by at least once a day. Sometimes more. And anytime you need us to be there, we can be. Even if it's on short notice. I'll make sure Walker gives you both of our cell-phone numbers, okay?"

"Okay," Mila said, trying, and failing, to smile. The thought of going home with Reid now, and of being left alone with him eventually, was filling her with an almost palpable dread. Still, it could be worse. It could be *a lot* worse. And, as she remembered how much worse it could be, her eyes traveled up and down the length of Butternut's Main Street, checking to see if she'd been followed. But . . . no. It was quiet. Just a rainy June afternoon in a small town. *A very pretty small town,* she thought. And it was true. Even on a gray day like today, Butternut's prettiness shone through. All the businesses on Main Street, for instance, had cheerful striped awnings, flower boxes, and brightly painted wooden benches for people to sit on. Taking this all in, Mila was reminded of the illustrations of small towns in children's books she used to stare at longingly as a child. She'd lived in the city then, of course, but not the nice part of the city. She'd lived in a drab, hardscrabble part of it, where no one thought to plant flower boxes or worried that tired people might not have a bench to sit on.

Mila turned her eyes back to Allie and Brooke just in time to see Brooke yawn a miniature yawn and bury her face against Allie's shoulder.

"Listen, I need to get going," Allie said apologetically. "I've got to pick up my son, Wyatt, at day camp, and I'm hoping it's not too late for Brooke to take a nap in her car seat. But Walker and I are going to switch cars, and he's going to drive you and Reid out to the cabin in the wheelchair-accessible van, all right? And, Mila?" she added, with a gentle smile. "Thank you. Thank you for coming. And thank you for staying."

"You're welcome," Mila said, with her best imitation of a smile, but standing there, under the dripping canopy, and feeling as gray as the rain itself, she thought, *Lucky for you I have nowhere else to go.*

Chapter 3

Afterward, as they drove out to the cabin in the van, Mila was relieved to discover that Reid, who had earlier seemed so eager to provoke her, had now apparently lost interest in her and instead had settled into a gloomy silence in the back of the van. Walker ignored him and peppered Mila with friendly, innocuous questions. Outwardly, she listened to him, and provided him with what she hoped were appropriate answers, but inwardly, she paid attention to the route he was driving, memorizing it, in reverse, in case she ever needed to leave the cabin in a hurry.

Left at the Moccasin Bar, she told herself, after they'd left the town and turned at a roadhouse whose neon sign blinked on and off even in broad daylight. *Right at Butternut Bait and Tackle. And left again at a sign for a resort called White Pines.* But when they reached the road the cabin was on—Butternut Lake Drive—Walker said to her, as if reading her mind, "Once you get to this road, it's hard to get lost. It's the only way in to the cabin and the only way out, too."

Mila nodded, but his choice of words sounded ominous to her, and she shivered, unconsciously, and drew her arms protectively around herself.

"Are you cold?" Walker asked. "I can roll up the windows."

But Mila shook her head. "No, it's nice," she said, gesturing to her half-open window. And it was. The air smelled clean and piney, and though it had stopped raining, when she turned her face to the window, it was bathed in a misty coolness.

They continued to drive in silence then, down a road that curved through dense forest as it followed the rough contours of a lake that only occasionally came into view on the left side of the van. Every once in a while, they'd pass a driveway, too, or a turnout for a logging road, but, for the most part, they passed nothing but unbroken stretches of pine and birch trees.

"Here's where the road starts to get twisty," Walker said, as he took the van into a steep curve. "It's like this for the next five miles. All the rest of the way to the cabin, in fact. You don't get motion sickness, do you?" he asked, glancing at her sideways.

Mila shook her head, but as she did so they went into another turn and she braced her hand against the dashboard.

"That's good," Walker said. "Because this road is hell otherwise. Wyatt, our son, is fine on it. But Allie and I joke that if Brooke turns out to be one of those kids who gets carsick, we're going to have to move into town." He smiled, but then he turned serious. "Just be careful driving on this," he said, lowering his voice. "Even in good weather, people have been known to take a turn too wide. And then there's the oncoming traffic. It's easy to inch into the other lane without realizing it. The next thing you know, you come into a turn and there's a pickup bearing down on you."

"I'll be careful on it," Mila assured him. Privately, though, she felt another wave of uneasiness.

But ten minutes later, after they'd turned into the long driveway, and the cabin had finally come into view, Mila's spirits lifted a little. The cabin, for one thing, was a cabin in name only, because while the word had called up for her an image of something that was at best rustic, and at worst, primitive, this place was neither of those things. It was large, and sleek, and modern, and yet, oddly enough, it was also completely at home here in the woods. Almost as if, instead of being built here, it had simply grown here, right along with the aspen and birch and pine trees that surrounded it.

Then, as soon as they pulled up in front, a woman came out of the house, wiping her hands on a dish towel. "Hi, I'm Lonnie," she said to Mila, as Mila climbed out of the van. She was a full-figured, blond-haired woman in late middle age with a wide, pleasant face and a friendly smile.

"I see you survived the drive," she said to Mila, and then without waiting for an answer she frowned and added, perplexed, "But you're so young."

"I'm not as young as I look," Mila said quickly, feeling again as if some kind of apology was in order.

But Lonnie only smiled. "Nothing wrong with being young," she said. "As anyone on my side of fifty will tell you. I just expected you to be more like the other two." She lowered her voice as she glanced over at Walker, who was operating the van's wheelchair lift. "You know, the other two aides were both sort of . . . matronly, like me," she explained.

Mila started to tell her she wasn't matronly, but Lonnie, at Walker's instructions, got Mila's suitcase out of the van and hurried her down the flagstone path to the cabin.

"Should I . . . should I help Walker with Reid?" Mila asked, looking over her shoulder.

"No, Walker's got everything under control," Lonnie said genially. "They'll use the kitchen door. It has a wheelchair ramp. Besides, I'm under strict instructions from Walker to take you on a tour of the cabin and then help you get settled in your room." She gestured for Mila to follow her into the cabin's main entrance. "We'll leave your suitcase here, for now," she added, setting it down inside the front hallway, and leading Mila into what was obviously the cabin's living room.

"*It's so big,*" Mila murmured, amazed at the scale of the room. She'd lived her whole life in a series of rental apartments, each one seemingly smaller than the one before it, and she was not used to spaces this large.

"Oh, it's big all right," Lonnie agreed, surveying the room as if for the first time.

But it wasn't *just* big. It was beautiful, too. Or maybe handsome was a better word, since there was something unmistakably masculine about it. It had a cathedral ceiling with exposed wooden beams, an enormous fieldstone fireplace that took up most of one wall, and another wall, at the foot of the room, constructed entirely of glass. Deep leather couches with soft sheepskin throws, richly patterned rugs, copper light fixtures, and lamps with oilskin shades completed a look that managed to be both rustic and warm at the same time.

"The fire's nice, too," Lonnie said, gesturing to the huge, crackling fire in the fireplace. "Especially on a day like today when there's a bit of a chill in the air," she added, and Mila wondered how much of that chill had come from the weather and how much of it had come from the occupant of this cabin.

"The deck's out here," Lonnie said then, traversing the length of the room to the glass wall, whose sliding door opened onto a wooden deck that seemed almost as large as the living room itself. Mila followed her and stood beside her as she looked out at the deck. She realized then that the cabin was built on a bluff above the lake, and that the deck was suspended in midair, with pine trees hovering above it and the water poised some distance below it.

"It's quite something, isn't it?" Lonnie chuckled, glancing at Mila. "Allie says that what Walker really wanted when he built this cabin was an adult tree house."

An adult tree house, Mila thought. That was exactly what it was like.

"There are the steps that go down to the lake," Lonnie said, pointing to a set of steps on the deck's left-hand side. "I'm sure you'll want to spend as much time down there this summer as possible. Especially if you need to cool off in the lake. Walker doesn't like air-conditioning and he didn't install it."

But Mila shrugged noncommittally. Why was everyone acting as if she was here on vacation? She didn't have time to think about that though once Lonnie resumed the tour. The living room made up the bulk of the cabin's downstairs, but there was also a study, a den, and a kitchen, each of which managed to seem both modern and warm at the same time—lots of clean lines, pale wood, and floor-to-ceiling windows. There was also a second floor, but Lonnie didn't take Mila up there. It was where Walker and Allie's and their children's bedrooms were, and, as Lonnie explained to Mila, they'd packed up and moved, for the time being, to Allie's family's old fishing cabin, the same one Allie had promised Mila was just three miles away.

"Now," Lonnie said, after she'd picked up Mila's suitcase in the front hall and brought her down a hallway tucked in behind the kitchen, "these are the guest rooms. Reid is staying in this one"—she indicated a closed door behind which Allie could hear Reid and Walker talking in low voices—"and this is the one you'll be staying in." She pointed to a door at the end of the hall, only fifteen feet away from Reid's room.

"They're so close," Mila said, without thinking. "Our bedrooms, I mean."

"Well, that's a good thing, isn't it?" Lonnie said. She added quickly, "I mean, if he needs your help, you'll be able to hear him." And Mila looked at her questioningly, wondering if she was referring to the nightmares Walker had told her about. But Lonnie was already opening the door to Mila's room, and, bustling inside it, she put Mila's suitcase on the luggage rack and started raising shades and turning on lights.

It was a nice room, Mila saw. Simple, yet somehow luxurious in its simplicity. It had only a bed, a bedside table, a dresser, a desk, and an armchair, but Mila thought it was more than adequate to her needs, especially since the muted color pallet and creamy bed linens gave it a restful quality she could appreciate in her present weariness.

"The bathroom's down the hall," Lonnie said, pausing to fluff up one of Mila's pillows with a proprietary air. "And there are extra towels and bed linens in the closet. Now, I'll leave you to get unpacked," she continued. "After that, why don't you come find me in the kitchen? I'll be leaving soon, at four o'clock, and before I go I want to show you a few more things. Nothing too complicated. The fuse box, the thermostat, the alarm."

"The alarm?" Mila repeated.

"Yes," Lonnie said, misreading her interest. "But it's perfectly safe out here. You don't even need to use it if you don't want to. Walker had it put in because one of the previous home health aides insisted on it. I guess she was spooked by being out in the woods like this."

"Well, you might as well show me how it works," Mila said casually, though she already knew she would set the alarm every night.

Lonnie left then, and Mila closed the door, walked over to the luggage rack, and opened up her suitcase. The first thing she unpacked from it were her test prep books for the nursing school entrance exam. There were several of them, and they'd taken up precious space in her small suitcase, but it had never occurred to her not to pack them. Now she placed them, along with lined paper, pencils, and a pencil sharpener, into the top drawer of the desk. After that, she put the few clothes she'd brought into the dresser drawers and arranged a small selection of toiletries on top of the dresser. Last, she took the ring box out from the bottom of her suitcase, and, without opening it, she placed it in the very back of the bottom dresser drawer, where it would be out of her sight.

As she closed the drawer and stood up, she caught sight of herself in the mirror hanging above the dresser, and, resisting the urge to look away, she studied herself in its reflection. First, she looked at herself head-on, then she tilted her chin, slowly, up and down, and turned her face to the right and then the left. She'd done a good job with her makeup, she decided, and it hadn't completely worn off on the bus, either. She could still see, of course, the faint shadow above and below her left eye, and the slight swelling of her upper left lip. But she didn't think either of these was visible to the untrained eye.

But the makeup couldn't hide everything, she reminded herself, reaching down and pulling up her blouse's left sleeve. Just a few inches above her wrist, the bruises started. A whole line of them, running up the inside of her arm to her elbow. They had faded from their original purple to a dull, ugly yellow, but it would be another week, at least, until they completely disappeared. She'd have to be careful to keep them under wraps until then, she decided, letting her sleeve fall back into place.

She knew she should go and find Lonnie in the kitchen now, but instead she wandered, a little for-lornly, over to one of the room's windows and looked out of it, onto a seemingly endless expanse of forest. The recent rain had left it looking lush and verdant, and the grass and the ferns and the trees together made up a thousand shades of green, from the palest moss green to the deepest pine green, each one layered intricately over the other and stretching away as far as the eye could see. And looking into that distance now, Mila was struck suddenly by how isolated she was here. And that was a good thing, she told herself, because what were the chances of him finding her all the way out here? Then again, if he *did* find her, late one night, it would be just her and Reid here. She pictured Reid in his wheelchair, pictured his hostility at the coffee shop, his glumness in the van. He wouldn't help her, she thought. No, she corrected herself, he *couldn't* help her. Even if he was inclined to help her—and he clearly was not—his physical condition wouldn't allow him to. If Brandon ever found her here, she decided, she would be really, and truly, on her own.

Later that evening, after Walker and Lonnie had left for the night, but before Mila took Reid his dinner, she sat on the edge of her bed, giving herself a silent pep talk. *You can do this, Mila. You know you can. Just remember, it's not about you. It's about doing the right thing. It's about honoring the contract you signed. The one that said you'd be responsible for Reid's well-being. Not his emotional well-being, of* course. Because that would be a tall order. That would require knowledge and skill well beyond her home health aide certification. But for his *physical* well-being. *And that means you need to be responsible for giving Reid his pain medication. Because right now, nobody knows how often he's taking it. Or how much of it he's taking. Or in what combinations he's taking it.* And if he were to have an accidental overdose, or, God forbid, a purposeful overdose—because, based on what Walker had told her about him, the man was obviously depressed—then it would be her fault. *And you don't want that on your conscience, do you?*

She did not. But she still could not bring herself to leave her room, walk down the hallway to Reid's room, knock on his door, and demand that he give her his prescription medications. And why not? she asked herself, getting up from her bed and pacing a little. Well, for one thing, she was afraid of him. Not *physically* afraid of him, of course. He couldn't hurt her. Not in the condition he was in now. Besides, there was nothing in his file to suggest he was violent, though there was plenty, of course, to suggest he was both rude and uncooperative. But she wasn't afraid of him for *that* reason, was she? *Yes,* a little voice inside her answered, as she remembered what he'd been like at the coffee shop that afternoon. The way he'd looked at her, as if he were seeing right through her, and the way he'd said that to her, too, about running away from a bad breakup . . . it was unnerving. Uncanny, almost. It was hard to know if he was being perceptive, or if he'd just made a lucky guess. Either way, though, she wasn't looking forward to having another conversation with him.

Then again, she thought, what kind of a nurse would she be, one day, if she couldn't stand up to her patients? If she couldn't act in their best interests, even if she was intimidated by them? *Not a very good one*, she had to admit. Besides, she was going to have to learn to be stronger than she'd been in the past, stronger and more assertive. She stopped pacing, closed her eyes, and counted silently to ten. Then, before she lost her nerve, she left her room and walked quickly to Reid's room. The door was closed, but she knocked on it, firmly.

"Reid?" she called.

There was no answer. She frowned. Could he be sleeping? It was possible. But it didn't matter. This couldn't wait. She knocked again, louder this time. Still no answer. Her resolve weakened a little. Maybe she should come back later? But no, she told herself. Later was too late.

She knocked again. "Reid?" she said. "Reid, it's Mila. I need to speak to you."

This time he answered. "Go away," he called out, obviously irritated.

She took a step back. Even after their earlier meeting, she was surprised at his rudeness. But she gathered her resolve. "I'm not going away," she said, hoping she sounded braver than she actually felt.

"Well, that's too bad," he answered churlishly. "Because I'm not opening this door."

"Well, then I'll wait here until you change your mind," Mila said, relieved that Reid had no way of knowing how fast her heart was beating. "And Reid," she added, "I can wait here all night."

She heard an exasperated sigh, but a moment later he wheeled himself over to the door and opened it a crack.

"What it is?" he growled, barely looking at her.

"I need to speak to you," she said, resisting the urge to take a step back.

"Not now," he said, already sounding bored by what had transpired between them.

"Yes, now," she said, as firmly as she could.

He sighed again, heavily. "Fine. Go ahead. But hurry up."

"Not like this," she objected, through the crack in the door. "I need to speak to you face-to-face."

There was a pause. "Are you quitting?" he asked.

"No, I am not quitting," Mila said. *But I would, if I had any choice in the matter.* "Reid, come on. This is silly," she said. "Open the door all the way."

And, after a moment, he did. "All right," he said, maneuvering his wheelchair out of the way, "you can come in. But make it quick. I'm busy."

And Mila, once she came into his room, almost laughed at this last remark. Because what could he possibly have been doing in here that she was interrupting? Even if there had been any diversions in the room—and, as Walker had already told her, there weren't many—the lights were off, and the shades were drawn, leaving everything, including Reid, in a kind of self-imposed twilight.

But the room didn't just seem lightless. It seemed airless, too. And she was tempted to open the shades, and the windows, but something stopped her, that something being the expression of open hostility on Reid's face as he studied her.

"I'd ask you to sit down," he said. "But I don't want to encourage you to stay."

And Mila, no longer surprised by his rudeness, thought, *You're a real charmer, Reid.* But she reminded herself, again, of why she was here. This wasn't about her ego. This wasn't even about *his* ego. This was about her doing her job, however hard Reid made it for her to do. So she ignored his remark and sat down in an armchair in the corner of the room.

He scowled at her and looked away.

She took a deep breath and steadied her nerves. She couldn't let him see how nervous she was. If he did, he'd take it as a sign of weakness. "Reid, the reason I'm here," she said, "is because I need to talk to you about your medications."

"What about my medications?"

"Well, I know you've been keeping them here in your room with you. But as of today, that's going to change. I'll be responsible for keeping them in a secure place, and I'll also be responsible for giving them to you at the right time, and in the right amount."

"What? No. No way," Reid objected. "I don't need someone doling those pills out to me. I can read a label. I'm not a complete idiot."

"I didn't say you were," Mila said reasonably. "In fact, I think you're perfectly intelligent." *And perfectly unpleasant, too.* "But your intelligence isn't in question. What is in question is whether you're taking your medication too frequently, or taking too much of it at one time. These drugs are called controlled substances for a reason, Reid. They're addictive. Or they can be, if you don't take them the way they're prescribed."

Reid, who'd initially angled his wheelchair away from her, suddenly spun it in her direction. "Did my brother put you up to this?"

"No," Mila said quickly. Too quickly.

"He told you to do this, didn't he?" Reid persisted.

Mila thought for a moment. "Yes," she said. "But I would have done it anyway. It's part of my responsibility as your home health aide."

Reid rolled his eyes. "That's debatable," he mumbled, looking toward a window whose shade was drawn.

"But we're not debating it, Reid," she said, trying to tamp down her nerves again. "So you're going to tell me where the medications are, and I'm going to leave your room with them. It's that simple." She glanced around the room, wondering if they were in plain sight. But they weren't, as far as she could see.

There was a long silence, as Reid angled his wheelchair away from her again. He was obviously hoping that if he ignored her long enough, she'd give up and leave. But she wasn't going to do that.

"Where are they, Reid?" she asked again.

Another stony silence.

She sighed. She'd known this wasn't going to be easy, but she'd hoped it wouldn't come to this. She was pretty sure this next tactic would work. But she was also sure it wasn't going to endear her to Reid. Then again, *nothing* was going to endear her to him. So what difference did it make?

"Reid," she said, "either I leave your room with those medications, or I call your brother and his wife and ask them to come over here so the four of us can discuss it together. Now. *Right now.* Because this can't wait another day."

Reid whirled around. He looked aghast. "Are you serious? They have a family, you know. They're probably sitting down to dinner right now."

"Well, their dinner will have to wait then. Besides, I think they'd agree with me that this is more important."

"Oh, for God's sake," he said, slumping in his wheelchair.

It was quiet in the room then, each of them waiting for the other to capitulate, though only one of them, Mila felt sure, was waiting with a pounding heart and sweaty palms.

Finally she stood up. "I'll call your brother," she said.

He sighed disgustedly. "They're in the bedside table drawer," he said, not looking at her.

"Thank you," Mila said crisply, and she stood up, walked over to the bedside table, and opened the drawer. Then she took out the prescription bottles one at a time, read the labels carefully, and, opening their lids, spilled the contents out onto her palm and counted them before returning them to their bottles. When she was done, she felt relieved. Not only had it not been necessary to call Walker and Allie for reinforcements, but Reid was only a couple days ahead, at most, on his different pain medications. He'd probably been gradually upping his dosage, she saw, but it wasn't too late, hopefully, for her to get him back on track before it became a real problem.

"Reid, when did you last take all of these?" she asked.

He shrugged. "I don't know. I don't take them on a schedule, really. I just sort of take them when I feel like I need them."

Mila's eyes widened, and she felt a lecture coming on, but she stopped herself before she could give it. Instead, she said only, "Well, that stops tonight, all right? From now on, you'll be on a schedule. And if you feel like you need a higher or a lower dosage, then, obviously, that's something you need to discuss with your doctor."

Another sigh from him. "Look, this has been great, really," he said sarcastically. "It's been so much fun spending this time with you. But I need you to leave now, okay? I mean, like, right now."

"Okay," she said, and she tried for a smile, but she couldn't quite pull it off. So she gathered the prescription bottles together, backed out the door, and closed it behind her. Then she went to the kitchen, where she opened one of the cupboards, cleared a small space, and put the medications inside of it. That would do for tonight. Tomorrow, she'd speak to Lonnie about finding a permanent place for them. After she'd put them away, she went back to her room, and sank down gratefully onto the bed. *There*, she told herself. *That wasn't so bad, was it?* But if that were the case, then why was she shaking all over?

Chapter 4

At midnight that night, Mila, who was sitting at the desk in the guest room, put down her pencil and closed her nursing exam study guide. Her back was starting to ache from sitting in the same position for so long, and she clasped her arms behind her to stretch her cramped muscles. She was tired, *dead tired*, as the bus driver had said, and she knew she should go to bed. Her responsibilities were over for the night. She'd taken Reid his dinner on a tray at seven o'clock, as instructed, and she'd come back to collect it at eight o'clock. It was completely untouched. But she couldn't fault him for not eating it. She'd had the same dinner—lasagna, salad, and garlic bread—alone at the kitchen table, and while it had looked good, and tasted even better, she hadn't been able to eat it either, and she'd ended up scraping most of it into the kitchen garbage can.

After she'd loaded the dinner dishes into the dishwasher and wiped down the kitchen counters, she'd locked the cabin's doors and set the alarm, which Lonnie had shown her how to do. Then she'd showered and changed into her nightgown. It had only been nine o'clock by then, and she'd known she wouldn't be able to sleep yet, so she'd studied instead. Or tried to study, anyway, because in her heightened state of alertness, every sound she heard—every branch creaking outside her window, every wave lapping on the lake's shore below, every car passing on the distant road—left her feeling on edge.

Mila, relax, she'd told herself. *You set the alarm. Nobody's getting into this cabin without your knowing about it.* But she couldn't relax, and she couldn't concentrate very well either. Still, as she worked her way slowly, and falteringly, through a section of practice questions, she reminded herself what was at stake here. If she was going to go to nursing school, she had to be prepared for the entrance exam. And being prepared for the entrance exam, which she'd take in the fall, meant spending every available minute studying for it this summer. She tried not to think about the logistics of all this, though. Tried not to think about the fact that taking the exam meant she'd actually have to emerge from hiding long enough to take it, and that applying to and getting accepted to nursing school meant actually having the freedom to attend it. Something she could never do in the shadowy half world that being in hiding had forced her into.

Now, though, she pushed that thought out of her mind, finished stretching her aching back and shoulders, and put her study materials back in the top drawer. But she didn't get up right away. Instead, she picked up a pencil and chewed thoughtfully on it as she thought about Heather. Her friendship with Heather was the reason she was studying for this test. God, she missed her. Missed her in a way she had not known it was possible to miss someone before tonight. She thought back, now, to the first time she'd met her, over seventeen years ago. Mila remembered it as clearly as if it had been yesterday. She'd been in the third grade then, and her teacher, Mrs. Williams, had taken her to her school's administrative office.

"Is the nurse here?" Mrs. Williams asked the school secretary. "This little girl is burning up," she said irritably. "I left a message for her mother, but she hasn't returned my call yet."

The secretary looked up, briefly, from a stack of papers on her desk.

"The nurse is in her office," she said. "She's new. Just knock on the door."

Mrs. Williams led Mila through the administrative office, to a door marked "Nurse," and knocked on it, sighing impatiently. And Mila stood beside her, feeling miserable. Her head ached terribly, and she felt so chilled that even with her scratchy wool sweater on she could barely keep her teeth from chattering. Worst of all, though, was the fact that she knew Mrs. Williams was angry at her. Angry at her for not feeling well. And angry at her for having a mother who wasn't returning her calls. Mrs. Williams already disliked her, Mila thought, and inconveniencing her like this wasn't going to help matters.

But as she was thinking about this, the door to the nurse's office opened, and the young woman who'd opened it smiled at both Mrs. Williams and Mila and asked, "Can I help you?" Mila blinked at her, wondering who she was. She couldn't be the nurse, she decided. She looked too young, and too casual, to be a nurse. She was pretty, with bright blue eyes and long shiny blond hair, and she was wearing the same kind of clothes Mila was wearing, a sweater and a pair of blue jeans. *No*, Mila thought, *this must be the nurse's friend.* Because while she didn't know a lot about nurses, it seemed to her that they should look official somehow. Serious. And this woman didn't look like either of those things.

"Are you the new nurse?" Mrs. Williams asked, and Mila realized that her teacher didn't believe it either.

"As a matter of fact, I am," the woman said pleasantly. "My name is Heather Drew. But you can call me Heather. And who do we have here?" she asked, kneeling down so that she was at eye level with Mila. That surprised Mila. She was used to adults looking down on her.

"This is Mila Jones," Mrs. Williams said, not giving her a chance to answer. "She has a fever. I called her mother, but, amazingly, she's not there. Her mother, by the way, is a real piece of work," she continued, in a lower voice, though not so low that Mila couldn't hear her. "I think she's a cocktail waitress. Or *something* like that."

Mila flinched. She wasn't as dumb as Mrs. Williams thought she was. She knew that she was implying that whatever Mila's mother really did, it was worse than being a cocktail waitress. Mila, usually timid, wanted to say something in her mother's defense, but she couldn't. Her head hurt too much. And her tongue felt funny in her mouth. Almost as if it had a weight on it.

And then Mila, through the fog of her fever, saw Heather frown. She didn't like what Mrs. Williams had said about her mother either, Mila realized. And for some reason, it made Mila feel a little better.

Heather stood up now, putting a hand protectively on Mila's shoulder as she did so. "That's fine," she said briskly to Mrs. Williams. "I'll take it from here. You go back to your classroom Mrs. . . . ?"

"Mrs. Williams," she said curtly. "And keep trying the mom," she added, over her shoulder, as she left the office. "Otherwise, you'll be stuck with this kid all day."

Mila swallowed, hard. She felt tears burning in her eyes. She hated the way Mrs. Williams talked about her. As if she wasn't even there.

And Heather, whose hand was still on Mila's shoulder, seemed to understand this. She knelt down again and smiled at Mila. "Don't mind Mrs. Williams," she said, softly, so the secretary couldn't hear her. "You wouldn't be very nice, either, if your face looked like a dried-up prune."

And Mila laughed, surprising herself. It was true, she thought. Mrs. Williams' face *did* look like a dried-up prune.

Now Heather placed her hand on Mila's forehead and whistled softly. "That's quite a fever you're running there," she said, standing up. "We better take your temperature."

She led Mila into her office and closed the door behind them. "Why don't you climb up there," she said to Mila, indicating an exam table. And Mila climbed up on it and waited, shivering, while Heather used one of those ear thermometers Mila had only seen at doctors' offices.

"A hundred and one," Heather said, frowning at the thermometer. "How long have you felt sick, Mila?" she asked.

Mila didn't answer. She was afraid if she told the truth, Heather would be angry.

"Did you feel this way when you left for school this morning?" Heather asked gently.

Mila nodded.

"And before you went to bed last night?"

Mila nodded again, keeping her eyes on the floor.

"And you didn't tell anyone?"

Mila shook her head no.

"Why not?"

"Because my mom can't work if I'm sick," Mila said quietly. "She has to stay home with me instead. And she needs to work. If she doesn't work, she doesn't get paid. And if she doesn't get paid . . ." Mila's voice trailed off. She didn't know what would happen if her mother didn't get paid. Her mother had never explained that. But Mila knew, whatever it was, it was bad.

She waited now, for Heather to say what Mrs. Williams had said, at least in so many words. That her mother was a bad mother. But Heather didn't say that. Instead, she asked, "Is it just you and your mom, Mila?"

Mila nodded.

"That's hard," she said sympathetically. "I'm sure your mother loves you very much. But she can't be in two places at one time, can she?"

"No," Mila whispered gratefully.

"Does your throat hurt?" Heather asked then, probing Mila's neck with her cool fingers.

Mila shook her head.

But Heather looked at her throat anyway, gently pushing down Mila's tongue with a tongue depressor and shining a little light into the back of her mouth.

"Your throat looks fine," she murmured, then used the same light to look in both of Mila's ears. "So do your ears. What about your stomach? Does that hurt?"

Mila shook her head again. "Just my head," she said. *And the rest of my body too.* A chill came over her then and she felt her teeth start to chatter. She clenched her jaw to make them stop.

"Poor thing," Heather said, helping Mila off the examining table and leading her over to a daybed in a corner of the office. "Why don't you lie down here for a minute, okay? I'm going to check your file and see if I can give you some medicine to help you feel better."

Mila lay down and Heather put a blanket over her. In a minute, she was back. "You don't have any allergies to medication," she said cheerfully, sitting down on the edge of the daybed. "So I'm going to give you some children's Tylenol, all right? It'll bring your fever down and help with the achiness."

Mila nodded and sat up.

"Can you chew these?" Heather asked. She was holding a Dixie cup with two bright purple tablets in it.

Mila nodded, taking the cup from her, and chewing and swallowing the tablets in spite of her funny-feeling tongue. "Good job," Heather said, favoring Mila with one of her warm smiles. "Now, why don't you rest here for a little while, okay? I'm going to call your mom. But don't worry if she can't pick you up right away. I can stay here with you for as long as necessary."

Mila wanted to thank her, but she was suddenly too tired to. So instead she closed her eyes and rested, just like Heather had told her to. And she must have fallen asleep, too, because when she opened her eyes, she knew immediately from the dusky winter light outside the office's windows that it was late afternoon. Her heart sank. Her mother still wasn't there. But Heather was there, sitting at a nearby desk, typing on a computer.

She must have sensed Mila looking at her, though, because she looked up and smiled at her. "You're awake," she said, getting up and coming over to the daybed. She sat down on the edge and felt Mila's forehead with her cool hand.

"Much better," she said approvingly, going to get the thermometer. And when she took Mila's temperature again, she was doubly pleased. "Ninety-nine," she said. "Almost normal. Are you feeling better, too?"

Mila nodded. She was. Her chills were gone, and her head only hurt a little now.

"I think, Mila, that what you have is the flu," Heather said, tucking the blanket around her again. "The plain old flu. And with lots of fluids, and lots of rest, you'll be back to your old self in a few days."

"That's good," Mila said unconvincingly. But that wasn't good. If she had to stay home for a few days, that would be a problem for her mother. Heather, though, seemed to read her mind.

"And don't worry about your mom missing work," she said. "I already spoke to her and she was able to trade shifts with one of her coworkers. She's going to be able to stay home with you tomorrow, and the next day, too, if you need her to. So the only thing you'll be responsible for, Mila, is getting better."

Mila felt relieved. Ordinarily, she was responsible for so many things. She had to walk herself to and from school every day, no matter what the weather was. She had to do all her homework by herself, even when she didn't understand it. And she had to make her own dinner in the microwave oven every night. It wasn't anyone's fault she had to do all those things. It was just the way it was. But then something else occurred to her. "When is my mom going to pick me up?" she asked Heather worriedly.

"Oh, a little later," Heather said, with a shrug. "As soon as she's done at work. But I told her I could stay here with you. If that's all right with you, that is."

"It's all right," Mila said, feeling suddenly shy. "But . . . but isn't there someplace you need to be?"

"Nope," Heather said. "I'm already where I need to be. Which is right here, with you."

"But don't you have a family?"

"I have a husband," Heather said. "But he understands. Now, Mila," she went on briskly, changing the subject. "How would you like a cherry Popsicle?"

"I'd love one," Mila said honestly. Heather brought her one from the freezer in the office, and she brought one for herself, too. Mila sat up on the daybed then, and Heather pulled a chair over, and they ate their Popsicles, and talked, while it got darker outside. And then, right as Heather was throwing their Popsicle sticks away, Mila blurted out, apropos of nothing, "When I grow up, I want to be a nurse, too."

"Really?" Heather asked, obviously pleased, coming to sit back down.

Mila nodded. It had never occurred to her before that she wanted to be a nurse, but as soon as she'd said the words, she'd known that they were true. "I'm . . . I'm good with my hands," she said to Heather, feeling shy again. "I'm good at making things, and cleaning things, and fixing things." And she was. But mostly, she was good at taking care of things, even if those things, so far, had consisted mainly of her stuffed animals, who suffered from a variety of ailments that often required her attention.

"Let me see those hands," Heather said now, and Mila, surprised, held her hands out for her. Heather held them lightly and examined them, "Just what I thought," she said, after a moment.

"What?"

"Those are nurse's hands," Heather said, with a gentle smile, letting go of them.

"They are?" Mila said, fascinated, looking down at them.

"Absolutely." And then, after a pause, she asked, "Do you like science, Mila?"

Mila, looking up from her hands, nodded enthusiastically.

"Good, because you'll need science to go to nursing school."

Mila thought of something then. "I like science," she said, "but I hate spelling. I'm terrible at it."

"Spelling, huh? Well, nurses need to know how to spell, too," Heather said.

"They do?" Mila said, feeling deflated.

"Uh-huh. But if spelling's a problem for you, I have an idea. Do you have a test every week?" Heather asked.

"Every Friday," Mila said.

"Well, then, why don't you come down to my office on Thursdays, at lunchtime, and we'll review your spelling words together. I'll have to get permission from Mrs. Williams first, but that shouldn't be a problem. And, of course, if I have a sick student here, we'll have to reschedule. I don't imagine that'll happen very often, though. The students at this school seem remarkably healthy. So what do you say? Thursdays, at lunchtime, right here?"

"I say yes," Mila said. A whole lunch period with Heather, every Thursday? Mila could hardly believe her luck.

"Good," Heather said, and she seemed as pleased as Mila. They talked some more, until Mila's mom got there, and by then Mila knew it was late. Late enough for Heather to have called her husband and told him to have dinner without her. But Heather didn't seem annoyed with her mom. She just gave her instructions about how to take care of Mila. Not in a bossy way, though. In a nice way.

"Is that woman really the school nurse?" Mila's mother asked her, as their old car rattled out of the almost empty school parking lot that night.

"Yep," Mila said, thinking that cherry Popsicles were now her favorite food in the whole world.

Two years later, on a balmy spring afternoon, Mila came sailing through the door of Heather's office. Heather was already sitting at the little table in the corner, unpacking her lunch.

"Sorry I'm late," Mila said. "I was waiting for Ms. Collins to give back the spelling tests." Mila was in the fifth grade now, but she still had lunch with Heather every Thursday, and she still had a spelling test every Friday.

"How'd you do?" Heather asked, as Mila sat down across the table from her.

"One hundred percent," Mila said, handing the test to Heather with a little flourish.

"Very impressive," Heather said, looking it over. "I guess Ms. Collins doesn't believe in gold stars, huh?"

Mila shook her head. "She said fifth graders are too old for gold stars."

"Well, she may have a point there," Heather said, taking the rest of her lunch out of an insulated lunch bag. "Would you settle for a homemade brownie instead?"

And Mila, taking a peanut butter and jelly sandwich out of a brown paper bag, flashed a smile at her. "Only if I can still have a cherry Popsicle," she said.

"Oh, definitely," Heather assured her, nibbling on a carrot stick.

Then, as they ate their lunches, Heather updated Mila on the various kinds of illnesses and injuries that had come through her office over the past week, and Mila talked about her life at home. Or rather, Heather asked her questions about it, and Mila answered them. It wasn't Mila's favorite topic of conversation.

"So how does your mother like her new job?" Heather asked.

"She says it's all right," Mila said. Her mom was cocktail waitressing at a new bar now, one where she hoped she'd get better tips. But so far, the tips had been just okay, and the bartender, her mom said, was a total jerk.

"And what about Mrs. Rogers?" Heather asked. "How are you two getting along?"

Mila frowned. Mrs. Rogers was the neighbor her mother paid to babysit Mila when she was working. "Mrs. Rogers," she told Heather now, "is the worst babysitter on the planet."

"Why do you say that?" Heather asked, peeling the foil lid off a yogurt container.

"Well, for one thing, she doesn't *do* anything," Mila complained. "She just sits on our couch and watches TV. And she's so old, she's practically deaf, so she has to turn the volume up all the way. When I go to bed, I have to put my pillow over my head to fall asleep."

"And what does your mom say about that?"

Mila shrugged. "She says Mrs. Rogers is all she can afford. She doesn't charge a lot, I guess, just to sit there and watch TV."

"Well, I guess it's better than having no one there at all," Heather said. "I mean, at least you won't be alone in an emergency."

"Ha," Mila said. "A whole army of zombies could march through our living room and Mrs. Rogers wouldn't even notice." She thought, but didn't add, that her mom might not notice either. She was either working, or she was sleeping. And on those rare occasions she was at home, and awake, she was complaining. Complaining about her customers being lousy tippers, or their landlord raising the rent, or their car needing a new carburetor. Mila knew it wasn't easy for her mom, but still, she couldn't help but wish that they could do something fun together every once in a while.

"Mila?" Heather said now, putting what was left of her lunch away. "There's something I need to talk to you about."

"Okay," Mila said, warily. She was old enough by now to know that conversations that started that way usually ended with bad news.

"Honey, I don't know exactly how to say this. I've known it for a couple of weeks now, but I was waiting for the right time to tell you. And then I realized that there wasn't going to be a right time."

"What is it?" Mila asked, and the peanut butter and jelly sandwich she had just eaten felt like a brick in her stomach.

"Mila, my husband and I are moving to Nebraska, where his family's from."

Mila blinked. For a moment, she thought she'd misunderstood her. But Heather went on.

"Rob's parents, who own a farm, are getting older, Mila. They can't do all the work by themselves anymore, and Rob and I are going to need to help them."

"How soon?" Mila whispered.

"At the end of this school year," Heather said, reaching out across the table and taking Mila's hands in hers.

Mila, though, turned her face away and looked at the office's wall. She was trying not to cry. But when Heather slid out of her chair, and came around to Mila's side of the table, and knelt down beside her, Mila felt a tear slide down her cheek.

"Stay here," Mila said softly. "Please. Or, if you leave, take me with you."

"Oh, honey," Heather said, hugging her gently. "I can't do either of those things. I have to go. My husband's parents need us. And if I took you with me, your mom would miss you, Mila."

Mila wiped away another tear with the back of her hand and Heather brought her a box of Kleenex.

"It's okay to cry," she said to Mila, and for a while that was what Mila did. She cried, quietly, and Heather rubbed her back and said soft, soothing things to her.

And when her crying finally stopped, Heather brought her a wet paper towel to wipe her face with. "You know, Mila," she said. "I feel a little bit like crying too," she confessed.

"You do?" Mila asked, surprised.

Heather nodded. "This is my favorite part of my workweek, having lunch in my office with you. When my husband told me he thought we needed to move, the first thing I thought was, 'But what will Mila do without me?' And then I realized that that was silly, and that Mila would do just fine without me."

But Mila shook her head. "No, she won't. I mean, no, *I* won't."

"Yes, you will," Heather said, smiling. "And do you know why, Mila? Because you have a dream. You want to become a nurse. And as long as you don't lose sight of that dream, you'll be fine. You'll be better than fine, actually."

Heather continued, "Besides, you don't have to do it alone. I'm still going to be a part of your life, Mila. Even if I can't have lunch with you every Thursday."

"How will you be a part of my life?" Mila asked, forgetting her misery long enough to be curious.

"We'll write to each other," Heather said simply.

But Mila looked at her blankly.

"We'll write *letters* to each other," Heather clarified. And then, "You have written someone a letter before, haven't you, Mila?"

But Mila shook her head. "I don't have anyone to write to," she said. And it was true. Her mother's parents were dead, and she'd never known her father or her father's family.

"Oh, Mila," Heather said, her blue eyes dancing with excitement. "You're going to love writing letters. And, more important, you're going to love *reading* letters. My grandfather and I used to write to each other when I was growing up, and to this day, I cannot open my mailbox without feeling a little bit of excitement."

Mila looked at her skeptically. "Is getting a letter that exciting?"

"It is when it comes from someone who's important to you," Heather said. And then, "Mila, promise me you'll write to me every week?"

"I promise," Mila said automatically. Heather had never asked her to promise anything before, and this, at least, was something Mila knew she could do, even if she couldn't necessarily do it very well.

"Good," Heather said, beaming at her. "And I promise I'll write you back as soon as I get your letter. And, Mila? I don't know if you'll still have spelling tests in middle school, but if you do, can you send me copies of them, please?"

"Okay," Mila said, slowly warming to the letter-writing idea. "And I can send you other stuff, too."

And she did. She sent her lots of stuff. After Heather moved away, at the end of the school year, Mila sent her a steady stream of letters, not to mention report cards, school pictures, essays, drawings, and even, as it turned out, the occasional spelling test. And Heather always sent back long, newsy letters. Letters about her life on the family farm she and her husband had taken over from his parents, and about her job as a nurse at a clinic in a nearby town. In those letters, she assured Mila that nothing interesting ever happened in rural Nebraska, but to Mila, Heather's letters were fascinating, especially when she wrote about her work at the clinic.

Mila saved every single letter and reread each one many times. At first, she tied them all together with

a red ribbon she had bought expressly for that purpose. But soon, there were too many of them for the
ribbon to fit around, so she put the letters in a shoebox
instead. And when they outgrew that, she moved them
to a file box. And every time Mila and her mother
moved during those years—and they moved a lot—
Mila dragged the box along with her.

She needed those letters. Those were hard years
for her mom, and for Mila, too. Her mom had trouble
keeping a job, and Mila soon understood why. When
she did work, she wasn't just serving cocktails, she was
drinking them, too. And as soon as the manager or the
bartender found out, she would get fired. Her jobs, and
her tips, kept getting worse, and so did the apartments
they moved into. Still, she pieced together a living, of
sorts, and Mila helped out whenever she could, first
babysitting, and then, as she got older, waiting tables,
usually at some little dive of a restaurant where the
management wasn't too concerned about her being old
enough to waitress legally, and where the customers,
in turn, weren't too concerned about the quality of the
food.

But through all this, Mila remained focused on
becoming a nurse. And when she was in high school,
and her mother started inviting friends over for loud,
raucous parties that lasted far into the night, Mila

locked her bedroom door, stuffed cotton in her ears, and studied until she was too tired to concentrate, then crawled into bed, clamped a pillow over her head, and fell into a fitful sleep.

She wrote to Heather faithfully, though, always careful to put a positive spin on her life, even when she knew from the worried tone of Heather's letters back to her that Heather understood more than she told her. Still, Heather's letters kept coming, week after week, and year after year, and the box Mila put them in kept getting heavier, until, until recently. . . . But she wouldn't think about that now, she decided. She *couldn't* think about that now. She would be strong, she told herself. And she would stay strong. Even if she could only do it for one minute at a time. She glanced back at the clock on her bedside table now. It was twelve fifteen. She would study for fifteen more minutes, she decided. She reached back into the drawer, took the study guide out, and flipped it open again. Then she bent over it, and, returning to the problem where she'd left off, she shut the rest of the world out. At twelve thirty, though, she stopped. There was something else she needed to do. Something that was going to give her much more satisfaction than getting a sample problem right.

Chapter 5

Mila got up from the desk, walked over to the dresser, took the ring box out of the bottom drawer, and then took the ring out of the box. She left the bedroom with the ring, padding softly down the hallway and stopping outside Reid's bedroom door. There was a faint yellow band of light visible beneath his door, but there were no sounds coming from his room. She waited there a minute before walking quietly to the kitchen, where, following Lonnie's instructions, she disabled the alarm she'd already set. Then she walked out of the kitchen, through the living room, and to the sliding glass door that led onto the deck. She unlocked it and opened it, slowly. She hesitated there, wondering if she should turn on the deck lights, but she decided not to. Some things, she thought, were best done under the cover of night. So she crossed the unlit deck to the set of steps Lonnie had pointed out to her that afternoon, and she started down them. As soon as she did, though, the night seemed to envelop her, and she felt suddenly defenseless in its bigness, and its darkness. Still, she kept going, climbing carefully down the stone steps, whose whiteness glowed faintly in the light of a thin crescent moon, and whose roughness felt cool beneath her bare feet.

When she reached the bottom step, she paused. The dock was much longer than she'd expected it to be. It jutted out, impossibly far, over the black, glassy surface of the lake. Did it have to be so long? she wondered anxiously. She'd always had a fear of deep water, and she knew that by the time she reached her destination, at the dock's end, the lake's depth would be well over her head. But she squeezed the ring in her hand to give herself courage, and when she felt it digging into her palm, she pressed on, careful to stay in the center of the dock, and careful, too, to stop a respectful distance from its end. And as she stood there, her bare toes gripping the smooth pine planks beneath them, she turned and looked back up at the cabin. It looked undisturbed, its outline only slightly blacker than the already black sky behind it. *Good,* she thought. She had the night to herself, and in more ways than one. She turned back to face the lake again, and, because she felt something was required of her now, something that would somehow mark this moment for the solemn thing it was, she gave a small, silent speech.

Brandon, I don't know if it will ever be possible to legally end our marriage, especially if legally ending it means that you'll know where I am. But the fact that somewhere there will be a piece of paper that says we're still married isn't important to me. What's important to me is that our real marriage ends tonight. For good, and forever. And another thing, Brandon. Even if you were to eventually find me here, I'll die before I'll ever let you hurt me again. That's a promise to you, and it's a promise to me, too.

And with that, she threw the ring into the lake, threw it as hard as she could, so hard, in fact, that she stumbled backward a little with the effort. But she caught herself and listened as the ring landed in the lake with a small *plink.* She pictured it, then, falling through the dark water, bumping gently against the lake bottom, and settling there on the sand or the silt or among the weeds. Would anyone ever find it? she wondered. She doubted it. As she was considering that question, though, the wind suddenly picked up, stirring the pine trees on the bluff behind her, ruffling the surface of the black water, and sending little waves slapping against the dock's pilings. She shivered and turned to go back up to the cabin. But as she climbed the steps, she imagined that she felt physically lighter without her wedding ring to weigh her down.

Reid shifted restlessly in his wheelchair and wondered, not for the first time, if his hearing was somehow more sensitive now than it had been before the accident. How else, really, to explain the fact that tonight, as he sat in a shadowy corner of his bedroom, he could hear every one of the cabin's after-dark sounds with near perfect clarity: every creak of the rafters, every rattle of the windows, every sigh of the wind in the chimney? Then again, he thought, maybe it wasn't his hearing that had changed since the accident, maybe it was him. Maybe he heard these sounds because he wanted to hear them, wanted to be reassured by their comforting familiarity. After all, these little creaks and sighs were the only things keeping him company during these otherwise desolate nights.

Tonight, though, tonight had been different. Tonight there'd been something new to listen to. Because unlike his other home health aides, Mila hadn't gone to sleep early or, as in Mrs. Everson's case, passed out early. No, she'd been on the move. She'd left her room about an hour ago, around twelve thirty, pausing first outside his bedroom door, where she'd stood and listened to him—listened to him listening to her—before she'd gone to the kitchen and turned off the alarm. *Is she leaving already,* he'd thought? And he'd felt a little surge of hope. But then he'd remembered the ultimatum Allie had given him at Pearl's that afternoon, and his joy had been tempered somewhat.

In any case, Mila hadn't left. Or rather, she *had* left, but she hadn't gone out the front door, and driven away, as he'd initially thought she might. Instead, she'd gone out the back door, the door that led to the deck and to the steps down to the dock. She'd stayed outside for about five minutes, and then she'd come back in, locked the sliding glass door, reset the alarm, and retreated back to her bedroom.

What had she done outside? he wondered now, absently turning his wheelchair first one way and then the other. Had she plotted her escape, by powerboat instead of by wheelchair-accessible van? Or had she looked at the stars? Or gone for a quick dip in the lake? He considered, and then rejected, each of these possibilities. He didn't know her very well, of course; he knew her only as well as you could know someone you'd had only two conversations with, and, in his case, they'd been two very *tense* conversations. But he couldn't picture her racing a stolen powerboat into the night, any more than he could picture her leisurely backstroking through the dark water. No, she was not a reckless person, and not a frivolous one, either, he decided. She was the opposite, in fact, of those things. She was cautious, careful, and watchful.

But . . . but she was something else, too, he realized with surprise. He'd noticed it that afternoon at Pearl's, when he'd made the remark about her stealing from her former patients, and he'd noticed it again this evening, here in his bedroom, when he'd initially refused to hand over his prescription medications to her. Both times he'd seen something in her eyes that was like a tiny flicker of light. *Of life,* he realized. And it had transformed not just her eyes, but the rest of her too. Transformed her from someone who was ordinary, if attractive looking, into someone who was . . . who was what? Well, who was anything *but* ordinary looking.

Reid, it's official, he thought now, giving his wheelchair an impatient spin. *You've lost your mind.* Completely and totally lost it. Because why else would you be expending so much mental energy on some woman, some *girl,* really, who just happens to be passing through your life? Some girl who won't be with you any longer than the other two home health aides were. And he sighed, knowing it was true. Knowing that she'd quit, the way the others had quit, and knowing, too, that he'd be shipped back to the rehab center, just as Allie had promised he would be.

He glanced bleakly at the clock on the bedside table. It was 2:00 A.M. now, time to begin the arduous nightly ritual of using his crutches to lever himself out of his wheelchair and into his hospital bed. Walker had watched him do it, once, and swore he'd never watch him do it again. It was too terrifying, he'd said. Reid didn't find it terrifying, though, so much as tiring. Exhausting, really. And pointless. Because what was the point of getting into bed if he didn't want to sleep? If he wanted, in fact, to stay awake, staying awake being the only way to ensure he didn't dream? Still, night after night, he went through these same motions. He got into bed, he turned out the light, and he lay in the darkness. Some habits, apparently, died hard. But maybe, he thought, brightening momentarily, maybe tonight would be different. Maybe he wouldn't sleep. Or maybe he *would* sleep but he wouldn't dream. If you could call what he did dreaming.

Because his dreams were too real to be dreams. They were . . . they were virtual re-creations of the accident and its aftermath. There was no other way to describe them. And it wasn't simply that his dreams got all the details right—the feel of the steering wheel digging into his chest, the taste of blood in his mouth,

the smell of motor oil leaking out of his car's engine—
it was that his dreams got *everything else* right, too,
the shock, the confusion, the claustrophobia, the pain,
and even, sometimes, the despair. It was there, all of it,
in his dreams. But most of all, the pain was there. He
would never have imagined it was possible to feel pain
in a dream. But he felt it, a pain so intense, and emanating from so many different parts of his body, that it
seemed to defy logic. He couldn't catalogue this pain,
couldn't organize it, couldn't describe it even. Except,
maybe, the pain in his left leg. There the pain ranged,
at any given moment, from excruciating to unbearable.
But most of the time, it was just unbearable.

The dream he dreaded the most was the one where
he was calling for help. In this dream, it was late afternoon on his third day in the car. He knew it was late
afternoon because he could see through the shattered
glass of his windshield that the shadows of the pine
trees were lengthening and darkening. Soon, it would
be evening, and, after that, nighttime. And nighttime was the worst time in the car. It was the coldest
time, for one, for while it had been an unusually mild
spring, and while he'd been wearing a jacket when he'd
gotten into the accident, the nights trapped in the car
were cold enough to make him shiver, uncontrollably,
thereby wasting what little energy he had left, energy

he desperately needed if he was going to get himself out of this alive.

But nighttime was also the time when he came closest to running out of hope. By the third afternoon in the car, he'd realized that no one was coming for him. Obviously, there'd been no guardrail on the road, which meant, in all likelihood, that there was no sign of his car going off the road, either. Getting out of the wreckage himself wasn't a possibility; his car had literally collapsed in on him, and he barely had room to fill his lungs with air, let alone move his arms and legs. Besides, even in the unlikely event that he found a way to work himself free of the wreckage and crawl out of it, he knew he wouldn't get far dragging what was obviously a broken leg over uneven terrain.

His cell phone wasn't any use to him either. Typically, he kept it in the car's drink holder, but the accident had thrown it into the backseat, out of reach, where it had buzzed, uselessly, with phone calls, e-mails, and texts for a couple of days until its battery had died. That meant that if he called for help, he'd have to do it the old-fashioned way—he'd have to shout for it. There was a problem with this, too, though. Because while he could occasionally hear the faint hum of a car or a truck going by on the road above him, it was far enough above him—around sixty feet, in his estimation—that it was unlikely anyone passing by on it would hear his calls for help. It was more likely, he thought, that he could attract the attention of someone on foot, a hiker, maybe, or a bird-watcher, though given the steepness of the terrain, and the thickness of the foliage, it was hard to imagine even the most intrepid outdoorsman or-woman wandering through the area where his car had landed.

Still, he had called for help. He'd called for it in real life, and he called for it in his dreams, too. He didn't do it because he thought anyone would actually hear him. He did it because he knew he wouldn't survive another night, and as tempting as it was sometimes to slip into unconsciousness one final time, he didn't want to go down without a fight. Not then, and not later, either. In his dreams. He looked warily at his bed and wheeled himself over to it, his motions slow and reluctant. The optimism he'd felt earlier was gone. There were no good nights anymore. There were only bad nights and less bad nights. And tonight would probably be the first kind of night.

At the same time that Reid, who'd finally gotten into bed, was trying to stay awake, Mila was trying to fall asleep. It wasn't easy. The vigilance that she'd worked so hard to maintain all day refused to relax itself now, and it was hours before she fell, exhausted, into an uneasy sleep. It wasn't long, though, before something tugged at her consciousness. She resisted it, but it tugged again, harder this time. It was a sound, she realized, opening her eyes onto the darkness of her room. A very strange sound. She sat up in bed, her body tense, her ears straining to hear it again. But there was nothing. Only silence. Could it have been . . . could it have been Brandon? she wondered, a cold, prickly sensation spreading all over her. Could he have found her already and broken into the cabin? But, no, if he had, he would have set off the alarm. And besides, the sound she'd heard hadn't been human. It had been, well . . . *animal.* Which made sense, really, when you considered that there was a whole forest outside her bedroom window.

She started to get out of bed then, to look out the window, but she heard the sound again, and she stopped, and sat perfectly still, listening to it. It wasn't coming from outside the cabin. It was coming from *inside* the cabin. From right down the hall from her room. "*Reid,*" she whispered, understanding, and she slipped out of bed, opened the bedroom door, and stood on its threshold. The sound stopped, then started again almost immediately. So *this* was what Walker had tried to warn her about after he'd picked her up at the bus stop that afternoon. *This* was one of Reid's night-mares. No wonder she'd mistaken his screams for an animal; they had a feral, wild, not-quite-human qual-ity to them. She shivered in her thin cotton nightgown and considered returning to the tempting warmth of her bed.

But Reid started another round of his strange, tune-less screaming then, and she knew she couldn't leave him that way. She turned on the lights in her room, and, her hands shaking slightly, pulled off her night-gown and pulled on a T-shirt and a pair of blue jeans. Then she walked haltingly down the hallway, trying to ignore the fact that her heart was pounding so hard now it was knocking against her ribcage. When she paused outside his door though, hand on his doorknob, she found she couldn't make herself open it. Now that she was this close, she could hear not just screaming, but actual words, too. Words like *help* and *please. Come on, Mila, just open it,* she told herself, and by some miracle she did. She edged into the room then and saw Reid was in his hospital bed, lit by the faint pool of light from a nearby night-light. He was quiet and still for a moment, and then he started to scream and to thrash around again.

She reached for the switch beside the door and flipped it on, but the light didn't wake him up. It did give her a better view of him, though, and she saw that he was drenched with perspiration and tangled up in his sheets. "*Help me,*" he said, his voice hoarse from screaming, and he struggled again, struggled so hard that it was almost as if he was drowning on dry land.

Mila stepped closer. She could reach out and touch him now, if she wanted to, but the truth was, she didn't want to, and what was more, she didn't know if she should. She racked her brain, trying to remember if they'd ever covered anything like this in her home health aide class, but she came up empty. Just then, though, Reid made a screaming noise again, and the sheer desperation, and sheer helplessness of it spurred her into action.

"Reid," she said softly, and she put a hand on one of his shoulders. "*Reid,*" she said, louder this time. "Reid, wake up. Please. I want to help you." *If* I can help you. But he slept on, in his strange, combative sleep.

She gripped his shoulder harder—it was encased in an undershirt that was soaked with sweat—and shook him, gently, at first, and then harder. "*Reid! Wake up!*"

He jerked awake then and stared at her with unseeing eyes.

"Reid, it's me," she said, trying to sound calm. "It's Mila. You were having a nightmare. I was worried about you."

Slowly, his eyes came into focus, but he was still breathing hard, and sweating harder. He looked around the room then, as if he'd never seen it before, and then looked back at her, and she could feel him mentally trying to place her.

"Mila," she said softly, answering his unasked question. "I . . . I got here today. Remember?"

He pushed himself up so that he was leaning back on his elbows, and he looked around the room again, and she got the feeling that he was making a conscious effort to come back here from wherever it was he had been before. It seemed to work, too, because when he looked back at her, it was as if he were seeing her— really seeing her—for the first time since she woke him up. "I remember who you are," he said, his voice sounding dry and sandpapery. "But I don't know why you're in my room."

"I . . . I was worried about you," she stammered. "I wanted to help you, I mean, I *want* to help you," she said, correcting herself.

He stared at her for another moment, then shook his head, as if she'd said something he didn't want to hear. "Did I tell you you could come into my room?" he asked, and his blue eyes were not only focused now but staring at her, in a cold, hard, flat way.

"What? No," she said, taking a step back from his bed. "You didn't tell me I could come in here. You were asleep. But you were . . . you were asking for help, Reid. In your dream."

He made a motion with his hand, an impatient motion, as if he were brushing all her words away. "Look, if I need your help—which I don't—I'll ask for it. Otherwise, leave me alone."

She hesitated, shocked by the hostility in his voice. How could a man who barely knew her dislike her as much as he already did?

"I'll . . . I'll try to leave you alone," she said, willing herself to be calm. "But I have to do my job."

There was a pause. Then he said quietly, so quietly that she had to lean in to hear him, "Then do your job. But stop trying to be helpful when you have no idea what you're doing. And don't ever come into this room again without being invited in. Is that clear? Or are we going to have to spell it out in your contract?"

"No . . . it's, it's clear," she said, her eyes burning with tears that had come out of nowhere. She backed out of the room, turned off the light, and closed the door behind her. She didn't remember walking back down the hallway, or closing her bedroom door behind her, or even collapsing onto the floor beside her bed. But she must have done all those things, because that's where she found herself, a few minutes later, lying on the floor, curled up on her side, and crying, *really* crying, crying in the way she'd wanted to cry ever since she'd left home that morning. All the defenses she'd so carefully constructed had been torn down now, and all of the optimism she'd so diligently nurtured had been blown apart. She was alone, afraid, exhausted, overwhelmed, and almost indescribably lonely.

And the worst part was, she didn't actually believe she could do this. *Any* of this. Didn't believe she could start over again, didn't believe she could put her past behind her, didn't even believe she could do the job she'd been hired to do. After all, how could she take care of a patient when she couldn't even take care of herself? *We're like the blind leading the blind,* she thought of the two of them as the sobs racked her body. Because while her injuries might be hidden from view, she knew, in their own way, they'd left her as damaged and as broken as Reid's injuries had left him.

Chapter 6

It felt like a lifetime ago, but, in fact, it had only
been six days earlier that Mila had waited outside
the offices of Caring Home Care, trying to catch her
breath, and standing, awkwardly, because the heel on
one of her shoes had broken. It was six o'clock on a
humid Friday evening, and she was already a half an
hour late for her appointment with Gloria Thompson,
the agency's owner. Everything that could go wrong on
the way there had gone wrong. She'd missed her bus,
flagged down a taxi instead, and then gotten stuck in
traffic. She'd paid the driver, gotten out, and run the
last three blocks to the office building, then ran up two
flights of stairs when the elevator wasn't waiting in the
lobby. It was on the last flight that the heel on one of
her pumps had broken off. She'd ignored it and limped

down the hallway instead, half expecting to see that the office was already closed. But no. She could see now through the frosted glass door that the lights were on, and she could hear someone moving around inside.

She held up her hand to knock on the door, but before she could, it swung open. "Ms. Jones?" the woman standing there said. She was petite, with brilliant white hair worn in a sleek chignon, and striking blue eyes that stood out against her olive complexion. She was at least seventy. Maybe older. But she radiated an energy and a vitality that was rare in a woman half her age.

Mila, too winded to speak, could only nod in answer to her question. Standing there, she tried to tuck in her blouse, which had come untucked from her skirt, and to push some of her perspiration-damp hair off her face, but then she gave up. She wondered how she looked to Ms. Thompson. Like a wreck, she decided. Like a person who couldn't even be trusted to care for a goldfish, let alone an actual human being.

Finally, between breaths, Mila said. "I'm sorry . . . I'm late . . . I know . . . You told me you have to leave by—"

But Ms. Thompson moved aside and gestured for Mila to come into her small but comfortable office. "Why don't you have a seat," she said, indicating one of the chairs facing the desk. And then, as Mila sank down gratefully into it she observed, "I see you broke your heel." Mila nodded, still trying to breathe normally. "I hate heels," Ms. Thompson remarked as she filled a glass of water from a pitcher. Mila hated them too, but she'd been trying to look at least semiprofessional when she'd gotten dressed to come here today.

Ms. Thompson handed her the glass of water and then sat down on the edge of the desk, facing her. And Mila murmured "Thank you" and sipped the water, and when she trusted herself to speak again, said, "I know you need to leave now. You said there was somewhere you needed to be this evening. I'm sorry if I've made you late for it." She stood up then. The interview, she assumed, was over before it had even begun.

But Ms. Thompson gestured for Mila to sit down again, and, fixing her with her penetrating eyes, she asked, "Ms. Jones, why was it so important to you that you see me now?"

Mila, disarmed by her directness, stumbled a little. "I, I've . . . I've always wanted to be a nurse," she said. "Since I was in the third grade. Since before that, really. I've always wanted to take care of people. And working as a home health aide would let me do that while I prepare for—"

But Ms. Thompson cut her off with an impatient gesture. "That's all very noble, Ms. Jones," she said. "But this is what I would have expected you to say if we'd met on Monday morning, as I suggested. But when you told me you needed to come in this evening, I assumed it literally could not wait."

"It couldn't," Mila said honestly. She knew there was no point in even trying to lie when she was on the receiving end of Ms. Thompson's laserlike focus.

"Good," Ms. Thompson nodded approvingly. "So why don't you forget the formalities. And forget, too, the speech about wanting to be a nurse. Which, by the way, I believe. After we spoke on the phone an hour ago, I called Mary Meyer for a reference. She said she's been teaching your certification class, in one form or another, for thirty-five years, and that you were one of the best students she's ever had, ever, and that you would make an excellent hire for this agency, not to mention an excellent nurse one day. So, as I said, it's not that I don't believe you when you say you want to be a nurse. It's just that I don't believe it's the reason you had to come see me right now, late on Friday just before closing, instead of on Monday morning, like I suggested over the phone. Am I right?"

Mila nodded, and then, without warning, her eyes glazed over with tears, and the view of Ms. Thompson, sitting on the edge of her desk, swam away, as if she were suddenly looking at her under water. Mila wiped impatiently at her tears, wondering why she'd chosen this moment, of all possible moments, to cry. She needed a job, damn it. Behaving like some blithering idiot wasn't going to get her one.

When her vision cleared again, though, Ms. Thompson wasn't sitting on her desk anymore. She was sitting on one of the office chairs next to Mila, holding out a box of tissues. Mila took one and blotted her tears. "I'm sorry," she whispered.

"Don't be sorry," Ms. Thompson said calmly. "Just tell me why you're here."

Mila hesitated, rehearsing another lie. But then she looked at Ms. Thompson's expression, which was firm but not unkind, tough but not judgmental, and she made a split-second decision. A decision she would be glad she'd made for the rest of her life. She decided to tell Ms. Thompson the truth. "I'm in an abusive marriage," she said simply. "And when I tried to leave my husband once before he found me. Now, he says he'll never let me leave him again."

Incredibly, Ms. Thompson didn't look surprised by this. She just nodded and said evenly, "Tell me about it."

"I . . . I don't really know how to," Mila confessed. "I've never told anyone about it before."

"No, I don't think you have." Ms. Thompson sighed. "But if you want me to help you, you're going to need to tell me about it. So start . . . start from the time you met your husband. And go from there."

So that was what Mila did. She started from the time she'd met her husband, Brandon, two years ago. She spoke slowly at first, haltingly. Since she'd gotten married she'd become a master of deception, first at hiding the truth from herself, and then, finally, hiding it from others. But Ms. Thompson knew how to ask the right questions. And she knew how to wait for the answers. And when those answers came, she was ready with more questions. And she didn't seem shocked by the answers either. In fact, she listened to them all unflinchingly.

By the time Mila was done telling her story, she'd gone through half a box of tissues, and the evening outside the office windows had turned to night. "I'm sorry I kept you so long," she told Ms. Thompson. "You've missed your other commitment, haven't you?"

"Oh, definitely," Ms. Thompson said, with a faintly amused smile. "But don't worry about it. It was my book club meeting, and since I have a terrible track record when it comes to actually having read the books we choose, my presence there tonight probably won't be missed."

Mila smiled tentatively. Now she had a question for her. "Ms. Thompson?"

"Yes?"

"Why did you want to know all of that? About my marriage, I mean. You've never even met me before."

"No, I haven't," Ms. Thompson said gently. "But I feel like I have."

Mila looked at her questioningly.

"When I spoke to you on the phone this afternoon," Ms. Thompson explained, "it was a little bit like . . . like speaking to myself. A younger version of myself. And then, when I saw you outside the office door, and I saw . . . well, I saw that you'd gotten a black eye, not too long ago, I knew why you seemed so familiar."

"It shows?" Mila said, skipping over the rest of what Ms. Thompson had said. Her fingers traveled, almost unconsciously, to her still tender eye. "I thought I covered it up pretty well," she said, her face burning with shame.

"Oh, I don't think it's visible to the untrained eye," Ms. Thompson said quickly. "But it was visible to me. Probably because I've had so many of them myself."

"Black eyes?" Mila repeated, not understanding.

"Black eyes, split lips, you name it, Mila. I've had them. *All* of them. Because I was in an abusive marriage too."

"But . . ." Mila started, and then she stopped. She didn't believe it. This woman, sitting in front of her, was nobody's victim.

"No, it's true," Ms. Thompson said. "And it went on for many years. Of course, this was a long time ago. A *lifetime* ago, I like to think."

"But . . . can I ask . . . I mean, how did it happen? I mean, you seem . . . you seem so strong," Mila said.

Ms. Thompson smiled, a little sadly. "Well, I had to be strong."

"But how did you . . . ?"

"How did I get away from him? With great difficulty." Ms. Thompson sighed. "I spent years trying to end the marriage. But my husband said if I tried to leave him, or divorce him . . ." She shrugged, leaving Mila to fill in the blank. "Mind you, Mila, I'm almost eighty," she continued, "so this was over fifty years ago. It was a different world back then. If you called the police over an incidence of domestic violence, they'd tell you it was a 'family matter,' and that they didn't want to get involved. And there were no battered women's shelters then, either, or at least none that I knew of. So as miserable as I was, I'd basically resigned myself to staying in the marriage . . . and then, then one day my husband met another woman, and she fell very much in love with him."

Mila's eyes widened with surprise. She fell in love with *him*? she almost said, but then she caught herself. She'd fallen in love with Brandon, hadn't she? Or at least at the time she'd thought so. She'd been so swept up in his passionate pursuit of her that she'd been sure it must be love.

"As it turned out," Ms. Thompson said, "that woman's loss was my gain. My husband let me go, and . . . well, I don't know what happened to him. Or to her." She gave a little shudder. "They moved away, and that was it. I never saw either of them again. I've often felt guilty, over the years, that I didn't try to warn her, somehow, about my ex-husband. But at the time . . ." She shrugged, a little helplessly. "At the time, she was my only way out."

Mila nodded slowly. *What an awful choice,* she thought. But then again, if someone had tried to warn her about Brandon in the beginning, would she have listened to them? Would she have believed them? She didn't think so.

"In any case," Ms. Thompson said, moving on, "I got a divorce, and I went to nursing school, and then, after I'd worked as a nurse for several years, I went back to school and got a business degree, and I started this agency. I've liked the work, tremendously. And it's left me enough time to do something else, too, something close to my heart."

"What's that?" Mila asked, her curiosity overcoming her shyness.

"I volunteer at a battered women's shelter. And I like to think I've helped some of the women I've met there start over again, too. That's what you want to do, isn't it, Mila? Start over?"

She nodded solemnly.

"It's not going to be easy," Ms. Thomson warned.

"I know that."

"And, once you do start over, you can't go back. First, you'll need to get as far away from your husband as you possibly can. And then, you can never, ever, get back in touch with him again. You understand that, don't you? No matter how much you miss him? Because, crazy as it may sound, you might find yourself missing him one day, especially if you get lonely enough."

"No," Mila said vehemently. "I'll never miss him. *Ever.* But right now, it's a moot point. I don't know how to get away from him. I have a little money saved. Enough to get myself somewhere. But once I get there, I'm going to need to have a way to support myself."

"Well, Mila Jones, you just might be in luck," Ms. Thompson said. She stood up, walked over to a file cabinet, slid one of the drawers open, and selected a file out of it. Then she came back and sat down beside Mila, flipped open the file, and scanned it quickly.

"I just got a fax today," she said, looking up at her. "It's from a home health care agency in Ely; I've done some work with them before. They've been having trouble finding a live-in aide for one of their clients."

"Ely? That's way up north, isn't it?" Mila frowned. "They couldn't . . . find someone who already lives up there?"

"It's a special case, I guess," Ms. Thompson said, still scanning the file. "A problem client. They've already had two unsuccessful placements with him."

"Him?" Mila echoed.

Ms. Thompson nodded, not looking up. "I think they thought I might know someone who could handle him."

Handle him? Mila's stomach contracted. She didn't like the sound of that.

"Oh no," Ms. Thompson said, looking up from the file and reading the expression on Mila's face. "I don't mean he's abusive. Well, not *physically* abusive, anyway. There's no indication of that. From what I can tell, he's just a jerk. A garden-variety jerk. Not pleasant to be around, maybe. But not dangerous, either."

Mila nodded, a little uncertainly, but she reminded herself that not every man was like Brandon. Most of them, in fact, were not. There'd been a time when she'd known that, too. She'd just forgotten it.

"I like this placement," Ms. Thompson murmured, more to herself than Mila, as she studied the file again.

"It would solve a lot of your problems. This patient lives in Butternut, Minnesota. That's over five and a half hours north of here. And not only that, but he lives outside of the town, too, on a lake. Butternut Lake. I gather it's fairly remote. But not a bad place to hide out for a while," she added, looking up at Mila again.

"No," Mila echoed, again uncertainly. She was thinking about living alone with a man in the middle of nowhere.

"When can you start?" Ms. Thompson asked her suddenly. Decisively.

"Start? You mean, start working there?"

Ms. Thomson nodded. "How long would it take you to tie up your loose ends here?"

"Not long," Mila said honestly. Thanks to Brandon, she had no life anymore. And consequently, no loose ends to tie up either.

"Good, I'll tell them you can start immediately," Ms. Thompson said. "Or by the middle of next week, anyway. Let's say Wednesday, all right?

"All right," Mila said, astonished at the speed with which everything was moving.

"In the meantime, I'll have to run a criminal background check on you, Mila. You don't have anything in your past I need to know about, do you?"

"Nothing," Mila said, shaking her head.

"And your driving record?"

"It's perfect."

Ms. Thompson nodded, already preoccupied by another issue. "I'll have to figure out a payment plan with the family," she said.

"The family?"

"Well, you won't technically be working for the patient," she explained. "You'll be working for his brother, who lives nearby." She frowned thoughtfully. "I'll have him pay the agency, and then I'll send you cash. Don't worry about the taxes; I'll work those out on my end. It will take a little . . . *creative accounting*. The important thing is that your name not appear anywhere. Not on a bank account, not on tax records, not on anything. Do you understand that?"

"Yes, but Ms. Thompson, my legal married name is Mila Stewart. So you'll need to do a background check on that name. But going forward I want to use my maiden name, Jones," Mila said. Ms. Thompson sighed and massaged her temples with the hand that wasn't holding the file. She seemed suddenly tired and Mila felt guilty, again, about keeping her past closing time. But, in the next moment, Ms. Thompson seemed to get a second wind.

"Okay, I'll tell the family you're working for that your name is Mila Jones, and all my records will be in that name," Ms. Thompson said.

"But, Mila," she said, closing the file and leveling her gaze at Mila, "you've got to be absolutely obsessive about secrecy. It used to be that you couldn't leave a paper trail, but now you can't leave an electronic trail, either. No cell-phone calls. No e-mails. No credit card charges. It needs to be as if you've simply disappeared off the face of the earth. Understood?"

"Understood," Mila said, without hesitation.

"Good. Because I don't think I need to tell you that if your husband were to find you, it wouldn't just endanger you. It would endanger the client, too. And since this particular client is recovering from a serious car accident, he wouldn't be in a position to defend himself."

"No, he wouldn't," Mila agreed, with an unconscious shiver of dread. She was picturing Brandon in one of his rages.

"Okay then," Ms. Thompson said, getting up and returning the file to the file cabinet. "Why don't you call me here on Monday morning, and I'll let you know what time to come in on Tuesday so we can confirm everything." Then she thought of something. "Did you call me from your home phone today?"

"Yes."

"Don't do that again," Ms. Thompson warned. "Call me from a pay phone. There's still a few of those around, believe it or not. Or better yet, buy yourself one of those disposable cell phones. Just don't let your husband find it. In the meantime, I'll speak to the agency in Ely. I should have all the details from them by the time I talk to you on Monday. And that should give you plenty of time to pack and arrange transportation for Wednesday. And remember," she said, ticking the next points off on her fingers. "Tell no one. Pay cash for everything. And destroy all your receipts."

Mila nodded, and, for the first time in weeks, she felt a sweet, almost dizzying sense of hope. But when she caught sight of the darkness outside Ms. Thompson's windows, it ebbed a little and she slid her cell phone out of her purse. Thank God. No missed calls from Brandon. He didn't like it when she missed his calls. That was how she'd gotten the black eye Ms. Thompson had noticed. But he also didn't like it when she wasn't there when he got home from work, and he'd be home soon. "I should get going," Mila said, feeling a familiar pulse of fear.

"Of course," Ms. Thompson said. "Just don't forget about any of the things we discussed."

Mila didn't forget. And by the time she came to Ms. Thompson's office, late Tuesday afternoon, everything was in place. She'd bought, with cash, a bus ticket to

Butternut, and she'd bought a secondhand suitcase, which was already packed and stored in a locker at the bus station. And Wednesday morning, after Brandon left for work, she'd leave for the bus station. On the way there, she'd throw away her cell phone and her cut-up credit card. She wouldn't throw away her wedding ring. That, she had a special plan for.

But sitting in Ms. Thompson's office that afternoon, that plan was the farthest thing from Mila's mind. She was anxious and exhausted. She'd worked hard over the last couple of days to keep up an appearance of normalcy with Brandon. To be pleasant to him, and even, God forbid, affectionate. But it had cost her. And, what was worse, it hadn't prevented another outburst from Brandon, who, in his paranoia, was convinced once again that Mila was being unfaithful to him.

"You look tired," Ms. Thompson said, perching on the edge of her desk and holding a couple of files.

"I *am* tired," Mila confessed. "And I'm worried, too. I mean, what if Brandon doesn't go to work tomorrow? He's done that before. Called in sick so he can spend the day with me. Or what if he pretends to go to work and follows me instead? He's done that before, too. Just to keep an eye on me."

"We can't know what he'll do tomorrow," Ms. Thompson said, "we just have to hope—pray, really—that he sticks to his usual schedule." She went on, "Now, I have two files here. One of them is for you." She handed it to Mila. "It's the patient's file. You'll have to hide it tonight, but tomorrow, on the bus, you can read it over and come up to speed on things." Holding up the other folder, she said, "This file is my file on you. But I'm not filing it with my other personnel files." Ms. Thompson indicated the file cabinet. Then she pointed to her desk. "I'm keeping it in my desk drawer. My *locked* desk drawer," she added. "I have help here, sometimes. My niece, Janet—who, between you and me, is not the brightest bulb on the Christmas tree—occasionally does some office work for me. But even she doesn't know where I keep the key to this drawer. And as for Brandon . . . well, if he were ever to turn up here, he'd have to get through me to get to that file."

"Well, then, he wouldn't stand a chance," Mila said, only half joking. Ms. Thompson, she imagined, could be very intimidating when the situation called for it.

"Okay, then, anything else?" Ms. Thompson asked, going to lock Mila's file in her desk drawer.

"No, nothing. Except . . . except thank you, Ms. Thompson. Thank you so much. For everything." Mila felt her eyes start to tear up, but Ms. Thompson, straightening up from the desk, said firmly, "No more crying, young lady. You've got work to do. You can call me when you get to the patient's house, and it goes without saying that you can call me any time after that, too, if you need any advice or have any questions."

Mila nodded and stood to leave, still fighting back tears. She was feeling so many different things at once. Elation, excitement, nervousness, and something else, too. Fear. Fear of Brandon. But also fear of this new, as yet unknown, man.

"Ms. Thompson," she said, hesitating, "is it really just going to be the two of us, me and the patient, all alone in that cabin?"

"Well, not all the time. There's a housekeeper, too. But at night, and on the weekends, yes, it'll just be the two of you." And then, understanding Mila's expression, she said, "But don't worry about him, all right? Even if he wanted to hurt you, he couldn't. He's in a wheelchair." And then, with the hint of a smile, she added, "If it came down to it, Mila, I'm pretty sure you could take him in a fight."

Chapter 7

"Is there . . . is there something wrong with the eggs?" Lonnie asked with a slight frown as she refilled Mila's coffee cup. It was two weeks after Mila's arrival at the cabin, and she was sitting at the breakfast table, trying, and failing, to eat the eggs Lonnie had scrambled for her.

"No, there's nothing wrong with the eggs," Mila said, eating a forkful of them to prove it. "They're delicious. It's just . . ." She paused, not wanting to hurt Lonnie's feelings. "It's just that I'm not used to having someone make my breakfast for me. I mean, I'm perfectly happy to do it myself."

"But that's silly," Lonnie objected, returning to the stove, where she was scrambling more eggs. "I have to make Reid's breakfast anyway. So I might as well make yours, too."

"But it's not just cooking my breakfast," Mila said carefully. "It's everything else you do for me, too. It's not necessary, really." But Lonnie, sliding the eggs out of the frying pan and onto a plate, disagreed. "It *is* necessary, Mila. It's my job. It's what I get paid to do," she said, taking three pieces of bacon out of another frying pan and putting them onto the same plate as the eggs.

"Besides, I like to stay busy," she added, putting the plate on a tray. And Mila sighed, quietly, and dropped the subject for now. She knew she wasn't going to make any headway with Lonnie this morning. It had already taken Mila two weeks of delicate negotiations to persuade Lonnie to let her make her own bed and launder her own clothes. Other things, Lonnie hadn't budged on. Mila still had to vacate her room for a half an hour every day, for instance, while Lonnie vacuumed the already perfectly vacuumed rug and dusted the already perfectly dusted furniture.

"How does this look?" Lonnie asked now, carrying Reid's breakfast tray over for Mila to inspect.

"It looks beautiful," Mila said honestly. "Worthy of any five-star hotel." And it was. In addition to a cup of steaming coffee, laced with cream, there was a glass of freshly squeezed orange juice, a plate of bacon and eggs, a side of toast with a pat of butter on each slice, and a pot of strawberry preserves beside it. Lonnie had even wrapped up the silverware in a linen napkin and tied it with a fancy twist and placed a small bud vase with some freshly picked wild violets in it in one corner of the tray.

"I hope he likes it," Lonnie said, a little wistfully, before she left the kitchen to take it to Reid's bedroom.

He won't, Mila thought, nibbling on a piece of her bacon. *He doesn't like anything.* But that didn't stop Lonnie from putting together those trays at breakfast time, and lunchtime, every day. And the food on them! Mila, for one, had never eaten so well in her life. For breakfast, French toast or pancakes or waffles made from scratch. Or biscuits and sausage smothered in gravy. Lunch was chicken pot pie in a flaky crust, or macaroni and cheese with toasted breadcrumbs on top of it. Lonnie left before dinner, but she left the refrigerator well stocked with carefully labeled Pyrex dishes, all filled with delicious food, all ready to be heated in the oven for Reid's dinner.

And that was Mila's responsibility every night, reheating Reid's dinner and taking it to him on a tray, though she didn't bother to make it look as elegant as Lonnie did. What was the point? Reid didn't care. He rarely finished his dinner and often only picked at it. Sometimes, when Mila went back half an hour later to collect his tray, the food on it looked as if it hadn't even been touched, and Mila was left to scrape it into the kitchen garbage can, feeling vaguely disapproving. How many meals, she wondered, had Reid wasted since coming home from the rehabilitation center?

Maybe his wastefulness bothered Mila as much as it did because she'd grown up in a household where breakfast cereal and canned soup were the norm at mealtime. Home-cooked food had been a rarity, reserved for special occasions, like birthdays. And even then, Mila's mother hadn't been much of a cook. But Lonnie? Lonnie cooked the kind of food Mila saw on cooking shows, and on the covers of glossy checkout counter magazines. Food that deserved to be eaten. No, food that deserved to be *worshipped*.

If Mila was honest with herself, though, she wasn't doing much better with Lonnie's dinners than Reid was. Because after she took him his tray, and sat down, alone, at the kitchen table to have her own meal, she could barely bring herself to have more than a few bites of it.

"Well, that was successful," Lonnie said now, coming back into the kitchen.

"Was it?" Mila asked, looking up.

"Not really," Lonnie confessed, her face falling a little. "He said he wasn't hungry, and not to bother him again this morning. But I left the tray there, anyway. You never know. He could change his mind."

"Well, at least you tried," Mila said, feeling a flash of annoyance at Reid. How could he be rude to someone as well meaning as Lonnie?

"More coffee?" Lonnie asked, bringing the coffeepot back over to the table. Mila started to say "no, thank you," since she hadn't even put a dent in the cup Lonnie had already poured for her, when the two of them heard the sound of tires crunching on the gravel driveway. Lonnie looked casually out the kitchen window, but Mila felt her whole body go taut with fear.

"Oh, look, it's the UPS man," Lonnie said, as the familiar brown truck rolled into view. Lonnie often had packages delivered at the house, since she was away from her own house for most of the day. Now Mila breathed a shaky little sigh of relief. *I have to stop doing that*, she thought. Panicking every time a car or truck pulled up outside. Because while Lonnie, bless her heart, wasn't that observant, Reid was. And Mila knew that even in the limited amount of time she'd spent with him, he'd noticed something odd about her behavior. She tried hard to appear relaxed. But every time she heard the phone ring, or a car rattle up the driveway, or a boat putter by the dock, she felt the bottom drop out of her stomach. She was certain then, all evidence to the contrary, that Brandon had found her. That *of course* he had found her. That he was never *not* going to find her.

She watched as Lonnie bustled out to meet the UPS man, then came back holding a package and shaking her head. "I'm afraid I ordered something else from one of those home shopping networks," she said, putting the package down on the counter. "I suppose they're counting on people like me," she added ruefully. "People who have nothing better to do at night than order some junk they've seen on TV." But she said this without any bitterness, or self-pity, and Mila realized, not for the first time, that Lonnie was one of those rare people blessed with a truly sunny disposition.

"Do you mind if I sit down and have a cup of coffee with you before I start the housekeeping?" she asked Mila.

"No, of course not," Mila said, and as Lonnie poured herself a cup of coffee, Mila realized how out of the habit she'd gotten at moments like this, the little give-and-take of everyday life. There'd been a time in her life when they'd been second nature to her. Chatting with someone in line at the grocery store. Striking up a conversation with someone on the bus. Exchanging pleasantries with your neighbor as you let yourself into your apartment. But during her marriage to Brandon, it had been easier to avoid these interactions, and simpler to not get involved with anyone, no matter how superficial that involvement might be. As Lonnie sat down across the table from her, Mila realized how much she'd missed this most basic human contact. Now if she could only learn to trust someone again, she thought. Even a little bit.

"How're you doing, Mila?" Lonnie asked, sipping her coffee. "You're not too lonely here, are you?"

"Not *too* lonely," Mila said, forcing herself to smile. That was a lie, of course. A spectacular lie. Because sometimes, she thought the loneliness was worse than the fear. Especially at night. At night, as she sat at the kitchen table, pretending to eat her dinner, or as she sat at her desk, trying to do the sample problems in her study guide, she could actually *feel* the weight of her loneliness pressing down on her, like the real, palpable thing it was.

It didn't help that it was so dark here at night. A city girl all her life, she'd never truly understood, until now, how dark the darkness could be. Sometimes, before she went to sleep, she'd stand at her bedroom window and try to see something—anything—beyond where the light from the cabin ended. But there was nothing to see. Only more darkness.

If the woods were dark, though, they weren't silent. They were, in fact, full of noises, noises that seemed designed to compound Mila's feelings of loneliness. The wind rustling in the trees, the mournful call of a loon, and even, occasionally, the faraway howling of coyotes; all these sounds, and others, too, had the effect of making Mila feel not less alone, but more alone.

Having Reid right down the hall, it turned out, did nothing to relieve this sense of isolation. She'd already known, of course, that being with someone else could be lonelier than being alone, and she was reminded of it again now. Neither she nor Reid had ever mentioned that first night, the night she woke him up from his nightmare. But the memory of it hung in the air between them. Still, they'd reached some kind of accommodation with each other: Mila, cool and professional, or at least *striving* for cool and professional, over the several layers of doubt and intimidation she actually felt, and Reid . . . Reid, sullen and silent. He barely tolerated what little time they spent together every day, and when they weren't together, Mila imagined she could still feel his hostility toward her, radiating right through his closed bedroom door.

"I think it was hard on the other two home health aides," Lonnie said now, breaking into her thoughts. "The loneliness. And, of course, being with him," she added, almost guiltily, glancing in the direction of his bedroom. "I mean, he can be difficult sometimes."

Sometimes? Mila wanted to say, but didn't.

"You know, he wasn't always like this," Lonnie said companionably, spooning more sugar into her coffee.

"No?" Mila asked doubtfully.

"Well, I didn't know him that well before the accident," Lonnie said. "I'd been doing housework for Walker and Allie for several years, but Reid didn't come up here that often. He was based in the Twin Cities, and, from what Walker said, he was all work and no play. But once in a while he'd come up, usually for some business at the boatyard, and, I must say, when he did . . ." Her voice trailed off, and she smiled and gave a little shake of her head. "Well, when he *did* come up here," she said, "he was something to look at."

Mila said nothing, but she was remembering what Allie had said to her that day outside the hardware store, about how women had found Reid so attractive. And Mila supposed that he was *still* attractive, though how you could even *notice* that attractiveness under all those layers of unfriendliness, she had no idea. Lonnie, though, seemed to be waiting for some response from her, so Mila shrugged and said the only nice thing she could think of to say about Reid. "He does have nice eyes. They're very . . . very blue." And it was true. They were such an intense blue, in fact, that even his too-long hair, which was always falling into his eyes, couldn't hide their blueness.

"Oh, his eyes are nice," Lonnie agreed. "But it isn't just his eyes. Or it wasn't, anyway, before the accident. And I know it wasn't just old ladies like me who thought he was handsome, either. Once, when Walker and Allie were away for the weekend, he came up here and brought a girl with him. Or a woman, I should say. Walker had asked me if I could do some cooking for them, and of course I said yes. I brought my son with me, too. He was about sixteen at the time, and Walker was paying him to do some odd jobs around here. Anyway, this woman, Reid's date, comes up from the dock and says hello to us, and, honestly, I thought my son's eyes would pop right out of his head." Lonnie laughed at the memory. "She was wearing the tiniest bikini I've ever seen. And it was *white*! Imagine that. Wearing a white bikini? It's not every woman's birthright, I remember telling my husband at the dinner table that night. But it was this woman's birthright."

"Later I asked Walker about Reid and her," Lonnie continued, after she'd paused to sip her coffee. "And he said they weren't together anymore. That it hadn't been, you know, a serious thing. But still, they seemed like they were having fun that weekend. Sunbathing, and swimming, and racing around in one of Walker's powerboats. I think about that, sometimes, when I see Reid in his wheelchair." Her expression suddenly grew serious. "It's hard to believe he's the same man."

Mila nodded thoughtfully. It certainly didn't sound like the Reid she knew either. But then something occurred to her. "I know he seemed different before the accident," she said to Lonnie. "I mean, obviously, he was more active then, and, you know, more social. But was he . . ." She searched for the right word, then decided there was really only one word for it. "But was he *nicer* before the accident?"

"Nicer?" Lonnie repeated, frowning.

"Not that he isn't nice now," Mila said quickly. *Liar.* "It's just that he's so irritable all the time. And who could blame him, really, when you consider what he's been through," she added. This was another lie. She didn't really believe his accident excused his rudeness. But she didn't want to make Lonnie feel uncomfortable, either. She was obviously a very loyal employee. So Mila tried again. "I guess what I mean is, was he more relaxed before the accident? You know, friendlier?"

Lonnie hesitated. "No, I wouldn't say he was relaxed before the accident. And, honestly, he wasn't very friendly, either. But he wasn't *unfriendly,*" she said. "I did try, the first couple of times I met him, to have a conversation with him. But then I realized he wasn't one for small talk. I could tell, I guess, that he thought it was kind of a waste of his time. You know, like there was something more important he needed to be doing.

But he wasn't rude, exactly. Just a little . . . abrupt, I guess you'd say."

Mila nodded. Just as she'd thought. So the accident hadn't changed Reid so much as it had scratched all the shine off his surface.

"Well, anyway," Lonnie said, draining the last of the coffee from her cup. "I'm sure he'll be back to his usual self in no time."

Mila didn't answer. Even to get that far, she thought, Reid had a long way to go.

Lonnie started to get up from the table then, but she hesitated and sat back down. "I've been meaning to ask you," she said, lowering her voice. "Is he still . . . is he still having the dreams?"

"You know about those?" Mila asked, surprised.

Lonnie nodded. "I spent a few nights here with him, in between his last two home health aides. And, honestly, I didn't know what to do when I heard him. It scared the living daylights out of me, I can tell you that. Walker had warned me about it, of course. But it's different, having someone tell you about it, and actually hearing it for yourself."

"So what did you do?" Mila asked.

"Nothing," Lonnie said, looking a little ashamed. "I was afraid to let him keep dreaming like that. But I was even more afraid to wake him up."

"I think you were right not to disturb him," Mila said honestly, remembering what had happened when she'd woken Reid up. "I don't know a lot about PTSD," she told Lonnie, "but obviously, if I'm going to stay here, I'm going to need to learn more about it."

"PTSD?" Lonnie repeated.

"Posttraumatic stress disorder."

"Is that why he has those dreams?"

Mila shrugged. "I'm not an expert, obviously. But I think so."

Lonnie looked a little frightened. "It sounds serious."

"It's treatable," Mila assured her. "On my next day off, I'm going to go to the public library in town and research it. Once I know more about it, I might be able to be more helpful to him." But she heard the doubt in her own voice. "Ultimately," she added, "I think he's going to need to see a specialist. A psychologist or a psychiatrist."

Lonnie nodded thoughtfully. "Well, in the meantime," she said, "if you want to do some research here, you can use the iPad in the study. I'm sure Walker wouldn't mind."

"No, that's okay," Mila said quickly. She'd poked her head in the study. But like most of the cabin, with the exception of her bedroom and the kitchen, it felt somehow off limits to her. Mila heard someone else driving up to the cabin then, and she felt her body tense up again.

"Oh, that'll be Walker," Lonnie said, standing up and taking her coffee cup to the sink to rinse out. And a moment later Mila saw that it was, in fact, Walker's pickup truck rolling into view. He often stopped by at this time of the morning, on his way to the boatyard in Butternut. Still, it wasn't until he'd parked and was pushing open the kitchen door that Mila finally felt her body begin to relax.

She stood up then, to say hello, but Walker waved to her to sit back down. "Don't let me interrupt your breakfast," he said. But he let Lonnie pour him a cup of coffee, and when he'd had a chance to drink some of it, he asked Mila, a little warily, "How's our patient this morning?"

"He's fine," Mila said, with a smile that cost her real effort.

"Good," Walker said, visibly relieved. "And you'll let me know if there's anything you need? Anything at all?"

"I'll let you know," Mila said, marveling at the fact that Walker and Reid were actually brothers.

"Good," he said. "Well, I'll just duck in and say hello to Reid now. Oh, and Mila"—he took a folded piece of paper out of his pocket and handed it to her—"about that appointment we discussed? Here are the directions to Reid's doctor's office. And I'll remind him, again, that you're going to be taking him on Friday, okay?"

Mila nodded, already worried about this outing. If Reid could barely tolerate her presence for five minutes, how would he ever be able to spend a whole morning with her? But she wouldn't think about that now, she decided, as Walker left the kitchen and Lonnie came to clear away her breakfast dishes.

"Oh, Lonnie, I can do that," Mila protested, reaching for them.

"Okay," Lonnie said. "But, Mila?"

"Yes?"

"In the future, don't feel guilty about my doing the cooking, or the dishes, or the housework. I *like* taking care of people. I like keeping busy, too. And now that my boys have all moved away from home, and my husband has . . ." Her voice trailed off now, and her normally cheerful expression clouded over.

"I'm sorry, Lonnie," Mila said softly, knowing that Lonnie's husband had died, suddenly, the year before.

"Don't be sorry," Lonnie said, smiling again. "Just let me do the dishes."

Reid was staring sullenly at his closed window shade when he heard Walker's quick, but decisive rap on his bedroom door. It was amazing how much you could tell about someone from the way they knocked on a door, he thought. Lonnie, for instance, had a knock that sounded cheerful. Cheerful and hopeful. Just like her. And Mila . . . Mila's knock seemed to him, somehow, to be both anxious and determined at the same time. It was a knock that said she didn't want to be there, knocking on his bedroom door, but that she'd be damned if she'd shirk her responsibility by *not* knocking on his bedroom door.

"Reid?" his brother said, through the closed door, when he didn't respond. But Reid ignored him. He heard Walker sigh heavily and knock again.

"Not now," Reid said. "I'm busy."

"Busy doing what?"

Busy avoiding people, Reid almost said. *Well-meaning, but otherwise annoying people, like you.* But he didn't say anything. He was hoping if he kept ignoring him, his brother would eventually go away. He'd done that before, though admittedly not very often.

"Reid, I'm coming in," Walker warned, before he opened the door and walked into the room. He took a quick look around it, as if inspecting the area for any illegal contraband, and then his gaze settled on Reid.

"Close the door," Reid said, by way of a greeting.

Walker closed it, then asked, "Mind if I sit down?"

"Would it matter if I did?"

"Probably not," Walker conceded, sitting down in the armchair in the corner. "How are you doing today?" he asked Reid.

Reid didn't answer.

"I see you didn't eat your breakfast," Walker said, glancing at the untouched tray on a nearby table.

Reid shrugged.

"Would it be all right if I had some of it?"

"Knock yourself out," Reid said.

Walker walked over to the tray and helped himself to some bacon and eggs. "You don't know what you're missing, Reid," he remarked between bites. "Even cold, these eggs are so good."

"What, no breakfast at your place?" Reid asked, annoyed.

"Not this morning. Things were a little . . . hectic over there."

"Hectic, huh? Does that mean there's trouble in paradise?"

"No, Reid. No trouble," Walker said as he ate another piece of bacon. "It's just hard getting everyone out the door in the mornings. But I'm sorry to disappoint you. I know how little faith you have in the institution of marriage."

Damn right, Reid thought, though how it could be otherwise, he didn't know. His parents' whole marriage, as far as he could see, had been one long public service announcement urging him and Walker to stay single.

"There is one thing, though . . ." Walker said now, spreading jam on toast. "One *tiny* little problem," he added, taking a big bite out of that toast.

"Well, whatever it is, it's not your appetite," Reid observed, watching Walker demolish the rest of his breakfast and then throw himself, satisfied, back into the armchair.

"No, that's not it," Walker agreed. "It's the whole . . . you know, 'sex after children thing.' The whole 'sex after baby thing,' really."

"Why, what about it?" Reid asked, not really wanting to know.

"Well, there just isn't enough of it," Walker said, lounging in the armchair. "I mean, don't get me wrong, what we have is still good, but . . ."

"Is it really that difficult to have sex when you have children?" Reid asked now, curious in spite of himself.

"It's not *difficult,*" Walker said. "It's just . . . we're never alone together anymore, and when we are, we're so damned tired. Like last night, for instance. By some miracle, we'd gotten both the kids to bed at a reasonable hour, and we were both still semiawake, so I'm lying in bed, waiting for Allie, and she comes in, and she looks . . . she looks good. I mean, she's wearing this new nightgown, and it's, you know, kind of sexy. Not in an over-the-top way, not see-through or anything, because that's not her style, but it's pretty, and I know she must have chosen it with this in mind—"

"Does this story have an ending?"

"Oh, it has an ending." Walker said, unfazed. He was used to Reid's rudeness. "It's just not a very happy ending. Allie got into bed, and we started kissing and—"

"Okay, you can skip this part."

"And I see this thing on her nightgown," Walker continues. "Right on the shoulder. And I realize that after she fed Brooke, Brooke must have spit up on her, without Allie realizing it. And I know if it's your own kid you're not supposed to feel this way, but, honestly, it was kind of gross. It looked like . . . old cottage cheese or something."

"That does sound gross," Reid agreed. "So what'd you do, ignore it?"

"No, I couldn't ignore it. A better man than me would have ignored it, but I pointed it out to Allie, and she went to put her nightgown in the laundry, and by the time she came back to bed . . ." He shrugged. "I was asleep. She tried to wake me up, but I was out cold. I'd been up since five A.M. that morning with Brooke. She's teething and for some reason—"

"Stop, please. I can't take any more," Reid said, holding up his hands. "Really, if the point of this is to impress upon me what a . . . domestic nightmare your life has become, consider it done."

Walker, usually immune to Reid's barbs, looked genuinely hurt. "That is *not* the point. And if you think that's how I see my life now, you're dead wrong. You just don't like it when I talk about the good stuff, Reid. Every time I try to tell you about something cute Wyatt or Brooke has done you cut me off and—"

"There's a reason I do that," Reid said, cutting him off again. "It's because when you start to talk about them that way you get this moronic, goofy expression on your face, Walker. I can't stand it, really. You look like a total idiot."

Walker was silent for a moment, studying him, an unreadable expression on his usually readable face. "Yeah, you would think that, I guess," he said, finally, with a shrug. And then, changing gears, he said, "But I didn't come here to talk to you about any of that, actually."

"Ahh, at last, the lecture of the day," Reid said. "I was wondering how long it was going to take you to get to that. But now that you have, can you hurry it up a little? Because the sooner you get it over with, the sooner I can get back to . . ." *To what?* he wondered.

Well, to nothing, he supposed. But it was a nothing that was easier to bear when he was alone.

But Walker ignored the last part of what he'd said. "The lecture of the day, huh?" he said, raising his eyebrows.

Reid nodded, barely.

"And what might today's topic be?"

"I don't know," Reid grumbled. "My poor attitude, maybe? Or my lack of interest in our business? Or—"

"Actually, you've got it all wrong," Walker said. "There's no lecture today. In fact, I'm here to congratulate you."

"Me?"

"Yep. You. Because you've reached a milestone, Reid. As of today, Mila's been here for two weeks. You never got that far with the other two home health aides. Or have you forgotten?" No, he hadn't forgotten. Especially since the second one, Mrs. Bolger—the one with the cloying personality and the too-sweet perfume—had quit in such a spectacular fashion. It was only a week into her stint when Reid made a particularly nasty comment that led to her resigning. But *before* she'd resigned, she'd told Reid exactly what she thought of him. And the funny thing was, it was the first time he'd liked her. No, not *liked* her, exactly. But found her entertaining. He hadn't known before then that she was capable of such colorful language. Such incredible profanity. It made her seem, if not interesting, then at least tolerable.

"I'm assuming things are going well with Mila, though," Walker said now.

"What do you mean by 'going well'?"

Walker hesitated. "I mean, you haven't antagonized her yet. Have you?"

Reid shook his head. "I don't think so," he said. And he hadn't. At least, not as far as he was concerned. He'd been direct with her, of course. To the point. Okay, maybe he'd gone a little beyond directness, maybe he'd bordered, *no, landed,* right on rudeness. But he'd agreed to let her be his home health aide, for God's sake. Not his personal companion.

There'd been only one time since she'd come to live there that his behavior had crossed the line. That first night, when she woke him up from his nightmare. He'd been furious then, and he hadn't held back, either, when he'd told her, in no uncertain terms, never to come into his bedroom uninvited again. And she'd been afraid. No, not afraid. She'd been *terrified.* He shifted uncomfortably in his wheelchair, remembering the expression on her face, and remembering, too, the crying he'd heard after she went back to her room. He rubbed his temples now, as if trying to rub away the memory of that sound. But he couldn't get rid of it, not when he knew he'd been the one responsible for it.

"Well, in any case, there's been no major incident yet that I know of," Walker said. "And that's a personal best for you, Reid. The last two aides only got a few days into this before we all had to have a little sit-down discussion about your behavior."

Reid nodded distractedly, thinking again about how afraid Mila had been that night at his bedside. And that wasn't the only time he'd sensed her fear, he realized. It was always there, right beneath the surface. It was in her guardedness. Her watchfulness. It was in the way she'd flinch, almost imperceptibly, if the phone rang or a car pulled up outside.

"Walker, what do we know about her?" he asked suddenly.

"Mila?" Walker said. "I don't know. The basics, I guess. And whatever else you've been able to learn. The agency, obviously, has its own screening process."

But Reid shook his head. He wasn't talking about the basics. He was talking about something else. Something that was hard to put into words. "No, Walker, I mean what do we *really* know about her?"

Walker looked nonplussed. "What do *any* of us really know about each other, Reid?"

But Reid shook his head. That wasn't an answer.

"Look," Walker said, after a moment. "I don't know what kind of information you want about Mila. But I can tell you that the agency did a criminal background check on her. And she passed it. With flying colors. They ran a check on her driving record, too. And Reid, she's never even had a speeding ticket before. Which, by the way, is more than you can say."

"No, I'm not saying I think she's a criminal," Reid said. "I'm saying that I think she's . . . she's scared. She's afraid of someone. Or something. It's like she's in danger. Or she *thinks* she is, anyway. And Walker, another thing, I think she's hiding here, at this cabin. I really do."

Walker stared at him. "Reid, she's a home health care worker," he said, "not a member of the witness protection program."

Reid waved this away, though.

Walker leaned closer to him then and studied him carefully. "Reid, you're not still doubling up on your pain medication, are you?"

"What? No," Reid said irritably. "Mila keeps that stuff under lock and key."

"Good," Walker said. "Because, honestly, you're acting kind of strange."

"Is it strange to have questions about someone who's living in your house?" Reid countered.

"It's not your house," Walker reminded him, not unkindly.

"Whatever," Reid said. "I just think she has a past, that's all. I mean, I was watching her hands the other day, and I could have sworn that her ring finger has a slightly paler strip of skin around it where a wedding ring used to be."

"Maybe it does," Walker said, finally exasperated by the direction this conversation was taking. "And maybe she did have a wedding ring on it, and she took it off because she's divorced. Or separated. Or whatever. But so what? It's not a crime, is it, to have a marriage fail? We all have a past, Reid. Even you."

"I guess so," Reid said, feeling suddenly tired. "But I still have unanswered questions about her."

"So *ask* her those questions," Walker said. "Ask her if she was married. Ask her anything you want, within reason, that is. I mean, that is what people do, Reid. They talk to each other. They ask each other questions. They answer each other's questions. They get to know each other. You should try it sometime. You might actually enjoy it."

"I can't ask her questions," Reid said. "And she wouldn't answer them, anyway. It's like she's got this protective wall around her or something."

"Well, that makes two of you then," Walker said.

But Reid only looked at the closed window shade. Something about Mila troubled him. But he wouldn't say any more to Walker about it.

"Look, Reid," his brother said now. "Answer this for me, okay? Has Mila done anything since she got here that's endangered you, or compromised your well-being?

Reid shook his head.

"Has she done anything since she got here that's made you think she's anything less than competent? Or well qualified?"

"No," Reid said. And now it was his turn to be exasperated. He hadn't said Mila was incompetent. She wasn't. Even he could see that. All he'd said was that he had some questions about her.

"Good," Walker said, getting up from the armchair and stretching lazily. "Because that's all I really need to know. And it's all you really need to know too, Reid." He gave Reid a brotherly pat on his way to the door, then paused. "Any chance I could get you to look at something later?"

"What something?"

"We need to sign a new lease on the Two Harbors Boatyard and—" But Reid was already shaking his head. Walker should know better, he thought, than to try to get him involved in running their company again. But to Walker his lack of interest in it remained a mystery. The only mystery to Reid, though, was why their company had ever interested him in the first place.

"Okay, forget I brought that up," Walker said. "If you need more time, take it. But what about a haircut and a shave, then? There's still a very good barber in Butternut, and, Reid, I have to be honest, this whole look"—he pantomimed a huge beard on himself—"it's not really working for you. Maybe some guys can pull it off, but you're not one of them."

But again, Reid wasn't interested. The whole idea of shaving seemed to him now a colossal waste of time, even when you had as much time on your hands as he did.

"Suit yourself," Walker said, imperturbable in his defeat. He started to leave then, but stopped and turned back. "By the way, don't forget that Mila's taking you to your doctor's appointment on Friday. I've already discussed it with her, all right?"

"Okay," Reid said. But he wasn't really listening. He was just relieved that Walker was leaving. He wasn't used to all this talking. Not since the accident. And not before the accident either. But at least *before* the accident he could always cut a conversation short by hanging up the phone, or by leaving the room. Now, of course, he was stuck. There was nowhere to run, and nowhere to hide. "Nowhere to run and nowhere to hide," he said out loud, his thoughts returning now to Mila. Because his intuition told him that this phrase might describe her situation better than his own.

Chapter 8

That Friday morning, Mila found herself once again confronting Reid's closed bedroom door. The sight of it never failed to inspire dread in her, and today was no exception. She tried to shrug it off, though. She'd told Walker she'd do this for him, and she was determined to follow through with it. Besides, while she might not be looking forward to spending time with Reid, she *was* looking forward to leaving the cabin. She hadn't left it yet, even on her days off, and she was starting to feel claustrophobic. Once, she'd thought "cabin fever" was just an expression. Now, she knew better.

Here goes nothing, she told herself, knocking firmly on Reid's door. And that was exactly what she got in response: nothing.

"Reid," she said, when her third knock had gone unanswered. "It's Mila. May I come in, please?"

"I'm busy" was his muffled reply.

"Well, can you finish what you're doing later?" she asked the closed door. *Especially since we both know that what you're doing is absolutely nothing.*

She heard Reid sigh loudly, then heard him wheel himself over to the door. He opened it, a crack. "What is it?" he asked, and Mila hesitated. Even by Reid's standards, he seemed irritable today.

He noticed her hesitation. "Can't this wait?"

She wavered again and thought about retreating to her room for the rest of the day. Hell, for the rest of the *summer.* But she stood firm.

"No, Reid, this can't wait," she said calmly. "Now, may I please come in?"

He glared at her, but he opened the door. Then he turned his wheelchair around and wheeled himself farther into the room. She hovered on the threshold, trying to resist the by now familiar urge to raise his shade and open his window. Outside, it was a postcard perfect summer day, but inside his dark and stuffy room you would never know it.

"Reid," she said, to the back of his wheelchair. "I'm going to be taking you to your doctor's appointment this morning, remember?"

There was a pause. Then he said, "No, I don't remember."

"Walker told me he spoke to you about it."

Another pause. "Well, he didn't."

She frowned. Of course Walker had spoken to him about it, and she almost said so now, but, sensing a long negotiation, she tried a different tack. "All right, well, as you know," she said, working hard to sound casual, "Allie and Walker left yesterday for Michigan. A friend of Allie's is getting married there tomorrow, and they decided to make a long weekend of it. So I'll be taking you to your ten o'clock orthopedist's appointment this morning. But Walker's shown me how to use the wheelchair lift in the van, and he's given me directions to your doctor's office in Ely, so I'm not anticipating any problems." *Any problems other than you, that is.*

At first, Reid said nothing. He just kept looking out the window. No, not *out* the window, because the shade was drawn. He kept looking *at* the window. "I don't think so," he said, finally.

"What do you mean 'you don't think so'?"

"I mean, I don't think you'll be driving me to my appointment today."

"And who would be driving you then?"

"Nobody. I won't be going."

"And why is that, Reid?" she asked, surprised by her own persistence.

He shrugged. "I just don't feel like going."

"Well, I'm sorry to hear that," she said, trying still to keep her tone light. Relaxed. "Because it's too late to cancel the appointment."

He looked disinterested.

"Reid, you can't miss a doctor's appointment," she objected.

"I won't miss it," he said. "I'll just reschedule it."

You mean somebody else will just reschedule it, Mila thought, but didn't say. She wasn't ready to give up yet. She needed this outing. Needed it almost more than she was willing to admit to herself. Because while leaving the cabin meant running the risk, however small, of Brandon finding her, it also meant a welcome return to the outside world, something that had begun to feel very far away. After all, in the little over two weeks since she'd arrived, she'd seen more deer than she had people. So she decided to take a page from Reid's book and pretend she hadn't heard him when he'd said he wasn't going.

"Okay then," she said, briskly. "We don't need to leave for another fifteen minutes. So why don't you do whatever it is you need to do before we go, and I'll come back then and—"

"I *said* I'm not going," Reid interrupted her, directing his words not at her but at the window shade. "Now *please* leave," he added, managing to make even the word *please* sound rude. "And close the door behind you."

But Mila didn't leave. Not today. Because today, for some reason, she was reminded of something Ms. Thompson had said about Reid after she'd read his file. *He's not abusive, Mila. He's just a jerk. A garden-variety jerk.* And it was true. He *was* a jerk. But he wasn't dangerous. Not like Brandon. Even Mila could see that, at least in her more rational moments. So why, she wondered now, was she so afraid of him? No, not *afraid,* she amended. *Intimidated.* Why was she so intimidated by him? *Because he made her feel incompetent,* she realized. Worse than incompetent, really. He made her feel totally inept. And inane. And annoying. And dimwitted. And a lot of other things, too. None of them good. But did she actually believe she was any of those things? No, she didn't. And the strange thing was, she didn't actually think Reid believed she was any of those things either. He just . . . *he just wants you to go away,* she realized. *He just wants you to leave him alone.* And the best way to do that, from his perspective, anyway, was to be a jerk.

The trouble was, they couldn't keep doing this, couldn't keep going in circles like this. Reid being a jerk, and Mila letting him be a jerk. Or at least letting the fact that he was being a jerk stand in the way of her doing her job. She could handle him, she told herself. She'd handled people like him before, arrogant, dismissive, rude people. During the years she'd waitressed, for instance, she'd met her share of jerks. Or people who were acting like jerks, anyway. She'd just learned not to take them personally. The frazzled mother with the cranky children. The sleep-deprived cabbie coming off an all-night shift. The lonely old man who was perfectly happy to take his loneliness out on a stranger like Mila. She'd met them all, and she'd dealt with them all, and she'd done it by trying to see through their behavior to the person behind it. But she hadn't done that with Reid, had she? She hadn't seen him as a real person. Hadn't spoken to him like a real person, either. Instead, she'd tiptoed around him, forgetting that behind all his condescension, and rudeness, and sarcasm, he was just a man. A man who was hurting. Inside and out.

"Are you still here?" Reid asked, glancing over his shoulder at her.

"I'm still here," Mila said from the doorway where she'd been standing. But now she came back into the room, and, determined to start over again, she sat down in the armchair in the corner. He glanced over at her, warily, and angled his wheelchair farther away from her.

"Look, Reid," she said patiently. "I know you don't want me to take you to your doctor's appointment. I know you'd rather Walker or Allie take you when they get back. I understand that. And I'm sorry. I really am. But I'm it for today. The good news, though, is that you're only going to have to put up with me for a couple of hours. And I can promise you I'll make those hours as painless as possible."

He turned his wheelchair, fractionally, toward her. "Can we not do this?"

"Not do what?"

"Whatever it is you're doing," he said, exasperated. "First you come in here pretending to be my friend, and then, when that didn't work, you were my psychologist, and now, apparently, you're my first-grade teacher, getting me ready to go on a field trip. But it's not working. Any of it. All you've done is waste my time and yours. And you know what, Mila? Sometimes, the truth is easier. Like right now, for instance, I'd actually prefer it if you didn't try to hide the fact that you dislike me."

"But I . . . I don't dislike you," she said, caught off guard. "And I don't think you dislike me, either." She said this last part, though, without any real conviction.

He only shrugged. "It doesn't matter," he said. "Because the upshot's the same. I'm not going with you today. And that's all I have to say on the subject. If you want to discuss this further, it won't be with me. You can call my brother on his cell."

"No, I *can't* call your brother on his cell," she said, surprising herself with the sharpness of her tone, and surprising him with it too, judging by the way he looked over at her. "I can't call him because I'm not interrupting the one weekend he's had off since your accident to tell him that I can't do my job."

"Not my problem," he muttered.

"You're right, Reid, it's not your problem," she shot back. "But only because you make it everyone *else's* problem. The way it'll be your doctor's office's problem when I cancel your appointment at the last minute today. And Walker and Allie's problem when one of them has to take you to your rescheduled appointment next week. And—"

"Are you done?" he muttered, angling his wheelchair farther away from her.

"No, I'm *not* done," she said, feeling her face flush hotly. He was more than a garden-variety jerk, she decided. And more than rude, too. He was ungrateful. And ungratefulness was something Mila had very little patience for. "And I know, Reid," she said now, "that Walker and Allie won't complain about taking you to your rescheduled appointment. I know because, as far as I can tell, they never complain about *any* of the things they do for you. But I wonder, sometimes, if it would be easier for them to do all those things if you showed them just a *little* appreciation. Just an *infinitesimal* amount of gratitude. Just a simple 'thank you,' maybe." Her voice sounded loud in the quiet room, and her heart, she realized, was beating faster, her blood thrumming in her ears. Still, she rushed on. "But gratitude isn't your specialty, is it, Reid? Because if it were, you'd already know you have a lot to be grateful for. *A lot* to give thanks for." She stopped finally. She had Reid's attention now, she saw. His full attention. She'd cut through the fog, the torpor, that usually surrounded him. And in its place was an almost electric anger.

"Grateful? Are you serious? What in God's name do you think I have to be grateful for?" he asked, making a gesture that included himself, the wheelchair, and the hospital bed.

"You're alive, aren't you?" Mila said simply. Her heart was still beating too fast, but she forced herself to take a deep breath and to speak more slowly. "Against all odds, you survived that accident. *And* the three days you spent trapped in your car. And everything that followed. I'd say you were pretty lucky, wouldn't you?"

"Yeah, well, forgive me if I don't feel very lucky right now," he said sarcastically.

"I know you don't, Reid. But maybe you *should*. Have you ever stopped to consider that? That even though you were unlucky to have gotten into that accident, you've been lucky ever since."

He didn't say anything. He didn't need to. The incredulous expression on his face said it all.

"No, it's true," she said, undaunted. "You're lucky, Reid. Lucky to have a family who cares about you as much as yours obviously does. Lucky to be able to recover here, in this beautiful cabin, on this beautiful lake, instead of in some depressing hospital or crowded rehab center. And lucky, too, to not have to worry about the things most people have to worry about after being in an accident. Like whether or not they'll still have a job to go back to, or still be able to pay their bills, or still have a roof over their heads. But all you have to do is focus on your recovery, knowing that as soon as you're ready, your life will be waiting for you to come back to it. I'd say that qualifies as being pretty damn lucky, wouldn't you?"

Stop talking, Mila, she told herself. *Please stop.* But she couldn't. She didn't want to. She felt strangely exhilarated. And strangely liberated. It had been so long since she'd done this. So long since she'd told anyone exactly what she was thinking, or feeling, and to hell with the consequences of telling them. "And

I would think that you could see how lucky you are, Reid," she continued now, "given how much time you obviously spend thinking about yourself. Given that, at least as far as I can tell, you *never* think about anyone *but* yourself. No, you're too busy drowning in self-pity. Too busy thinking that you're the only person in the world who's ever suffered any kind of setback or ever had any kind of obstacle they've had to overcome. The only person in the world whose life hasn't gone *exactly* the way they wanted it to." She paused, a little breathless. He was looking at her now, steadily, an inscrutable expression on his face, but he didn't say anything. Which was fine, really, since it was in that moment that she decided that Reid wasn't going to miss that appointment after all. He was going to it. And she would be the one taking him to it.

She had no idea what she expected him to do as she came up behind him, took hold of the wheelchair's handles, and maneuvered him out of his bedroom and down the hallway to the kitchen, but she expected him to do something, or to say something. To offer *some* form of protest. But he didn't. And neither did Lonnie, who, as they turned into the kitchen, had a stunned expression on her face.

Oh, of course, Mila realized. *The door to Reid's bedroom was open.* Lonnie had heard everything she'd said to him. And maybe, Mila thought, as she sailed through the kitchen, pushing Reid's wheelchair, maybe she should have felt embarrassed by that. But she didn't. She felt too . . . *too elated* to feel any embarrassment or regret. Why, she wondered, had she waited all these days to tell Reid what she thought of him? Why hadn't she told him the first night she'd gotten here?

"Lonnie," she said crisply, "can you get the door for us, please?" And Lonnie, bless her heart, only hesitated for a second before she nodded, hurried over to the kitchen door, and opened it.

"Thank you, Lonnie," Mila said, with a quick smile, but she didn't let her eyes linger too long on Lonnie's expression, which was still surprised but now a little anxious, too. Instead, Mila pushed Reid's wheelchair briskly out the door, down the ramp, and out to the van. And after she'd loaded it onto the van, and gotten herself settled into the driver's seat, she started up the van, turned down the driveway, and drove for several minutes in silence before finally glancing back at him. He was staring straight ahead, a stony expression on his face. He definitely didn't look happy, she thought, though after the dressing-down she'd given him, was that really so surprising? After all, she'd called him . . . well, actually, she'd called him *a lot* of things, and she'd implied he was a lot of other things, too.

Things like rude and selfish and ungrateful, and . . . She glanced back at Reid again and felt her recent euphoria start to give way to a new foreboding.

Oh my God, what have I done? she wondered a few minutes later. She shook her head, bewildered by her own actions. What had she been thinking? And, more important, what had she hoped to accomplish? And why had it been so important for her to take Reid to his doctor's appointment, anyway? Walker would never have blamed her if Reid had refused to go to it. And why, *why,* had it been so important for her to tell Reid, in excruciating detail, exactly what she thought of him? Because while Walker wouldn't have fired her for not taking Reid to his appointment, she realized now, with a cold, prickly fear, he most likely *would* fire her for what she'd said to him today. Fire her for insubordination, or lack of respect, or just general unprofessionalism. And then where would she be? Well, out of a job for one thing. And out of a place to live, for another.

And not just a place to live, either, she realized. But a place to live that was two hundred and forty miles, and a whole world away, from Brandon. Now, obviously, she would have to leave this place. But where would she go? She'd only been here for one two-week pay period, and the money that she'd earned so far wouldn't take her very far, or last her very long. And then there was the question of what she would do to support herself once she got to wherever it was she went. She couldn't ask Ms. Thompson to help her find another job, or even give her a recommendation for one. Not after she'd been fired from this job.

And all at once, the enormity of what she'd done settled over her like some thick, clammy blanket, and she knew she needed to pull over. She didn't trust herself to drive any farther. She slowed down, waited until she'd reached a straight stretch of road, and then pulled the van over to the shoulder and turned off the ignition. She felt light-headed, and slightly sick to her stomach, and she had to resist the sudden and over-whelming temptation to put her head down on the steering wheel.

"Why are we stopping?" Reid asked, intruding on her panic.

"Oh," Mila said, turning to him. "I'm just . . . I'm just stopping here for a second," she said. "Just to, um . . ." She shrugged helplessly. "Just to collect myself, I guess."

He frowned, waiting for more information, and Mila, knowing she was only postponing the inevitable, said, "I'm just going to sit here for a second until I feel ready to drive again, okay? And then I'll take you back to the cabin. When we get there, I'll call the doc-tor's office, and Walker, too. He can take you to your appointment when he gets back. And, in the mean-time, I apologize for forcing you to go with me today. Obviously, that was your decision to make. Not mine."

"So now we're not going to the appointment?" he clarified.

"No, we're not," Mila said. "And when I call your brother, I'll tell him about all the things I said to you, too."

"Why would you do that?" Reid asked. He looked genuinely mystified.

"Because . . ." She hesitated, surprised by his question. "Because it was wrong of me to say all those things to you," she said, forcing herself to maintain eye contact with him. "I was hired to help you. Not to pass judgment on you. And the things I said . . . they were out of line. *I* was out of line. But I'll leave as soon as Walker and Allie get back. Or as soon as they find someone else to take my place."

"You're . . . quitting?" Reid asked, rubbing his temples.

"Not *quitting*," she qualified. "Resigning. Resigning to save your brother the trouble of having to fire me."

"So let me get this straight," Reid said, after considering it for a moment. "You think if my brother knew what you'd said to me today he'd fire you? Assuming, of course, that you didn't resign first?"

She nodded. Hadn't she made that clear?

But Reid only laughed. Or at least that's what she thought he did. She'd never heard him laugh before, and she gathered he didn't do it very often anymore, because his laugh sounded strange. Unused, almost, and rusty. But when he was done laughing, he shook his head. "The only reaction my brother would have to your saying all those things to me is pleasure. *Pure* pleasure. And the only regret he'd have about it is that he hadn't been here in person to hear you say them. Trust me. He's wanted to say the same to me, and worse, since I got out of the hospital."

Mila stared at him in astonishment. "You're not . . . you're not angry?"

"Angry? No. I mean, I didn't enjoy it. How could I? It was pretty unflattering. But it did, at least, have the advantage of being true. Every goddamned word of it. And now, Mila, I think we need to get going, or we really will miss that appointment."

Mila nodded, too surprised to speak. But she turned the ignition back on and pulled off the shoulder of the road. She concentrated on her driving again, and Reid settled back into his usual silence. But something, she knew, had happened between them. Something had changed.

Back in the van after his doctor's appointment, Reid was surprised to discover that he didn't want to go back to the cabin yet. *That's strange,* he thought. That had never happened before. Usually, no sooner had he left it than he wanted to go back to it. Back to the cabin and, more important, back to his bedroom, with its closed windows, its pulled-down shades, and its securely locked door. Because as much as he hated being in that room—and he *did* hate it—he hated being there less than he hated being anywhere else.

Maybe his not wanting to go back to it now had to do with the weather, he reasoned, as the van hummed down a county road in the direction of Butternut. After all, it was a ridiculously beautiful day, so ridiculously beautiful, in fact, that even Reid, who'd been oblivious to this kind of thing since his accident, couldn't be entirely oblivious to it today. It was warm and sunny, and the air was soft and sweet and filled with the fragrance of the wildflowers that grew in the ditches alongside the road. And the sky, the sky was a brilliant blue, especially when seen against the puffy white clouds that occasionally, and languidly, floated through it.

But if Reid was honest with himself, the perfect weather was only part of the reason he didn't want to go back to the cabin. The smallest part, actually. Because the biggest part was *her.* The biggest part was Mila. Which was crazy, really, when he considered how much he'd resented her, and how hard he'd worked, over the last several weeks, to avoid her altogether. Or, more

accurately, to make *her* avoid *him*. Still, being with her
now was . . . well, it was not unpleasant, he decided.
Unlike his other home health aides, for instance, she
didn't feel the need to talk to him all the time, to fill
the space between them with inane, pointless conversations that neither one of them wanted to be having.
She was comfortable with silence, he saw, and that was
something he'd always considered to be an undervalued quality in people.

Now she glanced quickly over her shoulder at him
as she drove, but she otherwise said nothing. And he
appreciated that, too. Since the accident it had felt as
though people were constantly asking him questions.
Was he thirsty or hungry? Hot or cold? Was he in pain?
Did he need a blanket? A magazine? Or how about
another pillow to prop himself up with? It had driven
him crazy, all the verbal poking and prodding, especially since he didn't want *anything*, really, other than
to not be in pain, and to be left alone.

He watched as Mila turned smoothly off the county
road and onto one of the local roads. He liked watching her drive, he realized. And it wasn't just because
she was an excellent driver. It was because he liked
watching her hands. She was good with them, he saw,
and being good with your hands was, in his opinion,
another undervalued quality in this day and age.

On the face of it, of course, her hands looked ordinary. Small and pale, with short, neatly trimmed nails. But it wasn't the way someone's hands looked that told the story, he knew. It was the way they moved. And Mila's hands moved gracefully, with no false starts, and no wasted motion. She could drive a five-thousand-pound van as easily as most people could push a toy car, Reid thought.

Now Mila turned again, onto the street that led into the town, and they passed the BUTTERNUT POPULATION 1,200 sign, and then the gas station, and then, in the next block, the library and the recreation center. Soon they would drive through the center of town, past Pearl's and the Pine Cone Gallery and Johnson's Hardware, and then they would leave the town behind them. After that, it would only be another fifteen minutes before they were pulling up in front of the cabin, and Reid was wheeling himself back into his room, and closing the door behind him. And then . . . well, then he'd pick up where he'd left off, which was . . . which was really nowhere at all.

"Do you mind if we stop in town?" he asked Mila now, leaning forward in his wheelchair.

"Oh, no. Of course not," Mila said, slightly startled. It was the first time he'd said more than a couple of words to her since she'd pulled back onto the road after their conversation that morning. "Where do you need to go?" she asked, stopping at an intersection.

"I don't really *need* to go anywhere," he said. "It's just . . ." He grasped at a reason to not to go back to the cabin right away. "It's just that I'm hungry." Actually, he hadn't been conscious of being hungry before, but now that he'd said he was, he realized it was true.

"Oh, of course," Mila said apologetically, looking at her watch. "I didn't realize it was twelve thirty already. Where would you like to go?"

"How about Pearl's?" Reid asked.

"The place your brother brought me that first day?" Mila asked, as she proceeded through the intersection. And Reid groaned inwardly, remembering how he'd behaved then. But Butternut only had a few other options for lunch, and none of them were as good as Pearl's, so he said, "Yeah, that place. It's up ahead. On the right."

Mila said nothing, but she slowed the van, and then slid, as if by magic, into a parking space directly in front of Pearl's. "It looks busy," she said, noting the line of people spilling out the door and onto the sidewalk. "But the woman who owns it is a friend of Allie's, isn't she? She'll probably seat you right away."

That was true enough, Reid thought. But he didn't want any special treatment now, not when he'd had so much of it the last time he'd been there. And he flashed on an image of Caroline sweeping up the glass he'd broken, and soothing the baby he'd made cry, and bringing him a bendy straw to drink his new glass of water with.

"You know what," he said, "why don't we just get something to go?"

"To take back to the cabin?" Mila asked. She'd turned off the ignition, and now her hand hovered over the door handle.

"Um, I guess. Or maybe we could take it someplace else. There's a picnic area at the town beach," he said, improvising.

"A picnic area?" Mila asked in surprise, turning around in the front seat and studying him. "You want to have a picnic?"

"Why not," Reid said, a little defensively. "It's a nice day, isn't it?"

"It is, but . . ." She stopped, stymied. And Reid had to admit that his wanting to go on a picnic was a little incongruous, given that only a few hours ago he hadn't even wanted to leave his bedroom. But now he reached for his wallet and extracted a couple of bills from it and held them out to a still doubtful looking Mila.

"Would you mind going in?" he asked.

"No," she said, regaining some of her equilibrium as she took the bills from him. "What would you like?"

"How about the Butternut Burger, some fries, and a Coke," he said. "And, uh, Mila, you should get something for yourself, too."

"Oh, that's all right. I can have something back at the cabin."

"No, really, get something," he said. "I mean, otherwise, what are you going to do at the beach, just sit there and watch me eat?"

"No, of course not," she assured him. "I'll wait in the van."

"Oh," Reid said, taken aback. "I thought we'd have lunch, you know, together." He felt suddenly and undeniably awkward.

At the word *together* Mila's eyes widened slightly. More surprise, Reid saw. But she recovered herself quickly. "All right," she said. "I'll get us some burgers." And then she was gone, leaving Reid to mull over the curious turn the day's events had taken. And he had to admit, he was almost as surprised by them as Mila was.

But she was back before he knew it, carrying their lunches in a bulging and slightly greasy paper bag and looking as if she was determined to make the best of their impromptu picnic. And Reid, feeling oddly contented, gave her directions to the town beach, realizing as she pulled into the parking lot there a few minutes later that it was even prettier than he remembered it being. Set at one end of a sheltered bay, and fringed by great northern pines, the beach was a quarter-mile-long crescent of yellow sand that gave way to the blue waters of Butternut Lake. There was only a scattering of people there today, mainly parents with young children who had grouped their beach chairs, brightly colored umbrellas, and striped beach towels near the lifeguard's stand and the small, roped-off swimming area in front of it. Mila, though, seemed unnerved even by this small crowd, and Reid noticed that she was careful to park as far away from the other cars in the lot as possible, and that when she got out of the van and came around to slide his door open, there was a worry line creasing her otherwise smooth forehead. Once she'd gotten their lunches out and locked up the van, though, she seemed to relax. A little.

"There's a paved walkway over there that leads to some picnic tables," Reid said as he wheeled himself in its direction, and Mila fell in beside him. He remembered, now, the last time he'd been to this beach. It was a warm day in late spring, and Allie and Walker had brought him here, thinking that the fresh air and sunshine might do him some good. They hadn't. He'd wanted to leave as soon as they'd gotten here. It was only a few days after they'd moved him into the cabin from the rehabilitation center, and he was already resentful of their unflagging cheerfulness and already ashamed, too, of his resentment of it.

And the truth was, he wasn't in much better shape today than he had been that day, because by the time he got to the first picnic table, which stood in the shade of a nearby aspen tree, he was already winded. "Is this okay?" he asked, positioning his wheelchair at one end of the table.

"It's fine," Mila said, setting the drinks and the bag on the table and sitting down on one of its benches. She unpacked their lunches then and slid his Coke and his paper-wrapped hamburger and french fries over to him. He waited for her to start her lunch, but she didn't eat it right away. Instead, she took a tentative sip of her soda, and then she did that thing he'd seen her do at Pearl's the first time he'd met her. She made herself smaller somehow, dipping her chin down toward her chest and drawing her shoulders closer together. It was a tiny movement. A subtle movement. He didn't even know why he noticed it, really. Most people wouldn't have. But while it had annoyed him the first time he'd seen her do it, now it interested him. The way she closed herself up like that. Closed herself *off*. Maybe it interested him, he thought, because closing yourself off was something he knew about firsthand.

Thinking about that, he unwrapped his hamburger and took a bite and then, surprised, took another bite. It tasted like . . . it tasted like real food, he marveled. Since the accident food had seemed somehow unappealing to him. Eating was just another thing he did because other people expected him to do it. But he hadn't taken any real pleasure in it. This was different, though, he thought, and, suddenly famished, he took another bite of his hamburger.

Mila, watching him, unwrapped her own burger and took a small bite. "*Oh my God,*" she said softly when she'd swallowed it, "this is *so* good. Is everything at Pearl's this good?"

"Pretty much," he said.

"Do you think there are people in Butternut who eat one of these every day?" she asked, taking another bite.

"Oh, definitely," he said. "But they probably won't be with us much longer," he added. And she smiled, an almost smile, at him. It wasn't much, but he'd take it, he decided. It was the first tiny crack in the wall of her distrust for him that he'd seen since they'd left the cabin that morning.

They ate in silence for a few minutes, and then Reid noticed that Mila looked tense again. Her eyes flicked briefly in the direction of the parking lot, and Reid followed them and saw a car pulling in. He watched it park and looked as two parents and a passel of kids spilled out of it, all of them armed with coolers and sand toys and inflatable rafts. He glanced back at Mila, thinking that she couldn't possibly feel threatened by this family. And she didn't look as if she did, but still, there was something about the car's arrival that sent her guard back up, and she didn't go back to eating her lunch, but left it, instead, unfinished in front of her.

"Are you done?" she asked him a little while later, glancing at what remained of his own half-eaten lunch.

"No, not yet," he said. "I just can't get enough of these fries," he added, biting into one. Truth be told, after weeks of undereating, he was already full, but he wasn't ready to leave yet. Mila said nothing, but she looked at him a little strangely, probably remembering all the uneaten meals he'd sent back to the kitchen.

"You don't mind if we stay here a little longer, do you?" he asked.

"No, of course not," she said.

But when Reid came to the end of his lunch, he continued to dawdle. He didn't want to leave yet. Not until . . . not until he'd found out something about her. Because damned if he wasn't curious about Mila Jones. And then he thought of something his brother had said to him. *If there's something you want to know about her, Reid, why don't you just ask her?*

"Can I ask you a question?" he said.

She raised her eyebrows. "A question?"

"Uh-huh."

She frowned slightly. "I guess that would depend on what the question was," she said finally.

"Okay. That's fair. The question is, 'what is it that you do all day?' I mean, when you're in your room?"

She hesitated. "You know, I could ask you the same question," she said.

I try not to think, Reid almost said. *At least during the day. During the night, I try not to think and I also try not to sleep.* But instead he said, "Well, right now, I'm the one asking the question."

She seemed to consider it, then shrugged and said, "I study."

"You study?" That had never occurred to him before. "What do you study?"

She paused, played with a cold french fry, and then sighed. "I'm studying for the nursing school entrance exam. I have some practice books that I brought with me. So I do the sample problems in them."

"But . . . all day? I mean, most of the day? That's a lot of sample problems."

She shrugged noncommittally.

"How many test prep books did you bring with you?"

"A few."

"Haven't you done all the problems in them by now?"

She smiled faintly. "That's more than one question."

"I know. But there's something else I'm curious about," he said, not giving her time to object. "Why don't you ever go down to the dock?"

"I'm not here on a vacation," she pointed out. "It's bad enough that I'm already getting paid for time that I don't spend working, but getting paid for time that I spend relaxing . . . that doesn't seem right to me."

Reid nodded, slowly, thinking she had an admirable work ethic, but that it still didn't explain everything. "Okay, that's fair. But you don't even go down to the dock on your days off," he said. "You're not getting paid then."

She hesitated again, and he could see her weighing whether or not to tell him something. Finally, she said, "I don't know how to swim."

"You don't know how to swim at all?" Reid asked, shocked.

She shook her head.

"Didn't you . . . didn't you want to learn? When you were a kid, I mean."

"Of course I wanted to learn. When I was growing up, I used to walk by this pool sometimes, in the
summer, and it looked . . . it looked like fun," she said,
a little wistfully. "I used to . . ." But she caught herself
here, and stopped, and looked as if she was sorry she'd
said as much as she already had.

"But, I mean, couldn't you have taken swimming
lessons then?" Reid asked. "Or gone to a day camp
where they taught you how to swim?"

She shook her head. "No. I couldn't have taken lessons. Or gone to camp, either."

"Why not?"

"Because those things cost money," she said simply.
"And we didn't have any."

"Oh," Reid said, not knowing what else to say. He
forgot sometimes that not everyone's childhood was
as blessedly middle class as his own had been, though
after his father left and kept "forgetting" to send the
child support checks, money had been a little tighter.
Still, there'd always been enough for swimming lessons and day camps and stuff like that. Though now,
when he thought about it, he couldn't really remember when he'd first learned how to swim. It seemed to
him, in a way, that he'd always known how to swim.
That he'd been *born* knowing. And that was a good
thing too, because he and Walker had grown up on

a lake. Lake Minnetonka. One of his favorite childhood memories, in fact, was of him and his brother as
little kids, swimming in the still cold lake on an early
summer evening as their mother waited on the dock,
towels in her arms, begging them to get out of the
water. "Your lips are blue," she'd called out to them.
"You'll freeze to death." But she'd been laughing, too.
She'd still been young then, and pretty. It was before
their father had left them, and before the bitterness
had started eating away at her, like some terrible dis-
ease. He liked remembering her the way she'd been
on the dock that day. *God, she'd loved the water,* he
thought now. And she was an excellent swimmer, too.
In fact, it had probably been her, and not some camp
counselor, who'd taught him and his brother how to
swim.

"Couldn't your mom have taught you how to swim?"
he asked Mila.

She considered this. "Maybe. She knows how to
swim. But she didn't have time to teach me. She was
always either working, or sleeping."

"What about your dad?"

She looked uncomfortable, and he knew she didn't
really want to continue this conversation, but she said,
after a long moment, "My dad wasn't in the picture."

"Not . . . not at all?"

"No. I don't even know who he was," she said, concentrating on an imaginary design she was tracing on the picnic table's top.

He shook his head slightly. That was rough, not even knowing who your father was. Having him just bail out on you like that, probably before you were even born. His father, of course, hadn't stuck around for the long haul, either. But he'd been there for a while. Long enough to do the whole Boy Scouts thing. Long enough to go to some of their Little League games. Long enough to make it hurt, like hell, when he left them and stopped doing those things. And then, eventually, stopped seeing them or even calling them altogether. Maybe it would have been easier, he decided now, to never have known him at all.

"Now I have a question," Mila said, breaking into his thoughts.

"For me?"

She nodded. "I think that's only fair, don't you?"

"I guess," he said noncommittally. "If it's not too personal."

She raised her eyebrows. "You mean like asking me about my relationship with my father?" she said. And Reid frowned because, now that he thought about it, that *had* been pretty personal.

"Okay, shoot," he said.

He saw her take a deep breath, as if she was gathering her courage. "When you dream at night," she asked, "what is it that you dream about?"

Reid was instantly on edge. He hadn't been prepared for that question. "I don't . . . I don't remember my dreams," he lied, looking away.

"You don't remember *any* of them?" she asked gently.

He shook his head. And that was another lie. But what was the point, really, in trying to explain his dreams to her? She would never understand them. *He* would never have understood them, either, before the accident.

"When I hear you sometimes," Mila said, carefully, "you're calling for help."

Reid looked at her warily. Why was she bringing this up? he wondered. But a moment later, she seemed to think better of it too. "Never mind," she said, her tone still gentle. "It's none of my business. And you know what, Reid? You're right. Some questions *are* too personal to ask," and she smiled at him, a smile that seemed as much an apology as a smile.

Reid nodded, wordlessly, as a breeze shook the nearby aspen tree and sent little dappling shadows over the picnic table and the two of them.

"Are you done with those?" she asked, indicating the few now cold french fries that he'd left uneaten.

He nodded disinterestedly, his appetite gone. He watched as Mila gathered the remnants of their lunches and threw them in a nearby garbage can. He knew he should have offered to do it, but all of a sudden he was exhausted and anxious to get back to the cabin. Now, though, it was Mila who seemed to want to stay.

"The lake looks so pretty," she said, gesturing in its direction. "Do you mind if I take a closer look?"

He shrugged indifferently, but then he wheeled after her, at a distance, as she walked down the paved trail until it ended, in a turnout, right in front of the water. And even Reid had to admit that the view from there was stunning, especially the view of the opposite shore of the lake, where the deep blue of the water contrasted dramatically with the pale gray of craggy rocks and the dark green of towering pine trees.

The two of them were silent for a minute until Mila bent down and picked up a stone. It was a flat, round, smooth stone, and the beach and the beach grass were littered with other stones just like it.

"That would be a good skipping stone," Reid said absently, watching Mila examine it.

"Would it? Here," she said, reaching over and putting it in his hand. "Try it."

Reid held it in his palm and ran his thumb across the top of it. He didn't really feel like skipping stones right now, but this one was so perfectly suited for it that he couldn't resist. He adjusted his wheelchair so that its left side was facing the lake, and then he swung his arm, a little awkwardly, and, flicking his wrist, let go of the stone. It splashed a little too hard off the water, skipped once, and sank.

He was going to ask Mila for another stone, but she was already gathering up more of them. She handed him another one and he tried again. This time he got some power behind the stone, and it skipped, three times, barely skimming the surface of the water.

"Very good," Mila said, smiling, and she gave him another one.

He skipped several more of them, and then stopped, marveling that something that involved so little exertion could make him so tired.

"Why don't you try it?" he asked Mila.

But she shook her head. "It's another thing I don't know how to do," she said, still holding a few of the stones in her hands.

"I'll teach you then," he said, surprising himself. He was not, as a general rule, good at teaching people how to do things. He had no patience for it, and he didn't take any pleasure in it either. But he led Mila through the steps of skipping a stone, showing her how to stand, how to hold the stone, how to swing her arm and flick her wrist. She tried a couple of times before she got one to skip, but when she did, when one skipped twice over the lake's surface, she laughed delightedly and turned to him.

And when he looked up at her he saw it again, saw the light in her eyes he'd seen that morning when she'd been so angry at him. And, just as it had that morning, it transformed her completely, and, in doing so, it disarmed him completely. It was the reason he'd let her push him in his wheelchair out to the van without any protest. He'd been too surprised by the way her anger had transformed her to offer any real resistance. But she wasn't angry now. She was just . . . alive. Present. In the moment. And, if he were honest with himself, she was something else, too. She was pretty. Very pretty. Her eyes, which he'd thought were a plain brown, were actually, he saw now, brown flecked with a very pale gold. And her hair, which had seemed to be brown too, was really more of an auburn color, its red highlights shining in the sun. A breeze blew, then, and a strand of her hair escaped from her ponytail and blew against her smooth, pale cheek before she caught it and tucked it back behind her ear. My God, he thought, she was lovely. And it suddenly seemed incredible to him that he'd spent the last several weeks living with her without actually realizing it. Or *had* he realized it? And was it the reason he'd wanted to come here with her today, not because he hadn't wanted to go back to the cabin, but because he'd wanted to see that light in her eyes again?

"You're pretty good. Here, try this one," Reid said, holding out to her one of the stones she'd given him to skip. As Mila reached for it, though, Reid brushed at a lazy black fly that had landed on his arm, and when it bit him anyway, with a sensation more annoying than painful, he slapped at it, hard, without even thinking.

Mila let out a tiny yelp, though, and jumped back so suddenly that she almost tripped over some tall beach grass behind her. She recovered her balance quickly, but even so, Reid was stunned to see fear in her eyes.

"Hey, it was just a fly," he said quickly. "I didn't mean to scare you."

"No, that's okay," she said, and Reid saw that she wasn't afraid anymore, just embarrassed.

"Mila," he said, understanding something. "Did you . . . did you think I was going to hit you?"

"What? No. Of course not," she said. But she wouldn't look at him, and he knew she was lying.

"Yes, you did," he persisted. "You thought I was going to hurt you."

"Reid, I don't know what you're talking about," she said abruptly, twisting the hair that had worked itself loose from her ponytail back into place. "But we should be getting back," she added. And he saw that the light in her eyes was gone, and so, in a way, was she. Well, not *gone*. Just back inside of herself somehow. And as they made their way back toward the van he saw her familiar wariness return.

They were both quiet on the drive to the cabin, Mila concentrating on the road and Reid looking out the window. And by the time they got back, they'd both settled so far inside themselves again that Reid almost wondered if any of it—the picnic, the conversation, the skipping stones—had actually taken place. Except that he knew it had. He'd pocketed one of the stones Mila had given him, and he found it later that night. He started to put it on his dresser, but he stopped and held it in his hand instead, running his thumb over its lake-washed smoothness. And looking at it, he felt another piece of the puzzle fall into place. He knew why Mila was afraid. She'd been hurt. But who had hurt her, Reid wondered, and what had ever possessed them to do it?

Chapter 9

Mila met Brandon Stewart at a time in her life when she was surviving on black coffee, hope, and not much else. She was twenty-three years old, and completely on her own. Her mom, who'd had enough of Minnesota winters, had moved to Florida with her boyfriend as soon as Mila had graduated from high school. She'd told Mila that she could come with them, but Mila had stayed put. She didn't mind the cold, but she did mind her mother's drinking, and her mother's boyfriend, too—the way he looked at Mila had always made her feel uncomfortable.

So she'd found a walk-in-closet–sized apartment in a slightly sketchy neighborhood and enrolled at a local community college. Because she had to work full-time while taking classes, it took her four years, instead of two, to complete her community college degree. By day, she took classes, and by night she worked any number of jobs. In her last year of college, she was working the graveyard shift at a coffee shop where everything—the food, the dishes, and even the counters—seemed to be covered in a thin layer of grease. Still, working there wasn't that bad. It was slow during the early morning hours, and if its lack of customers was bad for tips, it was good for answering Heather's letters, and for studying for her classes, many of which were prerequisites for nursing school.

She was studying for one of those classes one night, sitting at the counter, her organic chemistry textbook propped open in front of her, when she met Brandon for the first time.

"Um, excuse me, miss?" she heard him say. "Do you think maybe you could take my order sometime tonight?"

And Mila, unaccountably annoyed by the interruption, glanced up from her textbook and looked at him. She'd been concentrating so hard she hadn't even noticed him come in and sit down at the counter, just three stools away from her.

"You do work here, don't you?" he asked, seeming more amused than annoyed.

"I *do* work here," Mila said, and, using a spoon for a placeholder in her textbook, she slid off her stool and walked around to the other side of the counter.

"I'm sorry about that," she said, reaching into her apron pocket for a check pad and a pencil. "What can I get for you?"

It was only then that she looked—really looked—at this customer. He was tall, and broad shouldered, with dark brown hair shaved into a buzz cut, and wide brown eyes set in a face that was tanned the year-round tan of someone who worked outdoors for a living. Which he did, judging from the flannel shirt, blue jeans, and work boots he was wearing. *Construction worker,* Mila decided, putting him neatly in his slot. But in the next second he surprised her. Most construction workers were hungry. All the time. They wanted to eat first and flirt later. This guy was different. He wanted to flirt first and eat later.

"Don't be sorry," he said. "I'm the one who's interrupting you," he added, gesturing at her textbook. "And that looks like pretty important stuff, Jody."

"Jody?"

"That's what it says on your name tag," he said, pointing to it.

She glanced down at it. "Oh, no, that's not my name. I lost my name tag, actually. But the owner makes us wear them, so I borrow Jody's."

"So, mandatory name tags, huh?" he said, glancing around. "I knew this was a classy place."

And Mila laughed, because under the unforgiving fluorescent lights, the coffee shop looked like exactly what it was. Which was a dump.

He smiled at her now. "Seeing you laugh was worth waiting for," he said. "If I could keep making you do that, I wouldn't care if you ever took my order."

Mila blushed now. She was used to customers flirting with her. But there was something about the way this customer was flirting with her that was different. He was doing it with an intensity, and a single-mindedness that was new to her.

"So what can I get for you?" she asked him again, indicating the menu that was sitting on the counter in front of him. But he didn't look down at it. He looked at her instead. Looked at her in a way that made her think he wasn't particularly interested in the day's special. Unless, of course, *she* happened to be the day's special.

"What's good here?" he asked finally.

And Mila blushed again. "Honestly? Not much. A cup of coffee's always a safe bet. And if you're really hungry, I can get our fry cook to scramble you up some eggs. It's hard to ruin those. But I think he's on a smoke break now." She glanced back at the empty kitchen behind her. "So if it's eggs you want, you may have to wait a few minutes."

"Uh, no thanks. I think I'll pass on the eggs," he said, still not taking his eyes off her. "But what about the pie?"

"The pie?"

"There's a sign outside that says 'Try Our Pie.'"

"Oh, that," Mila said. "That sign's been there forever. But the pie . . . the pie is actually not that great."

"So 'don't try our pie'?" he suggested.

She laughed. "You can see it if you want to." She brought him the pie in its plastic-domed pie cover and set it down on the counter in front of him. "What do you think?" she asked, removing the cover.

"Hmmm," he said, studying it, and probably thinking, like Mila, that it didn't look very appetizing. The crust, for one thing, looked kind of soggy, and the filling, which was some kind of gelatinous red substance, was just sort of leaking out of it.

"What kind of pie is it, exactly?" he asked.

"I'm not sure," she admitted. "Red, maybe?"

He laughed, and Mila laughed, too. "You know what?" he said. "I don't think I'll try your pie. But how about that cup of coffee?"

So Mila covered up the pie again and slid it down the counter. Then she went to get the coffeepot, relieved to have a moment to collect herself. Her face felt warm, and her stomach felt funny. She wished he would stop looking at her in that way he was looking at her. But then again, she would have been disappointed if he had.

She carried the coffeepot over to him and flipped over the cup sitting in front of him on the counter. Then she filled it up and pushed the cream and sugar over to him.

"Thanks," he said, looking away from her long enough to pour cream in his coffee. "Are you going to have a cup, too?"

"Me?"

He nodded, looking at her in *that* way again.

"Um, we're not allowed to socialize with the customers," she said, flustered. "I mean, not any more than is strictly necessary."

"No?" he said, amused. And then, "You know, there are a lot of rules here. Kind of surprising, don't you think, given the quality of the food?"

"Maybe," Mila murmured. But now *she* couldn't look away from *him*.

"So what do you say? One cup of coffee with me?"

An hour later, Mila was sitting on the stool next to his—his name, she'd discovered, was Brandon—drinking her third cup of coffee. She'd probably never sleep again, she thought, but right now, that was just fine with her. Because as long as she kept talking to him, sleep seemed completely inconsequential. And

Brandon didn't seem to be in any hurry to get to bed either. He'd gotten off work from the late shift at his construction job, and now he seemed perfectly content to sit here with Mila all night. Luckily for them, no one else had come into the coffee shop, and Javier, the fry cook, was in the kitchen, talking on his cell phone to his girlfriend in Guatemala.

"What was that book you were studying when I came in?" Brandon asked now, placing a hand lightly on one of her bare knees, which were just visible below the hem of the ugly pink uniform she was required to wear while waitressing there. (Another rule.) The way she was behaving tonight was totally out of character for her, she thought. She'd never crossed the line with a customer at work before. And now, she'd not only crossed it, she didn't even *care* that she'd crossed it.

"Um, I'm sorry. What . . . what did you ask me?" she said, as his hand lightly caressed her knee.

"I asked you what you were studying" he said, gesturing with the hand that wasn't on her knee to where her book was still sitting, a few feet away, on the counter.

"Oh, that," she said, following his eyes. "That's my organic chemistry textbook."

"Organic chemistry," he said, raising his eyebrows. "I'm impressed."

"Don't be. I'm only taking it because I have to. And it's killing me."

"So don't take it," he suggested.

"Oh, no, I have to take it," she said, marveling at how nice his slightly rough hand felt on her knee.

"Why do you have to take it?"

"It's a prerequisite for nursing school."

"You want to be a nurse?" he asked skeptically.

She nodded.

"Why would you want to do that?" he asked. "I mean, isn't that just, like, changing people's bedpans for a living?"

"No, it's not," Mila said, not bothering to conceal her annoyance. "Most nurses, in fact, don't change bedpans at all. But for the ones who do, it's only a small part of their jobs." She moved her knee then, out from under his hand.

"Oh," he said, looking surprised and contrite at the same time. "I'm sorry. I didn't mean to offend you. I obviously don't know a lot about nursing."

Her irritation waned, a little. "You're not alone," she said. "There are a lot of misconceptions about nursing."

"Well, then, maybe you can educate me about them," he said seriously.

"Maybe," she said, softening a little.

"Like tomorrow, maybe. Or should I say 'today,'" he added, glancing at his watch.

Mila shook her head. "Not today. I don't get off work until five A.M. Then I have to go home and go to bed. Then I have to wake up and go to class. And then I have to start all over again."

"That doesn't sound like very much fun," he said, glancing down at her bare knee like he wanted to put his hand on it again.

"It's not supposed to be fun," she said. "It's supposed to get me into a good nursing school." But she swayed a little bit closer to him. Even under the coffee shop's fluorescent lights, he looked good. *Really good.*

"So, 'work,' 'sleep,' 'study,'" he said, putting his hand back on her knee so softly that she had to look down at it to confirm it was actually there.

"That's my life," she agreed, and she suddenly felt too warm in her hideous polyester uniform.

"Do you think you could make time in your life for one more thing?" he asked, giving her a smile that almost made her fall right off her stool.

"Maybe," she said softly.

"Good," he said, giving her knee a little squeeze.

Mila made time for Brandon, but seven months after she'd met him at the coffee shop that night, she was locked in her bathroom, wishing she could get that time back now.

"Mila, please. Unlock the door," he said, from the other side of it.

But she shook her head violently, even though Brandon couldn't see her do this.

"Mila, please. Open the door," he pleaded. "Just for one second. I need to see you. I need to know you're all right." The anger was gone from his voice now, and the blind fury that had erupted from him had apparently subsided as quickly as it had boiled up. He sounded remorseful. Tender, even. But still, it was impossible to ignore what he'd done to her, especially when she had the fat lip to prove it.

"Go away," Mila whispered to the bathroom door, and she choked back another sob.

"Mila, sweetheart, please. I won't hurt you. I promise. I won't even *touch* you, if you don't want me to. But I need to come in," Brandon said gently. Cajolingly. "Look, I know there's no excuse for what just happened. And I don't blame you for being angry at me. But I need to talk to you, Mila, face-to-face. *Please.*"

Mila didn't answer him. Instead, she walked over to the mirror that hung above the bathroom sink and looked into it. She flinched. Her lip looked even worse than she'd imagined it would. One half of it was already swollen to twice its normal size. There was no way she'd be able to go to class tomorrow, and that went double for work. Nobody wanted a fat lip with their dinner order, she thought, as fresh anger welled up inside her, and new tears burned in her eyes.

She reached for a washcloth, ran it under cold water, wrung it out, and held it up to her lip. She winced. It hurt like hell. But she kept it there anyway, hoping it would bring down the swelling. After a few minutes, though, she gave up. The washcloth wasn't cold enough. What she really needed was a bag of ice, and she couldn't get that unless she was willing to leave the bathroom. And she wasn't willing to leave the bathroom. She was planning on staying there, in fact, until Brandon gave up and went home.

"Mila, say something, please," he said now. "Just so I know you're all right."

But she ignored him and sat down on the bathroom floor, resting her back against the side of the bathtub. She was tired. Beyond tired, really. And she wished, desperately, that Brandon would go just home so she could crawl into bed and have a good cry. As far as she was concerned, this was the end of their seven-month relationship. It could never survive this. Though even *before* this, she had to admit, it had been far from perfect.

In the beginning, she hadn't been able to see this. Everything was happening so fast. One minute, Brandon was flirting with her over a cup of coffee, and the next minute . . . well, the next minute stretched into hours, actually. Brandon wanted to be with her all the time, whenever she was free, and sometimes even when she wasn't free. Before she'd met him, she'd never missed a class or called in sick to work. But after she met him, she did both of those things occasionally. She knew it was wrong to shirk her responsibilities, but Brandon's feelings for her were so insistent, so passionate, and so all-consuming that sometimes she had trouble thinking clearly, trouble thinking *at all*, really, except, of course, for when it came to thinking about Brandon. Brandon, who'd told her he was in love with her—crazily, madly, wildly in love with her. And she believed him too. How else could she explain the complete single-mindedness with which he'd pursued her? Or the absolute devotion he'd shown to her after she finally gave in to him?

It was exciting, at first, not to mention flattering, to be wooed the way Brandon wooed her. There were the love notes he wrote to her and tucked into the pages of her college textbooks so that she would find them later while she was studying. And there were the presents he surprised her with, including the beautiful bracelet he slipped into the pocket of her waitressing uniform that she discovered when she reached for her check pad and pencil. And there were the grander gestures, too, gestures that reminded Mila of scenes from some impossibly romantic movie, like the time he drove her out to the country and surprised her there with a picnic that included champagne, strawberries, and several kinds of unpronounceable French cheeses.

Even in those early, heady days, though, there were signs of trouble. For one thing, Brandon needed to know where she was every second of every day. And if she wasn't in class or at work, he expected her to be with him. And only with him. She'd introduced him to a few of her friends, but she quickly realized that he had no interest in spending time with them. And what was more, he had no interest in *her* spending time with them either. In fact, he seemed to resent it when she did. So, gradually, Mila saw less and less of them, until her already limited circle of friends shrank to just one friend: Brandon.

But Brandon's possessiveness wasn't the worst thing about him. His jealousy was. It had started with him being suspicious of her male friends, no matter how innocent her relationships with them were. He was convinced, for instance, that Ted, her study partner in her anatomy class, had a thing for her. And nothing

Mila said could convince him otherwise. Finally, she told Ted she couldn't study with him anymore. She was sorry, too. They worked well together. But she was tired of arguing with Brandon about him.

Even after she stopped seeing Ted, though, Brandon found men in her life to be jealous of. An old friend from high school she and Brandon ran into at a movie theater once. Or a man from down the block whose dog Mila stopped to pet. It was worrying to Mila that Brandon could make even her most innocent social interactions seem fraught with intrigue. And lately, it had driven a wedge between the two of them that had Mila wondering if she could stay in this relationship any longer.

But here she'd been torn. There were good things about Brandon, too. He could be charming, and sweet, and, for all his seriousness, he could be funny, too. He always knew how to make her laugh, and not only that, but he always knew how to make her feel needed and loved, too.

But tonight, tonight had changed everything. Brandon was waiting for her when she came out of the coffee shop, and, at first, she was happy to see him. She'd gotten a biology exam back that day that she'd done well on, and she was in a celebratory mood. She told him, in fact, in his arms outside the coffee shop, exactly how she wanted to celebrate. But Brandon, she quickly realized, was preoccupied, and while she chattered all the way back to her apartment, he remained silent. Finally, when they got back, he spoke.

"Who was that man at the counter tonight?" he asked, sitting down on her living room couch. "The one with the Minnesota Twins baseball cap on."

And Mila groaned inwardly as she sat down on the couch beside him. They'd had this conversation before. Not about this customer. But about other customers. "Brandon, I don't know who he was," she said honestly. "Some guy who wanted a cup of coffee. He was probably getting off a late shift or something."

"So you think he was just there for the coffee?" he asked her, in a tone that implied she was naive.

She sighed, but then decided to use humor to try to diffuse the situation. Humor because logic, apparently, didn't work with Brandon.

"Actually, Brandon, he wasn't just there for a cup of coffee," she said conspiratorially. "He's FBI. He was there to meet a high-level informant. And our fry cook, Javier? That job is a cover. He's actually—"

"Okay. Very funny. I get it," he snapped. "You think I'm paranoid. But I saw the way that man was looking at you, Mila. And that's not the way you look at someone when all you want from her is a refill on your coffee."

"Brandon, he wasn't looking at me. He was reading a newspaper."

"Mila, I saw him looking at you. And I saw him talking to you, too."

"I took his order, Brandon. That's my job."

"No, you did more than take his order. You had a conversation with him. I saw you, Mila. I was watching you."

She paused. She had spoken to that man, briefly. But she'd spoken to him long before the end of her shift, long before Brandon was supposed to pick her up. "How long were you watching me, Brandon?" she asked then, not really wanting to know the answer.

He shrugged. "A while."

"How long is 'a while.'"

"A couple of hours."

"*A couple of hours?* Are you serious, Brandon? Why would you do that?"

"Because I wanted to know what you do at work when I'm not around, Mila."

"I wait tables, Brandon," she said, exasperated. "I think that's pretty obvious. And I don't like the fact that you were watching me do it without my knowing it. It's . . . it's kind of creepy."

"Creepy?" he repeated, tensing. "You think I'm creepy?" There was an air of menace in his voice that she'd never heard before. It frightened her a little.

"No, I don't think *you're* creepy," she said carefully. "I think what you *did* was creepy. There's a difference."

And then it happened, so fast that she didn't even see it coming. One minute they were sitting next to each other on the couch, and the next, the back of his hand was connecting with her face. She screamed, and her hand flew to her mouth. "Oh, my God, Brandon," she said through her fingers. "Why did you do that?" And before he could answer her, she ran to the bathroom and locked herself in. That was an hour ago, and their uneasy standoff had continued since then.

"Mila, please, let me in," Brandon was saying now. "Please. I am *so* sorry. I don't even know what happened. Really, I'm as shocked as you are. I've never done anything like that before. *Ever.* I swear."

"Brandon, just go home," she said finally. Wearily. "I'm tired, and I need to get some sleep. If I can get the swelling in my lip to go down, I'll have to go to class and work tomorrow."

"Your lip . . . your lip is swollen?" he asked. He sounded horrified.

"Yes, Brandon. It's very swollen."

"Oh, Mila," she heard him say softly. And then a moment later she heard something else. At first she thought she was imagining it. But when she got up from sitting on the floor and pressed her ear against the bathroom door, she realized she wasn't imagining it. It was actually happening. Brandon was crying.

She was so astonished that she forgot, momentarily, how angry she was. "Brandon," she said, unlocking the door and cracking it open. He was sitting on the floor of the hallway, his face buried in his hands. She came hesitantly out of the bathroom and knelt down beside him. Then she touched his face. It was wet. He gave another ragged sob and wiped impatiently at his eyes with the back of his hand.

"Brandon, you're crying," she said wonderingly. She'd never seen a man cry before, though admittedly, her experience with men was limited. She'd never known her father. And she'd only dated a few guys in high school and college. Those relationships, though, had been pretty uncomplicated. There hadn't been any crying in them, hers or theirs.

"Brandon, why are you crying," she asked now, feeling an unexpected tug of sympathy for him.

"I'm crying because I hurt you," he said miserably. "Why would I hurt you, Mila, when I love you so much?"

"I don't know," Mila said truthfully.

He looked up at her now, for the first time, and saw her lip. Another sob, low and hoarse, escaped from him. "Jesus, Mila, what have I done to you?"

"You gave me a fat lip," she said, her fingers moving to touch it gingerly. "And judging from the feel of it, it's getting fatter by the minute."

He went and got her a bag of ice then and coaxed her back onto the couch in the living room. Then he held the ice carefully against her lip. The pressure hurt, but the cold felt good. And when her lip got a little numb, it took the edge off the pain.

He talked to her then about everything that was happening in his life. The stress, he said, had been building up for a while. There was his new construction crew boss, who, for some reason, didn't like Brandon and would always make him do the hardest jobs, and then always complained about how he did them. There was his family, too. He didn't get along with his parents, especially his dad, who, he explained, was a real hothead who'd thrown him out of the house when Brandon was still practically a teenager. But mostly, he said, the pressure in his life had to do with Mila.

"With *me*?" she said when he told her this. "How am I making you feel pressured?"

"You're not doing it on purpose," he said. "It's just that . . . it's just that I love you so much, Mila. And I'm afraid you don't love me the same way. Or, worse"—his brown eyes searched hers—"I'm afraid there's someone else you love instead of me."

"Brandon, there's no one else," she said automatically. But she didn't say anything about loving him the same way he loved her, because she didn't know if she did. He seemed to love her so intensely. So . . . so *crazily,* almost. Much later, of course, Mila realized that what Brandon had felt for her wasn't necessarily love. It was instead a feeling born of a need to possess her, to control her. To *own* her, really. But in her naïveté, she believed he loved her, though not necessarily in a way she *wanted* to be loved. She tried to tell him that now.

"Brandon, I do care about you. Very much. But the way you care about me—"

"*Love* you," he interrupted.

"The way you love me," she continued, "it makes me feel uncomfortable sometimes. Like you're . . . like you're suffocating me. A little bit, anyway. And I can't understand why you feel so jealous all the time. Why, when I tell you I'm not attracted to other men, you don't believe me."

"It's probably because you're so beautiful," he said, almost reverently. "And so amazing. What man wouldn't want you, Mila? And knowing that, I just don't have any peace of mind, I guess. And I won't, either. Until I make you mine."

"Make me yours?" she echoed, with a slight frown.

Brandon nodded seriously. "Yes, Mila. I want to marry you."

She stared back at him uncomprehendingly.

"Well, you don't have to look so shocked," Brandon said, obviously hurt by her response.

"Brandon, I *am* shocked. We've never talked about this before."

"Well, maybe we should, Mila. I love you. I want us to get married. I want us to spend the rest of our lives together."

But Mila could only shake her head. "Brandon, you can't be serious."

"I'm completely serious," he said. "In fact, I've been thinking about it since the night I met you. Will you marry me, Mila? Will you be my wife?"

"Brandon," she said softly. "I can't marry you."

"Give me one reason why not."

"I'll give you a hundred."

"Okay, then, forget it. Don't give me a reason why not. Just answer a question for me, Mila. And answer it honestly."

She hesitated. "All right."

He took the ice pack off her lip and looked into her eyes. "Has anyone ever loved you the way I love you, Mila?"

"Brandon—"

"No, seriously. Think about it. *Really* think about it. And be honest with yourself about it, too. Has anyone ever loved you the way I have?"

Have they? she wondered. Her mother loved her, she supposed, in her own way. Her own ineffectual way. But when Mila was growing up, she'd made no secret of the fact that mothering Mila was, at best, inconvenient, and, at worse, burdensome. Not surprisingly, they'd never been close, and now that her mother had moved away, they'd drifted even further apart. And then there was Heather. Heather cared about her. Mila knew she did, and when she needed to be reminded of it, she reread Heather's letters to her. But while Heather was a big part of Mila's life, she thought now, Mila was a smaller part of Heather's life. After all, Heather had a husband, and two sons now, with a third son on the way. Add to that her part-time nursing job at a community clinic, and her full-time job working on a family farm, and it was easy to wonder how Heather even had time to *think* about her, let alone *write* to her.

Mila sighed. Her lip was still throbbing, but there was a new pain now, a dull, hollow ache that seemed to reside somewhere deep in her chest. It was loneliness, she knew, and it had been there all her life. Well, most of her life. Except for the times she'd spent in Heather's office. And except for these last few months with Brandon. Because when things had been good between them, when Brandon was at his best, that ache had receded. That ache had almost disappeared completely. Was that what it meant to be loved? Really loved? Did it make the loneliness go away? Or at least far enough away that you could forget, for a little while at least, that it was even there?

"Mila, has anyone ever loved you the way I have?" Brandon asked again.

"No," she said suddenly. "No, Brandon. They haven't."

"I didn't think so," he said, reaching out and stroking her hair. "And, Mila? I promise that what happened tonight will never happen again."

"It can't happen again, Brandon. I mean it. If it does . . ." *If it does, it's over,* she almost said, but she didn't want to spoil the moment.

"Mila, I swear. It won't. You have my word on it."

"Okay, then." She tested out a smile on him.

"Okay, 'what'?"

"Okay, let's get married," she said, feeling suddenly giddy and lighthearted.

"Really?" he asked, as if not trusting his luck.

"Really."

"Oh, Mila," he said, reaching for her. But he didn't kiss her. He couldn't. Her lip was still too sensitive. So he held her instead, and Mila held him back and tried, hard, to tamp down all those uncomfortable thoughts she'd had about their relationship when she was locked in the bathroom.

Chapter 10

The week after her picnic with Reid, Mila was studying her test prep books when she heard a light tap on her bedroom door.

"Just a second, Lonnie," she called out, but when she opened the door, she saw that it was Allie.

"Oh, hi," Mila said, a little uncertainly.

"Hi," Allie said, smiling. "Do you have a minute? Because if you don't, I can come back another time."

"Oh, no, it's fine," Mila said. "Now's as good a time as any," she added, opening her door wider and gesturing for Allie to come in.

"Thanks," Allie said, and as she walked past, Mila saw that she was carrying a small shopping bag.

Allie sat down on the chair beside the bed, and Mila perched anxiously on the edge of the bed. She wasn't used to having visitors in her room, and she was worried too that Reid might have told Walker and Allie about what she'd said to him the morning of his doctor's appointment. But no sooner had she considered this thought than she dismissed it. In the days since their picnic, there'd been no more conversations between her and Reid, but there'd been no more arguments, either, and the old hostility that Reid had exhibited toward her had been replaced by a new reserve. It wasn't a perfect working relationship yet—it was still too formal on his side, and too self-conscious on hers—but it was so much better now than it had been before that Mila couldn't imagine Reid trying to sabotage it.

"Is there something I can do for you?" she asked Allie, trying to relax. She liked Allie. She'd been as good as her word when she'd told Mila that she or Walker would stop by at least once a day to check on things; often, in fact, they stopped by more than once, sometimes separately and sometimes together. But so far, Mila's conversations with Allie had taken place in the kitchen and had been limited either to pleasantries or to the occasional progress report on Reid. And since Mila didn't usually have any progress to report on his behalf, these conversations still tended to be brief.

"Actually," Allie said now, "I was hoping there was something that *I* could do for you."

"Me?"

Allie nodded. "I brought you something," she said, handing Mila the shopping bag, and when Mila hesitated, she said, "It's a present. Open it."

"It's a present for me?"

"Of course for you," Allie said, amused.

With some reluctance, Mila reached inside the bag and peeled back the tissue paper inside it. She wasn't accustomed to getting presents. As a child, she'd only gotten them when her mother felt guilty about leaving her alone for too long. And as an adult, she'd only gotten them when Brandon felt contrite about "losing his temper" with her. She shuddered now, unconsciously, as she extracted an article of clothing from the tissue paper. No wonder she didn't like presents.

"Oh, it's a bathing suit," she said, holding it up.

Allie nodded. "I had to guess your size," she said. "But I have a pretty good eye for that kind of thing. I think it'll fit you. What do you think?"

Mila studied it. It was a one-piece, red with white polka dots and a jaunty little ruffle at the neckline. It was cute, she thought. And Allie was right. It did look like it would fit her. There was only one problem with it; she didn't need it.

"It's, it's really nice," she told Allie now, not wanting to seem ungracious. "But I don't know how to swim."

"I know," Allie said. "Reid told me."

"He did?" Mila asked, surprised. She wondered why Reid would tell Allie that.

Allie nodded. "Uh-huh. And he asked me if I could teach you how. For some reason, he remembered that I used to be a swim instructor during my summers off from college. So what do you say? Are you interested in learning?"

Mila hesitated, not sure how she felt about any of this, particularly the part about actually having to be in the water. What she finally said, though, was, "Allie, you can't possibly have the time right now to teach me to swim."

"Actually, I do," Allie said. "I just hired someone to work at the gallery two afternoons a week."

"But don't, don't you want to do something else with that time? Like, take a nap or something?" Mila asked, because as pretty as Allie looked, she looked tired, too. And, really, how could she *not* be tired when you considered all the things she was responsible for?

Allie only shook her head though. "Oh, no. I definitely don't want to take a nap. Do you know what happens when I try to take a nap, Mila? I lie on my bed, and stare up at the ceiling, and make mental lists of all the things I need to do. By the time I give up on the whole idea of falling asleep, I'm a complete wreck. No, I want to do something fun."

"And teaching someone how to swim is fun?" Mila asked doubtfully.

"Well, for me it is. I like doing it, and I'm good at it, too. Or at least I used to be good at it. But I think I probably still am. I'll let you be the judge of that, though, if you decide to take me up on my offer."

But Mila was still unsure. "What about Reid," she asked. "What will he do while you're teaching me?"

Allie shrugged. "Well, he'll probably do what he always does. Which is, sort of . . . nothing, I guess."

Mila frowned a little. Not because it wasn't true. Most of the time, it was. But she was remembering, for some reason, the way Reid had smiled as he'd skipped rocks over the sun-dappled water of the lake.

"I'm sorry," Allie said quickly, misunderstanding Mila's silence. "That was rude of me to say about Reid. I'm sure he does things to keep busy," she said, though she looked like she couldn't for the life of her imagine what those things were. "I guess what I meant, Mila, is that I think Reid can manage without you for an hour. Especially since the swimming lessons were his idea." Allie paused then. "Unless you don't want to learn how to swim," she added. "In which case, that's fine. Really, no pressure. It's just . . ." Her voice trailed off.

"Just what?"

"It's just, it seems like a shame, somehow, to spend the summer on this beautiful lake without being able to swim in it," Allie said. "And there's the safety issue, too. I mean, you can avoid *this* lake *this* summer, I guess. But what about in the future? What if there was a time you needed to know how to swim, but you couldn't?"

"I don't know," Mila said honestly. "It's never been an issue before."

"And it probably won't be. But what if it was?"

"I guess it could be, one day," Mila conceded. "But I feel like I should spend my time here working. And as it is, I already spend a big part of every day *not* working." She didn't say that there were days when, between Lonnie's efficiency and Reid's reclusiveness, she not only felt as if she should be getting paid *less*, she felt as if she shouldn't be getting paid *at all*.

But Allie obviously disagreed. "Trust me, Mila. I know Reid. And no matter how little time you're spending with him, the time you do spend with him qualifies as work. Hard work."

"Oh, it's not that bad," Mila said. "*He's* not that bad." And she marveled, once again, that since that day they'd spent together, she'd been feeling . . . feeling differently about Reid. Differently in a way she couldn't explain.

Allie only smiled, though, and tucked a strand of her honey brown hair behind an ear. "Well, *of course* he's not that bad," she agreed. "Walker and I know that.

We just didn't know if *you* knew it yet. So what do you say? To the swimming lessons, I mean?"

"All right," Mila said, smiling back at her. "But I can't promise I'll be a fast learner," she warned.

"That's okay," Allie said, standing up. "The summer isn't even half over yet. So, right here, down at the dock, on Tuesdays and Thursdays from two o'clock to three o'clock, all right?"

"I'll be here," Mila said, smiling, and feeling a little pulse of excitement. She was afraid of deep water, that was true, but they wouldn't start out in deep water, would they? Besides, even a nonswimmer like her could appreciate how temptingly cool and refreshing Butternut Lake looked on a warm, sunny day.

"Good," Allie said now. "I'll speak to Lonnie, too. I'm hoping to coordinate Brooke's nap with the lessons, but Lonnie will still need to watch her here."

"Lonnie will love that," Mila said, knowing how much Lonnie was looking forward to being a grand-mother one day.

"I'll see you Tuesday, then," Allie said, standing up.

"Thanks for the bathing suit, Allie," Mila said, feeling suddenly shy again as she walked her to her bedroom door. "It's really pretty."

"You're welcome," Allie said, and she was leaving when she stopped and turned around. "By the way,

Mila, that red will look great with your coloring," she said, and then she was gone. And Mila took the bathing suit over to the mirror above the dresser and held it up to herself, studying it thoughtfully. Allie was right, she realized with surprise. It *did* look good with her coloring. And she remembered now how badly she'd wanted a bathing suit as a child. Funny, though, she hadn't known how badly she'd *still* wanted one. Until now.

One minute, Reid was lying in his bed, willing himself to stay awake, and the next he was back in his car, after the accident, and night was coming on, and coming on fast. *I have to get help,* he thought, as he fought to keep the panic at bay. *I won't survive another night like this.* But he didn't know if he could trust his voice to call for help; the last time he'd done it he'd sounded like a croaking frog. He tried to swallow, but there was no saliva left in his mouth and his throat felt like it was lined with sandpaper. The thirst, in some ways, was worse than the pain. It consumed him in a way the pain did not, especially since he could hear a stream running nearby, and he could imagine its clear water gathering in drinkable pools.

But now he pushed the thought of water out of his mind. He needed to stay focused. He took a deep breath—as deep a breath as he could, given that the steering wheel was digging into his chest and several of his ribs, he knew, were broken—and then he called out, "Help me, please. Somebody help me!" *Christ,* his voice was barely audible, even to him. He tried again, louder this time, as loud as he possibly could. "Help me," he screamed, and still the words sounded no louder than a whisper. He couldn't give up, though. Not now. Not when he still had a little fight left in him. So he kept calling, over and over again, for what felt like an eternity, "Help me, help me. *Please, help me!*"

And this time, miraculously, somebody heard him. He knew they'd heard him because they answered him.

"*Reid?* Reid. It's okay. I'm here."

"You know my name?" he murmured, in amazement. He opened his eyes, but he couldn't see anything yet.

"Of course I know your name," the voice said gently. "I was worried about you."

And then, "You're all sweaty, Reid. Could I . . . could we take off your pajama top?"

Pajama top? He blinked and looked around as his bedroom, and then Mila, came into focus.

"Oh, it's you," he said, his heart still pounding.

"It's me," she said, a little warily. "Look, I know you told me not to come in here uninvited. But tonight, your dream . . . it was worse than the others. It went on for so long, and you were thrashing around so much, I was afraid you were going to hurt yourself. Or hurt yourself more than you're already hurt."

He nodded but said nothing. He was trying to breathe normally. Strangely enough, the dream still felt more real to him than this room, which seemed somehow watery and insubstantial. Mila, he decided then, was the most concrete thing here, and he tried to concentrate on her now. She'd turned on the lamp on his bedside table, and he saw in its light that she was dressed in a T-shirt and blue jeans, her auburn hair pulled back in a slightly messy ponytail.

"What . . . what time is it?" he asked.

She glanced at the clock on his bedside table. "It's three A.M.," she said.

"You're dressed," he pointed out.

"I got dressed before I came in here," she said. "Now, why don't we get you out of this, okay?" She gestured at his pajama top and Reid realized, for the first time, that it was damp with perspiration.

He didn't answer, but he didn't protest, either, when she started unbuttoning his pajama top. And then he watched, strangely detached, as she slid it off his shoulders and down his arms. It was such an intimate gesture, but Mila did it without any intimacy, her fingers moving with such lightness and sureness that their touch barely registered on his skin.

"Do you mind if I open the window?" she asked, laying his pajama top on the chair beside the bed. "It's a little stuffy in here," she added, almost apologetically.

"No, go ahead," he said, realizing she was wrong about the room being a little stuffy; it was actually swelteringly hot. But he'd gotten into the habit of keeping his window closed, whatever the temperature outside.

"It's such a nice night," Mila said, opening the window. "You should see the moon, too," she continued, almost conversationally, as she came back to his bedside. "It's absolutely enormous. And it's so bright. The lake looks like it has floodlights on it."

"When were you looking at the moon?" Reid asked. "I mean, weren't you asleep before . . ." *Before my screaming woke you up.*

Mila shook her head. "No, I couldn't sleep. I was studying my test prep books, and when I couldn't study anymore, I was looking at the moon."

"You were studying at three o'clock in the morning?"

"Well, it seemed better than just . . . not sleeping," she said, and there was something about the way she said it that made him think she was often awake at night. He considered asking her about this, one insomniac to another, but she chose this moment to reach down and press the palm of her hand, lightly but firmly, against his bare chest.

"Reid, you're burning up," she said, taking her hand away. "I know your brother's the only one you'll let give you a bath, but could I sponge you off just enough to cool you down? Just on your upper body?"

A breeze blew through the open window then, ruffling the window curtain and touching Reid's bare skin with its delicious coolness, and he thought about what Mila had said about how enormous the moon was tonight. "Yeah, all right," he said. "But could we do that out on the deck?" Because now, of course, he wanted to see that moon too.

Mila hesitated. "All right," she said. "We can do that. Just give me a minute, okay?" She left then and he heard her turn off the cabin's alarm, and open and close the linen closet in the hallway, and run water in the kitchen. And then she was back, with towels and an enamel basin full of water. She handed him his crutches, then, and positioned his wheelchair beside his bed, and looked away tactfully as he struggled into it. He had to work hard to keep his hands steady; the dream's adrenaline was still pulsing through him.

After he'd gotten himself into his wheelchair, he wheeled himself out of his room, down the hallway, and into the living room, where he first saw the moon through the wall of glass that faced onto the lake. "*Unbelievable,*" he murmured as Mila slid open the door to the deck, and he propelled himself over its threshold. The moon was hanging, huge and low and heavy, its white iridescence bathing everything it touched—water, trees, deck—in a pale, silvery light.

"I guess we don't need to turn on the deck lights," he said, wheeling himself over to the railing.

"Not tonight," Mila agreed, joining him there, and, commandeering a small table to put the basin on, she gestured for Reid to lean forward, and she draped a towel over the back of his wheelchair. Then she took the washcloth, dipped it into the basin, rung it out, and started to sponge him off with it, gently, first his shoulders, then his arms, and then his chest. And Reid, still tense from his dream, was, for a moment, tenser still. But gradually, he began to relax. Partly it was because Mila, who'd slipped effortlessly into her nursing role, was so unselfconscious about doing this that it made him feel unselfconscious about having her do it. And partly, it was because what she was doing felt so good, so different from his brother's clumsy attempts to bathe him.

"It's not too cold, is it?" Mila asked of the water in the basin, but Reid shook his head. *It's perfect,* he almost said, as she slid the cool, nubby washcloth over his chest. But he didn't say anything. He didn't want to interrupt her. She was settling into a rhythm now, dipping the washcloth in the bowl, ringing it out, and sponging his shoulders and chest and arms with it. He felt the memory of his dream receding, and, as it did so, he felt the fear, the panic, and the sheer adrenaline rush of it all ebb slowly away. And what flowed back into its place was an almost hypnotic calm, a calm Reid knew he hadn't experienced since before the accident.

And once again, he was fascinated by Mila's hands, just as he had been on the drive back from his doctor's appointment. Their movements were so fluid and so graceful that they were a pleasure to watch. How was it possible that those small, pale hands, with their neat, oval nails, could be so capable, so confident, and yet so gentle at the same time?

"Your hands," he said, without thinking, "you're good with them, aren't you?"

"Good with them?" Mila repeated, looking faintly surprised, and Reid realized that, like him, she'd been lost in the moment. Now she dipped the washcloth in the bowl, wrung it out, and sponged his shoulders with it. "I guess I am good with them. Someone told me once that I had nurse's hands," she added, musingly.

"Nurse's hands? Is that what they are?" he asked, as the washcloth moved over his arms again. "Well, that's good, isn't it? You want to be a nurse."

Mila nodded, sponging his chest with the washcloth now. And, without thinking, Reid reached out and took one of her hands, the one holding the washcloth, and gently pried the washcloth out of it. It wasn't that he wanted her to stop what she was doing. He didn't. But he wanted to take a closer look at her hand. He was careful not to look at her then as he held her hand by the wrist and, very slowly and very deliberately, turned it palm side up and looked at it from that angle. *Is this a nurse's hand?* Reid wondered, studying it. He supposed it might be. But right now, it didn't look like a hand that could ever do anything ordinary or prosaic. It looked beautiful. Smooth, and pale and lustrous in the moonlight. And it seemed to him to be almost impossibly lovely. Which was why he raised it to his lips and kissed it, on what seemed to be its palest and most tender point, right on the inside of the wrist.

He heard Mila suck in a little breath of surprise then, and he understood. He felt the same way. It was one of the few times in his life he had done something without knowing he was going to do it first. He waited for her to admonish him, or draw her hand away, or make some joke about what he'd done to lighten the mood, but she didn't do any of those things. And when he looked at her, he saw that she was watching him carefully. Intently. He couldn't read her expression. But she didn't look angry. She looked . . . she looked something else. Vulnerable, he decided. But not angry.

He let go of her hand, and he thought he saw it tremble, a little, as she drew it back. But he might have imagined that because when she began to sponge him off again, she did it with the same steadiness as she had before.

A few minutes later though, the wind strengthened, sending clouds scudding across the moon, rippling the surface of the lake, and stirring the branches of the great northern pines that towered above the deck.

"I think it's time to go inside," Mila said, putting the washcloth inside the basin and picking it up.

And Reid, knowing that it was over, sighed. Mila patted him dry with the towel she'd draped over the back of his wheelchair and followed him as he wheeled himself back inside. She paused to lock the sliding glass door behind them and detoured to the kitchen to reset the alarm. And then he was back in his room again. The room he was actually starting to hate.

"Do you need anything, Reid?" Mila asked him, from his doorway.

He shook his head, thinking that once again they'd returned to themselves, back to a studied calmness on her part and a familiar moodiness on his.

"Okay," she said. She started to close his door and then she stopped. "By the way, Reid, thank you for asking Allie to teach me how to swim. My first lesson is in a couple of days."

He nodded.

"Well, good night then," she said, and she closed his door and retreated to her room. But Reid didn't get back into bed. He stayed in his wheelchair, meditatively wheeling it back and forth, and thinking about the inside of her wrist. The skin there was so pale it was nearly translucent, and so soft it was like the velvety touch of the moonlight itself.

Chapter 11

"Here, put this on," Allie said, tossing Mila a bulky orange life preserver.

"Really?" Mila asked, holding it up. It looked like something a child would wear. A *large* child.

But Allie, standing in the doorway of the cabin's boathouse, only smiled. "Look," she said, "I know what you're thinking, and you're right. I could give you something to wear that would be easier on your ego. A waterskiing vest, for instance. But our first objective is for you to get comfortable being in the water, and, Mila, trust me, with this on, you'll *know* you're not going to sink."

Mila sighed, but she slipped the life preserver on over her new bathing suit and fastened and tightened all its straps.

"Good," Allie said, satisfied. "Now let's go." She led Mila out onto the dock that adjoined the boathouse, sat down on the edge of it, and lowered herself into the shallow water. "When you get your confidence up a little, we'll use the ladder at the other end. But for now, we'll just walk in, okay?"

"Okay," Mila said, and she smiled because Allie, in her sensible black tank suit and no-nonsense manner, had already slipped seamlessly back into swim instructor mode. All that was missing, Mila decided, was a whistle around her neck and a clipboard in her hands. But Allie was waiting for her, so Mila eased herself into the lake too. The water was only knee-high where she stood, so she didn't feel nervous yet, just faintly ridiculous in her cumbersome life preserver. Still, she was surprised to discover that even though it was only the first day of July, Butternut Lake was already pleasantly warm. *Funny,* she thought. Its deep, alpine blueness had always made it look cold to her.

"Did you see the moon a couple of nights ago?" Allie asked, as the two of them waded out into deeper water.

"I did," Mila said, thinking not of the moon that night, but of the impromptu sponge bath she'd given Reid on the deck. She saw herself, now, running the washcloth down one of his smooth, bare shoulders.

"In all the summers I've been up here, I've never seen the moon look that big before," Allie said. "Even Brooke was impressed by it."

Mila smiled, but now she was remembering something else: the way Reid's kiss, scratchy from his beard, had felt on the inside of her wrist. She shivered suddenly, though the sunshine was warm on her shoulders, and the breeze was as gentle as a caress.

"You're not nervous, are you?" Allie asked, seeing her shiver.

"Not yet," Mila assured her, but that was only because the sandy lake bottom was still firmly beneath her feet. As they walked out, though, the water inched steadily up, first to her navel, next to her breastbone, and finally to her shoulders. They were flush with the end of the dock then and flush with the ladder Allie had pointed out to her a few minutes ago. So people just climbed, casually, into water this deep? Mila wondered. But of course they did, she reminded herself. They already knew how to swim.

"Everything okay?" Allie asked.

"Uh-huh," Mila said. But she must not have sounded very convincing because Allie said, "Why don't we stop here. I think that's deep enough for today."

Mila nodded. She was of the opinion that it was deep enough for any day.

"Do you think you could try floating on your back now?" Allie asked.

"Floating?" Mila repeated, mildly alarmed.

"Yes, floating. All you have to do, Mila, is lean back; your life preserver will do the rest."

Mila swallowed nervously. She preferred to stand.

"Mila, trust me, you're perfectly safe. That life preserver would keep you afloat in a tsunami."

Mila sighed. She knew that Allie was right. But it didn't stop her from imagining herself sinking, like a stone, to the bottom of the lake.

Allie only smiled, though, a patient, encouraging smile that Mila knew was as much a part of her swim teacher's arsenal as the whistle and clipboard had been. She took a step closer to Mila and put her arm around her.

"Here, I've got you," she said. "Just lean back and relax. I promise, nothing's going to happen to you."

So Mila leaned back, into the life preserver and into Allie's arm, which was supporting the small of her back, and she realized, in the next moment, that she was floating, her legs stretched out in front of her, her toes poking out of the water.

"How's this?" Allie asked.

"It's . . . it's okay," Mila said, even though she felt a little strange, a little . . . *unmoored,* bobbing there on top of the water.

"Is it okay if I let go?" Allie asked.

Mila nodded, and she felt Allie's arm disappear from beneath her.

"Keep your back arched," Allie instructed. "Imagine that you're trying to keep your stomach above the waterline."

Mila tried this, and, amazingly, it worked. She continued to float on her back, legs stretched out in front of her.

"There you go," Allie said, sounding pleased, and she stayed nearby while Mila looked up at the sky, which, from this new perspective, seemed endless, an enormous light blue dome hinging neatly onto the dark blue flatness of the water. She took a deep breath, her first since she'd gotten into the lake. *This is nice,* she thought. *This is relaxing.* And it was. Together, the life preserver and the water seemed to be almost holding her. Cradling her. A breeze blew, and Mila rocked gently on it and closed her eyes. She stayed this way for a little while, thinking, at first, of nothing in particular, and then thinking of the night on the deck with Reid. She saw Reid's shoulders in the moonlight and felt the pressure of his fingers on her hand, the brush of his lips against her skin. When she opened her eyes, a moment later, everything seemed to have pulled away from her—the cabin on the bluff above them, the boat-house, the dock, even Allie—and all that was left in their place was water and sky, sky and water. She didn't feel the bulky life preserver anymore, either. Instead, she felt completely weightless.

"How do you feel, Mila?" she heard Allie ask, from somewhere on the periphery of all this blueness.

"I feel . . . I feel free," she answered.

"Reid? *Reid!* Wake up. It's okay. You're safe. You're here, you're at the cabin. Reid, please, open your eyes."

He opened his eyes, and Mila swam slowly into focus. She was leaning over his bed, her hands on his shoulders, a worried expression on her face. "Are you awake?" she asked.

He blinked and stared up at her. It was hard, he thought, much harder than she knew, to leave the wreckage of his car, with the woods pressing in on it, and the chilly night falling all around it, and to come back to this place. To this cabin, to this bedroom, to this person. To Mila.

"Are you all right?" she asked, her hands still on his

shoulders. He liked her hands there, he decided. He didn't want her to take them away. She didn't. He felt his heart slow a little, his breathing return to something approaching normal.

"Just say something, Reid. So I know you're okay," she said.

He said the first thing that came into his mind. "You look different." And she did. He was used to seeing her dressed in her nondescript clothes, her hair trained back in a neat ponytail, but tonight she was wearing a white cotton nightgown, and her auburn hair was loose on her shoulders. And there was something else, too. She looked as if she might have gotten a little sun during her first swimming lesson that afternoon because her cheeks had a faint pink coloring that he didn't remember being there before. She looked so young now, so unguarded, and so . . . *oh hell, who was he kidding,* she looked so lovely, too, and thinking this he felt that same shock of recognition he'd felt the day they'd skipped stones together at the beach.

"I look different?" she repeated and then she seemed, suddenly, to remember herself. "Oh," she said, letting go of his shoulders and folding her arms, self-consciously, across her chest. "You mean because I'm wearing a nightgown? I'm sorry, I would have gotten dressed, but I . . . I wanted to try something else tonight. With your dream, I mean."

"What was that?" he asked, wishing she would put her hands back on his shoulders.

"Well, I had this idea that if I woke you up as soon as you started dreaming, or at least as soon as I *knew* you'd started dreaming, I could kind of, you know, head it off at the pass. Stop it before it got too bad. Did it . . . did it work?" she asked. She'd uncrossed her arms and she was using her hands now to try to bring some order to her disheveled hair.

"Did what work?" he said distractedly. He was having trouble paying attention to what she was saying. Her thin white nightgown seemed to be almost glowing in the lamplight, and she was standing close enough to his bed for him to smell a faint but delicious scent emanating from her. Coconut, he decided. Some kind of body lotion, probably. Funny, he'd never liked the smell of coconut before, but on her, it smelled delicious.

"Was your dream better tonight, or, if not better, then less intense maybe? Or shorter?" she pressed.

"Um, I don't know about *better*," he said, remembering the dream. But then again, he thought, looking around, he wasn't covered with sweat, and his sheets weren't all tangled up, so maybe his dream had at least been shorter.

"Reid," she said, fidgeting nervously with her nightgown, "I've been doing some research on post-traumatic stress disorder, and I don't know if you know this but—"

"I don't have posttraumatic stress disorder," he said, interrupting her. He reached for the glass of water on his bedside table. "I'm not a soldier, and I didn't fight in a war."

"Reid, you don't have to have been a soldier to have PTSD," she said quickly, as if she thought he might interrupt her again. "People get it for all different reasons. I read one study that said that people who survive a heart attack are at risk for developing it, and I read another one that said that the wives of soldiers returning from Iraq and Afghanistan are also at risk for developing it, even though they've never been anywhere near—"

"I *don't* have PTSD," Reid said, again, and then, because his voice had sounded harsher than he'd intended it to, he added, in a milder tone, "Thank you, though, for your concern. But this is something I'm going to have to figure out for myself, all right?"

She hesitated, and he knew she wanted to say more on the subject, but he saw her decide against it. For now anyway. "All right," she said, with a little sigh.

And then, "Before I go back to bed, is there anything I can do for you?"

You can stay here, he almost said. Because he was suddenly dreading the prospect of being alone again. But he didn't know how to say this to her. Truth be told, he barely knew how to say it to himself. He thought about asking her to get him another glass of water. Or a couple of Advil, maybe, or a magazine . . . or something, *anything,* really, to make her stay a little longer, but already her hand was hovering over the switch on the bedside table lamp. "Try to get some sleep, Reid," she said quietly. "Some *real* sleep." And then she turned off the light and started to close the door.

"Don't go," Reid said, almost under his breath, and he thought for a moment that she hadn't heard him. But she stopped closing the door and came back into the room. She turned on the bedside table lamp and looked at him, her expression gentle, but questioning.

"I don't want to be alone," he mumbled, embarrassed, and he looked away from her again. "I don't want to have that dream again."

"Is it always the same dream?" she asked.

"Most of the time," he said, looking not at her but at the wall beside his bed.

"What happens in it?"

He studied the wall carefully. He'd never told anyone about the dream before. "I'm in the car. I'm trapped, and I'm . . . I'm shouting, I'm trying to get help. I know if it doesn't come soon . . . I . . . I won't make it."

"Does help ever come?"

He shook his head, and then he looked back at her warily. But she didn't ask him any more questions. Instead, she said, "I'll stay here." Indicating the armchair in the corner of his room, she added, "I'll sit over there."

"Will you be able to sleep there?"

She raised her slender shoulders. "It doesn't matter. I can always take a nap tomorrow."

"No, really, go back to bed," he said. "I probably won't be able to go back to sleep tonight anyway."

"Because of the dream?"

He nodded.

She looked thoughtful. "Look, why don't I stay for tonight," she said, after a moment. "I don't mind. And you try to sleep, Reid. If you have the dream again, I'll wake you up again, right away, okay?"

"Okay," he said, his relief palpable. "There's an extra pillow and blanket in the closet."

He watched while she helped herself to these and settled into the chair. He turned off the bedside table lamp, but when his eyes had adjusted to the darkness, he could see her outline, curled up in the chair.

She couldn't be comfortable there, he thought. But he'd be lying if he said he didn't want her to stay. He blinked sleepily, surprised at how tired he felt. He almost never went back to sleep after he'd had the dream. But tonight, with Mila there, he felt himself begin to relax, a little, and, eventually, he felt himself start the long, slow slide toward sleep. He tried, once, to stop it, but then it was too late, so he gave up and let go.

When Reid woke up the next morning, the room was flooded with sunlight, and the armchair was empty. He could hear Lonnie in the kitchen, making familiar sounds with pots and pans. And what about Mila? he wondered guiltily. Had she slept at all last night? He certainly had. He'd slept better, in fact, than he had in weeks. And if he'd had the dream again, it had left no impression on his consciousness.

You look like you could use a little more coffee," Lonnie said, refilling Mila's cup at the breakfast table that morning.

"Do I?" Mila said, barely suppressing a yawn. But it wasn't her tiredness that was worrying her. It was her neck. She rubbed the crick in it now, making a mental note to sleep in a different position if she ever slept in that armchair again. Still, it had been worth it. As far as she knew, Reid hadn't had the dream again, and when she'd left his room, in the gray light of dawn, he'd been sleeping peacefully, one arm thrown over his head.

"Do you think Reid liked his oatmeal?" Lonnie asked now, a little worriedly. She was standing at the kitchen sink, elbows deep in soapy water and that morning's breakfast dishes.

"I can't imagine he didn't," Mila said. "It was delicious."

"I don't know," Lonnie fretted. "I think I may have put too much brown sugar in it. You know me, I have a hopeless sweet tooth." But before she could reassure her again that the oatmeal had been fine, Mila heard the familiar rumble of the UPS truck coming up the driveway.

Lonnie heard it, too. "Oh, that'll be Hank," she said, reaching for a dish towel to wipe her hands on. Hank, Mila now knew, was the name of the driver who delivered Lonnie's packages to the cabin.

"I'll be right back," Lonnie said, using her fingers to fluff her blond hair a little before she rushed out the door. And Mila, going back to her coffee, smiled to herself. Lonnie got a *lot* of packages. Enough packages for Mila to wonder if her home shopping habit had more to do with her feeling lonely at night, as she'd told

Mila, or with the idea of Hank delivering packages in the morning. Probably a little bit of both, Mila decided, as Hank handed Lonnie a cardboard box. Like Lonnie, Hank was in his late fifties or early sixties. But whereas Lonnie was soft and round all over, his long, lanky body appeared to be all angles and edges in his brown uniform. They looked nice together, though, Mila thought, a little wistfully.

After a quick conversation, Hank got back into his truck and Lonnie came back inside. "Something else I don't need," she said to Mila, a little shyly, indicating the package.

"Oh, I'm sure you'll find some use for it," Mila said, putting her coffee cup down, and it was at that exact moment that Reid wheeled himself into the kitchen, his breakfast tray balanced in his lap.

"*Reid!*" Lonnie said, so surprised that she almost dropped her package. "What's wrong?"

"Nothing's wrong," he said.

But Lonnie, unused to his presence in the kitchen, didn't believe him. "It's the oatmeal, isn't it?" she asked, putting down her package on the counter and wringing her hands. "It had too much brown sugar in it, didn't it?"

"What? No," Reid said, looking a little mystified.

"The oatmeal was fine. I'm done with it so I just thought I'd bring my tray in and, um, get another cup of coffee."

"Oh, of course," Lonnie said, hurrying over to collect the tray from him. "I'm sorry I didn't check back with you sooner about the coffee. But you usually have just the one cup, and sometimes not even that." As she busied herself at the counter, refilling the empty cup, Reid looked at Mila and said quietly, "I hope you're not too tired today."

"I'm fine," Mila said, noticing how blue his eyes looked in the kitchen's morning sunlight. She felt strangely warm then, though the day hadn't heated up yet and there was a nice breeze coming in through the open kitchen windows.

"You don't need to wait for this, Reid," Lonnie said, nervously sloshing cream into his coffee and stirring it in so vigorously that some of it splashed onto the counter. "I can bring it to your room for you."

"No, that's okay," he said, wheeling himself closer to the table. "If you don't mind, Lonnie, I'll have it out here in the kitchen."

"If I don't *mind*?" Lonnie repeated, turning around. "Why would I mind? It's your place, isn't it? Or you brother's, anyway. Which is the same thing, really." She carried his coffee cup over to the table, set it down, and then started to rearrange the chairs. And Mila, feeling suddenly self-conscious about Reid's being there, too, stood up and tried to help her.

"Now, where would you like to sit?" Lonnie asked.

"Anywhere is fine." Reid shrugged. But Lonnie kept moving chairs around, and Mila kept standing there, not quite sure what to do with herself, either.

Reid sighed finally, and Mila waited for him to make a sarcastic remark. Or to announce that he'd changed his mind and that he'd be having his coffee back in his room after all. But instead he said, "Look, I didn't mean to interrupt your routine. So why don't you two just go back to doing whatever it was you were doing before I came in, and I'll figure out where to sit. All right?"

This seemed somehow to get though to them, because after a moment Lonnie left the chairs alone and went back to the sink and started washing the dishes again, and Mila sat back down at her usual place at the table and tried to pretend there was nothing out of the ordinary about Reid's being there.

"Jeez," she heard him mutter, as he wheeled himself closer and reached for his cup. "I just wanted some more coffee." But he didn't sound angry.

Chapter 12

Everyone has a breaking point, and Mila reached hers less than a year into her marriage to Brandon. It was a bitterly cold, late December afternoon, and the two of them had just carried their first Christmas tree into their apartment. It should have been a festive occasion, but Brandon was full of a silent fury that had Mila rushing into the kitchen as soon as they'd leaned the tree up against the living room wall.

"I'm going to make something hot to drink, cocoa, maybe," she said, pulling off her hat and gloves and coat and depositing them on a chair at the kitchen table. She went to fill the teakettle, but Brandon intercepted her at the sink.

"What was that?" he asked her quietly. So quietly it scared her.

"What are you talking about?"

"Don't play dumb, Mila. You know exactly what I'm talking about."

Her hand shook slightly as she set the teakettle down. He was right. She knew exactly what he was talking about.

"What was that, between you and our neighbor?" he asked.

"Brandon, that was nothing," she said, turning to him. "I've told you before. There is *nothing* going on between us. I mean, you were there. You saw it. *All* of it. He got on the elevator with us, and I didn't even say hello to him. I didn't even *look* at him. I ignored him. That was it. That was all."

"You did *not* just ignore him, Mila," he said, with barely suppressed rage. "You were flirting with him."

"I was *not* flirting with him," she insisted, anger rising in her. She tried to tamp it down now. If she'd learned anything over the last year it was that her anger only added fuel to Brandon's fire, and his fire already burned white hot all on its own.

"Stop denying it," he said, through clenched teeth. "Stop denying that even with your husband right there beside you, you sent him a message, loud and clear. You said 'I'm interested.' You said, 'I'm available.' You said,

'Hey, my husband's at work during the day, and I'm all alone. Why don't we—' "

"That's enough," she broke in, too full of disgust to let him go any further. "This is *ridiculous*. There is *nothing* between us. My God, Brandon, even *you* should be able to see that."

She didn't see it coming. She never saw it coming. It was an explosion of heat and light and pain, and she screamed once and brought her hand reflexively to her left eye. "This is *not* over," Brandon said, and he picked up the kettle and threw it against the wall above the stove with such force that Mila was afraid it would bounce back and hit her, too. But it clanged onto the floor instead, and Brandon stormed out of the kitchen and slammed the apartment door behind him. And Mila, who knew she needed to do something about her eye, and do it now, before it got too swollen, did nothing about it, and instead slid down, her back against the counter, until she was sitting on the kitchen floor.

She waited for the tears to come, but for once, they didn't. She decided it was because she was too angry to cry. Brandon's accusations, always unfair, seemed doubly unfair today. She had never flirted with their neighbor; she avoided him, and everyone else in their building, whenever possible. (She was convinced that they'd all heard Brandon shouting at her through the walls of their apartment or, worse, seen her with the black eye her sunglasses couldn't completely hide or the bruised cheek her makeup couldn't completely cover.)

Besides, not only was she not attracted to that neighbor, she wasn't attracted to *anyone* anymore, and that included her husband. The night before, for instance, when Mila was changing into her nightgown, Brandon had come into their bedroom, a towel wrapped around his waist, his skin still wet from the shower, and Mila had felt revolted at the sight of him. Maybe this was why she'd bought the nightgown she was putting on then. It was flannel, ankle length, with long sleeves and a high neck. And why not? Sex was the furthest thing from her mind. And she figured if she covered every inch of herself, maybe it would be the furthest thing from Brandon's mind, too.

Now, sitting on the kitchen floor, she took a deep breath and exhaled slowly, trying simultaneously to calm herself down and ignore her throbbing eye. But it wouldn't be ignored. Already it was so swollen she could barely see out of it. She got up to get some ice and realized she was still shaking all over. Not from fear, but from anger. There was so much of it that had built up inside her, and not all of it, it turned out, was directed at Brandon. Some of it was directed at herself.

How could she have been so stupid as to marry a man who'd already hit her once? she thought now, filling a plastic bag with ice. And how could she have been so idiotic as to believe him when he'd promised it would never happen again? Brandon was a classic abuser, and theirs was a classic abusive relationship. She knew this now; she'd researched domestic violence at the public library. The warning signs had been there from the beginning. Brandon's jealousy and possessiveness, his need to know where she was and who she was with at all times, and his attempts, mostly successful, to isolate her from her family and her friends.

But understanding this didn't change anything. She was still married to him, still sharing an apartment with him, still expecting him, at any minute, to walk through that front door. And she knew exactly what he'd be like when he did. When they were first married, he'd come home ashamed, and remorseful, and repentant. But lately, he'd come home still angry and, worse, resentful. He'd explain to Mila, at length, that what had happened was actually her fault, she'd backed him into a corner, provoked him, really, and given him no choice but to respond the way he had. And Mila, sickened by this logic, tried to remain as neutral as possible as she listened to his lecture. If he so much as glimpsed her disgust for him, the whole cycle would simply start over again.

But this wasn't going to be like all the other times, she realized, her heart pounding with the knowledge of what she was about to do. She left the bag of ice in the sink, walked to the bedroom, grabbed a suitcase out of the closet, and threw it on the bed. Then she started tossing clothes into it. She did this haphazardly, without considering what she might actually need wherever she was going. But she filled the suitcase and jammed it closed, put on a pair of oversized sunglasses that would hide her swollen eye, and detoured to the kitchen to pull on her coat. She paused to rifle through her handbag. Her wallet had only forty dollars in it, but for now, that would have to be enough; she didn't have time to go to the ATM. She stuffed the wallet in one of her coat pockets, stuffed her cell phone in the other, and, after a moment's hesitation, threw her apartment keys in the wastebasket. She wouldn't be needing those anymore.

And then she left. When Brandon came back, she'd be gone for good. The only problem, she thought, as she rode down in the elevator, was that she didn't have any place to go. Brandon, with his constant neediness and insane jealousy, had chased everyone in her life away. She considered calling Heather or even her mom, but decided not to. It wouldn't be fair to either of them. She'd gotten herself into this; she'd have to get herself out of it, too.

So the plan she'd settled on by the time the elevator doors opened was this: board a city bus, get off at the last stop, then board another one. And another one after that. Until she'd run out of buses. Or money. The point was to get as far away from Brandon as possible. After that, she'd figure things out. She wasn't worried about being able to support herself. She was young and healthy and willing to work hard. There was no reason why she couldn't start over again somewhere else, somewhere where there was no Brandon.

When she'd hurried though her apartment building's small lobby and pushed through the front door, though, the blast of icy evening air that hit her was almost enough to weaken her resolve. In her hurry, she'd forgotten her hat and gloves and scarf. But there was nothing she could do about it now. So she turned right and hurried down the block, glancing nervously over her shoulder at their building receding behind her. No sign of Brandon yet. She walked faster, as fast as she could without attracting attention, her suitcase careening down the sidewalk after her, her eye throbbing with pain. When she got to a bus stop six blocks from their apartment, she stopped. She never took this bus, so Brandon wouldn't think to look for her here. She sat down on the bench and tried to blend in with the dozen or so other people waiting for the bus. She was freezing. She pulled her coat collar up and pushed her hands deep into her pockets, then clenched her teeth so that they wouldn't chatter and prayed silently that the bus would come soon. She stood up and walked to the curb, craning her neck to see if she could see it in the distance. She couldn't. She sat back down on the bench and continued her vigil, praying silently for the bus to come. *Please come. Please come. Please, please.*

Finally, after what felt like a lifetime, Mila saw the other people waiting with her at the bus stop stir with movement. The bus was coming, its oversized headlights shining in the bluish twilight. She sat up straighter, pulled her suitcase closer, and watched as it approached. *Oh thank God,* she thought. Relief broke over her. Inundated her. Buoyed her. She was practically floating on it as she tightened her grip on the suitcase's handle and started to stand up. And that was when she felt a hand on her shoulder. A strong, possessive hand that gripped her too tightly to be friendly and that pushed her, forcibly, back down onto the bench. She cried out in surprise, but nobody noticed over the squeal of the bus's brakes.

"Mila," Brandon said softly into her ear, leaning over the back of the bench. "Did you really think you were going to be able to leave me? Just like that?"

And Mila, watching people board the bus, felt an unbearable sadness. "No," she said, quietly, after a moment. "I didn't really think so."

He came around and sat down beside her on the bench. Together they watched the bus pull away. Outwardly, Brandon was almost eerily calm and in control. Inwardly, she knew, he was full of a cold, black rage that was Brandon at his most volatile. And most dangerous.

"I came home, Mila," he said quietly, "and you were gone. And your suitcase was gone. And you'd thrown your keys in the wastebasket. Why would you do that, Mila? Why would you throw your keys away?"

She didn't answer.

"Well, I'll answer that for you, Mila," he said. "You threw them away because you didn't think you'd need them again, did you? You weren't planning on coming back. But you should have known I wouldn't let you leave." His voice was even as he continued, "Not now. Not ever. And, Mila? If you ever try to do this again, I'll do the same thing I've done today. I'll come and find you. Wherever you are. I'll follow you to the ends of the earth and back again, if necessary. But I will never, ever, *ever*, let you go. Do you understand me, Mila?"

She nodded miserably. She understood him.

"One more thing," he said, leaning closer. "I don't know what's happening between you and our neighbor, but if I ever find you with him or with any other man, I will kill him. So help me God, Mila, I will kill him." He let that sink in for a moment. "Now, let's go," he said, picking up her suitcase.

She followed him home. She was amazed, actually, that she was able to. Her limbs felt so leaden, and so heavy, that she could barely make them work. She wondered distantly if it was the cold that was making them feel that way, but she decided it wasn't. It was hopelessness.

Several months later, on a warm and balmy May morning, Mila was standing on her tiptoes, putting a winter blanket away on the top shelf of the closet, when something caught her eye. It was the cardboard box she kept Heather's letters in, and though it had been over a year since she'd opened it for any other reason than to put a new letter in it, she lifted it off the shelf now, and flipped its lid open. Then, still in her nightgown—it seemed pointless, lately, to get dressed in the morning, just as it seemed pointless to get out of bed—she knelt down on the floor and started to go through the box. One of the first things she saw was a photograph of her and Heather, taken by the school secretary when Mila was in fifth grade. She'd seen it many times before, but now, as she took it out and studied it, she felt as if she was seeing it for the first time. How different she'd looked then. Most of the difference, of course, was due to age. But not all of it was. No, there was something else, too. In the picture, she looked so . . . so full of life, she decided. So full of hope. She didn't look that way anymore. Not that she spent a lot of time looking in the mirror. She didn't. In fact, on the few occasions recently she'd caught a glimpse of herself in it, she'd been frightened by what she'd seen. Her reflection looked dull, flat, and lifeless.

She touched her fingertip to her image in the photograph, as if trying to recapture something from it. But she knew she couldn't. She'd had a dream then. She'd wanted to be a nurse. And though she'd finished her prerequisites for nursing school, she knew there was no point in even applying. She couldn't go. Not now. Not when it was all she could do to just hang on from one day to the next. So that dream was gone. Another casualty of her marriage to Brandon.

She thought sometimes about being a home health aide. She'd gotten her certification before she'd met Brandon. But again, what was the point? Brandon didn't want her to do it—didn't want her to do *anything,* she'd come to realize, but sit in the apartment and wait for him to come home. And so she waited, and she hoped it would make her unbearable marriage a little easier to bear.

Now she put the photograph of her and Heather back in the box and started to put the box away, too, but she changed her mind and dumped all the letters out onto the floor instead. Then she organized them chronologically, and, starting with the first one Heather had ever written to her, she reread each one of them. She read them slowly and carefully, almost as if she was trying to commit them to memory. Heather had believed in her, she realized, as she refolded an early letter and slid it back into its envelope. She'd seen something in a shy, insecure nine-year-old that no one else had ever seen before or since.

It took Mila the better part of the day to reread the letters—a day spent sitting on the floor of a cramped closet—but by the time she was done, she felt strangely energized. She hurried to shower and dress, and she took care to blow-dry her hair and powder over the remnants of a bruise on her cheek. She could do this, she told herself, as she carried the box of Heather's letters over to the front door, where it was still sitting when Brandon came home from work that night.

"You look nice," he said approvingly, giving her the once-over.

"Thank you," she said, making an effort to smile.

"*And* you're in a good mood. That's a nice change. You know how tired I get of you acting depressed all the time." He noticed the box beside the front door. "What's that?" he asked.

"Heather's letters to me," she said casually.

"What are you doing with them?"

"Recycling them."

"Why?"

She shrugged. "They were taking up too much space in the closet."

"But I thought they were so special to you." There was a slightly sarcastic emphasis on the word *special* that Mila tried to ignore.

"No, not really. Not anymore. I mean, you know how it is. People just . . . drift apart. They lose touch. I don't necessarily think it's a bad thing, do you?"

"Oh, no, definitely not," he said, and she saw that he was practically elated by this development. As hard as he'd tried, he'd never yet been able to come between her and Heather, and the letters they still wrote to each other were a constant source of irritation to him.

"Could you take these to the recycling room now?" she asked Brandon, indicating the box. She needed to be alone for a minute. All this lying was taking its toll on her.

"Yeah, okay," he said, and he left with the box. And Mila stood there and tried to not think about all the letters she would never see again. It didn't matter, she told herself. They were in her head, and in her heart. What mattered was that Brandon didn't come looking for her at Heather's house. Because she was leaving him again, only this time she was going to do it right.

The next day, Mila wrote Heather a letter. It was short—only five sentences—but it took her the whole day, and several drafts, to write. In it, she told Heather that she was starting a new job—she was a little vague about the details—and that she wouldn't have time to write to her again for a while. She was careful to sound positive and upbeat. She didn't want Heather to worry about her, though she suspected sometimes that she already *did* worry about her, and that while Mila was careful to hide the truth about her marriage, Heather had guessed it anyway.

Finally, though, Mila got the letter right, and in the soft, hazy afternoon light—Brandon would be working late that night—she walked down to the corner and dropped the letter in the mailbox. She felt a mixture of relief and sadness as she walked home, but outside her apartment building she saw a young woman helping an elderly man who was using a walker, and it reminded her of something. She hurried back up to her apartment and took her wallet out of her handbag, then searched through it until she found what she was looking for. It was a business card for Caring Home Care, an agency that placed health aides with patients who needed in-home care. Mary Meyer, the woman who'd taught Mila's certification class, had given it to her. She'd been impressed with the quality of Mila's work, and she'd told her that if she ever wanted a placement, she should call her friend Gloria Thompson, who owned the agency.

Mila slipped the business card out of her wallet and checked her watch. The chance of anyone being at Caring Home Care at five thirty on a Friday evening was almost nonexistent. But something made her pick up the phone and dial the number anyway.

Chapter 13

Three weeks after her first swimming lesson, Mila sat down beside Allie on the dock and tentatively dipped her toes into the water. "Brrr," she said, withdrawing them.

"I know," Allie said sympathetically. "The lake always gets colder after it rains. But it'll warm up again," she said, lowering her own feet into the water.

After a week of humid, overcast weather, there had been a torrential downpour the night before, and today the sky was a crystalline blue, and the air was so clear that everything seemed to shimmer in the sunlight. The rain had left a hint of coolness behind it, though, and the thought of getting into the now chilly lake wasn't very appealing to Mila.

"We'll just sit here for a few minutes," Allie said, as if reading her mind. "Just until we get warm enough to actually *want* to get into the water." With a contented sigh, Allie leaned back on the dock, resting on her elbows, and turned her face up to the sun. Allie, Mila noted, was in an especially good mood today, and she was tempted, for a moment, to ask her why. But she and Allie had never discussed anything personal before, and Mila was worried that that question might border on the personal, so instead she tested the icy water with her toes again.

"So, day after tomorrow," Allie said, her eyes still closed against the sun. "It's a big day, isn't it?"

"A very big day," Mila agreed, since it was the day that Reid would be trading in his full leg cast for a removable plastic brace, and his wheelchair for a pair of crutches.

"Do you think he's ready?" Allie asked. "For the change, I mean?"

"I think so," Mila said, knowing that having his cast off was going to mean more freedom for Reid, but also more work for him, too. He was starting physical therapy next week, and Mila had already seen the schedule for it. It was going to be grueling, but at least his pain from the accident had greatly diminished and he rarely needed his pain medication anymore.

"Well, at least the sponge baths will be over now," Allie said, with a glimmer of amusement. "I don't think either of the brothers will miss those. In fact, Reid told Walker that as soon as he gets back from his doctor's appointment he wants to take a twelve-hour shower." She added, "It's going to have to wait, though, because first Walker's going to bring him over to our cabin for a little celebration."

"Oh, that'll be nice," Mila said.

"I hope so. You'll be there, too, of course."

"Me?" Mila said, surprised. "But isn't it, you know, a family thing?"

"Not *just* family," Allie said, opening her eyes and turning to Mila. "We'll be having some friends over, too."

"But I'm not . . ." She stopped, not knowing how to say this without seeming rude.

"You're not a friend?" Allie chided her. "Of course you are." And then she grinned. "And you're not *just* a friend either. You're also my best swim student."

"Your *only* swim student," Mila said, laughing.

"Well, that may be, but I'd still like you to come to the party. Walker and I were just saying how much Reid's attitude has improved over the last month, and we both think you deserve the credit for that, Mila."

"Oh, I don't know," Mila said, studying with sudden interest a new constellation of freckles that had recently appeared on one of her shoulders. "I think Reid's just . . . more comfortable now," she said vaguely. "You know, in less pain."

"Maybe," Allie said, but she didn't sound convinced. Privately, Mila thought Allie was right about one thing though: Reid's attitude *had* improved, and if she had to point to the day it had begun to improve, she would point to the day of their picnic four weeks ago. Since then Reid's rudeness and sarcasm had given way to something different, to respectfulness, or to gentleness, almost, as if he thought Mila was someone who needed to be treated with . . . well, *with care*. And, as Reid's attitude had changed, so, too, had his and Mila's routine. If Reid had an appointment, Mila was as likely now as Walker to drive him to it, and, more often than not, Reid came to the kitchen at mealtimes instead of staying in his room. And then there were those nights when Reid had a nightmare so terrifying that Mila felt she had no choice but to wake him up from it, and then to stay, until morning, in the armchair in his room. But there was nothing unprofessional about their relationship, she told herself. Nothing inappropriate. They hadn't had any more personal conversations since the one they'd had on their picnic, and they hadn't had any more physical contact, either, since Reid had kissed her wrist on the deck the night of the full moon. So why, Mila wondered now, couldn't she bring herself to look at Allie as they talked about Reid?

"Well, it doesn't really matter *why* he's doing better," Allie said, swinging her feet vigorously enough off the dock to kick up little sprays of water. "What matters is that he *is* doing better."

"Absolutely," Mila agreed.

"And you seem to be settling it, too, Mila," Allie said, studying her with her astute hazel eyes.

Settling in? Is that what I'm doing? Mila wondered. As far as she knew, she'd never "settled in" anywhere before—not in the series of apartments she'd grown up in as a child, and not in the apartment she'd lived in with Brandon—but now, with Allie watching her, it occurred to her she might actually be doing just that at this cabin.

"I'm very comfortable here, thanks to you and Walker and Lonnie," Mila said to Allie, and that was true, but it was more than that too. Living at the cabin this summer, Mila felt it was almost as if something inside of her had started to unclench, like a tense muscle that was relaxing. And it wasn't only that she felt less on edge, though she did, of course—she'd stopped jumping every time she heard a car pull up outside during the day, or every time she heard one of the cabin's floorboards creak at night—it was also that she'd started to take pleasure in little things, too. Getting a tricky math problem right on a practice test, or listening to Lonnie's chatter over breakfast, or watching the nighttime shadows quivering on Reid's ceiling as she fell asleep in the armchair.

"Good, I'm glad you're comfortable here," Allie said, bringing Mila back to the conversation. "That tells me you'll be comfortable at our party, too. Because except for a few families, it'll just be us, me and Walker and Wyatt and Brooke and Reid. The same people you see here every day."

"I'd like to come to the party," Mila said, smiling. "But can I at least help you with it?"

"Nope," Allie said. "My friend Jax's daughter, Joy, is going to watch Brooke for me while I get everything ready, but there isn't actually going to be that much to get ready. I just need to marinate the chicken and the ribs. Caroline's bringing coleslaw and potato salad and biscuits from Pearl's."

"Lucky you," Mila said, remembering the mouthwatering Butternut Burger she'd had on her and Reid's picnic.

"Lucky *us*," Allie corrected her. "Now, for the logistics. Walker and Reid will have the van for the doctor's appointment, and they're coming straight from there to our cabin, so I'll come and pick you up here. Day after tomorrow. Probably around five o'clock, okay?"

"Okay," Mila said, feeling suddenly shy. But Allie was already shifting gears. "Are you ready to tread some water?" she asked Mila.

"As ready as I'll ever be."

"Good," Allie said, and she stood up and did a neat dive off the end of the dock, leaving Mila to ease her way down the ladder, and stand, shivering, in the shoulder-deep water, watching Allie swim a graceful front crawl that she'd promised Mila she would be swimming soon too.

"All right," Allie said, surfacing beside her. "Let's warm up treading water, and then we'll work on your flutter kick."

Allie had broken down the front crawl for her, and they'd practiced each element of it separately. This week, Allie explained, they would put them all together. "But can't I just dog-paddle?" Mila had asked her at one point, impatient to start swimming.

"Absolutely not," Allie had said. "I never let Wyatt dog-paddle, and I'm not going to let you do it either. When you swim—and you will swim, very soon— you're going to swim a real stroke, and you're going to swim it correctly."

Now, as Mila started treading water beside Allie, she stole a quick look up at the cabin and thought she saw, through the trees, the glint of Reid's wheelchair on the deck. She knew he watched her swimming lessons, though they'd never discussed it with each other. Still, she liked knowing that he watched them. It made her feel . . . but when she couldn't quite decipher how it made her feel, she dunked her head beneath the water instead and came back up into the sunlight, smiling, and pushing water droplets out of her half-closed eyes.

"Well, I'll be damned," Walker said, sliding open the screen door and coming out onto the deck. "When Lonnie told me you were out here, I didn't believe her. I said, 'Lonnie, that's not possible. My brother doesn't go outside anymore. Not willingly, anyway.' But obviously, I stand corrected."

"Obviously," Reid said dryly, edging his wheelchair back from the deck's railing.

"No, seriously, what are you doing out here?" Walker asked, coming over to him.

"I'm not doing anything," Reid said, irked by the defensiveness he heard in his own voice. "Not that I need a reason to be outside on a nice day." He turned his wheelchair slightly toward his brother.

"No, you're right," Walker said, suddenly contrite. "You don't need a reason to be outside. In fact, you *should* be outside. I guess I've just gotten used to you being inside. I mean, you're *always* inside."

"Not always," Reid said. *Not on Tuesdays and Thursdays between 2:00 o'clock and 3:00 o'clock in the afternoon.* "Aren't you supposed to be at a meeting with one of our suppliers now?" Reid glanced pointedly at his watch. "I thought you told me this morning that—"

"Canceled," Walker said blithely. "And I don't have to pick Wyatt up from day camp either because he's having a sleepover at a friend's house. So I decided to surprise Allie and Brooke. But Allie's not done yet with her swimming lesson"—he gestured at the lake—"and Brooke's still taking her nap, so it looks like you're stuck with me."

"It does look that way, doesn't it?" Reid said, with barely concealed irritation, though he knew that irritation was unfounded. Walker had no way of knowing how much Reid looked forward to watching Mila's swimming lessons, and, if he had known, he would have been nothing short of amazed. Reid was a little amazed himself. He'd watched the first lesson out of a mild curiosity, and he'd assumed that that would be the end of it. But he hadn't missed one since. They'd become the high point of his week. Oh hell, they'd become the high point of his *life*.

If Walker noticed his annoyance now, though, he chose to ignore it and instead went in search of a deck chair to drag over to Reid's wheelchair. And as he was doing this, Reid rolled a little closer to the deck's railing and stole a look down at the dock, wishing, for the one-hundredth time, that the view from here was less obstructed. But his brother had done the environmentally correct thing when he'd built this cabin, cutting down as few trees as possible, and sometimes, depending on where Allie and Mila were in the water, all Reid could make out through the trees were the splotches of color that were their bathing suits—Allie's black and Mila's red. Then again, he'd often thought, if he couldn't see them that well, maybe they couldn't see him that well either. Or at least that was what he told himself.

"How're the swimming lessons going?" Walker asked, rolling a deck chair over and sprawling out on it.

"I don't know," Reid lied, though of course he knew exactly how the swimming lessons were going. Mila's progress, in his opinion, had been nothing short of amazing. He watched now as she practiced the flutter kick, and Allie, standing beside her at the dock, made minor adjustments in her form and offered murmurs of approval.

"Allie's a good teacher," he said, without thinking.

"Is she?" Walker said, smiling. "I'm not surprised. I know she taught Wyatt how to swim." And if he thought it was strange that Reid, who claimed not to know how the swimming lessons were going, had known enough to make this observation, he didn't say so.

Reid glanced over at Walker then and noticed, for the first time, that he'd brought a file folder with him, which he'd set on the deck beside his chair. So he hadn't just come over to see Allie and Brooke, Reid thought, with an inward groan.

"What's in the file?" he asked Walker, not really wanting to know.

"This?" Walker said, feigning casualness as he picked it up. "It's a draft of the business plan for the new boatyard at Big Bear Lake."

"Oh, that," Reid said distractedly. There was the sound of laughter from the dock then, and he longed to know what Mila and Allie were laughing about.

"Do you think you might want to take a look at it?" Walker asked tentatively, holding it out to him.

"No thanks," Reid said curtly, though in fairness to Walker, it had been Reid's idea to buy that damn boatyard in the first place. Still, that had been a lifetime ago, hadn't it?

Walker blew out a long breath now and dropped the file back onto the deck, but Reid was relieved to see that he didn't seem to be overly disappointed. In fact, as he leaned back in his deck chair, he seemed to positively radiate contentment and well-being.

"What're you so happy about?" Reid asked.

"Me? Oh, nothing." Walker smiled. "I'm just thinking about last night."

"What happened last night?"

"Allie and I went on a date."

"In Butternut?"

Walker nodded.

"Let me guess. You went to the fish fry at the American Legion. Or was it karaoke night at the Elks Club?"

"You can make fun of Butternut all you want," Walker said. "But today, I'm not taking the bait. Actually we were supposed to go to the Corner Bar for hamburgers, but after we dropped the kids off at Jax and Jeremy's, I thought, 'Why the hell are we going out in public?' I mean, we could've talked, but we couldn't . . . you know, do anything else."

"Probably not without attracting the attention of other people," Reid agreed. He was only giving Walker half his attention. The other half belonged to Allie and Mila. They were standing in waist-deep water now, as Allie watched Mila do the arm movements for the front crawl.

"Anyway," Walker continued, "we went to the boat-yard instead. And I sent the night watchman home. And then . . . well, you know. Or you get the general idea, anyway."

"In the office?" Reid asked.

"No," Walker chuckled. "Not the office. In one of the boats on the showroom floor. The Chris Craft Corsair, actually. The Capri 21. That is one beautiful boat. And very comfortable, too, it turns out."

"You know we're going to have to knock twenty-five percent off her sale price now, don't you?" Reid said.

"Don't worry," Walker said amiably. "I brought a blanket in from the truck. But Reid, seriously, it was"— here he sat up on his deck chair—"it was amazing. I mean, not only did we not have to worry about being interrupted, but afterwards, we actually had a conversation without either of us falling asleep. And then, you know, we did it again. And then again after that."

"Okay, that's too much information," Reid protested.

But Walker only laughed. "You used to like hearing about my conquests, Reid."

"Yeah, well, I don't think it's considered a conquest if you're already married."

Walker laughed again. "Maybe not. But damn it, it *felt* like one."

Just then, they heard Brooke crying from inside the cabin, and, a moment later, Lonnie appeared with her at the screen door. "She just woke up," she said, "and she's a little fussy. I tried giving her the bottle Allie left for her, but I think maybe she wants her daddy to give it to her instead."

"I'd love to give it to her," Walker said. He stood up and clapped Reid on the shoulder. "Don't forget, day after tomorrow, you get your cast off. Then the party, right?"

Reid nodded resignedly. He'd already tried, and failed, to convince his brother a party wasn't necessary.

"Oh, Walker, don't forget the business plan," Reid said, pointing to the file his brother had left beside the deck chair.

"Right," Walker said, picking it up.

"And, uh, if you want, you can leave that on my dresser," Reid said. "I'm not promising anything, but I can probably take a look at it."

"Really?"

"Yeah. But don't get too excited, all right? I didn't say I was coming back to work."

"No, of course not," Walker said. And then, because he knew Reid too well to press his luck by saying any-thing more about it, he started to leave.

"Hey, Walk?" Reid called out to him.

"Yeah?"

"You know the barbershop in Butternut?"

"Yeah, it's a good one."

"You think you could run me over to it tomorrow?"

"God, yes," Walker said, instantly coming back. "You gonna get the works? Haircut, shave, the whole thing?"

"All right, calm down," Reid said, waving him away. "Go take care of your kid."

After Walker went back inside the cabin, sliding the screen door shut behind him, Reid was left alone to watch the end of the swimming lesson. There wasn't much to see. It was winding down now, both women moving leisurely toward the ladder. He'd stay out here a little longer though, he decided. At least until they started to come up from the dock. A breeze blew off the lake, stirring the trees that towered above the deck and bringing with it the scent of dry pine needles and the clean, tangy smell of lake water after it's rained. And Reid, looking down at Mila, her red bathing suit speckled by the sunlight, felt it again, the feeling he got sometimes when he watched her swimming lessons. It was a lightness, a buoyancy, a weightlessness, almost, that made him forget, momentarily at least, that he was in a wheelchair, and that he wasn't even walking right now, let alone floating.

He'd felt this feeling before, but it had been a long time ago. So long ago, in fact, that he had to make a mental effort to travel back that far in his mind. The last time he'd felt this way—*really* felt this way—was the summer he and Walker had bought their first boatyard. They'd paid almost nothing for it, only to realize later that they'd still paid too much for it. But they hadn't known that then. They hadn't known *any-thing* then, as far as Reid could tell, except, of course, that they loved boats. Building them, repairing them, customizing them. Anything having to do with them, really. And they'd thought that that would be enough to build a successful business. Well, that and the fact that they were willing to work like maniacs to do it. As it turned out, of course, that *had* been enough. But there was no way they could have known that then. Then, they should have been afraid. Should have been, but weren't.

The best part of that first summer, oddly enough, hadn't been the days, but the nights. The nights were when the two of them sat on the hood of Walker's pickup truck, which they parked outside the boatyard's office, and split a six-pack of beer while they listened to an old transistor radio Walker had found in an abandoned boat. They talked, far into the night, leaning back against the windshield of the truck, looking up at the sky, reluctant to go to sleep even after they'd finished the beer and the radio's corroded batteries had finally given out. They'd talked about the business, of course. About everything they wanted to do with that boatyard. And other boatyards too. This, when they'd barely had enough money to buy the cans of soup they ate for dinner, heated up on a hot plate in the boatyard's office. But they'd talked about other things as well. What other things they talked about, Reid wasn't quite sure now. Sports, probably. Women, definitely, though, as he recalled, they hadn't had a lot of time to meet any of them that summer.

Finally, though, the two of them would call it a night, climb into the bed of the pickup truck, and unroll their sleeping bags. Why had they slept in the truck, Reid wondered now, when they'd had the boatyard office right next door? But then he remembered. *Rats.* The office, the whole boatyard, actually, had been overrun by rats the size of small cats. They'd slept in the truck to get away from them.

He smiled now as he saw he and Walker as they'd been on those early summer mornings, after a night spent in the pickup. They'd crawl stiffly out of their dew-covered sleeping bags, which they'd hang out to dry on the hood of the truck, and then they'd eat handfuls of cereal right out of the box for their breakfast. They couldn't wait to get started then on rebuilding that boatyard, that pathetic little boatyard that Reid knew now should have failed. Should have, but didn't.

And the funny thing was, they'd been right to make big plans. Their business had succeeded beyond their wildest dreams. But the more it grew, Reid suddenly understood, the further he'd gotten from the way he'd felt sitting on top of that pickup truck that first summer.

But when had it stopped being so much fun? he wondered now. When did it become like everything else in life? Another problem to solve. Another item to check off a list. Another reason to stay up late, or wake up early, or work for sixteen hours at a stretch? He couldn't remember when it had happened; he just knew that it had. So why had Reid kept pushing himself so hard? Kept pushing both of them so hard? What was it that he'd wanted? And why hadn't anything he'd gotten ever been enough? He knew what Walker would say; he knew because Walker had already said it many times before. He'd say that Reid was trying to even some score with their dad, some score that could never be evened. It was their dad who'd introduced them to boats. When they were little, he'd always had one in the garage that he was working on. He'd let them help him sometimes, too, and he'd give them little jobs to do, little projects to work on. For their dad, though, boats were just a hobby, and as much as he would have loved for them to be a business, he didn't know how to make them one. He lacked something, the courage, maybe, or the drive, to turn his love of them into a full-time job.

And then he'd left. Left not just their mom, but them, too. He'd tried to stay in their lives, for a while, anyway. But then he'd stopped trying. Maybe it was because he and their mom kept fighting, even after the divorce, about child support checks, about visitation, about every little thing they could think to fight about it seemed. Or maybe it was because he'd met another woman and, eventually, had a daughter with her. He'd never introduced them to their half sister. They'd only heard about her, and not from their father, either, but from a friend of their father. By the time she was born, their dad had dropped out of their lives for good.

But no matter, Reid had told himself. He and his brother had taken something their father had loved to do and done him one better. No, done him *one hundred* times better. *One thousand times better.* They hadn't needed him. And they hadn't succeeded because of him, either. In fact, they'd succeeded *in spite of* him. But none of their success had ever given Reid the satisfaction he'd thought it would.

He remembered now the night of the accident, not the part after he'd gotten in his car, but the part before he'd gotten in his car. He stopped himself though. He wouldn't think about that now. Not when he was in this good of a mood. He looked down at the lake. Mila and Allie had dried themselves off, and, still wrapped in their towels, they were making their unhurried way to the set of steps that led up to the deck. Soon, very soon, he'd go back inside. But for a moment, he lingered there, feeling that unfamiliar, but welcome feeling. It was happiness, Reid knew. And it had come into his life again when he'd least expected it to.

Chapter 14

B y the time Brandon walked into the coffee shop that morning, Ed Tuck was already wedged into one of the back booths and already hard at work on what looked to be the breakfast special. Brandon knew that special well. It was what he'd ordered when Mila had worked at this place. It was the only thing on the menu, as far as he could tell, that was even halfway decent.

His stomach grumbled hungrily as he made his way down the narrow aisle to Mr. Tuck's booth. He was starving. But he knew he wouldn't be able to eat anything here. Too many memories. It would have been easier to pick someplace else to have this meeting. He knew that. But this place was symbolic. And if there was one thing Brandon could appreciate, it was symbolism.

"Good morning," Brandon said, sliding into the booth opposite Mr. Tuck.

"You're late," Mr. Tuck said, barely looking up from his plate, where he was using his toast to mop up the yolky remains of his fried eggs.

Brandon, annoyed, flipped over the empty cup of coffee on the table in front of him and signaled to the waitress. "It's my dime, Mr. Tuck," he said.

Mr. Tuck shrugged. "Maybe," he said, shoveling hash browns into his mouth. "But you already owe me a lot of dimes."

That was true enough, Brandon thought, his hand going reflexively to the envelope in his pocket. He'd already spent a small fortune on Mr. Tuck's services, and he hadn't even given him this last installment yet.

"Sorry I'm late," Brandon said. "I had to make up an excuse to get out of work."

The waitress came over then with a pot of coffee and filled Brandon's cup. She took out her check pad, but he shook his head. "Just coffee," he said, barely glancing at her. Funny how uninterested he'd been in women—even attractive women—since Mila had left. It was almost as if he didn't even see them anymore.

The waitress started to leave the table, but Mr. Tuck stopped her. "Ma'am, if you don't mind, I'll have a slice of the pie."

"For breakfast?" Brandon asked, the words out of his mouth before he could stop them.

"Why not? You only live once, right?"

Brandon sighed inwardly. Another charge on the tab. And he didn't believe the part about only living once. Judging from his waistline, Mr. Tuck looked like he'd already lived plenty, at least when it came to pie. And then he remembered something from Mila's days working at this place.

"I hate to tell you this, but the pie here is lousy."

"I'm not picky."

And that was a good thing, Brandon thought, when he saw the disgusting-looking wedge of pie the waitress set down in front of Mr. Tuck. But he seemed to like it just fine. So Brandon seethed, silently, alternately sipping his too-hot coffee and watching Mr. Tuck eat his pie. This man, Brandon thought with disappointment, had none of the style and panache he'd expected a private investigator to have. Instead, he had a bad comb-over, a puffy face, and watery eyes that made him look like he had a permanent cold.

When he was done with his pie, he wiped his mouth on a paper napkin and pushed his plate away. "Where's the money?" he asked Brandon.

"The money?" Brandon said, surprised, and then irritated at his directness. "Where's the information, Mr. Tuck?"

"I have it. But I want to see the money first." He reached into the briefcase sitting on the booth beside him and pulled out a sheet of paper, which he slid across the table to Brandon. "Here's my hours, and my expense report. I've deducted them from the retainer you gave me, but as you can see, Mr. Stewart, you still owe me two thousand dollars."

Two thousand dollars? Who the hell was this guy kidding? That was highway robbery. But Brandon said nothing. He didn't want to alienate Mr. Tuck yet. There'd be plenty of time for him to do that later, after he'd told Brandon where Mila was. So Brandon folded up the sheet of paper and tucked it into his pocket. "I'll look at it later," he mumbled, taking an envelope out of his other pocket. Then he opened it up, counted out twenty one-hundred-dollar bills, and handed them over to Mr. Tuck.

Mr. Tuck glanced quickly around the coffee shop, recounted the money, and pocketed it.

"So," Brandon said, leaning forward. "What have you got for me?" His heart was jumping in his chest, and it wasn't just the caffeine that was making it do that either. He'd spent seven weeks not knowing where Mila was, and today, he was finally going to find out.

"Well, first, why don't I tell you what I haven't got for you," Mr. Tuck said, settling back against the leather backing of the booth. "I don't have a record of a Mila Jones making an airline reservation or a rental car reservation. I also don't have a record of her opening a bank account, applying for a credit card, applying for government aid, getting arrested, or checking into a hospital. Nobody's run a credit check on her. And she doesn't have a job, either. Or, I should say, she doesn't have a job that's on the books. More than that, I can't say, Mr. Jones."

"But what exactly can you say?" Brandon asked, confused. "I mean, you found her, didn't you?"

Mr. Tuck shook his head. "No, what I'm saying is that I *didn't* find her. Not a trace of her."

"And you went . . . you went to Florida? And Nebraska?"

Mr. Tuck nodded and took another manila envelope out of his briefcase. He handed it to Brandon. "My assistant and I went to both places. It's all in this report. As discussed, we did twenty-four hours of surveillance on each residence. The apartment in Fort Lauderdale and the house outside Red Cloud, Nebraska. And let me tell you, Mr. Jones, it is not easy doing surveillance on a farmhouse in rural Nebraska without attracting attention. That's one of the harder jobs I've done."

"But, but how do you know she wasn't inside her mom's apartment? Or her friend's house?" Brandon persisted, something close to panic setting in. "How do you know she just didn't go outside during those twenty-four hours?"

But Mr. Tuck shook his head. "No, we got inside the residences. Or my assistant did, anyway. In Fort Lauderdale, she was a pizza delivery girl who'd gotten the wrong address. When your mother-in-law told her she'd made a mistake, my assistant said her cell phone had died and asked if she could use her phone to call the pizza place. Then she had a quick look around. She didn't see any sign of your wife. Your mother-in-law, by the way, was dead drunk, and this was at three o'clock in the afternoon."

"Yeah, she's got a problem," Brandon said impatiently. "Now, what about the other place, in Nebraska?"

"In Nebraska, my assistant posed as a driver who'd gotten lost. She stopped at the farmhouse to ask directions and then asked if she could use the bathroom and have a glass of water. It was hotter than hell there, as it turned out. But they were glad to give her something cold to drink. Nice family, by the way. Anyway, there was no one there fitting your wife's description."

"But, I mean, just because she didn't leave those places while you had them under surveillance, and just because your assistant didn't see her inside of them, how can you be positive that she's not still hiding out in one of them?"

"We can't," Mr. Tuck said simply. "Not without breaking the law. And that's what we'd be doing if we waited for everyone to leave a residence and then let ourselves in and searched it. That's called 'breaking and entering,' and I won't do it. It's not worth risking my P.I. license for."

"But, Mr. Stewart," he continued, using his fork now to scrape the remains of the gelatinous pie filling off his plate, "if you think your wife is at one of those residences, holed up in an attic or a basement, I can tell you right now it's very unlikely. People can't live that way. Not for long, anyway. Eventually, they let their guard down. Your wife, for instance, has had several weeks now to get comfortable wherever she's living. Trust me. She's not hiding in a closet. She's falling into some kind of routine. Grocery shopping. Picking up a cup of coffee. Maybe even socializing."

Socializing? The word made Brandon flinch. The very thought of Mila meeting new people, especially people of the male persuasion, was nauseating to him. She belonged here. At home. With him. Not off gallivanting somewhere, meeting men, flirting with them, maybe even . . . but here he stopped. He couldn't take that idea any further.

He gulped down some coffee and tried to clear his mind. He could let his guard down later, in the privacy of his apartment. He'd already punched several holes in the wall there since Mila had left at the beginning of the summer. "So," he said, running his fingers through his close-cropped hair. "Where do we go from here, Mr. Tuck?"

Mr. Tuck raised his eyebrows. "From here?"

"I mean, what do we do next?"

"We don't do anything next."

"What is that supposed to mean?"

"It means that my work is done. I looked for your wife. I couldn't find her."

"You're giving up?" Brandon asked, not bothering to keep the disgust out of his voice.

But Mr. Tuck only shrugged. "I told you the day you came to my office that there was no guarantee I'd find your wife. I told you I'd use every reasonable means at my disposal to find her. And I've done that."

"But isn't there anything more you can do?"

Mr. Tuck sighed, and, finally, having satisfied himself that not a single smear of pie filling was left on his plate, he put his fork down. "Look," he said, "if money is no object for you, I could do a little more legwork. Go to the bus station, maybe. Unlike airport ticket counters, they don't check IDs that carefully. Someone could easily use a fake one. Plus, it's easy to pay cash for a bus ticket. So, yeah, it would be a good way to travel if you were trying to run away from someone.

I could show her picture around the station. Ask if anyone's seen her. I might get a hit that way."

Brandon nodded eagerly. "Do it."

"Okay, but I'm going to need another retainer."

"Another one?"

"I spent the first one."

Brandon seethed. He'd already cleaned out his savings account to pay Mr. Tuck. "I might be able to get an advance on my salary," he muttered, draining the last of his coffee.

But after giving him a long, shrewd look, Mr. Tuck shook his head. "I think that would be a mistake. I think we both know you've already spent more money than you can afford to spend."

"Well, what the hell am I supposed to do?" Brandon asked angrily, bringing his fist down on the table with more force than he'd intended. Mr. Tuck sucked in a little breath, and several diners turned to stare.

"What you're supposed to do, Mr. Stewart," Mr. Tuck said, recovering from his surprise, "is to accept the fact that your wife has left you and move on with your own life."

"*Move on?* Are you kidding?"

"No, I'm not kidding. Because if the last several weeks have taught me anything, it's that your wife doesn't want to be found."

"My wife doesn't know what she wants."

"Maybe. Maybe not. But here's something else you may want to consider. Even if you do find her, you may not be able to persuade her to return with you. It's a free country, Mr. Stewart. You can't compel her to come home if she doesn't want to."

"Compel her? She's my wife, Mr. Tuck."

"That's true. But under the laws of this country, being your wife is not the same thing as being your personal property. She's a free agent. She can return home with you. Or she can choose not to."

"It's not a question of choice."

Mr. Tuck looked at him sharply. "Actually, it is. If you force her to go with you against her will, that's kidnapping. And it's a felony. You could do serious time for that."

Brandon tried to shrug that off. Though in truth he'd had a few brushes with the law already, and it had left its mark on him. Still, he was confident that once he found Mila, she'd come back with him. She'd have to. She was his wife.

Brandon signaled for more coffee, even though the cup he'd already drunk felt like it was burning a hole in his stomach. The waitress came over, but she looked nervous. She filled Brandon's cup and left immediately. Mr. Tuck didn't look too eager to stick around either.

He glanced at his watch and reached for his briefcase. But Brandon wasn't letting him off that easily. He'd taken Brandon's money. Now he could damn well listen to him.

"Mr. Tuck," he said quietly, leaning in close. "I know how most people see marriage today. They see it as disposable. If you hit a little rough patch, the way my wife and I did, it's over. You're supposed to just call it a day. Pack up and move out. Find somebody else. Maybe marry them, too. If that doesn't work out, you can always try again, right. But me? I'm old-fashioned that way. I believe marriage is forever. Until death do us part. And when I find my wife—and I *will* find her—I intend to remind her of that."

Mr. Tuck frowned then, as if Brandon had said something offensive. Or disturbing. Which, of course, he hadn't. He'd spoken the truth as he saw it. Nothing more and nothing less.

"Well, good luck with that," Mr. Tuck said quickly. He slid out of the booth, without shaking Brandon's hand, and he started to leave, but then he turned around and came back. "Mr. Stewart? My job for you is done," he said brusquely. "Don't call my office again." And then he was gone.

"Don't worry, I won't call your office again," Brandon said mockingly. "You've wasted enough of my time. Not to mention my money." He sat hunched over in the booth for a while, his coffee getting cold, the ebb and flow of the other diners swirling around him.

Finally, he glanced at the check, threw some money on the table, and got up to go. He had a plan. He'd take over where Mr. Tuck, that two-bit P.I., had left off. How hard could it be? He'd start by taking Mila's picture to the bus station. He'd come up with some story about why he was looking for her. Maybe he'd even say she was crazy, he decided, heading out of the coffee shop and down the street. Yeah, crazy was good. And not that far from the truth, either. After all, she would have to have been crazy to throw away every-thing they'd had together.

Chapter 15

"We just got those in," the salesgirl said, sidling over to Mila, who was standing in front of a rack of sundresses at the Butternut Variety Store. "What do you think?"

"I think they're . . . really cute," Mila said honestly. She had come into the store to buy a pair of flip-flops, but the sundresses, with their colorful floral prints, had caught her eye.

"They *are* really cute," the salesgirl agreed. She was a young woman who'd been restocking the sunscreen display and looking desperately bored when Mila had walked in, but now that she had some company she'd perked up considerably. "Ordering these dresses was my idea," she told Mila, in a confidential tone. "We already sold clothes here, if you call things like tube

socks and trucker caps clothes. But last spring, I said
to the owner, Mr. Rasmussen, 'Would it kill us to sell
something that women actually want to wear?'"

Mila nodded politely and slipped one of the dresses
off the rack, wondering if it was the kind of thing she
should wear to the party tonight. She held it up to herself, a little self-consciously, and looked around for a
mirror.

"Do you want to try that on?" the salesgirl asked.

"Could I?"

"Of course. There's a little dressing room in back.
But there's no mirror in it. Go figure, right? There's
one right outside it, though."

Mila followed her to a tiny dressing room and, pulling the canvas curtain closed behind her, wriggled out
of her clothes and into the sundress, as the salesgirl—
her name was Darla, she told Mila—chattered away
outside of it.

"Oh, it fits you perfectly," she said to Mila when
she came out of the dressing room, pointing her in the
direction of a full-length mirror.

But as soon as Mila looked in the mirror, she looked
away. It was almost as if she didn't recognize herself in
this dress. It had been so long since she'd worn something so . . . so feminine. And so pretty. After she'd
gotten married to Brandon, she'd stopped wearing

clothes like this. Fun, flirty clothes. Because while he might have liked to see her in them, he didn't want *anyone else* to see her in them, and that was a problem if she ever wanted to leave their apartment. Then, when she'd finally left Brandon, she'd packed only the most functional clothing she owned. Functional, of course, meaning boring.

"What do you think?" Darla prompted.

Mila looked back in the mirror. "I think maybe it's a little tight on me," she said, tugging at one of the sundress's straps.

"No, it's not. It fits you the way it's supposed to. Trust me."

"Maybe if I went up a size—"

"If you went up a size, it would be too big," Darla said firmly. "In fact, if I were you, I'd not only wear that dress out of here, but I'd throw away the clothes I wore in here, too."

"Why?"

Darla shrugged. "You have way too nice a figure to be wearing things that hide it," she said. And then she looked in the mirror at Mila and sighed. "If I looked like that in a dress," she said, "my boyfriend would probably have a heart arrhythmia or something." And then she laughed. "So maybe it's a good thing I *don't* look like that in a dress. Anyway, I have to get back

to stocking, but I think you'd be crazy not to buy it."
She left Mila alone to stare uncertainly at her reflection in the mirror. The dress wasn't exactly revealing,
she decided, but it showed a little more skin than she
was used to showing. She bit her lip then and looked
abruptly away. She was acting like a teenager. Staring
at herself in the mirror, agonizing over what to wear
that night, and impulsively trying on the first article of
clothing she'd seen in the store. And that was strange,
because even when she'd *been* a teenager, she hadn't
acted like one. She hadn't had the luxury of acting like
one. She'd been too busy holding their little family
together. Which begged the question, really, of why
she was acting like a teenager *now*.

She took one more look in the mirror, then frowned
impatiently and went back into the dressing room,
yanking the curtain closed behind her. But by the time
she'd changed and emerged with the sundress a few
minutes later, she felt something other than impatience
with herself. She felt something she'd been feeling, off
and on, all day. Fidgety. Restless. Wound up. It wasn't
an unpleasant feeling. Not exactly. But it was the
reason she'd done something today she'd never done
before; after Walker and Reid had left for Reid's doctor's appointment that afternoon; she'd asked Lonnie if
she could borrow her car and she'd driven into town.

The cabin, she'd decided, was too quiet, and too staid to contain her nervous energy. She needed to be where things were happening, and while there didn't seem to be a *lot* happening in Butternut, and what *was* happening seemed to be happening at its own leisurely pace, it was something, anyway. It was enough to distract her, and to keep her from thinking too hard about that little pulse of anticipation she felt, even now, as she left the dressing room.

She took the dress up to the register, but not before she picked up a pair of flip-flops, a couple of cotton nightgowns, and a cover-up to wear over her bathing suit. She felt guilty watching Darla ring up her purchases. She'd promised herself she'd save all the money she was paid this summer. But when Darla gave her the total, she felt a little better. It was very reasonable, much more reasonable than it would have been in Minneapolis, and when all was said and done, it would barely put a dent in the money that she'd earned so far.

Mila thanked Darla and left the store, pausing in the doorway to look surreptitiously up and down the block. No sign of Brandon, she thought with relief, and then she immediately chided herself for half expecting there to be a sign of him. As Ms. Thompson had pointed out many times before, the only way Brandon would find her here was if he traced her directly to Butternut. He wouldn't just stumble on her. Minnesota, after all, was a big state. Not *Texas* big, maybe. But still, big enough. Even with this thought in mind, though, she was walking quickly back to the car, keeping her head down, when out of the corner of her eye she saw a sign in the window at Butternut Drugs. END OF JULY SALE, it read. ALL COSMETICS 25% OFF.

She paused. She didn't own any cosmetics. Not anymore. They, too, had been a casualty of her relationship with Brandon. She looked beautiful to him without makeup, he'd told her, so if she wore any makeup, he said, it was obviously for the benefit of other men. She'd known this was ridiculous, and she'd told him so too. But as was so often the case with Brandon, she'd opted, finally, for the path of least resistance. The only makeup she'd kept was foundation and pressed powder, both of them ideal, it turned out, for covering bruises. Now, though, looking in the store window, she thought about how nice it would be to have a new lipstick, and she went into the drugstore and spent a very pleasant five minutes at the makeup counter choosing a lipstick and, at the last minute, selecting a mascara, too. And as she waited in line at the register, behind two teenage girls, she felt it again, the tiny but undeniable current of electricity that had been humming through her intermittently all day. It was both vaguely pleasant, and vaguely disconcerting at the same time.

"What time's he picking you up tonight?" she heard one of the teenagers ask the other.

"Eight o'clock. And you know what? I can't wait," her friend said. "He's so hot. I keep thinking about what it's going to be like to see him again. I don't know, maybe it'll be a complete disaster. But maybe not. Something might happen. And knowing that is driving me a little crazy. I mean, remember the night before our chem final? When we drank, like, five cans of Red Bull? That's how I feel right now. Like I'm totally overcaffeinated."

And Mila, listening to them, started to smile and then stopped. Because she knew *exactly* what that girl was talking about. She knew because she was feeling *exactly* the same way about tonight. She was feeling that same fizzy excitement, that same jittery anticipation. Call it the Red Bull effect. Call it whatever you wanted. It was the sense . . . well, like the girl in front of her in line had said, it was the sense that *something might happen.* And knowing she was feeling that way about Reid, and about the party tonight, and knowing that she was behaving like some infatuated adolescent, instead of the mature adult she had thought—or at least *hoped*—she was, almost made her groan out loud, right then and there, standing in line at Butternut Drugs.

But she didn't. She paid for her cosmetics and walked out of the store and back out onto Main Street. And then she drifted distractedly down the sidewalk, only tangentially aware of her surroundings. *You like Reid, don't you?* she thought, simultaneously fascinated and appalled by this new knowledge of herself. *You like him* a lot. *And what's more, you're attracted to him, aren't you?* Attracted to a man who, seven weeks ago, she couldn't even stand to be in the same room with. *Yes,* she answered, *yes on both counts.* But how had it happened? So . . . so suddenly? But it hadn't happened suddenly, she realized. It had been happening gradually since the day they'd had the picnic at the beach. And she saw an image of him from that day, an image of him skipping stones, his upper body moving with an easy grace that even his wheelchair couldn't contain, his dark blue eyes focused not on the stones he was skipping so effortlessly over the water, but on her. On Mila.

She flashed on other images, too, from the last month. An image of her running a washcloth over Reid's bare chest on the deck the night of the full moon. Another one of her curled up in the armchair in his room in the middle of the night, knowing that they were both awake, and both sharing a strange, silent intimacy with each other. And an image of her sitting with him at the dinner table last night. His brother had taken him to a barbershop in Butternut late yesterday afternoon, and when they'd come back in the evening, right as she was taking dinner out of the oven, Mila had felt so disoriented by Reid's changed appearance that it was all she could do not to drop the pan of lasagna she was holding. He looked so different. So completely different. For the first time since she'd met him, she could actually see his face. And he'd looked handsome enough to swoon over. Where the tangle of his too-long hair had been, and the scruffiness of his beard had been, there were now only the clean, smooth, strong lines of his forehead, his cheeks, his jaw, and his chin. He was a little pale, of course, from all the hours he'd spent inside since the accident, and he had a scar, too, that she'd never seen before, running in a faint, jagged line across his forehead. But even so, he'd been a revelation to her. And the best part of that revelation, she'd decided, were his eyes. Because now that his hair was no longer falling into them, she could see them in all their deep, bright, blue glory.

After Walker had left yesterday evening, Mila and Reid had sat down at the kitchen table and had dinner, and then they'd had some kind of conversation, about something, though what it was, Mila couldn't for the life of her remember now. What she could remember were the pauses in the conversation, the spaces between words, the little silences during which tiny currents of . . . of attraction had eddied between them and around them.

Oh, my God, what was she thinking? What was she *doing?* She stopped and leaned against a lamppost for support, and its solidity gave her some measure of comfort. Comfort and resolve. She didn't know what she'd been doing, but she knew what she was going to do now. She was going to stop pretending that she and Reid were going on a date tonight. Because they weren't. They were going to a party. That was it. That was all. And whatever was happening between the two of them was going to stop happening. *Now.* She was his employee, for one thing, or his brother's, anyway, but it added up to the same thing. And she wasn't available, for another. Because although she wasn't wearing her wedding ring anymore, she might as well have been. Her little speech to herself at the ring-throwing ceremony the first night at the cabin aside, she was still technically married. And even in the unlikely event that she could forget that fact, she couldn't ignore the fact that she had no future with Reid. (Even if, as crazy as it seemed now, she thought she might want one with him.) But no, it wouldn't be fair to him to put him in the kind of danger he would be in if Brandon ever found her with him.

Thinking about all this, she felt suddenly dizzy, and, leaning on the lamppost, she wondered for a moment if she was going to faint. But the dizziness passed, and Mila, searching for its source, realized that she'd been too preoccupied to eat lunch today, and too distracted, sitting across the table from Reid, to eat breakfast, either. (She'd pretended, instead, to nibble on a piece of toast.) *No wonder I'm dizzy,* she thought, with relief. *I'm hungry.* And the Red Bull effect? That was probably just low blood sugar. And, holding on to this slender hope, she looked around for a place to eat and almost laughed when she realized that this whole time she'd been standing directly outside of Pearl's. It was well past lunchtime, but, as luck would have it, Pearl's was still open and still catering to a few late afternoon stragglers. So Mila went in and, avoiding the table she'd sat at on that first unpleasant afternoon, selected a booth in the back and slid into it, settling her shopping bag beside her. She took the menu out of the menu holder, ostensibly to study it, but she ended up studying the cook behind the counter instead, the one she'd seen the day she'd come in here to order her and Reid's hamburgers. The man was *enormous.* And there was that same waitress, too, the pretty one with the heart-shaped face and curly hair who seemed sweet but, at the same time, hopelessly confused.

She came over to Mila now. "Hi," she said, "I'm Jessica. What can I get for you?"

"Um, let's see," Mila said, looking back down at the menu.

"The Butternut Burger's good. Frankie—he's our cook—grinds the meat fresh every day," Jessica said proudly, looking at Frankie.

"I'll bet he does," Mila said, taking in Frankie's gargantuan arms, which were larger in circumference than her own waist. He smiled back at Jessica now, an adoring smile, and Mila realized that she was watching two people who were obviously very much in love with each other. *Great,* she thought. *Just what I need to be seeing now.* "You know what," she said to Jessica, a little abruptly. "I think I'll just have the vanilla milk shake."

"One vanilla milk shake," Jessica murmured in concentration as she wrote out the whole order on her check pad, and then she hurried away, bumping into a table as she went, and leaving Mila to worry about how she fared when the restaurant was actually busy. *Oh well,* she thought. *I probably wasn't a very good waitress either. Especially since I always had a chemistry textbook or a letter to Heather waiting for me to come back to between orders.*

But thinking about writing letters to Heather made her feel sad, so she tried to think about something else and immediately thought of Reid, which made her feel jittery all over again. *Low blood sugar,* she reminded herself, and when Jessica brought her milk shake, which was delicious, she drank it as dutifully as if she were taking medicine. And she *did* feel better afterward, but she still felt that same strange little quiver of excitement she'd felt all day. She sighed, paid her bill, and, leaving a generous tip for Jessica, she walked back to Lonnie's car and drove back to the cabin, grateful for once that the twisty road required all her attention.

After she'd walked into the kitchen and thanked Lonnie for letting her borrow her car, she lingered there for a little while, chatting with her and, at Lonnie's insistence, showing her the dress she'd bought that afternoon.

"You don't think it's too . . . too dressy?" Mila asked shyly, holding it up to herself. She didn't really mean dressy, though. She meant something else.

"Too dressy?" Lonnie repeated. "No, honey, it's perfect," she said, with her by now familiar and reassuring smile. "I'm glad you're going out tonight," she added. "It's about time you had some fun up here this summer. Honestly, I don't know how you've survived all these lonely nights out here all by yourself."

"Well, not *all* by myself," Mila corrected, not looking at her as she put her dress back in the shopping bag.

"Oh, of course," Lonnie amended. "You've had Reid to keep you company, too. And I must say, he's doing so much better, isn't he, Mila? I like to think," she confided, "that it has something to do with my home cooking. You know, now that he's actually eating it and not just picking at it."

"You know what?" Mila said. "I think your home cooking is definitely doing the trick." Privately, though, she now had another theory about Reid's improving mood.

"Oh, by the way," Lonnie said, "Allie called while you were out. She told me to remind you that she'd pick you up at five. I wish I could come, too, but my church is having a potluck tonight and I've already baked five dozen lemon squares for it."

"Your church is very lucky then," Mila said, and she left Lonnie in the kitchen and went to take a shower. Afterward, she blow-dried her hair with a little more care than usual and then slipped on her new sundress. She didn't look at herself in the full-length mirror in her room, though. She was afraid if she did, she'd lose her nerve and take it off. But she did use the small mirror above her dresser to put on a little bit of mascara and lipstick. And then she went back to the now quiet kitchen—Lonnie had left already for the night—and tried to keep her nervousness at bay while she waited for Allie to pick her up. But when Allie was late, and her nerves had had time to ratchet up another notch, she decided to call Ms. Thompson at Caring Home Care. Mila had gotten in the habit of calling her at least once a week, and, no matter how busy Ms. Thompson was, she always made time to talk to her.

"Mila," she said now when she heard her voice. "I'm so glad you called."

"I'm not interrupting anything, am I?"

"No, of course not," Ms. Thompson said, though Mila could hear her rustling papers in the background. "I'm just refiling all the filing my niece, Janet, did today." She sighed audibly. "Is it wrong to call someone who's your own flesh and blood a dolt?"

But Mila didn't know how to answer that so instead she asked, "How's your book club going?"

"Oh that," Ms. Thompson said with another sigh. "Well, I haven't been drummed out of it yet, if that's what you mean. But I sense a growing impatience with me just the same. Honestly, I don't know how those women find the time to always read the book, Mila. I really don't."

"Are they all still working, like you?" Mila asked.

"Oh, God no. Most of them had the sense to retire years ago. Something I should probably be considering doing, too," she added, though Mila somehow knew that Ms. Thompson would never retire. Not voluntarily, anyway.

"What about you, Mila?" she asked. "How are you doing?"

"I'm doing fine," she said carefully.

"And your patient? How's he doing? Still being difficult?"

"Um, no. Not at all. And he's not—he wasn't ever, really—as bad as I've made him out to be," she said, knowing she couldn't explain to Ms. Thompson, or herself, for that matter, the way she was feeling about Reid right now. "He's getting his cast off today," she said, redirecting the subject. "And his family's having a little party for him tonight at their cabin. I'm actually waiting, right now, for his sister-in-law to give me a ride there."

"You're going to a party?" Ms. Thompson asked.

"Well, a barbecue, actually."

"By the lake?"

"Uh-huh."

"That sounds like fun," Ms. Thompson said encouragingly. "And you know what? You deserve to have fun, Mila. You haven't had nearly enough of it lately, have you?" And Mila hesitated, thinking that what Ms. Thompson had just said to her sounded a lot like what Lonnie had said to her a little while ago. But she didn't say anything, because at that exact moment Allie's car pulled up outside. "My ride's here," she said, her stomach feeling fluttery again.

"All right, well, have a good time. And call me back soon," Ms. Thompson said. "It'll give me something to look forward to."

"I'll do that," Mila assured her, and then she said good-bye and hurried out to the waiting car.

"I'm sorry I'm late," Allie said as Mila climbed in beside her. "All our guests just arrived at the same time." Glancing over at Mila, Allie added before she headed up the driveway, "I like your dress. It's really pretty."

"Thank you," Mila said, relieved to see that Allie was wearing a sundress, too. "How did Reid's doctor's appointment go?" she asked casually as they turned onto the main road.

"Fine, I guess," Allie said. "They're not back yet."

"No?" Mila said, surprised. But Allie shrugged, unconcerned. "I think Walker was going to run a few other errands while they were in Ely," she said. "I'm sure they'll be back soon."

They drove the remaining five minutes to Allie and Walker's cabin in silence, and when they'd driven down its long gravel drive and pulled up in front of it, Mila was relieved to see there were only a handful of other cars there. *Good,* she thought with relief, so *it isn't a big party.* And it wasn't, as it turned out, a big cabin, either. It was small and rustic, and very charming, in its way, but it didn't look big enough to accommodate a family of four and Mila said as much to Allie.

"It's been a tight squeeze," Allie admitted as they got out of the car. "But it's been good for us, too, to all be so close together this summer. So *literally* close together. It was the same way for my family when I was growing up."

Mila nodded. The cabin did look like a sweet place, she thought, but it had still been generous of Allie and Walker to turn over their larger and more luxurious cabin to a convalescing Reid for the summer. "Come on," Allie said now, companionably taking her arm, "I want you to meet our friends."

Mila felt her natural shyness intensifying then, but she let Allie lead her around the cabin to where a lawn sloped gently down to the lake and to a small boathouse and dock. On the lawn was a large grill and a long picnic table that was covered with a blue-and-white-checked cloth, weighted down by picnic food that looked so delicious it could only have come from Pearl's. The guests, not surprisingly, were scattered around this table, sipping drinks, nibbling on finger food, and talking, and their children were at the other end of the lawn, clustered around a tetherball game, which Walker and Allie's adorable nine-year-old son, Wyatt, seemed to be playing with an almost ferocious determination. It was nice, Mila thought, all of it. Pretty and summery and festive. The sky was shaded the palest pink of early sunset, and the air was tinged with the smell of recently cut grass and charcoal smoke and filled with the sounds of conversation and laughter. And Mila got the feeling she'd gotten sometimes as a child, the feeling that she was on the outside looking in, and that something other people took for granted—in this case, friends getting together for a barbecue on a summer evening—was for her nothing short of amazing. *God, I want this,* she thought. She wanted now, more than ever, to be a part of something, a family, a group of friends, a town, anything, really, to banish the loneliness that had been the one constant in her life. But what were her chances of ever having anything like this? she wondered, looking around. Almost nonexistent, she decided. No, she amended. *Completely* nonexistent. As long as Brandon was looking for her, and she knew he was looking for her, scenes like this would always be unattainable to her.

She tried to brush away these thoughts, though, as Allie introduced her to all the guests, some of whom were already familiar to her. There were Jax and Jeremy

Johnson, who owned the hardware store in Butternut, and their four adorable daughters, who ranged in age from four to sixteen, and whose names, like their parents' names, all began with the letter *J*. The oldest of their daughters, Joy, looked very happy to be toting Brooke around with her everywhere, and Brooke, it seemed, was very happy to be toted around by her in return.

And then there were Jack and Caroline Keegan, who owned Pearl's and whom Lonnie—who liked to gossip about Butternut's residents, though never in a malicious or mean-spirited way—had told Mila about over coffee at the breakfast table one morning. Apparently, Jack had left Caroline and their daughter, Daisy, almost twenty years before, when Daisy was only three, only to return again last summer and work his way back into their lives and their hearts. According to Lonnie, he and Caroline had gotten remarried in the winter and had a small wedding reception with only their family and closest friends in attendance. As Allie introduced her to them, Mila looked for signs of their tumultuous past, but she couldn't find any. Jack was as handsome as Caroline was pretty, and they both looked happy and relaxed, holding hands and smiling at each other as if they'd never been apart before. Or maybe, she thought, they looked that way because they *had* been apart before, and now, after all those years, they had a true appreciation of what it meant to be together again.

"I was at Pearl's today," Mila told them, after she'd shaken hands with both of them. "And I had the best vanilla milk shake I've ever had."

"That's nice to hear," Caroline said, smiling. "I like them, too, but I prefer chocolate. Drinking them, though, is an occupational hazard for me, so I try to save them for special occasions."

"Speaking of special occasions," Allie said, "Jack and Caroline's daughter, Daisy, called them today to say that she and her boyfriend, Will, are engaged."

"Oh, congratulations," Mila said.

"Thank you," Jack said, looking pleased. "We're very happy for them."

"We are happy," Caroline said, in a qualifying tone. "But unlike Jack, I'm also a little worried. I mean, Will's stationed in Virginia, and Daisy will be going to graduate school in Michigan, and I just think it's going to be hard for them to be engaged to each other when they're so far apart."

"They'll be fine," Jack said reassuringly. "And in the meantime," he told Allie and Mila, "I've got my eye on a little cabin for them. I'd like to fix it up and surprise them with it after they get married here next summer. That way, if they don't have time for a real honeymoon, they'll at least have a place of their own to stay the weekend of their wedding."

"Jack, that is *so* sweet," Allie said, beaming at him. "And, as wedding presents go, I think a cabin's going to be much more useful to them than a juicer. Now, if you'll excuse us, I need to introduce Mila to the rest of our guests." With that, she dragged Mila away to meet some more families. And Mila tried to be polite, and tried to seem interested, but the truth was, she was intensely preoccupied by Reid's impending arrival. And just when she thought she couldn't stand it anymore, Allie looked up from the conversation they were having and said, "Oh look, here they are now."

Mila's eyes followed hers to the driveway, where the van was pulling up, and she felt her nerves ratchet up another notch. *I can't stand this anymore,* she thought, and though the night was warm, she realized her palms were sweating, and she tightened them around the icy can of Coke she was holding. She followed Allie over to the van, though, and only hung back a little as they got close. Then she watched as Walker got out and opened the passenger-side door. Positioning a pair of crutches beside it, Walker helped Reid out of the van and assisted him in hooking the crutches under his arms. And that was when Reid looked up and looked straight at Mila.

She didn't walk right up to him, though. She waited until Allie had congratulated him on getting his cast off, and until Walker had made sure Reid was comfortable on his crutches. And then, once they left him and went to put the chicken and ribs on the grill, Mila walked over to him, almost reluctantly. Reluctantly because all the Red Bulls she hadn't drunk that day were really kicking in now, and between her excitement and her nervousness she didn't quite trust herself to behave naturally around him. Especially since he looked so different on his crutches than he had in his wheelchair. He was taller, for one thing, several inches taller than Mila, and he was somehow more dynamic, too, and more in control.

"Hi," she said, feeling her face flush.

"Hi," he said, and then, "I like your dress."

"Thanks," Mila said, and then without thinking she blurted out nonsensically, "Darla made me buy it."

But Reid only smiled. "Well, then you should send Darla a thank-you note."

Chapter 16

"So you never told me what you thought of this," Reid asked, running his hand across his newly smooth jawline. He'd said hello to the other guests, and then he'd asked Mila if she'd come sit down with him on a bench that overlooked the lake. He'd told her that he wasn't used to being in social situations like this anymore, and that he needed some space, but the truth was, he wanted to be alone with her.

"I like it," she said, smiling. "What about you?"

"Me?" he asked, and he realized he'd already forgotten what they'd been talking about. He was having trouble thinking tonight. Or thinking *clearly*, anyway. And it was the sight of Mila that was confusing him. *Confounding him*, really. She looked . . . she looked so different tonight. She *always* looked good, of course, but right now, at this minute, she looked nothing short of incredible. There was the dress she was wearing, for one thing. It was so pretty, and so feminine, and what it revealed of her—from the soft curve of her breasts, to the narrow tapering of her waist—made him realize how little of her her other clothes had revealed. And then there was her auburn hair, which fell in a smooth and shiny curtain to her almost bare shoulders, which were tanned a lovely golden brown. She must have gotten that tan during her swimming lessons, he mused. It gave her complexion a warm and healthy glow and set off her amber eyes, with the golden flecks of light in them. But there was something else about her eyes . . . had she curled her eyelashes, he wondered, or put on eyeliner? He really didn't know much about these things, but whatever she'd done, it made her eyes look especially bright and luminous tonight.

"Do you like not having a beard?" Mila prompted him now. "Or are you going to miss it?"

He shook his head. "No, I won't miss it. I mean, I've gotten out of the habit of shaving every day, so that'll be an adjustment. But at least I won't look like a terrorist anymore, as my brother so helpfully pointed out."

Mila laughed then, and as soon as she stopped, Reid wanted to make her laugh again. She didn't laugh nearly enough, he decided. Neither of them did. But his eyes must have lingered on her for too long, because she seemed suddenly self-conscious, crossing and uncrossing her legs. Reid saw the problem. When she crossed her legs, her sundress rode up a few inches above her knees. So she left her legs uncrossed now and, pressing her knees together, tugged ineffectually at the hem of her dress, trying to make it cover those knees. But it wouldn't. Reid smiled. Her knees were adorable. *She* was adorable.

Still, in an effort to rescue her from her self-consciousness, he asked, "Are you having a good time here?"

"Uh-huh," she said, looking around. "It's nice. I don't know any of these people that well, except, maybe, your brother and sister-in-law, but they all seem so nice. So . . . so normal."

As opposed to what? Reid almost asked. But he stopped himself. He knew Mila well enough by now to know she wouldn't elaborate on that comment.

"It *is* nice," he said instead, looking around, and he was surprised to realize that he meant it. "It's funny," he went on, "I used to think things like this were a waste of time."

"Parties?"

He shrugged. "Anything like this. I didn't really see the point of it, I guess."

"Well, to eat and to drink," Mila said, raising an eyebrow.

"Yeah, but it's a lot of trouble to go to, isn't it? Wouldn't it be faster and easier to eat and drink at home?"

She shook her head, amusement and disbelief mingling in her expression. "Well, then, to be with other people. To not be alone," she added.

Reid nodded. "Yeah, that was the part that was the hardest for me to understand. The being with other people. All the useless small talk, and the polite banter. I thought, 'who needs it, really?' "

"Well, these people, for one," Mila said, her eyes traveling over the assembled guests. "And as for the useless small talk, Reid, I don't really think that's what's happening here, do you? I mean, I think these people care about one another. Quite a bit, actually."

Like I care about you, Reid thought. But he got her point. Something like this felt different for him now that he was here with Mila.

"What about you?" he asked, suddenly. "Do you like things like this?"

She nodded and then smiled, a little sadly he thought. "I do. Maybe because, as a child, I was never invited to them. And even if I had been, my mom would never have taken me."

"Because she didn't have the time?"

She nodded. "No time, and no family or friends, either."

"No friends?"

"Not really. Not real friends. More like drinking buddies, I guess you'd call them."

"But you must have had friends," Reid pressed.

"I . . ." She hesitated. "There was someone I was close to when I was growing up. But we lost touch and . . ." Her voice trailed off. She shrugged then and seemed to suddenly become interested in watching a game of capture the flag the kids were playing.

And Reid surprised himself by saying, "Well, maybe your family didn't go to things like this, but you'll have your own family one day, won't you? And then you'll go to as many parties as you want to. You can have them yourself, every day, if it makes you happy." As he was saying these words, he realized how badly he wanted her to be happy.

She looked at him, a little strangely. Then looked away again. "I'm not going to have a family," she said.

"Really?" Reid said. "Because it . . . it seems like it would be a natural thing for someone like you to do. You know, someone who's obviously so good at taking care of other people."

As he said this, though, her expression became one of sheer, almost heartbreaking wistfulness. But then that disappeared and in its place was Mila's usual expression. Guarded, reserved, and neutral.

"I don't think having a family would be right for me," she said carefully.

"How could you know that now?" he asked.

"Some things you just know," she said, looking away. "Marriage and children aren't for everyone. Some people, like me, should probably just go it alone."

"Mila Jones against the world?" Reid asked gently.

"Something like that," she said, and, for a moment, her guard slipped again and the sadness was back. And Reid felt a sudden urge to take her in his arms and kiss her, kiss away her sadness, and her fear and her doubt and anything else, for that matter, that stood in the way of her being perfectly happy. He imagined doing it then. He would start with her eyelids, he decided, her closed eyelids, and he would kiss them as gently as he knew how to. Then he would work his way down, from her temple to her jaw to her neck, to the soft hollow at the base of her neck, to her collarbone, to her shoulders, and finally, when he couldn't stand the anticipation any longer, he would kiss her lips, her lovely, lovely lips . . .

"Let's get out of here," he said suddenly.

Mila looked startled. "Reid, we haven't even eaten yet."

"Isn't there something we could heat up back at the cabin?" he started to ask, but at that moment, Walker came sauntering over to them. "Dinner's ready," he said, smiling at them.

"Why don't I get something for both of us," Mila said quickly, standing up.

"I'm not really hungry," Reid said to her retreating back, but she ignored him.

Walker looked after her a little quizzically. "She looks different tonight," he said, turning back to Reid.

Reid nodded.

"She looks nice."

Nice? Reid almost said. *She looks beautiful, you idiot.* But Walker had caught something in his expression and was staring at him a little too intently.

"Reid," he said, frowning. "You're not . . ."

"Not what?"

"You're not getting too close to Mila, are you?"

"Have you ever known me to get too close to anyone?" Reid asked.

Walker didn't need to think about that. "No," he said. "No, I haven't."

"Well, then, there's nothing to worry about, is there?" Reid said, hoping this would put the subject to rest.

"I guess not," Walker said, apparently reassured. "I better see if I need to put more ribs on." With a quick smile, he walked away.

Mila was back then, carrying plastic forks, knives, and napkins and two paper plates laden with spareribs, coleslaw, and biscuits.

They ate with their plates on their laps, and Reid was surprised to discover that he was hungry, and that everything tasted delicious. A soft, purple dusk had settled over the lake, and on the picnic table the candles quivered and jumped in the evening breeze. Someone had brought sparklers for the children, and they ran across the lawn with them, trailing their comets of bright sparks behind them.

Mila and Reid had been sitting in silence as they ate, but now Mila asked, "Can I get you some dessert? I think one of Jax's daughters made cupcakes."

"No, thanks," he said.

"I'll be right back," Mila said, taking their plates away. And when she came back and sat down beside him again, he resisted the urge to reach for her hand, which was what he really wanted to do.

But she turned to him then, and something passed between them, something so sharp and so electric that it left Reid feeling a little stunned. How was it possible to feel that charge, that current, he wondered, when you weren't even touching someone? And then he had a thought. A depressing thought, really. What if Mila hadn't felt it, too? What if it had been one-sided, one-sided on *his* side. He'd understood this so well once, this whole game of seduction. He'd been good at it too. Very good, as he recalled. But now he felt as if it were all a complete mystery to him.

That's because it's not a game anymore, he told himself. *It's real.* And whatever he'd thought he'd known about it had no bearing here. Except . . . except maybe he wasn't completely wrong about Mila. Maybe he hadn't totally imagined her attraction to him. Because in the next moment, she leaned closer to him, smiled, and said, "You know what, Reid. You're right. Let's get out of here."

By some unspoken agreement, Mila and Reid went out on the deck after they came back from the party. The sky had darkened from purple to black, and the stars were shimmering pinpricks of light. "I'll get that," Mila said when Reid started to lug a deck chair over, but she was amazed at the ease with which he was already moving on his crutches. He had a natural athleticism she saw; it would serve him well now that his physical therapy was due to begin.

They sat on side-by-side deck chairs for a little while, neither of them saying anything, but both of them acutely aware of the other's presence. Their attraction, Mila realized, was a real, palpable thing, and there was something exhausting, finally, about not giving in to it. About not doing the things she'd wanted to do all night: touch him, kiss him, hold him. Finally, when she thought she couldn't stand it anymore, Reid turned to her and very gently brushed a strand of hair off her cheek. "May I kiss you, Mila?" he asked.

God yes, she wanted to say, but what she said instead was, "Do you always ask permission before you kiss someone?"

"No. I've never asked anyone before. But I'm asking you now."

She smiled—at the seriousness of his expression, and the formality of his question. But even as she smiled, she understood the reason for his seriousness. Reid knew something about her, something she had never told him. And he understood, intuitively, how slowly he would need to move with her. How carefully.

"May I?" he asked. "One kiss?" And since it was almost impossible for her to enumerate all the reasons why he shouldn't kiss her, she didn't even try to. Instead, she said, "Yes," and closed her eyes, hoping that everything would somehow feel less real this way, and she would feel less burdened by the consequences of what she was doing. But when he kissed her, he didn't kiss her on the lips, as she'd expected him to. He kissed her instead, first on one closed eyelid and then on the other. "These aren't part of the official kiss," he said, kissing her now on her left temple. "These are . . ."

"Unofficial kisses?" Mila suggested, as the kisses traveled down from her temple to her ear.

"That's right," Reid agreed, between kisses. There was a whole string of these kisses, too, marching steadily down, to her jaw, and then to her neck, and then to the little hollow at the base of her neck, and each one of them was so soft and so feathery light that she almost squirmed with the anticipation of what was to come. What was to come, of course, was a kiss on the lips. A kiss that was, as promised, just one kiss. On the face of it, anyway. But, in reality, it was actually many different kisses. There was the gentle kiss that he had started out with, a kiss that hardly left any impression on her lips at all. A kiss that was more of a preview of what it would be like if he kissed her than an actual kiss itself. And that was followed, a little later, by a teasing, playful kiss, a kiss that almost made Mila smile. It was a kiss that was an invitation to have fun, she realized, and since fun was something that had been missing in her life for so long now, it was a kiss that was almost impossible to resist. And that kiss was followed by a new kiss, an exploratory, thoughtful kiss, a kiss that made Mila think that Reid was trying to memorize, by touch, her lips, and her mouth and her tongue. After that, he started running his fingers through her hair, in a gesture that was both gentle and sensual, and his kiss deepened, his tongue stroking her tongue, luxuriantly, in a way that seemed to suggest that they had all the time in the world and nothing else to do but kiss each other like this. It made Mila's insides quiver, and it made her bury her hands in Reid's newly short hair and tug on it with her fingers. There was a low sound in his throat when she did that, and he took her face in his hands, and kissed her with such urgency that Mila felt a searing heat rip through her. Because if a man kissed you this way, you couldn't help but wonder how he would make love to you. . . . She pulled, suddenly, away from him.

"What's wrong?"

"Nothing's *wrong*," she said, out of breath. "But, Reid . . ." She shook her head, as if to clear it.

"I'm sorry. I said one kiss. And I wanted you to remember it. I wanted to make it count."

She didn't say anything. She couldn't. So she tried, instead, to restore some order to her hair, and to her thoughts, both of which were chaotic and wild. Her hair was tangled on her shoulders, and her thoughts, her thoughts were running something like this: *That was cutting it* way, way *too close.* One more minute of a kiss like that and she would have followed him anywhere. Though the most logical place for her to have followed him, of course, would have been to his bedroom. Or, more specifically, to his bed. And she saw an image then of her sundress, bra, and panties in a little heap on the floor beside Reid's bed.

"I think I . . . I think we'd better call it a night," Mila said now. "I'm really tired. And I know you must be too." It sounded lame, even to her, but Reid only nodded. She stood up to go inside, and Reid followed her. And after she'd closed and locked the sliding glass door, and set the alarm in the kitchen, she walked with him as far as his bedroom door and said good night to him.

"Good night, Mila," he said, with the same seriousness with which he'd asked if he could kiss her.

She headed down the hall to her room, and Reid went inside his room and started to close the door, but she had a change of heart and turned back.

"Reid?" she called.

"Yes?" he said, coming back out into the hallway.

"That kiss? You made it count. Trust me. You *really* made it count." She went into her room then, closed the door, and leaned back against it. She could still feel his hands in her hair, and his mouth on her mouth, and she was reminded of what she'd overheard that teenager say in the drugstore earlier that day, about having the feeling that "something might happen" that night. *Oh, something had happened all right,* she told herself. *Something had definitely happened.* But now that it had, there was no way to make it *un*happen. And standing there, she reminded herself, as she had that afternoon, that it was impossible. Getting involved with each other would be unprofessional on her part, and dangerous on his. Still, it was hours before she stopped reliving his kiss, and hours before she stopped making a map of all the places his lips had touched.

Chapter 17

"Are you all right?" Mila asked, leaning over Reid's bed in what by now had become a familiar ritual.

"I'm fine," he started to say, but he stopped himself, since the condition he was in would seem to contradict that statement. His heart was pounding, his adrenaline was spiking, and his throat . . . *uh,* his throat was so parched and rough he could barely swallow. He knew he'd been screaming tonight, probably for a long time.

"I'm sorry," Mila said.

"*You're* sorry?"

She nodded. "I don't think I woke up right away," she said. "Usually, I'm a light sleeper, but . . ."

"But you're exhausted," Reid finished for her. "And you should be. You've spent the last three nights sleeping in a chair, Mila."

She shrugged. "It's not me I'm worried about, Reid."

He drew in a real breath now, the first since she'd woken him up, and felt his heart rate begin to slow.

"I'll get the pillow and the blanket," Mila said. But Reid stalled, wanting her to stay close to him.

"This is new," he said of her nightgown, which was a sleeveless white cotton one, with an edging of lace at the neckline, and a pattern of tiny pale pink roses on it. It was both modest and lovely, he decided, taking a little of its material between his fingers. It was just like Mila.

But Mila, watching him, removed his hand gently from her nightgown and looked at him as if to say, *We've been over this already.* And they had. They'd been over it at the breakfast table a couple of days ago, the morning after their kiss on the deck. Lonnie had gone outside to collect one of her packages, and Mila had said, a little formally, as if she had already rehearsed it, "Reid, last night was a serious breach of professionalism on my part. And I can't allow it to happen again. Not if I'm going to continue to live here and work here."

That was all she'd had time to say before Lonnie came back inside, but it had been enough. Because Reid's worst fear, it turned out, was not that that kiss wouldn't happen again, and happen again soon, it was that Mila would leave. So he said nothing, and he was careful to observe the new distance she'd put between them. Personally, though, he was skeptical about how long they could maintain it. Their attraction, it seemed to him, was like a rubber band stretched tight and ready to snap at any moment.

But Mila wasn't feeling that attraction right now. Right now, she looked tired, her pretty brown and gold eyes shadowed by faint circles.

"You don't have to stay," Reid said. "Really, go back to bed. I'll be fine."

"No. I told you that first night I would stay after you had a dream like that, and I meant it." She started to head for the closet to retrieve the pillow and the blanket, but he said quickly, "Look, Mila, there's a bed right here that you can sleep in."

She stopped and turned back. "You mean the bed that you're already in?"

"Well, I'm not taking up the whole thing," he said, amazed at his own audacity.

She was amazed at it too. "Reid, you *cannot* be serious."

"Why not? I don't . . . want to be alone," he said, conscious of the effort it still cost him to admit this. "And you don't want to spend the rest of the night sleeping in a chair. And besides, this bed is huge."

Indicating the hospital bed that he didn't really need anymore but that the medical equipment rental company hadn't picked up yet, he added, "Really, there's more than enough room in it for the two of us."

"Reid, I'm not sleeping in your bed with you," she said, crossing her arms across her chest.

"Even if it really is to sleep? Even if I give you my word that that's all we would do?"

"It's not that," Mila said, in a way that made Reid think it was, at least partly that.

"Then what it is?"

"It's that it would be completely inappropriate for me to sleep in the same bed as a patient."

"Even if it contributed to that patient's overall sense of well-being?" Reid asked, knowing full well that he was pushing the envelope here.

"Even then," she said, her eyebrows quirking up again in a way that seemed to say, *Nice try, Reid.*

She retrieved the pillow and blanket, turned off the bedside table lamp, and settled into the armchair. And Reid stared at the dark ceiling. He knew he'd overstepped her boundaries with that suggestion, but he'd be lying if he said he didn't think about it, about the two of them being in the same bed together. He did think about it. He thought about it all the time. Not necessarily *sleeping* together, though the sleeping would be nice, too, once they were both exhausted enough to sleep. He sighed and wondered what it would take to deliver Mila into his bed with him right now. *A miracle,* he decided. Which was why he was so surprised when, a minute later, Mila got up, turned on the bedside table lamp, and said, without any preamble, "How much do you want me to sleep next to you tonight, Reid? And I do mean *sleep.*"

He blinked. "A lot," he said.

She studied him, her expression intense and speculative. "All right," she said finally. "I'll do it. I'll sleep next to you, in your bed, on one condition."

"Which is?"

"That you'll see a doctor that I've heard about."

"What kind of doctor?" he asked, instantly tense.

"A psychologist, actually, and he comes highly recommended. He's very experienced treating people with PTSD."

He groaned audibly. "Not this again."

"Yes, this again."

"I told you. I don't have that."

"That's a matter of opinion. But if we can't agree on it, I can always go back to the chair," she said, reaching for the light switch.

"No," he said hastily. "Don't do that. I'll . . . I'll see him, okay?"

Her hand stopped in midair.

"I'll see him *once*," he amended.

"You'll see him once *and* you'll keep an open mind about seeing him again," she countered.

"I don't know about that."

"Okay, then you'll *try* to keep an open mind about seeing him again."

"You drive a hard bargain," he said.

She shrugged, almost imperceptibly.

"All right," he said grudgingly.

"All right?" she repeated, her eyes suddenly alight. He nodded.

"Well, move over then," she said, with a smile.

And Reid, trying to contain his delight, moved over, dragging his uncooperative leg with him. Mila retrieved her pillow from the armchair, started to get in beside him, and then stopped. "Reid, if you think tonight is going to pick up where the night on the deck left off, you're going to be disappointed."

"I don't think that," he assured her. "Really, it's not going to be a problem for me. I'll stay on my side of the bed and you'll stay on yours."

"Good," she said, satisfied. She laid her pillow next to his pillow, and then she slipped in beside him. As he'd predicted, there was plenty of room for both of them. More than enough so that they could lie beside each other without actually touching each other. But still, the very presence of her in his bed was exotic, and strange. He tried to seem nonchalant, though, as she plumped up her pillow, pulled the covers over her, and, after reaching to turn off the bedside light, settled into the bed, facing him in the darkness.

"Good night, Reid," she said, and he thought he could hear a trace of humor in her voice.

"Good night, Mila," he answered.

He closed his eyes, and the room was quiet, except for the soft, regular sound of her breathing. He listened to it carefully, as it slowly relaxed and then settled finally into the easy rhythm of sleep. After that, he opened his eyes and watched her in the faint, gray light of the room. He felt an incredible urge to touch her then, to brush a strand of hair off her face, or to pull the slipped-down strap on her nightgown back up onto her shoulder. But he did neither of those things. He'd promised to stay on his side of the bed, and he intended to do so. Still, he savored her nearness. The faint coconut scent of the lotion she was wearing. The sweet tickle of her breath reaching him from several inches away. Never would he have believed it was possible to share this kind of intimacy with someone without actually touching them.

And then he remembered a placard on the wall of a dive bar he and his friends had frequented in college.

It had said, "Never play poker with a man named Doc. Never eat at a restaurant called Ma's. And never sleep with a woman who has more troubles than you do."

He smiled wryly to himself, knowing the "sleep" this referred to was not sleep in the literal sense of the word. In his and Mila's sense of the word. Still, it gave him pause. *Did* Mila have more troubles than he did? Well, not *more* maybe, but she had at least as many, and they weren't insignificant troubles either. She was afraid, for one thing. And since she didn't strike him as a coward, he assumed that whatever, no, *whoever* she was afraid of, was pretty goddamned scary. And she'd been hurt, too. Badly. Maybe so badly that having a relationship—a normal, healthy relationship—wasn't in the cards for her. Though, in truth, a "normal, healthy" relationship was something he himself knew almost nothing about.

Still, it was crazy for him to think about having a future with Mila. He knew that. Both of them were scarred in their own ways. Both of them were struggling to find some semblance of normality. And both of them had a long way to go before they got there. *If* they got there. Alone, they had their work cut out for them, and together . . . together they might not be the stronger for it. Together, they might be like the drowning victim who drowns the person who tries to save them.

Lying there beside Mila, he told himself all these things. And he told himself why falling in love with her was a bad idea. A very bad idea. And he lined up all the reasons why he shouldn't get involved with her. Lined them up in an intimidating column that would have disheartened even the most romantic of men, let alone a born cynic like himself.

But none of this mattered. Because lying there with her, he had that feeling again, that feeling he had when he watched her swimming lessons. That slow, percolating happiness that bubbled up through the layers of his indifference until it burst through, finally, onto the surface of his consciousness. It was the clearest, purest, lightest feeling he'd ever felt, and it kept him awake until daybreak. It was then, as the pale morning light began to fill the room and he drifted into sleep, that he realized it had been one of the best nights of his life. No. Not *one* of the best nights. *The* best night.

As luck would have it, the psychologist Mila had found for Reid, Dr. Michael Immerman, had an opening the next week, and on a cool, wet afternoon in late July, Mila drove Reid to his office, in a nondescript office park outside the town of Ely. After the appointment, as they stood waiting for the elevator, Mila asked casually, "How'd it go?"

Reid, leaning on his crutches, shrugged. "He talked, a little, about what he does. I didn't talk at all."

"You didn't . . . you didn't say anything?" Mila asked, feeling a sting of disappointment.

Reid shook his head.

"You just . . . sat there?"

He nodded, almost imperceptibly.

"So I guess you won't be going back," she said, looking not at him but at the elevator display. She didn't want him to see how let down she felt, especially since she thought she wasn't being entirely fair to him. After all, he'd kept his end of the agreement. He'd gone to the appointment. He hadn't promised anything more, had he? Which was why she was surprised now when he said, "Actually, I made another appointment with him for next week."

Mila stared at him. "Why?"

"Well, for one thing, he doesn't seem like a *complete* crackpot," he said. "And for another, a good roommate is hard to find." He smiled at her and lowered his voice. "Especially one who fits into my bed as perfectly as you do."

Mila blushed and looked around, but there was no one else nearby. "You're going to have to say something to him eventually, you know," she said, as the elevator doors slid open.

"Probably," Reid agreed, as they got onto a full elevator. And Mila, working hard to seem nonchalant, didn't bring the subject up again. She knew it was important not to pressure him. She'd gotten him this far, but she couldn't get him any further. Reid, and Dr. Immerman, would have to do the rest. Riding down in the elevator, though, and driving back to the cabin, she felt so happy and so lighthearted that it was all she could do not to hum the song Lonnie had been singing as she'd washed the breakfast dishes that morning.

Chapter 18

A couple days after his first appointment with Dr. Immerman, Reid was sitting at the desk in the study when Walker appeared in the doorway.

"Hey," Reid said, looking up from the file in front of him. "I was just taking a look at the business plan you gave me."

"What do you think?" Walker asked, coming over to him. He was pleased, Reid knew, to see him working again.

"I think I'm going to need a little more time," Reid said. Which was true. Because when he'd told Walker he was "just taking a look at it," he'd meant it literally, as in just staring blankly at it while he thought about Mila instead. She was over at Allie and Walker's cabin, where her swimming lessons had been moved for the rest of the summer. With August right around the corner, Butternut's peak tourist season was upon them, and Allie was too busy at the gallery to take Tuesday and Thursday afternoons off anymore. Instead, Mila would be going over to her cabin on those evenings, after Brooke and Wyatt had had their dinners but before it was too dark to comfortably see outside. Reid understood the rationale behind this, and he understood, too, that Allie couldn't have known how much he liked watching the lessons, but still, he felt a little sulky, knowing they were continuing without him and knowing, too, how close Mila was to swimming.

"Hey, don't worry about the business plan," Walker said, sitting on the edge of his desk. "Take as much time with it as you need." Then he added, "It's not even the reason I came over. I want to take you back to the cabin with me. I think Allie and Mila have something they want to show you."

Reid looked at him questioningly, but Walker, feigning ignorance, only shrugged. His brother had always been a lousy liar, Reid thought, but right this minute he was going to let it slide. "Let's go," he said, reaching for his crutches.

By the time Reid and Walker drove over to the other cabin and walked down to the dock, there was a feeling of excitement in the air. Wyatt, for instance, was jumping up and down, and even Brooke, resting securely on Allie's hip, seemed more wriggly than usual.

"Uncle Reid," Wyatt said, still jumping, "my mom and Mila have a surprise for you."

"Do they?" Reid said, smiling and reaching over to pat Wyatt's mop of unruly brown curls. "Well, I can't wait to see what it is."

He glanced over at Mila, who was standing at the end of the dock, and she waved to him shyly. She looked excited, too, but she also looked nervous. She'd obviously been in the water already. She had a beach towel wrapped around her waist, and her still wet hair was pulled back in a ponytail. But towel aside, there was still plenty of her bathing-suit-clad body visible to him, and Reid tried, mightily, not to gawk at her. God, he loved that bathing suit. Loved it even better from close up than he had from far away.

"All right, let's get started," Allie said briskly, handing Brooke over to Walker. "Are you ready, Mila?" she asked, walking out onto the dock. Mila nodded, and it was then that Reid realized that Allie wasn't wearing a bathing suit, and that she hadn't been in the water yet, either. He frowned. He thought she got into the water with Mila during their lessons.

"Have a seat," Walker said to Reid, sitting down on a nearby deck chair and settling Brooke onto his lap.

Reid sat down distractedly. He was watching Allie and Mila, who were conferring quietly with each other. Then Mila stole a quick look at Reid, dropped her towel on the dock, and climbed down the ladder into the water.

"Isn't Allie going in with her?" he asked Walker.

"Nope."

"Why not?"

"Just watch," Walker said, jiggling Brooke on one knee and pulling Wyatt over to sit on the other.

Allie sat down on the edge of the dock and spoke to Mila, who was standing in the shoulder-deep water. "You know what you're doing," she said encouragingly. "Just take it slowly. And whatever you do, remember to breathe, okay?"

Mila nodded, and then, with an expression of quiet determination on her face, she turned around, pushed off from the bottom of the lake, and began to swim a slightly awkward front crawl.

"Oh my God," Reid said after a moment. "She's doing it. She's swimming."

Walker smiled. "She started swimming last week, but she wanted to be able to swim out to the float and back before she showed all of us."

Reid nodded, watching her. Now that she'd settled into her stroke, it was less awkward. More graceful. She was swimming in a straight line, too, more or less, from the end of the dock to the swimming float a short distance away. But the water out there was deep, he realized, deep enough to be over her head.

"She's not . . . she's not going to get tired, is she?" he asked Walker. "Because she can't touch the bottom out there."

"She's fine. She's not going very far, and Allie wouldn't let her go even *that* far if she didn't think she was ready."

"You're right," Reid said, relaxing a little. "She's doing fine." *Better than fine,* he thought, his pride in her building steadily as she swam. She reached the swimming float and stopped there for a moment, catching her breath, and then she turned around, pushed off the float, and swam back to the dock.

"That was fantastic," Reid said, more to himself than to anyone else, and, ignoring Walker and Allie and Wyatt, who were all cheering for Mila, he pulled himself up on his crutches and started down the dock. Mila climbed up the ladder, wrapped her towel around her, and, after hugging Allie, she started toward Reid, meeting him halfway.

"You did it!" he said, wanting to reach for her, but knowing if he let go of his crutches, he'd fall.

"I did it," she agreed, coming up to him, her face alight with happiness. "And, Reid, I love it! I love it so much! One day, when your leg is stronger—"

But he didn't let her finish. He leaned in to kiss her cheek, her smooth, cool cheek, and then, at the last second, he shifted direction, fractionally, and kissed her mouth instead. If he'd stopped to think about it, it might have occurred to him that kissing her this way, in front of everyone, wasn't a great idea. But he didn't stop to think about it. He didn't want to. And neither, apparently, did Mila, because after hesitating for a moment, she kissed him back.

After that, everything but the two of them seemed to disappear. The dock, the lake, the whole world, and everybody else in it. And when Mila pulled away from him, breathless, he was amazed to see that everything, and everyone, was still there. He looked over at Allie. She was mildly surprised, but also, Reid thought, very pleased. She had seen this coming. Then he looked at his brother. He hadn't seen this coming, or hadn't wanted to see it coming, Reid thought. There was a long silence then, during which the only sounds were Brooke gurgling and Wyatt still jumping up and down.

"Well, I don't know about anyone else," Walker said finally, "but I could use a drink."

"If I live to be a hundred, I will never, *ever*, forget the expression on my brother's face after I kissed you," Reid said with satisfaction as Mila let them into the cabin's kitchen. But Mila said nothing. Reid paused, resting on his crutches, his brow creased with sudden concern. "You're not upset about what happened, are you?" he asked as she closed the door.

"I'm not upset with you, Reid," she said, though she was careful now to put a safe distance between them. "I'm upset with myself. Letting that happen was poor judgment on my part." She leaned against the kitchen counter, her arms folded protectively over the bathing suit and cover-up she was still wearing. "I don't know what I was thinking."

"I don't think you were thinking," Reid said. "I think you were just doing what felt right to you in the moment."

"Well, that's not a very good formula for living your life, is it?"

"I don't know about that," Reid said. "Some people would say it's a *very* good formula."

She frowned, though, preoccupied by something. "What did your brother say to you when he was helping you into the van?"

He hesitated. "He said . . . he said 'I hope you know what you're doing.'"

"Do you, Reid?"

"I know exactly what I'm doing," he said, looking at her in that way he had of looking at her. That way no one else had ever looked at her before. It was as if he were seeing her as the person she actually was, instead of seeing her as the person he wanted her to be, or hoped she would be. And she almost asked him then, *What is it, exactly, that you're doing, Reid?*, but the truth was, she was afraid of how he might answer the question.

So instead she said, "We need to turn some lights on in here. It's almost dark." But when she headed for the light switch next to the door, Reid objected.

"I like the light in here now," he said, and she stopped, because she realized she liked it too. Outside, the sky was lavender, and inside, everything seemed to be bathed in its gentle light. It seemed a shame, she thought, to drown out this twilight softness.

"This is my favorite time of day," Reid said.

"It is?" she asked. "Why?"

"Because it's the one time of day you feel like anything could happen," he said, not taking his eyes off her.

Exactly, Mila thought. *That's the problem.* But he smiled at her now, and she felt that irresistible tug toward him that she knew was as emotional as it was physical.

"I think Lonnie left something for dinner," she said, resisting it. "Should I heat it up?"

"If you'd like some of it," he said.

"No, not really," she said. Because what was the point of heating up food she had no intention of actually eating? And what was the point, finally, of postponing the inevitable between them? Because standing there with him, she realized she couldn't do it anymore, couldn't resist the sheer force of their attraction to each other. She had tried, since their first kiss on the deck, and it was wearing her down. It was *exhausting* her. And she wondered why they were still talking, instead of doing what they both knew they were going to do, and then she realized, for the first time in her life, that talking—just talking—could be as sensuous as touching. Or at least it could be with Reid. She felt that warm, almost liquid sensation sliding through her body now, as if his hands and lips were already on her.

Why didn't he come to her? she wondered. There was only six feet separating them, maybe less, from where they both stood, leaning against the kitchen counter. But he made no move to close the distance between them, and, suddenly, she understood why. He was waiting for her to come to him, waiting because it needed to be her choice. As persuasive as Reid could be, he would never pressure her to do something she didn't want to do. Never ask her to be someone she didn't want to be. And, in that sense, he was Brandon's polar opposite. He was a man who could take no for an answer. A man who wouldn't take yes, in fact, unless she could give him that yes wholeheartedly. With all her being.

Somehow, knowing this gave her the courage to walk over to him now, angle herself between his crutches, put her hands on his shoulders, and kiss him, full on the lips, without any inhibition. And he kissed her back, but this kiss, she quickly discovered, wasn't part of his repertoire of kisses from that night on the deck a week ago. This kiss was something else entirely. It was . . . it was so many things. It was hungry, and deep and sweet, and tender, and needful. It held nothing back, and it gave everything away. And within thirty seconds, Mila knew this kiss couldn't end as innocently as the last one had, with the two of them saying a chaste good night at Reid's bedroom door. But that was all right. She didn't want it to end that way. She wanted everything from this man, she realized, with a little shock. She wanted everything at once.

He must have known that, too, because no sooner had he started kissing her than he started to unbutton her cover-up, which was really just an oversized white cotton shirt that buttoned up the front. She let him unbutton it, and let him slide it down her shoulders and her arms, and drop it onto the floor, where it settled at her feet. Then, still kissing her, he caressed her bare arms, and shoulders, and collarbone, until finally, when she thought she couldn't stand it anymore, he began to caress her breasts, very softly, but very deliberately, through the stretchy fabric of her bathing suit.

She shivered and felt her nipples harden immediately. He concentrated on one of them, stroking it softly at first and then harder, until the friction he'd created between her bathing suit and her nipple made Mila break away from their kiss with a little moan of pleasure. He kissed her again then and dipped a hand inside of her bathing suit top and, after cradling her breast tenderly in his palm, he stroked her nipple harder, in a way that sent a rush of warmth through her body.

"Let's go to my room," he said into her neck. "Or your room."

"I, I don't know. It's not . . . it's not a . . ." *It's not a good idea,* she meant to say, but she lost her train of thought. What Reid was doing to her felt so good, so unbelievably good, that she couldn't form a single coherent sentence. So she stopped trying to and instead dug her fingers into his hair and arched her back so that she could feel more of his body against her body.

"Oh God, Mila," he groaned. "Let's go."

Mila started to shake her head, but he kissed her lips again, and it was quiet in the kitchen for a while, quiet as he slowly peeled the top of her bathing suit down, leaving her breasts bare in the dusky light, and his hand free to explore them with his expert touch. "Mila," he said, finally, his voice throaty with the same excitement she felt, "it's given me so much pleasure, watching you learn how to swim this summer. Now let me give you a little pleasure. Just . . . just a little." He skimmed his lips along her collarbone.

A little? Was he serious? If this was *a little* pleasure, what was Reid's idea of *a lot* of pleasure? Because right now her pleasure was so intense that she was about to spontaneously combust. With Reid, it was all about pleasure. *Her* pleasure. He wasn't asking anything of her. Anything at all. Except that she feel the exquisite sensations he was coaxing from her body.

He had worked her bathing suit down around her waist, and done it so seamlessly that the only reason she noticed it now was that the evening breeze, blowing in through the open kitchen windows, felt suddenly cool on her bare skin. And his fingertips glided over that skin with a featherlike lightness, from her collarbone, down between her breasts and all the way to her navel. His other hand was busy, too. The man was clearly not deterred by the fact that he was on crutches, she realized. He was simply letting his underarms bear the bulk of his weight so that both his hands were free.

Which was why he was able to use that other hand to gently stroke the inside of her thighs, a soft, insistent stroke that would have been mesmerizing if it wasn't also so electrifying.

Another moan escaped her, and she wavered then, for one second, on the edge of surrender. It would be so sweet, so very sweet, to let them finish what they'd started. But even as she was thinking this, she saw an image in her mind of her wedding ring, lying on the bottom of the lake. It didn't look the way it had when she'd thrown it in at the beginning of the summer. It wasn't bright and shiny anymore. It was slightly tarnished, coated with algae, and partially buried in the soft muck of the lakebed. But there it was. No less real for all that. And as soon as she saw it in her mind, she untangled herself from Reid.

"I'm sorry," she said, trying to catch her breath and reflexively folding her arms over her bare breasts, whose pale skin seemed to be glowing faintly in the near darkness. "I can't do this," she mumbled as she clumsily yanked at her bathing suit straps and reached for her crumpled cover-up on the floor. She couldn't help but feel faintly ridiculous now. Only one of them, after all, was partly undressed.

But Reid, seeing how self-conscious she'd become, shook his head. "Mila, no. Don't ever be embarrassed by the way you look. You are so beautiful. Every single inch of you is so beautiful."

"Thank you," she whispered, because she could see by the expression on his face that he actually believed what he was saying. He reached out and gently ran a finger down the side of her face and kissed her so tenderly it made her heart ache. "I just . . . I just want to love you," he said then. "Please, let me love you, Mila."

But as soon as she heard those words, she felt her eyes tear up. "I'm sorry," she said again, and, pulling away from him, she hurried out of the kitchen before real tears started. And she made it all the way down the hallway, into her bedroom, and under the covers of her bed before they came. Really came. She buried her face in the pillow and tried to cry quietly.

She hadn't cried since the first night she'd arrived at the cabin. And that night, she'd cried for different reasons. She'd cried because she was alone, and afraid, and bereft of hope. She'd cried, too, because she was married to an abusive man, and she saw no way, legally, at least, out of her marriage to him. Tonight, she was crying because she knew now, beyond a shadow of a doubt, that she was in love with a man, a man with whom she could have no real future, not when she knew she would have to spend the rest of her life on the move, trying to stay one step ahead of a man who wouldn't rest until he'd found her. And she was crying because the words Reid had said to her, *Let me love you, Mila,* were the kindest, loveliest, and most beautiful words anyone had ever said to her.

Chapter 19

After Mila was done crying, she felt both curiously empty, and completely exhausted, so exhausted, in fact, that she could barely muster the energy to change into her nightgown, brush her teeth, and crawl back under her covers. But no sooner had she fallen asleep than something dragged her, violently, awake. *What is that?* she thought, sitting up in bed, her heart pounding, her covers thrown off, her feet already on the floor. *What is* that noise? But she knew. She'd never heard it before, but as its shrill electronic pulse filled the cabin, she realized that she'd been waiting—no, she'd been *expecting*—to hear it all summer. It was the alarm, and something, or someone, had tripped it.

"*Brandon*," she whispered into the darkness, and the simple act of saying his name frightened her more than the alarm's incessant blaring. Her next thought, though, wasn't of Brandon, or even of herself. It was of Reid. *Oh, my God, Reid. No!* She scrambled out of bed and tore down the hallway to his room, but when she got there, she found an oddly disorienting scene. The door was open, the lights were on, and Reid was out of bed, leaning on his crutches and holding his iPad in his hands and typing something onto it. He looked mildly annoyed, but otherwise, perfectly calm.

"Mila?" he said, right as the alarm stopped shrieking. "What's wrong?"

"What's wrong?" she repeated, holding on to the doorjamb to steady herself. Her breath was coming so fast it was hard for her to talk. "Reid, the alarm . . . It woke me up . . . why'd it stop?"

"I turned it off," he said.

"Why?" she asked, her legs rubbery beneath her.

"Because if it goes off for more than forty seconds, the security company calls the police."

"But, Reid, they *should* call the police," Mila said. "Call them back. Right now. *Please*. Or better yet, call 911."

Reid put the iPad down on his dresser and came over to her. He looked worried. But not about the alarm. About her. "Mila, it's okay," he said, his eyes finding hers. "It was a false alarm. Nobody broke in, if that's what you're worried about."

"How, how could you know that?" Mila asked, and she heard an edge of hysteria in her own voice.

"I know that because the sensor that went off tonight—it's for one of the basement windows—has already malfunctioned twice. Both times, though, were before you got here. The first time, the police came out. But it was nothing, Mila. It was a waste of their time. The security company was supposed to send a tech out to replace the sensor, but they never did. I'm sorry. I should have told you about—"

"But, Reid, what if it's . . . what if it's *not* a faulty sensor," she said, her voice dropping to a whisper. "What if someone's actually here?" *What if Brandon is actually here?* she wondered. *Watching them? Listening to them?* She glanced down the shadowy hallway. It was empty but it still seemed ominous. She shut Reid's bedroom door, and locked it, then dragged a desk chair over and wedged it under the doorknob. A lot of good any of that would do them if Brandon was actually here, she thought, her heart still beating wildly. But it seemed better, somehow, than doing nothing at all.

Reid, who'd watched her do all this in silence, now put a firm hand on her shoulder. "Mila, look at me," he said, when her eyes wandered back to the door. "It's okay. There's nobody here but us. It's a faulty sensor. And, honestly, even the first time it went off, I wasn't concerned. It's very safe out here. Trust me. The last time there was a break-in on Butternut Lake, it was in the dead of winter. Some high school kids with a keg jimmied open a window at a rental cabin and had a party there. Seriously, that's it. That's crime on Butternut Lake. The only reason my brother even had an alarm installed was because the first home health aide, Mrs. Everson, was worried about marauders. She actually used the word 'marauders,'" he added, amused, but Mila couldn't see the humor in this now.

"Reid, you don't understand," she said, watching the door.

"You're right, I don't," he agreed. "Explain it to me."

"There isn't time now," she said, impatiently, wondering if she should call the police herself. But some corner of her brain—some rational corner—knew that Reid was probably right, that it was probably just a faulty sensor, and that everything would probably be okay. But there was that word. *Probably.*

"I need to go down to the basement myself," she said suddenly. "I need to make sure there's"—her voice dropped again—"there's nobody down there."

"You mean, other than the spiders?"

But she ignored his remark and started to move the chair away from the door. She was afraid if she didn't leave his room soon, she'd lose her nerve and not be able to leave it at all.

"All right, look, I'll go," Reid said. "You wait here."

"Reid, no. You can't go down a flight of stairs on your crutches."

"Why not?"

"Because you could fall."

"Well, that's what I'm worried about you doing. I mean, look at you, Mila. Your legs are shaking so hard your knees are practically knocking."

"I'll be fine," she said, unlocking the door and opening it.

"Mila—"

"I don't have time for this," she said, standing in the open doorway. *And neither do you.* "I have to go."

He started to say something else, but she cut him off.

"Reid, please, no more arguing. Just promise me something, okay?"

He hesitated. "Okay."

"Promise me you'll lock the door behind me. And promise me if you hear"—*if you hear me scream* she almost said, but she changed it—"if you hear anything, anything at all, you'll call the police."

"All right," he said reluctantly. "And, Mila? As you come down the basement stairs, there's a row of windows on the wall directly in front of you. The one with the faulty sensor is all the way on the right."

She nodded and left him then, closing the door behind her and waiting until she heard him lock it before she started down the hall. Then she walked stealthily to the kitchen, turning on the lights as she went and stopping when she got there to consider whether she should take some kind of weapon with her. A hammer, maybe. There was one of those in the utility drawer. Or the baseball bat she'd seen in the hall closet. But no, she decided. Brandon was stronger, and faster, than she was. If she tried to use a makeshift weapon against him, he could easily turn it on her. Or worse. He could turn it on Reid.

She walked over to the basement door and turned the doorknob quickly, very quickly, almost as if it were hot and might blister her hand if she touched it for too long. Then she pushed the door open and turned on the light. *One step at a time,* she told herself as she started down the stairs. And she could see Reid's point now. Her legs were shaking so violently she was afraid they would buckle beneath her. But she kept going, and once she reached the bottom of the stairs, she saw ahead of her the row of windows Reid had mentioned. The one on the right looked fine. *Looked* fine, but it still needed to be inspected, as did the rest of the basement.

So she walked toward the window, fully expecting Brandon to materialize out of some shadowy corner or, worse yet, put a hand on her shoulder from behind. She glanced quickly over her shoulder, but there was nothing to see but more basement and the steps leading back up to the kitchen. So she kept going, her cotton nightgown brushing against her legs, the concrete floor cool and damp beneath her feet. Her breath was coming fast and shallow, and her body, even in the chilly basement, was bathed in sweat. But she needed to stay calm, she told herself, or, at the very least, she needed to not panic. Because if Brandon was here, somewhere, she was going to need to keep her wits about her if she wanted to protect Reid.

After what seemed like an eternity, she reached the window, and a tiny but welcome wave of relief washed over her. Nobody had come through this window. Not tonight, and not any other night recently, either. There was an unbroken spiderweb spanning the entire thing, and for some reason, Mila reached up and ran a hand through its sticky strings.

Thank God, she thought, leaning against the wall. And after a minute, she walked, across the basement and back up the steps. But when she came out into the kitchen, she hesitated. Reid was there, leaning on his crutches, waiting for her.

"I know I said I'd stay in my room," he said, with an apologetic shrug. "But I was worried about you. Is everything okay?" he asked, watching her carefully.

She nodded, suddenly embarrassed. "It's fine. You were right, by the way. Nobody broke in through that window. I don't think it's been open for a long time. There's a spiderweb over it."

He nodded. But he didn't move. "Mila, what's going on?"

"Nothing," she said, coming farther into the kitchen. "I just . . . I just got a little freaked out, that's all. This cabin, out here in the woods, and you and I all alone in it. . . . I mean, do you know how many scary movies start with that premise, Reid? *A lot* of them. And I've probably seen too many of them." She smiled, or tried to smile, anyway.

But he looked unconvinced. "I don't mean what's going on *tonight*, Mila. I mean, what's going on *in general*. What happened before tonight? Before you came here? Why are you so afraid?"

"I'm not, I'm not afraid," she said, fidgeting with her nightgown.

He didn't say anything. Instead, he stood perfectly still, watching her, and waiting for her to tell him what was wrong. And, for one wild moment, she almost did. It was so tempting, in its way. She'd start at the beginning, start from the night she met Brandon at the diner, and go from there. His jealousy, his paranoia, his violent outbursts, her running away the first time, and him stopping her, her meeting Ms. Thompson, and her running away again. But if she told him all of it, what then? He might accept it, and her, unquestioningly. Or he might . . . he might tell her that it was more than he could handle. And if he told her that, would she blame him? After all, what kind of man, knowing the truth, would sign on for a life with her? A life lived in fear, a life lived waiting for Brandon to find them. *No man,* she answered herself. Not even Reid. And if she told him now, what was happening between them might be over, over before it had even really begun. And, self-ishly, she couldn't bear that thought.

"You're not going to tell me, are you?" he asked now.

She shook her head guiltily.

He sighed, but he didn't argue the point. Instead, he said, "Do you want a drink? There's a very good bottle of whiskey in the liquor cabinet. I know because I gave it to my brother for Christmas."

"No. No, thank you," she said, and then she remembered something. "You know what I would like, though?"

"What?"

"A cherry Popsicle."

"Really? Why?"

"A friend of mine . . . someone I knew once, introduced me to them. And I don't know why, but for some reason, having one always made me feel better."

"Did it?" he said, looking a little bemused. "Well, we don't have any here. But I could ask Lonnie to put them on the grocery list."

Mila smiled at him, a little shakily. Apparently, just *talking* about cherry Popsicles was enough to make her feel better.

She must not have *looked* better though, because Reid was still staring at her worriedly. "Are you sure you're all right?" he asked.

"I'm fine, really," she said. "Don't worry about me."

"Easier said than done," he said, with the closest thing to a smile she'd seen from him since the alarm had gone off.

She closed the door to the basement, and they left the kitchen, Mila going first, and Reid following behind her on his crutches. She stopped outside his bedroom door. "I'm sorry I panicked. Obviously, I overreacted."

He shrugged. "I'll call the alarm company in the morning, and I'll have them send someone out to fix that sensor."

She nodded.

"Are you really going to be able to go back to sleep tonight?" he asked.

"Of course," she said. *Not a chance,* she thought.

"Well, you know where to find me," he said with a smile, indicating the open door to his room.

After they said good night, she walked back down the hallway to her room but knew she didn't want to get back into bed. She was still too keyed up, and she felt a little grimy, too, from the cold sweat she'd broken out into, and from the gritty floor of the basement and the sticky spiderweb over the window. She went into her bathroom, turned on the shower, stripped off her clothes, and stepped under the spray. She stood there for a long time, letting the hot water sluice over her, and then she grabbed a bar of soap and a washcloth and scrubbed herself. After she got out of the shower, she dried herself off, rubbed her wet hair with a towel, and changed into another pair of panties and another nightgown.

She got into bed then, but she didn't turn off the bedside table light. She didn't do anything but sit there, for a long time, letting a new realization sink in. She sighed then and got out of bed. The night wasn't over yet.

Reid was sitting on the edge of his bed when he heard a light tap on his door. "Mila?" he said.

The door cracked open. "Can I come in?" she asked.

"Of course," he said. She came in and he saw that she'd taken a shower—her hair was still damp at the ends—and changed into another nightgown. And her color was better now, almost back to normal. But he knew she was still afraid. He could feel her fear in the room with them, almost as if it were a third person.

He patted the edge of his bed, meaning for her to sit down on it, but she eyed it uncertainly and kept standing.

"Do you ever feel like we see each other more at night than we do during the day?" she asked him, with something close to a smile.

"Sometimes. But I don't really care when I see you. As long as I *do* see you."

She smiled at him then, a shy smile, and he knew she felt the same way about him. She sat down gingerly on the very edge of his bed.

"Are you okay?" he asked, already knowing that in some important way, she was not okay.

She nodded. "Yes. But I need a favor."

"Anything."

"I don't want to be alone tonight."

"Then be with me," he said simply. "It's not as if I sleep that much anyway. What do you want to do? We could watch a movie. Or play cards. Do you like cards?"

"I . . . they're okay. But that's not really what I had in mind."

"No?"

"Can I . . . can I stay in your bed with you?" she asked, her cheeks coloring almost imperceptibly.

"Oh," he said, after a moment of confusion. Delightful confusion. At least until he realized what she must mean. "Yeah, of course," he said. "I know the drill. I'll stay on my side of the bed, and you'll stay on yours."

But she shook her head. "No, not tonight. Tonight, I need you to hold me."

He nodded, slowly, but realized he still needed to clarify something. "Just hold you, Mila? Nothing more?"

"Yes. Is that all right? I mean, I want, I *need*, actually, to be with you, but not the way I was with you in the kitchen before. Just . . ."

"Just holding," Reid finished for her. "I can do that," he said, though inwardly he was less confident. They had slept together before without even touching each other. But that was before . . . well, before tonight. Before the kitchen. Now, it would be harder. Still, if that was what she needed from him, that was what she would get from him. Even if it killed him. And it might actually kill him, he thought ruefully, as he lay down on his bed and made room for her.

"Thank you," she said softly, lying down beside him, and after she'd arranged the covers over them, she reached over and turned off the light.

He turned on his side and propped himself on one elbow. "How do we do this, exactly?" he asked, looking at her in the dark and feeling like an idiot.

She laughed. "I don't know. I don't think there's an instruction manual. Why don't you lie down and I'll lie down next to you and we'll take it from there."

So Reid lay down and wondered why he always felt as if everything he did with Mila he was doing for the first time. He thought, *Is it possible I've just asked her how I should hold her?* That was ridiculous. Holding a woman was like Seduction 101, and he was pretty sure he'd done well in that class the first time he'd taken it, back in high school

But with Mila, he thought as she lay down next to him, everything was different. He didn't want to just hold her; he wanted to hold her as perfectly as it was possible to hold someone. So he waited while she nestled against him, and then he helped her arrange and then rearrange their limbs, until they were both comfortable.

"Is this okay?" he finally asked. He was lying on his back, and she was cradled in his arms, her head resting at the base of his neck, her breasts crushed gently against his chest, her legs resting beside his legs, but not on top of them.

"It's fine," she said, into his neck. "But can you sleep like this?"

"I'm practically asleep now," he lied.

"Good," she said, snuggling closer.

For a long time after that, they lay perfectly still, Mila at last relaxing into his arms, and Reid trying, with every ounce of his being, to not become aroused. He did this by thinking about things far outside of the room. The least exciting things, really, he could think of. He thought about an insurance policy he needed to renew on one of the boatyards. And about the upcoming quarterly tax filing for his and Walker's company.

And when his mind came back to this room, back to this bed, and back to Mila, he realized that the danger had passed. Mila was asleep, her body resting in his arms, her breathing regular as her chest rose and fell against his. *God, she smells so good,* he thought, inhaling deeply. She smelled like pure soap and clean towels. And it went without saying that she *felt* wonderful, too. He couldn't resist, now, running his hand along one of her bare arms. Her skin was so soft, he marveled, and even now, on a chilly night, it felt warm to his touch, as if it were somehow lit from within.

He returned his hand to the small of her back, where it had been resting, and let his body relax beside the gentle weight of her. He hadn't thought he'd be able to sleep tonight. He'd fully expected to lie awake until morning, watching over her. But gradually, he felt the tension ebb out of his body, until he was suspended somewhere between wakefulness and sleep. And that was when he realized something. Something amazing. His and Mila's hearts were beating in time with each other. He could feel them, pressed together, separated only by the thin cotton of his undershirt and her night-gown. How was this even possible? he wondered. He'd heard of it before, of course, but only in cheesy love songs, or on tacky greeting cards. *Two hearts that beat as one.* He'd never given much thought, though, to the idea that it could actually happen.

He tightened his arms around her. "I love you, Mila Jones," he said. But the only answer was the steady rhythm of her breathing.

Chapter 20

The morning after the alarm went off, Mila and Lonnie were in the kitchen together when they heard a truck rumbling up the gravel driveway.

"It's Hank," Lonnie said, looking out the window as the UPS truck came into view. She was at the kitchen sink, up to her elbows in soapy water, but she snatched up a dish towel to dry her hands on and was out the door before the truck had even stopped. Mila, who was sitting at the breakfast table, picking at the remains of her French toast, watched Hank get out of his truck. He seemed as eager to see Lonnie as she was to see him, though it was the third time this week he'd been to the cabin. Mila wondered if he even had a package to deliver. But he did. He handed it over to Lonnie, and after a few minutes of conversation, he got reluctantly back into his truck and drove away. When Lonnie came back into the kitchen, she was humming.

"It's a package for Reid," she said to Mila, setting it down on the table. "Do you want to take it to him when you're done?"

"All right," Mila said, feigning interest in her French toast. She knew there was no way Lonnie could know about her and Reid's unconventional sleeping arrangement last night, but for some reason she still felt self-conscious around her this morning. Mila hadn't seen Reid yet; he'd been sleeping when she'd left him this morning, and by the time she'd showered and come to the kitchen, he'd skipped breakfast and had Lonnie bring him a cup of coffee in the study instead.

"It's wonderful that Reid's working again," Lonnie said, going back to the sink. "When he first came here, straight from the rehabilitation center, he wasn't interested in *anything*. Can you believe what a difference a summer makes?"

"No, I can't," Mila said honestly. And the difference wasn't confined to Reid, either. She hadn't thought she'd be able to sleep last night after the cabin's alarm had gone off, but she'd been wrong. She'd slept more deeply than she had all summer. She'd felt so safe in Reid's arms, so protected, and so . . . *so cherished*, she realized, with a little jolt of surprise. So completely and utterly cherished. What would it be like, she wondered, to feel that way every night of your life, and every day, too?

"So what do you think?" she heard Lonnie ask her now from across the kitchen.

"About what?" Mila said, embarrassed. She hadn't heard a word of whatever Lonnie had been saying.

"About Hank asking me out for dinner," Lonnie said, frowning slightly as she came over to the table.

"I think it's wonderful," Mila said honestly.

"I think so too," Lonnie said, sitting down across from Mila. "The thing is, though, I haven't dated a man in twenty-five years. I'm not sure I remember how to."

"It'll come back to you," Mila said encouragingly.

"Will it?"

"Absolutely."

But Lonnie looked unsure. "Do you think," she said, after a moment, "that instead of going out to a restaurant with Hank I could have him over to my house for dinner? I think I'd feel more relaxed." She added, almost shyly, "And I think he'd like my chicken pot pie."

"Lonnie, he'll *love* your chicken pot pie," Mila said. "Just thinking about it makes my mouth water."

"Then there's only one other thing I'm worried about."

"What's that?"

"I'm worried that if he comes over, he'll want to sit in Sven's—my late husband's—armchair. It's right in the middle of the living room. And my God, Sven loved that chair. If he was home, he was sitting in it. And now, when guests come over, they seem to gravitate toward it. Why, I don't know. It's nothing to look at. You know the kind. Brown leather, all cracked and worn. Sort of like an old shoe," she said, with a chuckle. "But it *is* comfortable. I'll grant it that. And I have a feeling that if Hank comes over, he'll sit right down in it. And it'll just feel . . . I don't know, wrong somehow. Disrespectful to Sven's memory."

"And you don't want to give it away?" Mila asked gently, hoping she wasn't overstepping her boundaries here.

"Oh no, I couldn't. Not yet, anyway."

"Could you . . . put it in another room? A bedroom, maybe?"

Lonnie wavered, then shook her head. "No, that would feel wrong, too. Like I was banishing it or something."

Mila thought about it some more. "I know," she said. "Keep the chair. And leave it exactly where it is. But before Hank comes over, put something on it—a pile of folded laundry, maybe—so he can't sit down on it."

"That might work," Lonnie said thoughtfully. "But what about the next time he comes over? If there is a next time, I mean."

"More laundry?" Mila suggested.

"But I live alone," Lonnie pointed out. "How much laundry can one person have?"

Mila laughed. "It doesn't matter. Just put something there until you're ready to let another man sit in it."

"And if I'm never ready?"

"Then you'll put one of those velvet ropes across it. The way they do to the antique chairs in museums."

Now it was Lonnie's turn to laugh. "Well, I better be getting back to work," she said, getting up from the table. "Are you done with that?" She motioned to Mila's breakfast plate, which had only a crust of French toast left on it.

"I'm done," Mila said, as Lonnie cleared it away. It was still hard for her, even after two months, to let Lonnie wait on her this way. But now she reached for the package on the table. "I guess I'll take this in to Reid, then," she said, with elaborate casualness. "Oh, and Lonnie? The house alarm malfunctioned again last night. Reid said he was going to call someone to come out today and fix the faulty sensor."

She carried the package to the study and tapped lightly on the closed door, her heart beating annoyingly

fast. Not with fear, like last night, but with excitement. "Come in," Reid called immediately, and Mila
remembered the long sulky silences that used to greet
her whenever she knocked on Reid's bedroom door.
Lonnie was right. What a difference a summer had
made.

"Hi," she said, cracking open the door. "The UPS
man delivered this." She held up the package. "I
thought you might need it."

"Oh, thanks," Reid said, smiling and leaning back in
the swivel chair. His left leg, in its brace, was stretched
out in front of him, and his crutches were propped by
the side of the desk. "I've been expecting that."

Mila came into the office, feeling suddenly shy. It
happened every time she saw Reid now. No matter how
much time she spent thinking about him when they
weren't together, she was completely unprepared for the
reality of him when they were together. Objectively, of
course, she knew he was good-looking. But knowing it
was different from feeling it. And this morning she was
struck, with a whole new force, by the sheer physicality
of his presence.

It was amazing to her, really, that someone who had
been in such a devastating accident such a short time
ago could radiate such good health now. He'd put back
on the weight he'd lost after the accident, and it looked

good on him. His new tan, which he'd gotten watching Mila's swimming lessons, looked good on him too. He smiled at her, and his smile caught at her heart, and the feeling was sweet and bittersweet at the same time. Sweet because she knew that she loved him, and bittersweet because she knew that she shouldn't.

She came over to him then and handed him the package. "I don't want to disturb you," she said, starting to leave.

"You're not disturbing me."

"I did last night," she said guiltily, turning around.

"The alarm going off disturbed both of us."

"*After* the alarm went off, I mean. I'm sorry. I'm a grown-up. I should be able to sleep alone." That wasn't all she wanted to apologize to him for. But that list was long and complicated. Too complicated, probably, for this conversation.

"Well, I should be sleeping alone too," Reid said. "But that hasn't stopped me from asking you to spend the night with me, has it?" He picked up the package and held it out to her. "This is for you, by the way," he said.

"For me?" she said. It was addressed to Reid.

"Well, I ordered it for you. Go ahead, open it," he said, reaching into his top desk drawer and handing her a letter opener. She used it to slice through the flap of the padded envelope, then reached inside and pulled out two new test prep books. "You ordered these for me?" she asked, looking up in surprise.

"Uh-huh. I knew you'd been studying the same ones all summer. I thought you were probably ready for something new."

"I don't have these two yet," she said, excited by her new windfall. But then she caught herself. "Reid, you know you didn't have to do this," she said.

"I wanted to."

"Well, I'll pay you back," she said.

"Whatever," he said.

"No, I mean it."

"Okay, fine. But I'm going to owe you, too."

"For what?"

"For providing me with a new source of entertainment."

She looked at him questioningly.

"Starting tonight, I'm going to be administering your practice tests," he said. "And scoring them, too."

"Why would you want to do that?"

"Because it'll be fun."

"It doesn't sound fun."

"Well, maybe not for you. But only because you'll be the one doing all the work."

She hesitated, touched by his offer, but he misread her hesitation. "Mila, look, it's not a big deal," he said. "Friends help each other out sometimes, that's all."

Do friends also sleep in the same bed together? she wanted to ask him. But she already knew the answer to that. They did not.

Something about her expression made him smile at her, though, and she felt it again, that tightening around her heart. "What are you thinking, Mila?" he asked.

"I'm thinking that it was incredibly thoughtful of you to order these books for me," she said. But what she was *really* thinking was that if she spent the night in the same bed with him again, there was no way she was going to be satisfied with having him just hold her.

"Time," Reid said, looking up from his watch later that evening.

"Already?" Mila said in dismay, dropping her pencil onto her open test prep book.

"Uh-huh."

"Can I have five more minutes?"

"No."

"Why not?"

"Because you're not going to get five more minutes when you take the real test."

"You're right." Mila sighed, rubbing her eyes.

"Here, let me see that," Reid said, reaching for her answer sheet across the card table they were sitting at in the study. He compared her answer sheet to the answer key in the book while Mila massaged her temples and wished they were spending this chilly evening playing a board game, or watching television, or doing almost anything other than what they were doing now. She'd liked doing the practice problems before tonight, but that was because she'd done them alone, without timing herself, and without thinking too much, either, about what taking the actual test would be like.

"Not bad," Reid said, looking up from the answer key. "You got nineteen out of twenty-one right. But that's out of the problems you did. You never got to the last four problems."

"No kidding," Mila said, feeling discouraged. "But I don't think I'll ever finish all the problems in the time allotted."

"Of course you will."

"Reid, it can't be done."

"Of course it can," Reid said.

"How do you know that?"

"Well, *I* don't know it. But the people who design the tests know it. Besides, Mila, you're accuracy is good. It's excellent, in fact. You just have to do the problems faster."

"And how am I going to do that?"

"By timing yourself every time you do one of those sections, and by learning to pace yourself so you never spend too much time on any one problem. And by not getting discouraged," he added. "Take tonight, for instance. This was just your first try being timed. I'll time you on a different section now, and then another one after that, and you can see if your scores get better. I think they will."

"Reid, you have got to be kidding about my doing another one of those now," Mila protested.

"I'm completely serious," he said.

"But my brain . . . my brain already feels like it's about to explode."

"Well, it might feel that way," he said, "but I think even without a nursing degree you know that's not actually possible." He reached for her test booklet and flipped through it until he found what he was looking for, then passed it back over to her.

"Here, try this section," he said. "You have twenty minutes to do it in."

"Can I have twenty-one?" she asked.

"You know what?" he said, feigning seriousness. "Just for asking that, I'm going to give you nineteen."

She laughed. "And what are you going to be doing for those nineteen minutes?"

"I'm going to be watching you do those problems."

"That sounds fascinating."

"You'd be amazed, actually, at how fascinating I'm finding it," he said, and he smiled at her, a smile that made her think of everything else they could do in nineteen minutes.

"Are you ready?" he said, tapping on his watch.

She nodded and managed, finally, to stop staring at him long enough to glance down at the problems on the page in front of her.

"All right, go!"

Chapter 21

*G*oddamned *waste of time,* Brandon thought, as he dropped some quarters in the vending machine slot and pushed the "coffee" button. This was the third time in the last ten days that he'd been at the bus station, showing Mila's picture around to ticket agents, bus drivers, maintenance people, and even, as it turned out, the occasional homeless person and vagrant. And so far . . . nothing. Not a single hit. So either Mila had never been to this dump before, or all the morons who worked here, and all the losers who hung out here, had lousy memories. As he heard the plunk of the paper cup landing and the hiss of the coffee filling it up, he remembered what Ed Tuck had said about knowing when to quit.

That smug bastard, he fumed. There was no way he was taking his advice. No way in hell. Because while the nine weeks that Mila had been gone might feel like a long time, it wasn't long enough for her trail to be completely cold. It wasn't enough time for her to completely disappear. There was still somebody out there, somewhere, who knew where she'd gone and how she'd gotten there. He reached down and picked up the cup of coffee and took a tentative sip. He grimaced. It was awful. He tossed it angrily in a nearby garbage can and then shoved the whole can over, littering the floor with empty soda cans and crumpled chip bags.

"Whoa, what do you think you're doing?" a cop said, materializing out of nowhere. "Pick that up now and put the garbage back in it."

So he took a deep breath and waited while his vision cleared. "Officer, I'm sorry," he said. "I lost my temper. I'm having a bad day."

"Well, go have a bad day somewhere else," the cop said.

"Yes, sir," Brandon said, trying to keep the panic out of his voice. He must have succeeded, because the cop didn't say anything else. He just waited while Brandon picked up the garbage can and put whatever had spilled out of it back into it.

The cop, satisfied, nodded toward the exit. "Now, get lost," he growled. And Brandon, in a cold sweat, headed toward the exit. *That was close,* he told himself. He'd had a thing about cops since he'd gotten arrested a few years ago, before he'd met Mila. An ex-girlfriend of his had stupidly called the cops, and because it was a Friday night he'd spent the weekend in jail. He hadn't known then he was claustrophobic. He knew it now. Just the thought of being in a jail cell again made his skin crawl.

He pushed through the bus station door, but once outside, he took a quick look over at the bus bay and saw, almost immediately, a bus driver, a white-haired old guy, he'd never seen before. He was helping passengers unload their baggage. Brandon waited until he was done, glanced around to make sure the cop wasn't around, and then walked over to him.

"Excuse me, um, Bob," he said, reading the man's name tag, and smiling the smile he reserved for those occasions when he wanted something from someone. "Can I ask you a favor?"

"You can ask," the man said mildly. "But I'm going off duty soon."

"This'll just take a minute," Brandon said, keeping the smile fixed in place as he reached into his blue jeans back pocket and took out the photo of Mila. It was one he'd taken of her soon after they'd met. He'd surprised her that day with a picnic in the country, and in the picture she was sitting on a blanket, smiling into the camera. He couldn't look at it now without feeling a wave of fury. Blind, hot fury. They'd been so happy together. Both of them. But her especially. All you needed to do was look at her to see how happy she'd been then. So why had she gone and wrecked everything by leaving him?

But as he held the photograph up for the driver to see now, he was careful not to look at it himself. He needed to stay focused on the task at hand. "Have you seen this woman before?" he asked. "She might have taken a bus from this station several weeks ago. Probably around the first week of June."

Bob considered the picture. "May I?" he asked, reaching for it.

"Of course," Brandon said, letting him take it. Inwardly, he seethed, He hated old people. They were so slow. This guy, for instance, was acting as if he had all the time in the world. Whereas Brandon needed to get back to work. Either that, or get fired for taking too much time off.

"Why are you trying to find her?" Bob asked now, glancing up from the picture. "I mean, if you don't mind my asking."

"I don't mind," Brandon lied. *You nosy bastard.* "I'm looking for her because she's sick. She's very sick."

"She looks okay to me," Bob said.

"Mentally, I mean. Mentally, she's very sick," Brandon said quickly. "She's had some kind of a psychotic break. She could be a danger to others, and she's definitely a danger to herself. We need to bring her back home so she can get the treatment she needs." He tried out his concerned expression on Bob.

"I see," Bob said. "And you are?"

"Me? I'm her brother."

Bob took one last look at the picture and shook his head. "I've never seen her before. And if I *had* seen her, I'd remember her. I have an excellent memory for faces."

"Well, aren't you lucky, Bob," Brandon muttered, not bothering to be polite anymore. And as he stuck the photo back into his pocket he thought about how good it would feel right now to punch Bob. A hard, clean punch, right to the jaw. Or no, on second thought, a one-two punch, right into that doughy stomach of his. But he remembered the cop and turned away from Bob.

He'd had enough of the bus station for one day, he decided. In the meantime, he'd go back to the apartment tonight and ransack the place again. There must be something, however small, that he'd missed the first two times he'd done it.

"It ain't over till it's over, Mila," he muttered, heading back down the block. "And it ain't over yet. Not by a long shot."

Chapter 22

"And the dreams? What about the dreams? Are they becoming less frequent?" Dr. Immerman asked, leaning back in his swivel chair.

"The dreams . . . the dreams are definitely getting better," Reid said, after a moment's hesitation. He hadn't really been listening to what Dr. Immerman was saying. He'd been thinking about Mila, who was sitting in the waiting room, on the other side of the office door. But now, with a conscious effort, he turned his mind back to the therapy session. "It's been at least a couple of days since I had one of the dream," he said. "And it was different from the others."

"Different how?" Dr. Immerman asked. He was already familiar with the content of Reid's dreams. Reid had described each one of them to him, several times over, in what had sometimes felt, to Reid, like excruciating detail.

"Different because even as I was having it, I knew, somehow, it wasn't real. I knew that I would wake up from it eventually."

Dr. Immerman nodded. "That's good. That's very good, Reid."

"It *is* good," Reid said, though there was also a downside to it he wouldn't be discussing with Dr. Immerman. Now that the dreams were less violent and less prolonged, Mila had stopped sleeping in his room at night. The last time she'd slept there, in fact, had been a week ago, the night the cabin's alarm had gone off. Since then he'd been careful to give her the space and the time he sensed she needed. It hadn't been easy, though. There were times when he wanted her so badly that he experienced it almost as a kind of pain. A *different* kind of pain, it was true. A *new* kind of pain. But a pain just the same.

He sensed now that Dr. Immerman was waiting for him to say something more, and, as it turned out, he did have something more to say, he just didn't know how to say it. "There's, uh, something else I wanted to tell you," he said, shifting uncomfortably in the armchair he was sitting in. He wasn't very good at apologizing. He never had been, and he probably never would be. But there were times like now when it couldn't be avoided. "I wanted to say that I was sorry for not being fair to you. At least not during our first few appointments."

"How so?" Dr. Immerman asked, raising his eyebrows.

"Well, for one thing, I was pretty cynical about this whole process. And I didn't try to hide it either."

"You were entitled to your cynicism," Dr. Immerman said mildly.

"Maybe. But I was also here under false pretenses."

Now Dr. Immerman cocked an eyebrow.

"I . . . I wasn't here because I thought I had a problem," Reid admitted. "I was here because . . ." He smiled, remembering the first night he and Mila had spent together. "I was here because I was bribed."

Dr. Immerman eyebrows came together to form a V, something they did when they were waiting for more information. It was amazing how expressive the man's eyebrows could be, Reid thought. Because of them, he was able to speak whole sentences without saying a single word.

"Mila told me I needed to come here," Reid explained. "*Had* to come here, actually," he added, glancing in the direction of the waiting room. "So when I agreed to come here that first time, and when I agreed to come back after that, and to come twice a week after *that . . .*" He shrugged. "I did it, at first, to make Mila happy."

"Mila is the woman who brings you to your appointments?" Dr. Immerman clarified.

Reid nodded.

Dr. Immerman's eyebrows came together now. "Well, I think we can both agree that the reason why you initially came here is less important than the fact that you did."

Reid nodded. That sounded sensible. Despite his previous skepticism about therapists and therapy, Reid had to admit that almost everything Dr. Immerman said sounded sensible.

"We only have a few more minutes left of your session, Reid," he said now, glancing at the clock on the wall, "but I wanted to talk to you about something new today. Something we haven't talked about before. There may not be time to cover it all now, in which case, we can pick up wherever we left off at our next session."

"Okay," Reid said, his old wariness returning. For some reason he didn't like the sound of this.

But Dr. Immerman pressed on. "I wanted to talk about the night of the accident."

"Is there anything left to talk about?" Reid asked. "I mean, we've already been over it so many times."

"I don't want to talk about the accident itself," Dr. Immerman said. "Or the aftermath of it. Not right now. I want to talk about what happened *before* the accident."

"Before the accident?"

"Yes. About the events leading up to it."

"I don't know what you mean by 'events,'" Reid said, focusing not on Dr. Immerman but on the wall above him and slightly to the right of him.

"I mean, what you were doing before you drove off the road that night. Before you got in your car, even."

"I wasn't drinking, if that's what you're thinking."

"That's not what I'm thinking."

"And I wasn't texting, either. That's everybody's second guess."

"Well, it wasn't mine. You mentioned to me once that you may have fallen asleep at the wheel. Is that really what you think happened?"

"No," Reid said, a dull, almost numb feeling settling over him. "No, that's what I tell people. But that's not what happened."

"What did happen?" Dr. Immerman asked gently, his eyebrows knitting themselves into a totally new formation.

But now it was Reid's turn to check the time. "Aren't we done here?"

"Not quite."

"So we still have enough time left for me to have a major psychological breakthrough?" he joked.

"We might," Dr. Immerman said. But he wasn't smiling. He, and his eyebrows, looked completely serious.

Several days later, on a sultry August afternoon, Reid sat at his desk in the study trying to concentrate on a financial statement Walker had e-mailed him. Lonnie had already left, and Mila was at Allie and Walker's cabin for a swimming lesson. It had been threatening to storm since morning, but Allie had still wanted Mila to come over. She felt guilty about only having had time to teach her one stroke so far, and she was hoping, because Mila was such a quick learner, that she could teach her another one before the end of summer.

The end of summer . . . that was one subject that Reid and Mila had never discussed. She hadn't brought it up, and he'd sensed that she hadn't wanted him to bring it up either. Still, it was already the second week in August. They couldn't keep pretending that summer wouldn't be ending soon, could they? Then again, he thought, maybe they could. And he remembered, for some reason, the adorable little freckles he'd noticed on her shoulder the last time he'd seen her in her nightgown. But just as he was making a mental note to kiss each one of those freckles the next time he got the chance, there was a tap on the study door. *Walker,* he thought. He'd asked him to come by on his way home from work.

"Come on in," Reid called, and his brother came in, looking for all the world like the kid Reid had grown up with. He'd been working on his own restoration project at the boatyard, apparently, because he was wearing a ratty T-shirt, blue jeans, and work boots, and he looked happy. The way he looked when he was with his family or working on a boat. And Reid felt a sudden protectiveness over his brother, and a sudden regret at what he had to tell him now. Was it really necessary? he wondered. But he knew it was. Reid needed to tell him this, and Walker needed to hear it. Right now, though, it was hard for Reid to know what would be worse. The telling or the hearing.

"Hey, Reid," Walker said, dragging a chair over to the desk. "What's up?" And when Reid didn't answer him right away, he asked. "What did you want to talk to me about?"

"Yeah, um, about that," Reid said, struggling with how to begin.

"Does this have anything to do with what happened between you and Mila after the swimming demonstration?" Walker asked, sitting down.

"Yes and no," Reid said.

"Because we still haven't talked about that," Walker reminded him.

Reid nodded, but he couldn't, for the life of him, think how to begin.

Walker shifted around in his chair. "Are you going to tell me what this is about or not?"

"I'll get to it," Reid said, marveling at the fact that he and Walker seemed to have changed places over the course of the summer. Before the accident, Reid had been the one who was always impatient, always in a hurry, always rushing from one place to another, and Walker was the one who was always counseling patience. And now? Well, there was nothing like spending time in a wheelchair to teach someone the true meaning of patience.

Now Reid took a deep breath. He'd start at the beginning, he decided. The beginning of that night. The night that ended with him trapped in the wreckage of his car at the bottom of a ravine. "The night of the accident," he said, "I was at a bar and I saw—"

But Walker cut him off. "You were at a bar? You told me you weren't drinking that night."

Reid shook his head. "I wasn't. I mean, I ordered a drink, but I left before I could drink it."

"So no drunk driving?"

"No."

"Good, Because I can't tell you how many people have asked me if you'd been drinking that night. And I've told them all no. So you better not have been lying to me."

"No, I wasn't lying about that. But I was lying when I told you I may have fallen asleep at the wheel."

Walker raised his eyebrows. "So . . . what happened?"

"Me. I happened. I was . . . I was in a bad place when I got into my car that night. A very dark place, I guess you'd say."

Walker looked alarmed. "You're not saying that you did it on purpose, are you?"

"That I was suicidal? No, of course not."

"Good," Walker said, relieved. "Because that's the other question people have asked me."

Reid sighed. He'd tried to go back to the beginning, but he realized now he hadn't gone back far enough. "Okay, look," he said, starting again. "I'd gone to a bar that night, not to drink, but to meet a woman, a woman I'd met at my gym. I'd said we should go out sometime, and she'd suggested this bar. Anyway, I was running late that night, so she was waiting when I got there. She'd already ordered a drink, so as soon as I sat down with her I ordered a whiskey and . . ." He stopped, wishing he had a whiskey now. He was as nervous as hell . . .

"Christ, Reid," Walker grumbled. "Can you just get this story over with already?"

"Yeah, all right," he said, determined to keep going this time. "Anyway, the bar we were in wasn't just a bar, it was a restaurant, too. A nice one. A little fancier than I'm used to, than I *prefer,* actually, but like I said, I didn't choose it. So we're sitting there, my date and I, and the hostess brings this party of three in and seats them at one of the tables in the bar area. They have a dinner reservation, but their table isn't ready yet, so they're going to have a drink there while they wait, and . . ."

"And?"

"And one of them . . . one of the members of the party of three was dad."

"Oh," Walker said, his face falling.

"Yeah. 'Oh.' That was about my reaction too."

"What was he doing there?"

"He was there with his wife, Crystal, and their daughter. Our half sister. You know, the one dad never introduced us to?"

"I know," Walker said tensely. And then, "And you recognized him? After all this time?"

"Yeah, I did. He didn't look that different, actually. A little thicker around the middle, maybe. A little balder. And the hair that was left, a little grayer. But, yeah, basically, he looked the same." He leaned back in the swivel chair and tried to find a more comfortable position for his leg. "So they're sitting there, at this little table, the three of them, and I realized it's a special occasion. Crystal has a cake box with her, and she asks the hostess if she'll take it to the kitchen. Then, when the cocktail waitress comes over to ask if they want anything to drink, Dad makes a big deal about ordering a bottle of champagne. He says it's to celebrate his daughter Chloe's graduation from college."

"Chloe," Walker repeated, softly, almost to himself.

Reid nodded. "You knew that was her name, didn't you?"

Walker nodded. "I remember when she was born. I remember because after that, Dad stopped seeing us. Or *trying* to see us, anyway, since he and Mom were always fighting about it. And then after that, they moved to a different suburb," he said, with a little shrug, "and that was it. Well, except for that time I saw Dad at that Minnesota Twins game. But he didn't have Chloe with him then . . ." His voice trailed off, and then he said, with renewed interest, "What does she look like, Reid?"

"Chloe? She looks a lot like you, actually."

"She does?" Walker said, fascinated.

"She does. A feminine version of you, of course. She's very pretty. But back to the story. So Dad orders a bottle of champagne, and the waitress asks him what kind of champagne he wants. And Dad says—I swear to God, he says this—'Just bring us the most expensive bottle you have.' I almost fell out of my chair. 'The most expensive bottle you have'? This from the man who had to be taken to court to make him pay a couple of hundred dollars a month in child support? That bottle probably cost more than a whole *month* of child support."

"Probably," Walker muttered. And then, "Did he see you, Reid?"

"No. Not then. Not later, either. I mean, I was staring at them the whole time. And I wasn't more than fifteen feet away from them. And not once did any of the three of them even notice me. They were so absorbed in each other. So happy, Walk. It was like they were in their own little world. And the whole time, Dad was just beaming at her. At Chloe. He was so proud of her. You could tell. And when the champagne came, he asked the waitress to let him open the bottle and fill the glasses, and then he made this toast about her. About what a great kid she'd always been, and what a great adult she was going to be. Stuff like that. And Crystal keeps reaching over and patting his hand. And then I realize that Chloe's tearing up. She's so touched by this display of fatherly devotion that she's actually crying. And I'm sitting there, staring at him, and thinking. 'What about us, Dad? What about me and Walker? Where were you when we graduated from high school? Or college? Where were you for our Little League games? Or birthday parties? Or sports banquets? And where the hell were you for every other goddamn thing that happened to us after you left? And what was it that Chloe had that we didn't have?' "

Walker, whose face was stricken, looked away. "Well, she's a girl, for one thing," he muttered. "Maybe Dad always wanted a daughter."

"Maybe. But that doesn't explain why he'd just write us both off, permanently, does it?"

"No."

"Okay, so, I'm staring at them. And eavesdropping on them. And my date is getting annoyed. She asks me if I know them. If I want to say hello to them, or whatever. And I just wave her off. I know I'm being rude. But I can't concentrate on our conversation. And finally, she just gets up and leaves. Just storms out of there. Which other people seem to notice. But not our happy family. They are totally oblivious to it. And, Walker? At that moment, I hate them. I really hate them. All three of them."

"No, that's not right," Walker said. "Don't hate her. Chloe. It's not her fault. I mean, for all we know, she doesn't even know we exist."

Reid sighed. "I know. I didn't really hate her then. I don't hate her now, either. But I was jealous of her, Walk. I don't know why, when Dad's obviously such a loser. Why would I even care if he loved us? Why would I even want someone in my life who left his kids like they were old junk, you know, the kind of stuff you just kick to the curb on moving day?"

Walker winced at that analogy. "I don't know if that's fair, Reid. It's true he didn't make much of an effort—"

"*Much* of an effort?" Reid snorted.

Walker ignored him. "But Mom didn't exactly make it easy for him, either, as I remember. She was always canceling his scheduled visitation at the last minute. Or changing the days and the times. And then, when he came to pick us up, she was waiting there, ready to pounce."

Reid shrugged. "Okay, fine. She made it hard for him. I don't deny it. But would you just have given up on us the way he did?"

"I don't know. Maybe. Eventually."

"If you and Allie got divorced, and you had problems with custody, or child support, or whatever, you'd let Wyatt and Brooke go without even putting up a fight?" Reid clarified.

"No," Walker said flatly. "Never."

"I didn't think so."

"So what happened? After your date left, I mean?"

"Nothing, really. I sat there, watching them. And getting angrier by the minute. There were a lot of things I thought about saying, or doing, but in the end, I just left."

"Maybe you should have said something, Reid."

"Like what? 'Gee, Dad, it's nice to see you. It's only been, what, twentysomething years? And this must be my half sister, Chloe, who you never bothered to introduce us to. I guess you had even less time for us after she was born, huh?' "

Walker sighed. "Yeah, all right. I guess whatever you said to him, it was bound to be awkward."

" 'Awkward' doesn't begin to cover it, Walk. The worst part was, the things I thought of saying to him don't even bear repeating. That's how angry I was. I was shaking all over. Part of me wanted to just go over there and punch him, you know? And part of me . . . part of me wanted to say to him 'How nice that you're here celebrating tonight. But did you know, Dad, that you're not just a dad anymore? You're a granddad, too. That's right. Your son, Walker, the one from your disposable first family, has a son and a daughter of his own now, too. And you're missing that, Dad, just like you missed everything else in our lives.' And then another part of me wanted to send them a second bottle of champagne, same kind as the first, and then go over there and say something like, 'Oh, it's no big deal. That's chump change for me.' And then I'd casually mention the fact that you and I own fourteen boatyards in three states. And that we could probably buy and sell him several times over. And that unlike him, who wanted to build boats but was too goddamn cowardly to do it full-time, we're living his dream. We've got everything he ever wanted."

"Well, not everything," Walker said quietly.

"What is that supposed to mean?"

"It's supposed to mean that he wanted a family, Reid. A real family. And he found one. Not with us. But, still. And you, on the other hand, Reid, have been very vocal about *not* wanting a family of your own. You've only wanted one thing, as far as I could tell, and that was to be successful."

Reid shrugged. "I don't disagree with that. And I'm going to get to that, too. But first, I need to tell you about the rest of the night. The part leading up to the accident. You already know about the part after the accident."

"Okay," Walker said, looking wary.

"So I finally leave the restaurant. Just throw some money on the table and storm out of there. They've left the bar area by then, and they're sitting at a table in the main part of the restaurant, and I just kind of look in on them before I go. It's more toasts, more happiness. And for a second, just a second, Walk, I think about storming in there and flipping their table over. Champagne and all. But I don't. I head out to the parking lot, I get in my car, and then . . . and then, I don't remember. Honestly, I don't. I was so angry that the next couple of hours are just kind of a blank to me."

Walker frowned. "What do you mean, 'a blank'?"

"I mean, I can't remember where I went. I drove around, I guess. But mainly, I was replaying memories of all the times he wasn't there when we were growing up. Like the time you couldn't go to your Boy Scout father-son sleepover, because he never showed up. And you spent the whole day dressed in your Scout uniform, sitting on the front steps, with your sleeping bag and your backpack beside you. Just waiting for him to pick you up. And it was dark outside before Mom persuaded you to come back inside and—"

"Okay, that's enough," Walker snapped. "No more rehashing memories, okay? Believe me, that one, especially, I'll take to the grave with me."

"Exactly," Reid said, feeling suddenly exhausted. "We both will. Because sometimes, Walk, watching you get hurt was worse than getting hurt myself."

Walker nodded. "I know that. But, for the record, you made up for a lot of that, Reid. You were a good older brother. You did your part. You did *more* than your part, actually. You were half brother and half father to me."

"I don't know about that. But getting back to that night . . . I think I drove around for a couple of hours. Remembering stuff like that. And having these revenge fantasies. I think I was driving a little maniacally, actually. I remember other drivers kept honking at me. I was speeding, probably. Weaving in and out. I wasn't drunk. But if I was driving like I was drunk, it's a moot point, isn't it?"

"Yeah."

"I wish to hell I'd gotten pulled over. But I didn't. How like the police to not arrest you when you need to be arrested," he added, with an attempt at laughter. "Anyway, the next thing I knew, I was going into a turn too fast, and I knew I wasn't going to be able to pull myself out of it. Those five seconds from the time I went over the embankment to the time I landed at the bottom of the ravine, those were the longest seconds of my life."

"I can't imagine the three days that followed went very quickly either."

"No, they didn't. But you know what? I'm not sorry they happened now."

Walker looked dismayed. "Reid, how can you say that? You almost died. And you still have months of recovery ahead of you."

"I know that," he said quietly. "Believe me, I know it. But honestly, Walker, my only regret now is that the accident took such a toll on you and your family. I can't imagine what it was like for you. What it's still like for you."

But Walker waved his concern away. "That's what family's for, Reid."

Reid nodded slowly. "I know that now. And I know something else, too. I can't go back to being who I was before the accident, Walker. The workaholic who never even unpacked his suitcase between business trips. Who thought take-out Chinese was its own food group. Who lived in an apartment building for five years without once learning the name of a single neighbor. And whose longest relationship with a woman before now was six weeks long."

"Well, if you're going to put it that way, it does sound kind of depressing," Walker joked, a little lamely.

Reid sighed. "No, not depressing, Walker. Soul crushing."

"Soul crushing? That's being a little overly dramatic, isn't it, Reid? Your life before the accident might not have been perfect, but you seemed to like it well enough. Running a successful company. Dating a lot of attractive women. Plenty of men would have traded places with you."

"Well, they would have been in for a big disappointment. Because the only people who came to visit me in the hospital were you and Allie. And while I love you both very much, it wasn't enough. Not for the sum total of one man's life."

Walker was quiet for a moment. Then he asked hesitantly, "So things are going to be different now?"

Reid smiled. "That's the plan."

"And I take it Mila has something to do with that plan?"

"She has everything to do with it. Because it wasn't until she came here, at the beginning of the summer, that the fog from the accident started to lift, and I began to realize that, as bad as my life seemed when I came to in that car, it was worse before it."

"Look, Reid," Walker said, running his fingers through his hair. "Nobody is more grateful to Mila than I am. I mean, the difference between you now

and you at the beginning of the summer is pretty goddamned miraculous. But, Reid, do you *really* think you
should be rushing into anything?"

"I'm not rushing into anything. I'm just serving
notice that things are going to be different now," he
said calmly. "I'm not running myself into the ground
anymore to prove myself to a man who doesn't give a
damn about me. Or you, for that matter."

"Thanks," Walker said, trying, and failing, to smile.

"So, yeah, things are going to be different," Reid
said. "I'm going to work nine to five, like a normal
person. Take vacations. Maybe even start fishing. Isn't
that what you've always wanted me to do? Join the
Church of Fishing?"

Walker smiled, his first real smile since they'd
started talking. "Honestly, yes. I'd love to get you out
there. We could start with some basic lures and work
our way up—"

"Hey, slow down," Reid interrupted him, laughing.
"I'm not quite ready to start casting off yet. But I need
you to know, Walker, that whatever happens next,
Mila's going to be a part of it."

"Have you told her that?"

"No. Not in so many words. But she knows how
I feel about her."

"And how does she feel about you?"

"She hasn't said, exactly. But I think she cares about me. No"—he caught himself—"I *know* she cares about me."

Walker didn't dispute this, but Reid could tell something was bothering him. "What?" Reid asked, a little defensively.

"Nothing, it's just . . . well, it's the age difference for one thing. She's what, in her midtwenties? You're at least fifteen years older than her, Reid."

"Oh, that," Reid said, surprised. He honestly hadn't given it any thought yet. "I'm not worried about that," he told Walker now. "Mila's an old soul."

"What does that mean?"

"Just what it sounds like," Reid said, with a shrug. "She's wiser than her years."

"All right, then, so what's next for the two of you?" Walker asked, a little challengingly. "Where do you go from here?"

Reid hesitated. He and Mila had never discussed a future together. But still, he knew they *had* one. It was just . . . complicated. He tried to put it into words for Walker. "I get . . . I get the feeling Mila has some loose ends to tie up before we can make plans with each other. You know, just some things from her old life— her life before this summer—that she needs to take care of."

Walker looked somber. "That's what I'm afraid of, Reid. I mean, how much do you know about her? *Really* know about her?"

"How much do any of us *really* know about anybody? Isn't that what you said to me when I brought up Mila's past at the beginning of the summer?"

Walker smiled now, a little ruefully. "I did say that, didn't I?"

Chapter 23

"Lonnie, if you don't mind, I'm going to take the cordless phone into my room for a few minutes," Mila said after breakfast the next morning. "I just need to make a quick call."

"Of course I don't mind," Lonnie said, looking up from the bread dough she was kneading. But then she paused in her work and studied Mila for a moment. "Are you all right, honey?" she asked. "You look a little peaked."

"I . . . I didn't sleep well last night," Mila confessed.

"You were probably too hot to sleep," Lonnie said sympathetically, glancing out the kitchen window at the gray, muggy morning. "Honestly, I wish Walker had gotten air-conditioning put in when he built this place. He says he doesn't like it, and that you only need it up here a couple of weeks a year, anyway, but still, *during* those weeks . . ." She shook head. "Then again," she said, wiping her floury hands on her apron, "if it gets any more humid, it'll be raining, and that, at least, might clear the air."

Mila knew what she meant. The sky was so low and so heavy with rain clouds it appeared to be almost touching the lake, and the air felt thick and still. Nothing was moving . . . nothing. Not the water on the lake, which formed a perfect sheet of pewter glass, and not the leaves on the trees. It had Mila on edge and praying for a violent thunderstorm. Anything to break the tension. But beyond an occasional flicker of lightning, or a distant rumble of thunder, nothing happened.

But she thanked Lonnie for breakfast and took the cordless phone into her bedroom, closing the door behind her. Then she perched on the edge of her bed and dialed Ms. Thompson's number.

"Caring Home Care. How may I help you?"

"Hi, Ms. Thompson. It's me."

"Mila, I'm so glad you called," she said.

"I'm not interrupting anything, am I?"

"Oh no, not at all. I haven't even started working yet. I was just finishing my coffee, and taking a look at my book group's pick for the month."

"Do you think you'll read it this time?" Mila asked, knowing that Ms. Thompson had a poor track record when it came to her book group's selections.

"I tend to doubt it," Ms. Thompson said, with a little sigh. "But I have a new strategy, Mila."

"What's that?"

"I'm going to time my arrival at the next meeting so that I'll get there *after* they've discussed the book, but *before* they've finished the Chardonnay."

Mila laughed. "Well, good luck with that," she said. There was a pause in the conversation then while Ms. Thompson coughed. She'd had a cough last week, too, Mila remembered, but it had gotten worse. It had a deep, bronchial quality to it now that worried Mila.

"Have you gotten that checked out?" she asked Ms. Thompson when she'd finally stopped coughing and caught her breath.

"Oh, no. I'm fine," she said dismissively. "That's nothing."

"Well, it doesn't sound like nothing. I think you should see someone about it."

"Mila, I'm a nurse," Ms. Thompson said, in a clipped tone. "I think I'm a pretty good judge of how sick I am."

"Of course you are," Mila said quickly, though privately she had her doubts about this.

"Look, I don't want to talk about me anyway,"

Ms. Thompson said, still slightly breathless from her coughing fit. "I want to talk about *you*. How is your patient, for starters?"

"He's . . . he's fine," Mila said, feeling her face grow warm. *Liar. He's better than fine,* she thought. *He's perfect.* And everything else would be perfect, too, if she didn't have to leave soon.

"Mila, what's wrong?" Ms. Thompson asked. "I mean, what's *really* wrong? Besides the obvious, of course."

Mila hesitated, thinking the words but afraid to say them out loud.

"Mila," Ms. Thompson prompted, in her no-nonsense way.

Mila looked nervously at her door, which was silly. No one could hear her through it. "I'm in love with him, Ms. Thompson."

"*Oh,*" Ms. Thompson said, surprised. And then she chuckled softly. "Remember when I told you, in my office that day, that this patient was a jerk? I guess I was wrong about that."

"You *were* wrong about that," Mila said, a little regretfully. "He's not a jerk. He's . . . the opposite of a jerk. Whatever that is."

There was a pause in the conversation, then Ms. Thompson asked, "Does he know about Brandon?"

"No," Mila said, ashamed. "And you don't have to

say it either. I'll say it for you. It's cowardly of me not to have told him. What's happening between us . . . it's a mistake. At best, we have no future together. At worst, I'm putting him in danger. You'd think my knowing that would have been enough to keep me from falling in love with him, but it wasn't," she added, a little bitterly. "I couldn't help it. I *can't* help it. And now, when I . . . when I leave, he'll be hurt, Ms. Thompson. And I'll be the one who hurt him. Believe me, I know how selfish I am."

"No, not selfish, Mila. Just human," Ms. Thompson said, then stopped to cough again. When she came back to the conversation, she went on, "Besides, I'm relieved to know you can still have those feelings for someone. Sometimes women who've been through what you've been through find it difficult to put their trust in someone again. So difficult, in fact, they don't even try to do it."

Mila didn't say anything, but she knew somehow that Ms. Thompson was talking about herself. And it made Mila feel even more sad than she already felt.

"I know things are complicated," Ms. Thompson continued. "But for now, just, just try to be happy, all right? And who knows? Maybe Brandon will give up on you. Maybe he already has."

"I don't think so," Mila said, anxiously biting her

lip. "I don't think he's even *close* to giving up on me. I mean, I know this sounds strange, but it's almost as if I can *feel* him looking for me. It's not like I'm psychic or anything. But I know him so well. And he's not going to stop looking for me until he finds me. He's just not."

"Well, you may be right about that. But, as my mother used to say, 'don't borrow trouble.'" Here Ms. Thompson started to cough again. But when she stopped, finally, she continued as if there'd been no interruption. "In the meantime, I need to know if you want me to keep looking for another placement for you."

"I . . . that would be good," Mila said, though the thought of leaving this place—this lake, this cabin, but most of all, of course, this man—left her feeling very nearly bereft. Still, she was running out of excuses to stay. Reid wasn't going to need a home health aide for much longer, and, in fact, he didn't even really need one now. Thanks to his physical therapy, he was getting stronger every day, and soon the plastic brace would be coming off his leg and he'd be walking unaided again. And then there was Mila. She'd saved enough money now to take her anywhere in the country, and to support herself there, for a little while anyway, while she built another life.

"I thought I'd found something for you in Milwaukee,

starting after Labor Day," Ms. Thompson said, "but that fell through. I'm sure I'll get another lead soon, though."

"I'm sure you will," Mila said, feeling miserable. Then, not wanting to sound ungrateful, she said, "Thank you, Ms. Thompson. Thank you so much for all you've done for me. And, another thing, too. It's a little late, I know, but just for the record, I'm sorry."

"Sorry for what?"

"Sorry for falling in love with a patient."

"Why?"

"Well, it's not very professional, is it?"

But here Ms. Thompson only sighed. "Mila, honey," she said. "You and I are *way* beyond that now."

Later that afternoon, Mila was sitting on one of the living room couches, a test prep book propped open on the coffee table in front of her. Reid had gone into town with Walker to run some errands, and Lonnie was in the kitchen, humming as she made something for their dinner that night. Mila was trying to concentrate on one of the problems in her book, but she found she couldn't. She was too hot. She'd initially tried to study on the deck, hoping she might be cooler outside, but the mosquitoes had chased her back in again. And now, even with the enormous ceiling fans whirring overhead, the air in the room felt sluggish, and when she shifted her perspiration-damp legs, they stuck uncomfortably to the leather couch. She was just about to give up studying and go pour herself a glass of iced tea when Reid came into the living room on his crutches.

"You're back," she said, and she smiled at him in spite of herself. No matter how often she saw him, she never got tired of seeing him again.

"I'm back," Reid agreed, and she was so distracted by the way he returned her smile that it wasn't until he'd reached her that she noticed that one of his hands that was holding a crutch handle was also holding a small, brightly colored cardboard box.

"Are those—"

"Popsicles," he nodded, using his crutches to lower himself down beside her on the couch. "I picked them up in town."

"You . . . remembered?" she asked.

He nodded. "The night the alarm went off, you said cherry Popsicles always made you feel better," he said, opening the box. "And you seemed like you could use one now."

"Reid, I'm sorry if I haven't been very good company lately," she said. And she hadn't been. She'd been anxious, tense, and, now that she thought of it, probably more than a little self-pitying.

"No, you've been fine," he said. He'd been rummaging around in the box, and now he extracted a Popsicle in a white plastic wrapper and held it up to the light. "I think this one is cherry." He handed it to her.

She unwrapped the Popsicle, and because he was watching her expectantly, she smiled and took a bite out of it. "Reid, it's delicious," she said honestly.

"Is it? I'm glad. This was the last box of Popsicles at the IGA. They're the perfect hot weather food, I guess."

"I'm not sure they're actually considered a food," Mila said, amused. "They're something like 99 percent artificial. Once you get past that, I think they work well in any kind of weather. Some of the very best cherry Popsicles I've ever had, in fact, have been in the dead of winter."

"Really? Well, how does this one stack up?"

"Pretty well," Mila said, savoring its familiar sweetness, though the rush of happiness she suddenly felt probably had more to do with Reid than with the sweet treat. "You have to have one, too," she said, reaching for the box.

"No, that's all right. If I have one, there'll be one less for you."

"That's okay," she said, searching through the box. "If we get really desperate, we can eat the orange and grape ones, too." She found another cherry Popsicle and handed it to him, and he slid it out of the wrapper and bit into it. "Wow," he said, after a second. "I don't think I've had one of these since I was twelve years old."

"Do you like it?"

"I love it," he said seriously. But the way he was looking at her made her think it wasn't the Popsicle he was talking about.

Chapter 24

That night, in Minneapolis, Brandon swung his refrigerator door open and reached in for a beer. But his hand came back empty. No beer. No nothing, really. He swore and slammed the door shut. He thought about using what little money he had left to go to the grocery store and buy a six-pack but decided against it. Drinking would have to wait. Eating, too. Because he wasn't spending another night in this apartment without getting to the bottom of this. Despite what Mr. Tuck had said, nobody, not even Mila, could disappear into thin air. She had to be somewhere, didn't she? And tonight he was going to figure out where that was.

He walked back into the living room, which was so hot it was almost suffocating, and sat down on the couch. Then he turned his attention back to the cardboard box on the coffee table. Inside of it was every single bill, certificate, document, letter, or photograph that Mila had left behind. And she'd left almost everything behind, as far as he could tell. The only things she'd taken with her were her birth certificate, her Social Security card, and her driver's license. That was it. Everything else was here, from childhood report cards to recent credit card statements. And he was convinced that somewhere in this box was the clue to wherever Mila was now. He'd already been through it several times, but he was willing to go through it again. And again after that, if necessary.

After all, he had unlimited time to do it in now. He'd lost his job that morning, due to "unexcused absences." (Although what, he'd wanted to know, was more deserving of an unexcused absence than the fact that he was looking for his missing wife?) Still, he hadn't been that disappointed. The lack of money would be a problem—the bills were starting to pile up—but at least getting fired freed him up to search for Mila full-time. And not only that, but it meant that now he truly had nothing left to lose. Except, maybe, his life. And that was somehow fitting. Because he'd decided that he'd either find Mila and bring her home, or he'd die trying.

Now, he used his T-shirt to wipe the sweat off his face and started to go through the box again, one item at a time. He struggled, at first, to focus. It had been weeks since he'd slept more than a couple of hours at a time. But he worked like this until the box was almost empty. By then, it was almost dark in the stifling living room, and he had a knot between his shoulder blades from bending over the papers.

He got up to turn on the light and stretch. He came right back to the box, though. No rest for the weary. No food and no drink, either. He'd do this twenty-four hours a day if he had to. He wasn't willing to consider, now or ever, the possibility that he wouldn't find Mila. When he took the next piece of paper out of the box, though, it wasn't with high hopes. He'd seen it before. It was a certificate Mila had gotten from her home health aide class showing that she'd completed seventy-five hours of training and skills testing. He shook his head, mystified. He'd never understood why she wanted to work in health care. It had seemed to him a career that was at best boring, and, at worst, just plain disgusting. But maybe she'd changed her mind about it, he thought, because by the time their first anniversary had rolled around she'd stopped mentioning nursing school. He'd been relieved. He'd never had any intention of letting her be a nurse. Anything that would take her away from him, even for short periods of time, was unacceptable. Besides, being a nurse would have brought her into contact with other men. Medical technicians, doctors, patients. And while Mila had insisted that she'd never been unfaithful to him, he still didn't trust her. He needed her at home. Where she belonged. And where he could keep an eye on her.

Now he set the certificate down on the coffee table and started to take the next piece of paper out of the box. But he changed his mind and looked at it again. It didn't have a lot of information on it. Her name. The name of the community college that she'd taken the class at. The date she'd received the certification on. But if it wasn't going to lead him to Mila, he thought, it might at least answer one question he'd been asking himself: what was Mila doing to earn a living now?

After all, according to his calculations, she'd taken less than two hundred dollars with her when she'd left him. And if she wasn't staying with her mom or Heather, she had to somehow be earning her own keep. She could be working as a waitress, of course. She knew how to do that, and it was the kind of job where you could get paid cash, under the table, if necessary. But for some reason, he didn't think she was waitressing. It was too public. Too out in the open. And if she was really hiding from him, which she obviously was, working in a busy coffee shop was the wrong way to do it.

But working as a home health care aide . . . that was different. You'd spend most, if not all your time, in someone else's home. Taking care of someone who wasn't able to take care of themselves, which meant taking care of someone who probably wasn't up to spending a lot of time out in public, either. In some ways, it would be the perfect cover.

He thought about Mila doing this now and found that it actually brought him a measure of relief. His greatest fear—his only fear, really, beyond not getting Mila back—was of her meeting another man. He'd imagined her doing this in the months since she'd left, and it always left him feeling the same: first sick with jealousy, then white hot with rage. But if Mila was a home health aide, he reasoned, the chances of her having met someone her age were slim to none. He pictured her now wiping the drool off some senile old man's chin, and it pleased him. She'd thought she'd wanted to run away, but by the time he found her, he figured she'd probably be thrilled to come back home.

But as comforting as he found this thought, he banished it from his mind. He needed to focus. He stared at the certificate and tried to think calmly. Logically. What could this piece of paper tell him about where Mila was? Well, for one thing, he decided, certifications for things like home health care aides probably varied from state to state. Just because Mila was licensed to be an aide in Minnesota didn't necessarily mean she was licensed to be one in Michigan or South Dakota. So chances were good that she was still in Minnesota. But if that were the case, then how had she found a job? She could have found it over the Internet, but if she had, she hadn't used their home computer to find it. He'd already taken it to some computer geek to check the browser history. Of course, there were other ways of finding jobs. Help wanted ads, bulletin boards, employment agencies . . . *employment agencies.*

Brandon pushed himself up off the couch and headed for their bedroom where their desktop computer was. But he stopped midway there. The computer was gone. He'd sold it to pay Mr. Tuck. He hesitated, then turned and headed for the kitchen instead, where he ransacked the cupboard until he came up with a copy of the Yellow Pages. He took it back to the couch with him and thumbed through it until he found what he was looking for. Home Health Agencies. There was a whole page of them. He ran a finger down the columns of listings look-ing for . . . looking for what? He didn't know. But he'd know it when he found it. His finger slid over a listing for Caring Home Care, then paused and came back to it. What was it about that name that sounded familiar? He thought, hard, closing his eyes. Then he rifled through one of the stacks of paper on the coffee table and pulled out a record of his account that he'd printed from the phone company website. It was an itemized list of phone calls made from their landline in the month before Mila left. He'd called all the numbers on the list to identify them and then he'd written the name of the person or business in the margin next to the number. Scanning the list now, he saw one of the numbers had been for Caring Home Care. When he'd first dialed the number and the woman on the other end of the line had answered with Caring Home Care, he'd hung up immediately. He'd assumed that Mila had dialed a wrong number. Of course, he'd also assumed, wrongly, that Caring Home Care was a housecleaning business. The only reason he'd written its name down was in the interest of being thorough. His eyes scanned the record of the call. It had been made at 5:30 P.M. on May 30, and it had lasted three minutes. Too long, he decided, to be a wrong number, but long enough to discuss job possibilities.

"Bingo," he said softly, and he felt a rush of adrenaline that might have been amplified by hunger or sleeplessness. He glanced at his watch. It was eleven o'clock at night. He doubted the agency would be open before nine o'clock the next morning. But he'd be there then. And he wasn't leaving until he knew everything the people there knew about Mila.

Chapter 25

The next morning, Reid slowly stirred awake. He was aware, from the gray light behind his eyelids, that it was morning, and he was also aware, from a steady tapping on the window, that it was raining. So the rain had finally come, he thought, rolling over onto his side, and, as he did so, he became aware of something else. He wasn't alone in his bed. There was someone else in it with him. And there was really only one person who that could be.

He opened his eyes and, miraculously, there she was, sleeping beside him.

"Mila?" he whispered, reaching out tentatively to stroke her cheek. He hated to wake her up when she looked so peaceful, but he needed to confirm that she was actually there. She was. Her eyes opened, and, seeing him, she smiled and snuggled into his arms, then sighed contentedly. "Good morning," she said.

"When did you get here?" Reid asked cautiously, brushing a strand of hair off her cheek. It was the first time since the alarm had gone off that they'd slept in the same bed, and he did not quite trust his luck.

"Mmmmmm," she said, nuzzling her lips against his neck. "Sometime during the night."

"What . . . what made you decide to come in here?" he asked, though he didn't want to interrupt the thing she was doing to his neck with her lips.

"I woke up and it was raining," she said. "And it was cool again, for the first time in days. And I wanted to be with you. And I thought, 'Well, what are you waiting for? He's right down the hall,'" She gave a little laugh. "I hope it's okay," she added, and her lips started doing that thing to his neck again.

"Are you kidding? Of course it's okay. I *want* you to be here," he said. "I want you to be here every night. You know that, don't you, Mila?"

She pulled away from him and smiled, and he realized that for the first time in a long time, she didn't look anxious or fatigued or worried. She looked . . . *she looked amazing*. And he didn't know if it was because the heat wave had finally broken, or she'd slept in the same bed as him, or she'd just *slept*, period, but she looked as relaxed and as happy as he'd ever seen her look before. Her skin, for instance, was rosy and warm, and her golden-brown eyes were shining. Her auburn hair was brushing her almost bare shoulders, and her sleeveless white cotton nightgown showed off her tan.

"You are so beautiful—" he started to say, but she put a finger to his lips to silence him, and then she leaned over and kissed him so he couldn't say anything else.

And Reid kissed her back and marveled at how delicious her mouth tasted. It was as sweet and as fresh, he imagined, as the rain falling outside the window. And her body, pliant and relaxed against his, told him that she had let down her defenses. She wanted him. And he wanted her. *Oh God, he wanted her.* But he needed to go slowly, he reminded himself. Very slowly. She'd been through so much, though what exactly she'd been through, he didn't know. Still, he could hazard a guess. He knew she'd been hurt. Badly. And he knew she was afraid. But he thought he knew something else, too: if he could translate the way he felt about her into the way he made love to her, he could erase a little of her hurt and fear. Erase it and replace it with something else.

So he pulled her, lovingly, into his arms, and kissed her as tenderly as he knew how to. He would take his time, he decided. *Really* take his time. But Mila, it turned out, didn't want him to take his time. She pressed herself against him, kissed him more deeply, and ran her hands up under his T-shirt, touching his chest and stomach and back with some indefinable combination of impatience and delight.

"Let's take this off," she said, breaking away from their kiss, and easing his T-shirt up over his head. "I want to feel you against me."

"I want to feel you against me, too," he said, or *groaned*, really, at the thought of his bare skin touching her bare skin. He reached down then and took the hem of her nightgown in his hands and peeled it up, slowly, over her body, until everything was revealed to him—her slender legs, her cream-colored panties, her flat stomach, and, finally, her small, perfect breasts.

When he'd pulled her nightgown all the way off and dropped it on the floor, he pulled her back into his arms. She anchored herself firmly against him so that her breasts crushed softly against his chest, running her hands over his back. "You're so warm," she said.

"You're warm too," he said, kissing the nape of her neck in a place he already knew was especially sensitive. He did this for a little while, using his tongue, until she started to squirm, and then he reached down and caressed one of her breasts with his fingertips, feeling her smooth nipple harden beneath his touch. She made an appreciative sound in her throat, and he stroked her nipple harder, until she let out a little moan that excited him almost beyond measure. Then he leaned down and kissed that same nipple, tracing it with his tongue, and took the very tip of it between his lips and sucked on it gently. Mila cried out, louder this time, and brought her hands up to the back of his head and arched her back so that he would take more of her nipple into his mouth. He obliged her, happily, and as he did so he felt her whole body move beneath him in an undulating wave of excitement.

After a few moments, though, he started to edge his mouth downward, toward her navel, then thought better of it and came back to the other nipple. It wasn't fair, he'd decided, for only one of them to get all the attention. So now he kissed and tongued and sucked this nipple, too, until Mila moved beneath him again, burying her fingers in his hair and tilting her hips against his hips. She was hungry, he thought with satisfaction. And greedy, too. He left his mouth on her nipple and skimmed a hand down to her panties, then caressed her through the silky material.

"*Reid*," she whimpered, not in protest but in need, and he decided that this article of clothing needed to come off, too. He freed up his other hand, which had stayed behind to stroke a swollen nipple, and, using both hands, he started to peel down her panties with the same care that he had peeled off her nightgown. In about sixty seconds, he thought, she'd be naked, and he'd be the only one wearing any clothes. But maybe not for long. Because even as he was thinking this, Mila's hands were moving down his stomach, her fingers dipping briefly into the waistband of his pajama bottoms, and then settling on the outside of them, and squeezing his hardness through them in a way that made Reid groan loudly. He slid her panties down, until, without warming, he felt her stiffen in his arms and she sat up in bed.

"What is it?" Reid asked.

"It's a car, in the driveway," she said breathlessly, looking out the window. She glanced at his bedside table clock. "Reid, it's eight o'clock," she said, astonished. "It's Lonnie."

"Damn it," he said without thinking, and then, grabbing Mila's hand, he said, "Don't go."

"Reid, I *have* to," she said. She pulled up her panties, then groped around on the floor for her nightgown.

"Please don't," he said, already missing the feel of her body against his.

But she shook her head. "Reid, we can't make love with Lonnie in the next room."

"*Yes,* we can," he said, but Mila ignored him as she picked up her nightgown and pulled it over her head, covering up, in reverse order, everything she had just revealed to him: first her breasts, then her stomach, then her legs.

She started to get out of his bed, but when she looked at him, something about the expression on his face made her laugh.

"Reid, I swear," she said, "you look like a little boy who just dropped his ice cream cone."

"Oh, no, Mila," he said seriously. "This is *much* worse than that. Trust me."

She smiled at him affectionately and, kneeling on the bed, kissed him one more time, letting her tongue linger in his mouth for a moment before pulling regretfully away. And then she was gone, and Lonnie was letting herself into the cabin, and Reid was left to wonder if Mila had ever been there at all. Except he knew, of course, that she had been there. Her side of the bed was still warm, and he was so aroused by the taste and touch and feel of her that it was all he could do to fall back on the bed, his body aching with his need for her.

By late morning the rain had stopped, and by early afternoon, the sun had burned off the low-bellied clouds, the cottony mist over the lake, and the fat,

quivering drops of water that hung from the pine needles on the pine trees, and the day was as beautiful
as any day that Mila had seen that summer. Even at
four thirty in the afternoon, as she puttered around in
the kitchen, everything outside the cabin, and inside
of it, too, seemed to be suffused with the same warm,
golden light, a light that was the exact same color,
to Mila's mind, as the little jars of clover leaf honey
Lonnie bought at the farmers' market in Butternut.

It was an afternoon that practically begged you to be
outside, but Mila was perfectly content inside, doing a
few of the chores Lonnie hadn't had time to do before
she'd left that afternoon. She hummed as she languidly
wiped down the kitchen counter with a dishcloth, then
paused to rinse the cloth out in the sink and, as a cloud
of steamy water rose up to meet her face, she remembered the scene in Reid's bed that morning. She turned
off the faucet, wrung out the dishcloth, and wandered
over to the kitchen window, letting the sweet breeze
blow over her and savoring the earthy smell of the
woods after the rain.

She was happy, she realized, happier than she'd been
all summer. Happier than she'd ever been before in her
life. After she woke up but before she went to Reid's bed,
she'd made a decision. She wasn't going to live this way
anymore, with one foot in a painful past and the other

in an uncertain future. Tonight, she was going to start living in the present. She was going to tell Reid everything about her life before she'd met him. *Everything.* And then, she was going to tell him one more thing. She was going to tell him that she loved him. After she told him that . . . well, after that, it would be in his hands. He'd have to decide what would happen next. But she wasn't afraid, as she had been once, that he'd ask her to leave. She thought she knew how he felt about her now. And it was the same way she felt about him. She sighed happily and glanced at her watch, then went to take out of the refrigerator the shepherd's pie Lonnie had made that morning. She wanted them to eat early that night, because the sooner they had dinner, the sooner they could talk, and the sooner, she hoped, they could finish what they'd started this morning. She was done waiting. Once she told Reid about her marriage, she'd decided, that marriage would be all but dissolved, in her mind anyway.

God, she missed Reid, she thought, sliding the pan of shepherd's pie out of the refrigerator. She missed him even though she'd only seen him a little while ago. He was in the study, looking over something Walker had e-mailed him. She thought about going to him now. He wouldn't mind the interruption, she knew. In fact, he would welcome it if it was from her. But there was something else she needed to do first. She needed to call Ms. Thompson before Caring Home Care closed for the day. She wanted to check up on her and see if her cough was any better. And if it wasn't, she'd need to lecture her, again, about seeing a doctor. After all, Mila might not be a nurse yet, but she knew a nasty cough when she heard one.

So she picked up the cordless phone and climbed onto the high stool that Lonnie liked to sit on while she peeled vegetables at the kitchen counter, and after she'd dialed Ms. Thompson's number, she waited for her familiar voice at the other end of the line. But when someone did answer, with "Hello, Caring Home Care," it was a voice she didn't recognize.

"Oh, um, hi," Mila said, feeling disoriented. Nobody but Ms. Thompson had ever answered the phone before. "Is Ms. Thompson there, please?"

"No, she's not. But maybe I can help you."

"Is . . . is she all right?" Mila asked haltingly. But she already knew she wasn't all right.

The voice on the other end of the line hesitated, then said, "Ms. Thompson has pneumonia. We all told her—I'm her niece, Janet, by the way—to go to the doctor, but she wouldn't listen to us. By yesterday evening, though, she was having trouble breathing so my dad drove her to the emergency room. They checked her right into the hospital."

"Oh, my God, I'm so sorry," Mila murmured, her eyes filling with tears. "But she's going to be all right, isn't she?"

Janet hesitated again. "I, I don't know. It's very serious. She's in the ICU right now. But we're all pulling for her," she added. "I'm going to visit her later today, as soon as I'm done here."

"That's good," Mila said, wiping a tear away. "Well, I won't take up any more of your time."

"Oh no, that's fine. I'm just trying to come up to speed. The only thing my aunt has ever let me do here is file, but for the short term, at least, I'm going to be filling in for her. By the way," she said, "I didn't catch your name."

"I, I didn't give it to you," Mila said, after a moment's struggle. "It's Mila. Mila Jones. But Ms. Thompson and I have a . . . a special understanding," she went on, wondering how she would explain this understanding to Janet. But Janet interrupted her.

"Oh, Ms. Jones," she said, eagerly, "I'm so glad you called. Your brother was here first thing this morning."

"My brother?" Mila repeated, her mind a blank.

"Uh-huh. Kevin, right? He came into the office. He said he'd been out of the country, you know, doing a tour of duty, and he'd lost your contact information."

It was so quiet in the kitchen then that Mila could hear every single drip from the still wet dishcloth she'd hung up on the sink's faucet. "I don't have a brother," she heard herself say.

"Are you sure?" Janet asked.

"I'm sure," she said, in too much shock to even register the absurdity of this question.

"Oh. Because I could have sworn that that's what he said. That he was your brother," Janet said, sounding only vaguely disconcerted. "But maybe he said cousin. Or something else. Honestly, I can't remember. Anyway, I had the hardest time finding your file, Mila. It wasn't with the other files. I told your brother—or whoever he was—that I didn't think the agency had placed you with anyone, because I couldn't find any record of you. But he was so insistent. He said he had some family news. He said it was urgent. So I looked again, not in the file cabinet, but in my aunt's desk drawer. The one she keeps locked. And she's never even told me where the key is," Janet said, a little petulantly. "But I found it. Your brother, or whatever, helped me look, and it was under a potted plant on an end table. So, long story short, your file was in the drawer, along with your contact information, and I gave it to him. You know, 'cause I could have sworn he said he was your brother and he seemed so desperate to find you . . ."

There was a silence on the phone now, and Mila, whose brain was still not working, gave herself a little shake. "What time was it when he came in this morning?" she asked. But her voice sounded strange, even to her.

"Ummm, let me think. He came in . . . right as I was opening. Around nine o'clock, I guess." A phone rang in the background then, and Janet asked, "Do you mind if I put you on hold for a second? I need to take this other call."

But Mila didn't answer. She hung up the phone and reached to set it down on the kitchen counter, but she missed it and dropped the phone instead. It clattered to the floor. And then that same floor seemed to be rising up to meet her. Or was she sinking down to meet the floor? Either way, she felt her body sink onto the tiled floor, and she was grateful to have something solid beneath her. She heard the phone ring then, loud and jangly, just inches from where she lay. But she couldn't answer it. She didn't have the strength. Instead, she lay perfectly still and felt the cool floor against her warm cheek. And then, after that, she felt nothing at all.

Chapter 26

When the cordless phone on his desk rang, Reid, glad for the interruption, answered it immediately. It was Walker calling from the boatyard office.

"Did you get the spreadsheet I e-mailed you?" he asked.

"I'm looking at it right now," Reid said, though even as he was saying this he was swiveling his chair away from the desk and the spreadsheet on his iPad.

"And?" Walker prompted.

"And . . . and I'm sorry. I can't make head or tails of it."

"Reid, you know how to read a spreadsheet," Walker said, in disbelief.

"I *knew* how to read a spreadsheet," Reid amended. "Now, apparently, I've forgotten or . . ."

"Or what?"

"Or I just don't want to read it," he admitted, glancing back at his iPad. "I mean, seriously, Walk, how is it even possible for anything to be that boring?"

"You didn't use to find them boring. You didn't use to find our business boring either," Walker pointed out, sounding mildly offended. "You used to find it pretty goddamned interesting."

"And I still do," Reid said, quickly. "But, Walker, answer me this, okay? When was the last time you had a cherry Popsicle?"

"A cherry Popsicle?" Walker repeated. And then he sighed. Loudly. "I'm assuming this has something to do with Mila."

"It does," Reid agreed, tilting back in his chair. "And, Walk? If you haven't had any recently, you might want to try them again."

"Okay, thanks. I'll bear that in mind. But in the meantime, Reid, when are you coming back to work? *Really* coming back to work?"

Now it was Reid's turn to sigh. "Soon, Walk. I promise. It's just . . . it's just that I'm finding it hard to concentrate."

"No kidding," Walker grumbled.

"Like now, for instance, when I should be thinking about the spreadsheet, I keep thinking about last night instead. I was giving Mila these practice tests, you know, for the nursing school entrance exam, and I was supposed to be timing her while she took them, but . . ." Reid smiled, remembering this. "But I kept forgetting to look at my watch. Because when she concentrates, she does this thing with her mouth. It's sort of like a half frown, half pout, I guess. She doesn't even know she doing it, but she is, and, Walk, it's adorable."

There was silence now on the other end of the line, but Reid imagined he could hear Walker rolling his eyes.

"Anyway, that's the problem," Reid said, leaning farther back in his chair.

"Mila's mouth is the problem?"

"Not her mouth but—"

"But the thing she does with it when she's concentrating?"

Reid laughed. "Well, yeah. But no, not really. The problem is, when I'm not with her, I can't stop thinking about her."

"Reid, you're *with* her all the time."

"Not *all* the time," Reid qualified. "I'm not with her right now. I haven't been her for . . . for thirty-seven minutes now," he said, studying his watch.

"That long, huh?" Walker said, but he sounded suddenly tolerant. He sounded, Reid thought, like a man who knew what it was like to be in love. "All right, well, go be with her then," Walker said. "And do . . . well, do whatever it is you two probably spend most of your time doing anyway."

"Oh," Reid said, tilting his chair abruptly forward. "Oh, no. We're not doing that," he said. "I mean, we're not doing that *yet*, anyway."

"You're not?" Walker said. He sounded genuinely shocked.

"No. Why, do you think that's strange?"

"Not strange, but . . . yeah, actually, I think it's a little strange. After all, it's not as if you two have lacked for opportunities to be alone this summer."

"You're right, we haven't. But Mila's old-fashioned that way," Reid said, though the truth, he knew, was more complicated than that.

"Huh," Walker said, considering this, and then, "Nothing wrong with being old-fashioned."

"Nope," Reid said, though as he said it, he flashed on an image of a near naked Mila in his bed that morning, arching her back, and pinning her hips against his, alive to his kiss and every touch, and he had to admit that "old-fashioned" was probably not a phrase he would have used to describe her then.

"Look," Walker said now, "you're obviously not getting anything done, anyway. So why don't you take the rest of the day off. But tomorrow, it's back to work, all right? I can't keep carrying you, Reid."

"I know that. And you won't have to, I promise."

"All right. I'll talk to you—" But Walker's voice cut out then.

"Hello?" Reid said. "Walker?" He pressed the talk button on the cordless phone and listened but there was no dial tone. The line was dead. That was strange. Sometimes, up here, a storm could bring a phone line down, but it was clear as a bell outside right now. Still, there were other things that could interrupt phone service. It'd probably be back up again soon, he thought, and he lost interest in the problem. He swiveled his chair around again and put the cordless phone back in its charger. He'd take Walker's advice now and go be with Mila. He missed her already. Missed her like crazy. She'd been so different today, he reflected. Ever since they'd woken up together, she'd been so relaxed, so untroubled, as if a burden had suddenly been lifted from her. He reached for his crutches beside his desk chair, but before he could get up, the study door banged open and Mila came rushing in.

"Oh my God, Reid, are you okay?" she asked, coming over to him.

"What? Yeah, of course, I'm fine. But, Mila, what's wrong?" Her face, he saw, was completely drained of any color. "What happened?" he asked, alarmed.

"Thank God you're all right." Her eyes scanned the room. She sat down on the edge of the desk, and, as if she still didn't believe he was all right, she leaned over and touched his face, running the back of her trembling hand against his cheek.

He reached out instinctively and held her hand, trying to still its shaking. It was surprisingly cold. He rubbed it between both of his hands. "Mila, seriously, you're scaring me. What happened to you?"

"I . . . I fainted, I think. But I don't know how long I was out for. I came to and I—"

"What do you mean you fainted? Are you ill?"

But she shook her head. "No. But, Reid? We don't have a lot of time. We need to leave. *Now.*"

"Where are we going?" he asked, mystified.

"I'm taking you to Allie and Walker's. You'll be safe there, I think."

"And what about you?" he asked, his heart quickening. He'd never seen her this way before. She'd been frightened the night the cabin's alarm had gone off. But this was worse.

"I don't know about me. The main thing is to get *you* away from here, and then to get *me* away from you. He can't see us together, Reid."

"Who is *he*, Mila?" he asked. And then, "You've got to back up, okay? You've got to tell me what's going on here."

She nodded jerkily. "All right, but then we've got to go, okay? And, Reid, no questions. There's no time for questions."

"No questions," he agreed.

"I'm married," she said, looking at him steadily. "I left my husband because he was abusive. And I took this job because it was as far away as I could get from him."

He nodded, suddenly and strangely calm. He wasn't surprised by any of what she'd just said. All of it, in fact, made perfect sense to him. All summer long, Mila had been like a jigsaw puzzle he'd been trying to put together. Now, at last, she'd given him the final piece. And it was a relief to put it into place, to complete the puzzle and to know that there was nothing about that puzzle that could make him love her any less than he loved her right now.

Mila kept talking. Rapidly. Shakily. "The woman who owned the agency, Ms. Thompson, promised to keep the fact that I was working here confidential. But when I called today, to check in with her, her niece answered the phone and told me that Ms. Thompson's in the hospital. And she said that Brandon, my husband, was in the office first thing this morning, with some lie about being my brother, and that he found my contact information. Reid, he knows where I am. If he left Minneapolis this morning, he could be here by now." She stopped speaking, out of breath.

"Mila," he said, taking both of her hands in his. "Calm down. It's going to be all right. I promise."

"It's *not* going to be all right," she said, her voice rising. "He can't find us here together, Reid. You have no idea what he's like. I mean, he went off the deep end once because I rode up in an elevator with another man. If he finds out I've been living here with you, alone, all summer . . ." She shook her head, and blinked a few tears.

He let go of one of her hands now, slid the top desk drawer open, took out the extra set of keys to the van and pressed them into her palm, closing her fingers around them. "Mila, *go.* Now. By yourself. Go to Allie and Walker's. If I come, I'll slow you down."

But she shook her head. "I won't leave you here alone."

"I can handle him."

"Reid," she said, her voice rising and more tears spilling down her cheeks. "You don't understand him. You're assuming he's a rational person, but he's not. He's totally *irrational.* He's hurt me before and he could do worse to you. You're going to have to take my word for it, okay?"

He nodded. He believed her. Nothing else could account for her fear.

"In fact, Reid, we should just call the police right now," Mila said, reaching for the cordless phone on his desk. "I mean, he could be here any minute, right?"

Her eyes flitted toward the empty doorway to the room.

But as Reid watched her, as she hit the talk button and put the phone up to her ear, he had an awful realization. "It's dead, isn't?" he asked, as she hit the talk button again.

She nodded, and, not taking her eyes off him, she put the phone back slowly, on the desk.

"It went dead right before you came in," Reid said quietly. He leaned forward in his desk chair and picked up his iPad.

"Reid," Mila whispered. "I think he's already here. Cutting the phone line . . . That's him. He works construction. He knows how to do that kind of thing."

Reid looked at his iPad. Walker's e-mail was still open in front of him. He clicked on reply and started typing.

She looked positively gray now. "Reid, where's your cell phone?" she whispered.

"I left it on the kitchen table this morning," he said, and he finished typing and pressed send.

"I'll get it," Mila said, turning to go. And before he could stop her she left the room, closing the door behind her.

He checked his iPad again. No reply from Walker yet. *Please let Walker still be at his desk and still be checking his e-mail.*

Breathe, Mila. Breathe, she told herself, and as she walked through the living room she drew in a ragged little breath. *Now keep breathing, because you'll be useless to Reid, and to yourself, if you faint again.* When she walked into the kitchen, she saw Reid's cell phone on the breakfast table, caught in an intricate pattern of sunlight and shadows. And something about the way the light danced along a jagged edge made her look at the windowpanes on the kitchen door. That's when she saw that one of the panes had been broken, but before she could register what this meant, she was grabbed from behind.

"*Brandon,*" she whispered through his hand, which was now clamped over her mouth.

"That's right, Mila." His voice was a menacing whisper. "What did I tell you? I told you I'd never let you go. I meant it." As he said this he turned her around and pushed her back up against the wall, and, pressing his forearm against her chest, he pinned her there. "Don't even think about screaming," he said.

She tried to focus on him, tried to formulate a plan, but she couldn't think clearly. He started ranting, telling her how she'd wrecked everything, ruined their life together. He had no job, no money, no nothing. Nothing but her, and she'd left him. She was coming back with him now, though, and she would have to fix things. Put them right. He said other things, too, things that were harder to follow. They were disjointed. Chaotic. And so, too, was his appearance. His hair was greasy, and his T-shirt stained, both of which were unlike him. He'd always taken care of the way he looked before.

His tirade ended abruptly. "Who's that man?" he asked, his eyes coming into focus.

Mila felt a new stab of fear. "There's no man," she said, shaking her head.

"Yes, there is. I saw a man in the other room. I saw him through the window."

"I don't know what you're talking about," she said, her heart beating faster.

"Yes, you do. He's sitting at a desk. Who is he?" He moved his arm up, so that it was pressing against her neck. "Who is he, Mila?" he repeated, pressing harder. "Answer me."

"He's a patient," she rasped finally, her hands trying to push his arm away.

"Hold still," he said in her ear. "Or I'll hurt you." And then, "I don't think he's a patient. He looks all right to me."

She shook her head. She had to get Brandon to leave before Reid knew he was here. If Reid knew he was here, he would try to protect her, with potentially disastrous results. She would go with Brandon now, she decided, but she would only stay with him long enough to get him away from Reid.

"Let's go," she whispered to him, still fighting for breath.

But he shook his head. "Who is that man?" he asked her again. "Have you been living here with him?" More pressure on her neck.

"Let go of her." *Reid,* she thought, and her fear was mixed with relief. Brandon swung around, and she sucked in some welcome air. Reid was standing ten feet away, in the kitchen doorway. Brandon jerked her away from the wall, and holding her arms tightly behind her, he turned her so that she was between him and Reid.

"Who the hell are you?" Brandon said.

Reid ignored the question. "You need to leave." His voice was calm, but his taut body looked poised to strike.

Brandon yanked Mila closer to him. "We're both leaving. I'll be back for you later."

Mila felt a surge of panic, and she started to struggle against Brandon. But he only tightened his grip on her.

"You're not taking Mila. The police are on their way. And unless you want to spend the night in a jail cell . . ."

"You're lying," Brandon taunted. "The police aren't coming. I cut the phone and Internet lines, and your cell phone's right there," he said, his eyes darting to the kitchen table.

"I didn't need those. I used my iPad."

Mila felt Brandon tense. He tightened his arms around her. "We're going together," he said in her ear.

"Did you hear that?" Reid said quietly. "That's a police siren."

"I didn't hear anything," Brandon said, but he cast a nervous glance toward the door. In the next second, Mila heard it: the faint whine of a siren. She wondered if, in her desperation, she was imagining it. But then Brandon heard it, too. "Son of a bitch," he said, under his breath and he scanned the room rapidly, his eyes stopping on the knife holder on the kitchen counter.

"Brandon, go," Mila said, trying to distract him. She knew that the longer he was there, the more likely things were to spin out of control. "This isn't going to end the way you want it to," she said. "It was *never* going to end the way you wanted it to. I'm not your wife anymore."

"You'll always be my wife," he said, but as he said it there was a hunted quality about him. He was afraid, Mila saw, with surprise.

"If you don't leave now, you'll be arrested," Reid said. "You won't be with Mila. You'll be sitting in a jail cell."

Brandon wavered, and in the silence that followed the sirens sounded again. They were getting closer. But Mila knew from experience how far sounds carried out here. The police might still be five miles away. Then again, Brandon didn't know that.

He turned her to him, and his grip on her arm tightened. "I found you once. I'll find you again," he said. And he shoved her, hard, against the wall, and then he was gone, the screen door banging shut behind him. Mila groped for a kitchen chair, but Reid was already beside her.

Brandon took off through the woods to the place where he'd left his pickup parked on an old logging road a quarter of a mile from the cabin. By the time he reached it, he was scratched and bleeding and he had badly twisted one ankle, but the pain barely registered. He fumbled for the keys in his pocket, his breath coming fast, his whole body trembling with a mixture of anger and fear. With great effort he pulled open the door, climbed into the driver's seat, and shoved the key into the ignition.

Just then he heard the sound of sirens again and a surge of adrenaline shot through him. *They're not going to get me,* he told himself as he slammed on the accelerator with such force that the pickup lurched up the logging road and shot onto the main road. *They can't get me. I'm not going back to jail. I'm not an animal. I won't be locked up like one.*

He took a turn wide, not caring that he was taking up the whole road. He had no idea where he was going, only that he was heading away from the town. A truck passed him coming from the other direction and practically grazed his pickup. The driver honked and signaled something to him. He knew he needed to slow down. To make a plan. To figure out what he would do next. But he couldn't fix on anything. His brain felt crowded. Muddled. He realized he didn't even know what day it was. What time it was. He'd left that morning to bring Mila back, but nothing had gone according to plan. He'd thought she would leave with him. She was *supposed* to leave with him. She was meant to be with him. In the past, she'd always done what he'd told her to do. The last time she'd run away, he'd brought her back. She'd come willingly then, hadn't she? But she seemed so different this time. He didn't know this Mila. What had she meant, for instance, when she'd said things were not going to end the way he'd wanted them to? But they *had* to end the way he wanted them to. There was no other future for him than a future where Mila was always there, always waiting for him.

He took the next turn too fast and slid onto the shoulder before pulling back. Christ, this road was twisted. Why would Mila have come to this crazy place anyway when she could have been safe at home with him? *Christ*, it was practically the end of the world, he thought, as blinding green forest flashed by on either side of him.

A wave of dizziness came over him then. He should have eaten something. He'd wanted to get here so badly, though, he hadn't had time. And now . . . now he had to start over. Rest. Eat. Plan. And then go back for her. There was so much he had to do over. To do right. The dizziness got worse. He saw Mila at the cabin with that man. Saw her refusing to come with him. Saw her wrecking everything they'd had. "Why'd you do it?" he muttered, speeding up. His car veered, and instead of righting it, he stepped harder on the accelerator. The last thing he saw as his car went off the road was a blur of green branches and the dark, roughened bark of a tree trunk rising up to meet his windshield.

Chapter 27

Mila lay on her bed, facing the wall. She was willing herself not to think about what had already happened, or what might happen in the future. She had no idea, either, how long she'd been lying there for, but it must have been at least an hour, judging from the shifting light outside. It would be evening soon. She could hear Reid and Walker, still talking in the kitchen.

After Brandon left, but before the police arrived, she'd had a few minutes to talk to Reid. She'd told him then how sorry she was, how she never should have put him in this kind of danger. But he'd stopped her from saying any more. It wasn't about blame or guilt, he said. It wasn't about him or her. They were in this together. And that was the way he wanted it to be.

Then there was a flurry of activity. A police car pulled up outside, followed shortly by Walker's pickup truck. She and Reid had spoken to the police. The police, who luckily had been in the area when they got the call from Walker, hadn't passed any cars on their way to the cabin, so they knew that Brandon had left the driveway heading north on Butternut Lake Drive. They'd radioed another car to try to intercept him coming from the other direction. And Mila had worried, silently, about the possibility of Brandon taking one of the logging roads, and hiding out there until after dark, but she'd said nothing about this to the police.

When the police left, she'd told Reid, who was obviously worried about her, that she wanted to lie down. She was exhausted, but more than that, she knew the brothers needed time to talk. Walker was visibly upset, and who could blame him? She could hear them now, and she concentrated on Reid's voice. Something about it made her feel safe. Reassured.

Finally, though, she heard a car drive up. She got up from the bed and walked over to the window. It was a police car, and for one wild moment she wondered if Brandon had been arrested and was sitting in the backseat. But no, there was no one in the backseat. She watched as two officers got out, and then she went and sat back down on the edge of the bed. *He got away,* she thought wearily.

She sat there as the minutes ticked by. Reid and Walker's voices were joined by the policemen's voices, and then, finally, there was the sound of everyone leaving. Reid must be alone, she thought, and she went to the kitchen to find him. She saw him before he saw her. He was standing at the kitchen table; a bottle of whiskey and two small glasses, one of which was empty, were on the table.

"Mila," he said, when he saw her in the doorway. His expression, which had been one of preoccupation, instantly softened.

"Come sit down with me," he said. "I was about to finish my drink. My brother had the idea of finally opening that bottle of whiskey I gave him. Do you want a glass too?"

She shrugged a tiny shrug, but he took this for a yes and went to get a third glass, then poured a little whiskey in it. She was surprised by his casualness, though it was tempered by concern for her. Still, under the circumstances, he seemed almost too calm.

She looked at him quizzically as she sat down at the table. "What did the police say?"

He sat down with her and pulled his glass over to him but didn't take a sip. Instead he reached for her hand. "He's gone, Mila."

"He got away?" Mila asked.

"No," he said, his hand tightening on hers. "He's dead."

She shook her head, not understanding.

"He hit a tree a couple of miles from the driveway. The police passed the crash site after they left here the first time. Judging from the impact, it looks like he was going way too fast for these roads. He wasn't wearing a seat belt, either. They think he broke his neck. In which case, he died instantly."

She stared at Reid, her mind a perfect blank. But it must have been functioning on some level, because she picked up the glass of whiskey. She took a sip, and swallowed, then felt it burn, first as it went down her throat and then as it landed in her stomach. She put the glass down.

"Why don't you try drinking the whole thing at once," Reid suggested.

So she did. She gulped the rest down, and this time the burning sensation made her eyes water, and the taste, so foreign to her, made her whole body shudder.

Reid then drank what was left in his own glass. Unlike Mila, though, he didn't wince when he drank it. She wished that the whiskey brought some relief. But it didn't. Her head felt a little cloudy, her stomach a little warm, but, mostly, she felt the same. She felt numb. Completely numb, and it scared her.

"Reid . . . I don't feel anything," she confessed.

"Anything from the whiskey?"

"Anything at all."

"I think you're in shock, Mila."

"I think . . . I think you're right," she said softly. "But it feels wrong, somehow. He's gone and I feel . . . I feel nothing. Nothing at all." Not even *relief*, she almost said, but didn't.

"I think the feelings will come later," Reid said.

"When?"

"I don't know."

"Do you think they'll come a little bit at a time, or all at once?"

"I don't know that, either. But I know they'll come, eventually."

"I . . . think I'll lie down," she said suddenly, knowing even as she said it that sleep was out of the question.

"That's a good idea," Reid said encouragingly. "You must be exhausted."

She nodded.

"I'll be in my room, if you need me," he said.

"Okay," she said, standing up.

She got ready for bed, changing mechanically into her nightgown. She didn't expect to sleep, but she must have fallen asleep, because the next thing she knew, she was sitting bolt upright in bed, her heart pounding, her breath coming fast.

"He's gone," she said, out loud, in the dark room, and, for the first time, the words resonated with her. For the first time, she understood them. And then the feelings came, as Reid had said they would. And they came all at once, one on top of the other, so that she didn't have even a moment between them to label them, examine them, or understand them. And they were all there: relief, anger, horror, sadness and regret, and even a little guilt. And she knew now she wanted to be with Reid. She went to his room and opened the door. He was still awake.

"Mila," he said, sliding over in his bed and reaching for her at the same time. And Mila came into the room, and let him take her into his bed, and his arms, in one fluid motion, and hold her tightly to him. And, Mila, wordlessly, held him back, held him as if her life depended on it, which in a way it did.

She nestled against him, her face buried in his chest. And then the tears came. Just a few, at first, rolling hotly down her cheeks. She sniffled and blinked them away. But they wouldn't be stopped. There was more then, a great flood of them.

And Reid held her and let her cry. And Mila was so grateful to him. He never once suggested she stop. He never made a show of bringing her tissues, or a glass of water, or a cup of tea or anything like that. And he never said anything, either. Any of the meaningless things people say at a time like this. He never said that everything would be all right. That things would get better. That it was a blessing, really, that it had all happened the way it had.

He just held her, on and on and on, as her tears soaked through his undershirt. And as the night sky lightened in the east, and then slowly pinkened, and as the sun rose, burning the morning mist off the lake and leaving the grass shimmering with dew, Mila cried. She cried for herself, for the years she'd lost living with Brandon, and for the bruises that had faded from her body but would never fade from her memory. And she cried for Reid, who'd never asked for any of this but had become a part of it anyway, and for Ms. Thompson, who was in the intensive care unit, and for Heather, whom she missed terribly.

Mila cried for all these things and more. And at some point, and against all odds, she fell asleep in Reid's arms. He had held her, without words, or judgment, for hours. And only later did Mila realize that she had done what he'd wanted her to do the evening he'd first seen her swim. She had let him love her.

Chapter 28

"Well, I'll be damned," Reid said, squinting at the far shore of the lake. He was leaning on his crutches at the living room window, watching a sunset that even by Butternut Lake standards was spectacular. But it wasn't the sun, an enormous orange globe hovering above the horizon, or the sky, awash in pinks and golds and reds, that had caught Reid's attention. It was a birch tree across the lake whose upper leaves were already splashed with gold. There was always one tree like this. One tree that began to turn before all the others. It was almost as if it had been put there, Reid thought, to remind the residents of the lake how truly short, and truly ephemeral, the rest of summer would be.

"Reid, if it's all right with you, I'll be leaving now," Lonnie said, from the doorway to the living room.

"Oh, of course," Reid said, turning to her.

She came over to the window then, and stood, for a moment, watching the sunset with him. "Did she, did she say what time she was getting here?" she asked.

"She said she'd be here about"—he glanced at his watch—"fifteen minutes ago. She probably ran into some traffic. I'm sure she would have called if she was going to be much later than this," he added.

"Of course," Lonnie said. "But when you spoke to her, how did she sound?"

"She sounded tired, but otherwise all right."

Lonnie nodded, relieved. "Well, she'll have plenty of rest once she gets back here, and plenty of good food, too. I've been cooking all day."

Reid smiled. In Lonnie's opinion, there were very few problems in the world that couldn't be solved by a home-cooked meal.

"Well, I'll be heading home now," she said. "Do you want me to turn the lights on in here before I go?" The living room was filling with a faint pink light, its corners retreating into shadows.

"No, it's fine," Reid said. "And Lonnie?"

"Yes?"

"Thank you."

"For what?"

"For everything you've done this summer."

"Oh, no need to thank me," she said, pleased, but at the same time a little flustered, too.

"I'll see you tomorrow," she said, and then she was gone, leaving Reid alone to watch the sun sink a little farther beneath the horizon and to think back over the last week. The morning after Brandon's death, he woke up alone. Mila, who'd spent most of the night crying in his arms, was already gone. He cursed himself for falling asleep, then got out of bed and dressed hurriedly. When he came into the kitchen, Lonnie was scrambling eggs at the stove, and Mila was sipping coffee at the kitchen table. And he knew, from the subdued atmosphere in the room, that Mila had already given Lonnie a rough outline of what had happened the night before.

Reid declined Lonnie's offer of breakfast, then sat down at the table with Mila. When he looked up again, Lonnie had disappeared. That was when Mila—pale and puffy eyed but otherwise calm—had told him that Allie had come over earlier and offered to drive her to Ely and then Duluth that morning. She needed to give a statement to the police in Ely, and, as Brandon's next of kin—he was, not surprisingly, estranged from his parents—she needed to identify his body at the Duluth coroner's office and then arrange to have a funeral home transport the body back to Minneapolis. Reid was shocked. It had never occurred to him she would feel any responsibility for Brandon now, but on this point she was adamant. She was equally adamant about renting a car in Duluth afterward and driving back down to the city that night. There, she would make arrangements for Brandon's burial, pack up their former apartment, and visit her friend, Ms. Thompson, in the hospital.

Reid had suggested he come with her to do all of this. They could take the van, he'd pointed out, and once they'd gotten to the city they could stay at his condominium. But Mila had politely refused his offer. This was something she needed to do alone, she explained. And Reid had known, from the set of her jaw, that it was useless to argue with her. Still, he'd been relieved when she'd promised to come back to the cabin as soon as possible. In a week, she hoped, or maybe less. So Reid had said good-bye to her and watched Allie's car pull out of the driveway, and then he'd gone back inside a cabin that, even with Lonnie's cheerful presence in it, felt utterly empty.

The next seven days of his life had crawled by. And the nights? The nights were longer than the days, each one of them its own separate eternity. Thanks to Mila and Dr. Immerman, he'd been sleeping again recently, but with Mila gone, his insomnia returned with a vengeance. He tried everything to fill the sleepless hours.

Reading, watching television, playing solitaire on his iPad. But nothing he did made the time go by any faster or made the cabin feel any less deserted. How had he ever lived alone all these years? he wondered. But that wasn't the real question. The real question was, how had he ever lived without Mila?

Missing someone was new to Reid. So, it turned out, was worrying about someone. But he worried about Mila. He worried about her all week. He worried about her being alone. He worried about her being lonely. He worried about whether she was eating enough, or sleeping enough. And he worried about something happening to her, worried about her becoming ill or, God forbid, getting in a car accident.

When he wasn't worrying about her, he was wishing he could be with her. Wishing he could help make her life at least a little easier right now. But as it was, at odd moments of the day or night, he'd imagine her alone in her old apartment, packing away the contents of an unhappy marriage into cardboard boxes, and he'd feel a rush of pity for her. Or he'd picture her meeting with a funeral director, and uncomplainingly choosing a coffin for a man who had very nearly ruined her life, and he'd feel a surge of anger at the unfairness of it all.

"Reid?" He started as Mila's voice called to him from the front door. He'd been so deep in thought, he hadn't heard her drive up to the cabin or let herself into the kitchen.

"I'm in the living room," he called, turning on his crutches. He saw her silhouette in the doorway.

"Why are you in the dark?" she asked.

"I don't know," he said, surprised to see that the last of the day's light had already drained from the room. The sun had set, leaving only a blush of pink on the horizon, and a pale moon was etched above it. He started to come to her, but she was already coming to him, switching on lamps as she did so. He stopped and watched her. She was wearing a very pretty cotton print dress that he didn't recognize, and her hair was pulled up in a loose twist that managed to look both casual and elegant at the same time. As she came closer to him, he saw, too, that she looked thinner than she had when she'd left, and paler too, and that her eyes were shadowed with fatigue. For all that, though, she looked lovely to him. Lovelier than he ever remembered her looking before.

"You're here," he said, and he reached for her as best he could on his crutches.

"I'm here," she agreed, with a tired smile, and as he drew her into his arms and kissed her there was a shyness about her that disarmed him slightly. Still, he was savoring the nearness of her, when he asked, "How was it?"

"It's . . . it's over," she said, and there was something about the way she said it that told him she didn't want to talk about it anymore now. "I'm sorry I'm late," she added, "but I decided to make a last-minute stop."

"Where?" he asked, brushing a strand of hair off her face.

"Well, on the drive up I realized I was still, technically, your home health aide. So I stopped in at the boatyard and told your brother that I was resigning."

He smiled. "How'd he take it?"

"Pretty well," she said, stepping closer and nuzzling his neck with her lips. "He took it pretty well. What about you, Reid? How've you been?" she asked.

"Um, okay," Reid said, and her lips on his neck felt so good that he wondered, momentarily, if the dress she was wearing had buttons on it or a zipper. But there was something he needed to do now, before . . . well, before he answered the button/zipper question.

"I've actually been thinking, a lot," he said, and Mila, sensing his change of direction, stopped kissing his neck and took a step back from him.

"What have you been thinking about?"

"About you. About *us*, actually. About our future, and about where we go from here."

The corners of her mouth lifted in amusement. "You've never been one for small talk, have you, Reid?" she asked.

He shook his head. "No. Is that a problem?"

"Not even a little bit of one," she said, her eyes gentle.

"Good. Because, as I said, I've been thinking, and while I don't really know how to say this the right way, the *romantic* way, I mean, I'm going to say it anyway. I want you in my life, Mila. I *need* you in my life. And I think you need me in your life, too. Or at least I hope you do." He stopped, unsure of how to continue.

"Go on," she said encouragingly.

"So . . . I want you to come back to Minneapolis with me," he said. "God knows, I've loved being here with you this summer. In this cabin. On this lake. It was like being in our own little world. And part of me wants us to stay here like this, forever, but part of me knows we can't. I mean, for starters, my brother and his family need their house back. There isn't even enough room for Wyatt's Legos in the cabin they're staying in, let alone enough room for the four of them. But there's something else, too. We need to start the rest of our lives. And we can't do it here. Not all of it. I need to get back to work, and for the first time in a long time, I actually *want* to get back to work. And not just *work* work, either, as in work for my company. But other work, too. You know, physical therapy, and the other kind of therapy, if I still need it. And you're going to be applying to nursing school, aren't you?"

She nodded but didn't say anything. He pressed on. "Anyway, what I thought was, if we're both moving back to Minneapolis, why don't we do it together. Live together, I mean. I have a condominium there, as you know. It's not much to look at, really. The building it's in is nice. It has a gym in it, and a pool. But the condo itself . . ." He shrugged. "It's a little . . . impersonal, I guess. There's not much in it. Just some furniture that I rent. I never took the time to decorate it. I didn't see the point, to be honest. But we can decorate it now, if you like. Buy some house plants, or pillows for the couch or whatever it is people do . . ." He trailed off. Interior design was well outside his area of expertise. "Then again," he said, "if you really hate my condo, and you might, we can buy something else. A house even, if you think that would make you happy. Something we could both call home." He stopped. *Home.* Until recently, home was not a concept he had ever associated with himself.

He waited now for Mila to say something about the two of them living together, or buying a house together, but when she did say something, it wasn't about either of those things.

"You rent your furniture?" she asked, perplexed.

"Well, yeah," he said. "It just seemed simpler somehow. But we don't have to *keep* renting it. We could buy it. Not that same furniture, of course, because it's all kind of beige and corporate looking. But we could buy different furniture. I'm getting off track, though." He fought back an unfamiliar nervousness over what he was going to say next. "And, uh, another thing. If you don't want us to live together—*just* live together—if you want us to do *more* than that, we could get married. It's not something I ever thought I'd do. Not before I met you, anyway. But if it's important to you, Mila, we'll do it. We'll do it right away, if you want us to."

And then, realizing how his words must have sounded to her, he stopped abruptly. Had he actually just proposed to her by saying, among other things, *It's not something I thought I'd ever do?* Christ, what was wrong with him? He'd had a week to work on that. *A week.* And that was the best he could do? He studied her expression now, looking for some clue as to how she felt about what he'd said, and he saw her face had colored slightly, probably with embarrassment, though maybe with disappointment.

"Yeah, I know," he said, quickly. "That wasn't a great proposal. I'm sorry. I guess I should have planned it better. You know, done something with rose petals.

Made a trail out of them, or scattered them around somewhere, or whatever it is people do with them."

Mila laughed, surprising him. "I don't know what people do with rose petals, Reid. But I don't need them. I need *you*," she said, stepping closer to him. "I love you." Reid leaned down and kissed her then, a long, lingering kiss on the lips, and he felt the rest of what he needed to say to her slipping away. But he couldn't let it, he decided. It was too important.

"Mila, one more thing, all right?" he said, pulling away from her. "I know how much you want to be a nurse. And I want you to know that if that's your dream, it's my dream, too. If there's anything I can do—*anything*—to help you realize it, I'll do it. The admissions process, the studying, anything I can help you with, I will. I won't make you go it alone. I mean, obviously, to a point, you'll have to, but I'll still be there with you, from beginning to end. Every step of the way."

He stopped. There, he'd said it. All of it. Everything he'd been thinking about all week. It was out of his hands. Still, when he tried now to read her expression, he couldn't. She was doing something with her hair, he saw, loosening it from the knot it was in and then shaking it out so that it came tumbling down to her shoulders. It had gotten longer this summer, and lighter, too, and it's red and gold highlights shone in the lamplight.

"I want to talk about this, Reid. All of this. I really do. But I don't want to talk about it right now," she said, slipping out of the flats she was wearing and reaching her arms gracefully behind her and unzipping her dress. *So it had a zipper,* Reid thought. Still, his brain felt a little slow now. A little foggy. "What . . . what are you doing?" he asked.

"What does it look like I'm doing?" she said, and with a little shimmying movement she worked first her shoulders and then her arms free of her dress.

"It looks like you're getting undressed," he said.

"Very good," she said, the now familiar light dancing in her eyes. And in that moment, it struck him that if he could keep that light in her eyes all the time, it would be enough for him. He wouldn't need to accomplish anything else. She worked her dress down now, over her waist and hips, and then let go of it and let it skim down her legs. It landed around her ankles, and she stepped out of it and gave it a graceful little kick so it wouldn't be in their way. Her bra and panties, he saw, were a matched set, cream colored, and satiny, with delicate scalloping around the edges. They were just right for her, he decided, unmistakably lovely, but, at the same time, unmistakably modest. And he was glad he'd bought a box of condoms at Butternut Drugs.

It was sitting on his dresser right now.

She stepped closer to him, and he caught the faintest scent of the coconut body lotion he had come to love. The contrast of her skin tone—creamy white where her bathing suit had covered her, and pale gold where it had not—was particularly captivating. He swayed toward her on his crutches and imagined he could feel the warmth emanating off her body.

But he didn't touch her. Not yet. He couldn't. He could only stare at her, mesmerized. He felt like a starving man who was being served every single course of a twelve-course meal simultaneously. *Where to start. Oh God, where to start.* He swallowed and reached out a hand; then, with his finger, he traced a line across her navel, from one hip to the other. She sucked in a little breath when his finger touched her, and as he drew it across her navel, she reached behind her with both hands, as if to unfasten her bra, but she hesitated and changed her mind. She'd lost her nerve, Reid saw. Her striptease was over. But he didn't mind. He wanted to take off those last two pieces of clothing himself.

"Mila, can I ask you a question?" They were out on the deck, lying on one of the cushioned chaise lounges, their naked bodies wrapped in a sheepskin throw. They'd considered going to one of their bedrooms to make love, but, in the end, the night was so beautiful that they'd decided to come out here instead.

"A question?" Mila murmured now. Her head was resting on his chest, and she was so blissfully relaxed, and so completely satiated, that she didn't know if she'd be able to summon the energy to answer a question or not.

"Yes, a question," he said, kissing the top of her head. "There's something I've always been curious about." She lifted her head, fractionally, off his chest and looked at him, then couldn't help smiling at him. His hair looked wonderfully rumpled after all their lovemaking.

"Where did you go that first night you were here?" he asked. She frowned, not understanding.

"When you left the cabin, I mean. It was around midnight, I think, when you went outside. At first I thought you were leaving, for good, but then, about five minutes later, you came back inside."

"Oh, that," Mila said, finding the strength to prop herself up on one elbow. "I threw my wedding ring in the lake."

"You did?" He was fascinated.

"I did," she said, and now she reached up and tenderly traced the scar that ran across his forehead. "I thought if I couldn't end my marriage legally, I could at least end it symbolically. So I made a little speech—to myself—and I threw my ring off the end of the dock. And, as far as I know, it's still there, sitting at the bottom of the lake. Do you think anyone will ever find it?"

"Not unless they're looking for it," he said. "It's probably under a couple of inches of silt by now." She nodded, relieved, and put her head back down on his chest. It seemed right to her, somehow, that the ring was there. That it would always be there. And that she and Reid would always be the only two people who knew about it being there. She'd often thought about that ring over the course of the summer, but lying here now, in Reid's arms, she knew she wouldn't think about it anymore. And that felt right too.

They were quiet for a little while then. Mila listened to Reid's heartbeat and felt the rise and fall of his chest against her cheek, and Reid ran his fingertips up and down her back, from the nape of her neck to the little indentation at the small of her back. His light, caressing touch was relaxing at first, and then, gradually, it became something else, and she stirred in his arms, wanting, and then needing, him again. But Reid had another question for her.

"How is it possible," he asked, turning onto his side, so that they were facing each other, "that we waited the whole summer to do this?"

"I have no idea," she said, savoring the feel of her skin against his skin and pulling the throw more tightly around them against the cool night air. "But it was worth waiting for, wasn't it?" she asked.

"*Of course* it was worth waiting for," he said, kissing her. "But part of me wishes we'd done this your first night here. And every night after that, too. And not just once a night, either, but several times a night."

Mila laughed, but then she pointed out playfully, "I don't know about our making love my first night here, Reid. As I remember it, you didn't even want to be in the same *room* with me that night, let alone be in the same bed with me." She'd meant to tease him but saw now he was troubled by what she'd said.

"Oh, God," he said. "I hate remembering that. The way I treated you then, and the first couple of weeks after that, too. I don't know how I could have been that cruel, but—"

"You weren't cruel, Reid," Mila said, interrupting him. "You were just . . . lost."

He thought about that as he started to run his fingers through her hair. "You're right," he said finally. "I was lost. But you found me, didn't you, Mila? You saved me."

"I saved *you*?"

"Yes, you saved me," he said. "That first day, when you walked into Pearl's, I was in a dark place. A very dark place. I was going through the motions, I guess, but I didn't really see the point in going through them anymore. I was like a dead man walking, except, of course, that I wasn't walking." He smiled wryly. "But you changed that, didn't you?" he said, kissing her, very gently, on the lips. "You made me rethink everything. Every decision I'd made since I woke up in that hospital bed. And a lot of the decisions I'd made before that, too."

She saw an image of him then, the way he'd been that day, but it was hard to reconcile it with the way he was now. The man sitting in that wheelchair at Pearl's could never have made love to her with the same passion or tenderness as this man had. But there it was. He was one man, and it had been one summer, though who would have ever known it was possible for a life to change so much in so little time?

Then again, she thought, she had changed as much, if not more than he had this summer. And she saw an image of *herself* as she'd been that same day at Pearl's, choosing a chair that faced the door, jumping every time anyone pushed it open, jangling its little bells, and cringing whenever anyone at the table said her name out loud. And now . . . well, now she wasn't that person anymore. She just wasn't, though she liked to think, of course, she'd kept the best parts of herself, kept them for her and for Reid. As for the doubt and the fear and the loneliness, well, those parts of herself she could live without now.

"Reid, if I saved you," she said, touching his face again, "then it goes without saying that you saved me, too."

"Mmmm, why don't we just call it even, then," he said, a little distractedly. And she was distracted too. He was slowly peeling the sheepskin throw away from her body.

"What are you doing?" she asked, though it was perfectly obvious what he was doing.

"I just want to see how your skin looks in the moonlight," he said. For a moment, she wanted to be under the throw again, but instead she closed her eyes and let him uncover her.

"I love you, Mila Jones," she heard him say softly, and he started running his fingertips up and down again, only now, instead of tracing a line down her back, he was tracing a line down her front, from the hollow of her neck, down over her collarbone, down between her breasts, and down to her navel. Then he stopped and started the line in reverse. She shivered.

"Are you cold?" he asked.

"No," she said. "Not cold. Just thinking about something."

"What's that?"

She opened her eyes then and saw that he was as naked as she was, having tossed the throw onto the deck, and that the moonlight was bathing not just her but him, too, in its milky glow.

"I know you said you wanted to leave tomorrow," she said, watching his fingers skate lightly down over her navel. "But do you think we could stay one more day. Or even two?"

His fingers reversed themselves. "Why?"

"So we could spend more time making up for lost time."

He smiled. "We'll stay here for as long as you'd like," he said, leaning down to kiss her. For a long time after that the night was quiet, except for the two of them and the soft lapping of waves against the dock below.

Epilogue

"*Walker! Allie!*" Reid called to his brother and sister-in-law, who were working their way down one of the aisles in the crowded auditorium.

They waved and turned into his row. "Great seats," Walker said as they sat down next to Reid. "Front and center."

"I got here a couple of hours ago," Reid admitted, before he leaned over Walker to say hello to Allie.

"You look good, by the way," Walker said when Reid was done chatting with Allie and had sat back in his seat. "How's your leg doing?"

"Good. Good enough for me to run five miles yesterday."

"Very impressive," Walker said.

"Mila didn't think so," Reid said, with a laugh. "She thought I could have gone a few more. But she's very proprietorial about this leg," he added, patting it. "Remember how hard she pushed me in my physical therapy sessions that fall after the accident?"

"I remember," Walker said. "Where is Mila, by the way?"

"With her class, over there." Reid said, gesturing to their left, where the first several rows on that side of the auditorium were cordoned off and filled with members of the graduating class, resplendent in their blue caps and gowns.

"Is she excited?" Walker asked. Reid nodded.

"She couldn't sleep last night. Although that was partly my fault," he added, lowering his voice. "I wouldn't *let* her sleep last night." He smiled, remembering their hours of lovemaking. By the time they'd finally fallen asleep, entwined in each other's arms, it had been 7:00 A.M. and the alarm clock was soon going off.

Now Walker shook his head, the expression on his face half admiring and half amused. "Reid, are you two still behaving like a couple of newlyweds? After two years?" Reid glanced at the gold band on his ring finger. Had it been that long? It didn't feel like it. But

Walker seemed to be waiting for some kind of response, so he said, "Mila's starting her job next week, and being a critical care nurse is going to be pretty intense, especially at first, so we've been trying to make up for lost time, ahead of time."

"Huh," Walker said. And then, "I'm sure there's a logic in there somewhere."

But Reid didn't answer. Someone was waving to him from the side aisle, and now he smiled and waved back. "You remember Heather, don't you?" he asked Walker and Allie as an attractive, middle-aged blond woman entered their row.

"Of course," Allie said. "She was at your wedding."

"You made it," Reid said, rising to give Heather a hug and a kiss.

"Of course I made it," she said, sitting down next to him. "I wouldn't have missed it for the world. But I have to confess, I'm not used to driving in all this traffic anymore."

"Do you even have stoplights in Red Cloud, Nebraska?" Reid teased. But she ignored his remark and turned to Allie and Walker instead.

"You've known Mila for a long time, haven't you?" Allie asked her, after they'd exchanged hellos.

Heather nodded. "I was the school nurse at her elementary school."

"Heather's the reason Mila became a nurse," Reid interjected.

"Oh, I don't know about that," she demurred. "But I can tell you that Mila was a very special child. And when she told me, in the third grade, that she wanted to be a nurse, I never doubted for one moment that she'd become one."

"The third grade?" Allie said, in surprise. "And you stayed in touch all these years?"

"We lost touch once," Heather said, glancing at Reid. "For a little while. But after that, we never let it happen again."

"They still write to each other," Reid said.

"Real letters?" Walked asked. "I wasn't aware that people wrote those anymore."

"Some of us do," Heather said good-naturedly. "You should try it sometime. But honestly, as much as I love getting letters from Mila, being here to see her in person is much more exciting."

"She must be thrilled you're coming," Walker commented.

"She doesn't know yet," Heather said, smiling at Reid. "My son's high school graduation is tomorrow, and I was afraid if I drove—which I usually do—I'd be cutting it too close. But Reid made me airline reservations. I'm literally just flying in and out. And not only that, but he practically had me sign a confidentiality agreement, too," she added, her exasperation tempered by affection.

"I want Mila to be surprised," Reid said simply.

"Oh, she'll be surprised," Walker said, and then, lowering his voice, he added to Reid, "You're full of surprises."

Reid looked at his watch now and shifted nervously in his seat. The ceremony was about to start, and he still had one seat left to be filled. He sighed and looked around. Why hadn't she let him drive her here? he wondered. Or send a car service for her? But she was stubborn, he knew. It was one of the things he and Mila both loved about her. In the next moment, though, he saw her, and she saw him. She started down the row, slowly, leaning heavily on her cane, and he wanted to help her, but he knew her pride wouldn't allow him too. Even at eighty-two, Gloria Thompson made very few concessions to old age, though the cane, which she hated, was one of them. When she reached them, the four of them stood up to greet her warmly, and after they'd all said their hellos, she settled herself between Reid and Heather. As the lights in the auditorium dimmed and a hush fell over the crowd, she put her hand on top of Reid's hand and asked quietly, "How's our girl?"

"Our girl is just fine," he said, squeezing her slightly gnarled hand. And he felt it again. That gratitude he always felt toward Gloria and Heather and his brother and Allie. It was true that Mila had never had a conventional family, and what family she did have had long since dropped away. It had been a couple of years now, for instance, since her mother had returned one of her phone calls. But no matter. Because together, the people in this row (and Wyatt and Brooke, too) had become Mila's family. Someday, soon, Reid hoped they would add to this family, but not yet. Mila had some other things she wanted to accomplish first.

The graduation ceremony began now, and Reid watched, absorbed, until the dean of the nursing school began to give out the diplomas. After what seemed like a lifetime, she got to the *J*'s, and, by the time she called Mila's name, he was clapping so hard his hands hurt, and the only thing that kept him from standing up was the knowledge that it would annoy the people seated behind him. He watched as Mila shook the dean's hand, took her diploma, and looked to the front row where Reid had told her they'd be sitting. Her eyes found his, and then registered the excitement of seeing them all there, and then the surprise of seeing Heather. It was there in her expression. It was all there. The happiness, the surprise, the excitement, the pride, and the love. But most of all, the love.

HARPER LUXE

THE NEW LUXURY IN READING

We hope you enjoyed reading
our new, comfortable print size and found it
an experience you would like to repeat.

Well – you're in luck!

HarperLuxe offers the finest in fiction and
nonfiction books in this same larger print size and
paperback format. Light and easy to read, HarperLuxe
paperbacks are for book lovers who want to see
what they are reading without the strain.

For a full listing of titles and
new releases to come, please visit our website:

www.HarperLuxe.com

SEEING IS BELIEVING